喚醒你的英文語感 !

Get a Feel for English !

測評學習
最新二版

英語認證測驗
國際標準版

TOEIC
Model Tests

New TOEIC 新多益
全真測驗
速戰速決400題

作者 入江泉 / 審訂 宮野智靖

命題趨勢全掌握，得分訣竅快易懂

貝塔│語測
檢測學習平台

iRT＋題測 高點│美語系列

序

英語是國際溝通的一項重要工具，為與時俱進並如實檢測應試者，多益測驗歷經幾次題型更新。於 2018 年更新之題型包括 Part 3 和 Part 4 加入「圖表題」和「詢問主旨‧用意題」，Part 6 新增「插入句題」，Part 7 則融入了「手機傳訊對話題」、「詢問主旨‧用意題」和「插入句題」，且閱讀文章增加至最多三篇。除了題型上的變革之外，在試題細節上也有新考法。比方說，Part 3 包括三人對話、篇幅較長的對話或是像 Haven't you heard? — Heard what? 這樣的簡短問答。這是相當好的變化。透過學習更加實用的對話，考生參加多益測驗不再單純以考取高分為目的，更能從英語學習本身獲得更多的樂趣。而本書著眼於上述改變要點，緊扣最新多益考情趨勢，針對舊版內容做了全面的檢視，當然也納入了符合新制的試題類型。不僅如此，作者也將其自身實際參加測驗時的心得大量分享於各環節。

本書包含兩回完整模擬測驗及詳盡解析，致力於維持最高品質的擬真試題，並輔以明瞭易懂的解說。請讀者做完試題後，不僅答錯的題目，連同答對的題目之解析也務必仔細詳讀。因為即便作答正確，也不代表是真正理解，而有可能是下列三種情況：一、充滿自信地解出答案；二、雖然不太確定但還是答對；三、猜對答案。希望讀者能將上述狀況加以分析，反覆研讀翻譯和解析、甚至多次自我測驗，以徹底強化應考實力。如此一來，勢必能有效發揮本書兩回全真試題的功用，並確認自身程度，揪出自己較不擅長的 Part 或題型，進而妥善分配各 Part 解題時間，參考上面舉例的各種學習法，充分利用本書。

除此之外，特別介紹書中精心歸納之「七大題型應考要領」和網羅多益最新頻出商業用語的「高頻商英字彙 200」。尤其推薦詳讀「應考要領」，其中收錄了最新考情趨勢之相關資訊，包含重要考點、難解文法、難記詞彙以及有助於在最後關鍵時刻搶分的答題技巧。請讀者務必讀通、讀熟，以期在正式考試時能發揮出最大效果！

最後要藉此版面表達我由衷的謝意。感謝一直以來給予我機會執筆多益模測書籍的關西外國語大學短期大學部的宮野智靖教授，以及出版社編輯部的各位夥伴。

作者　入江 泉

CONTENTS

目錄

BOOK 1　完全解析本

BOOK 2　全真測驗本

本書使用方式與特色

BOOK 2 全真測驗本

* 收錄兩回完整多益模擬試題，每回 200 題、共 400 題。
* 全擬真命題，試題情境多元、內容逼真詳實，搭配與實際多益測驗幾近的書籍開本和內頁編排，充分掌握應試臨場感。

BOOK 1 完全解析本

* 內含全試題之中文翻譯和詳解，並提示重要考點與答題陷阱。
* 彙整各題常考單字與片語及其音標、詞性，有效增強字彙力。
* 雙色印刷，架構清楚，方便閱讀，輕鬆使用。
* 連同試題一併收錄，只要帶著 BOOK 1 就能進行複習。

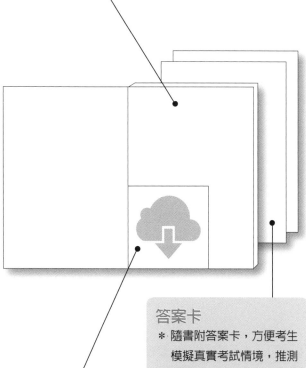

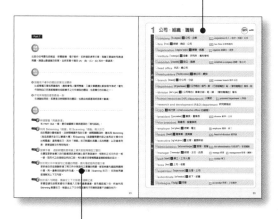

答案卡

* 隨書附答案卡，方便考生模擬真實考試情境，推測目前實力。

七大題型應考要領

* 搭配例題剖析非知不可的搶分解答技巧。
* 聽力部分之例題的語音亦有提供 MP3 音檔。

高頻商英字彙 200

* 嚴選八人類兩百多個最重要的商英字彙，幫助第一次參加多益測驗或還沒有工作經驗的大學生克服應試難關。
* 所收錄之詞彙發音亦收錄於 MP3 資源裡，並標示音標、詞性和搭配用法。邊聽邊記單字，效果最好。

雲端專屬學習資源免費下載

聽力 MP3

* 收錄七大題型應考要領、高頻商英字彙及兩回全真試題之聽力測驗內容。MP3 音軌皆標示於書中相對應之處。另為了讀者使用方便，特將音軌細分成數軌，幫助對照練習。
* MP3 001-058 第一回模擬試題聽力部分
  MP3 059-116 第二回模擬試題聽力部分
  MP3 ex01-ex16 七大題型應考要領及高頻商英字彙
* 比照官方試題，試題語音包括美加英澳四國口音，並於 BOOK 1 完全解析中以國旗標示。

線上題庫免費練題

* 精選 100 道文法題，可無限次數反覆練題，徹底釐清文法觀念、改善答題弱點。

關於多益測驗（TOEIC L&R Test）

※ 2023 年 2 月資料

　　TOEIC 為 Test of English for International Communication 之縮寫，是美國教育測驗服務社 ETS（Educational Testing Service）所開發的全球性英語溝通能力測驗，廣受好評。在台灣，多益成績也是大學畢業、語言訓練、公司內部晉升等的認定標準。多益測驗的特徵在於，不以合格‧不合格二分法評測應試者的英語能力，而是以 10～990 分的方式將應試者的英文溝通能力分出不同等級，答題方式為劃記答案卡，是一套相當客觀的考試。包含答題提示，測驗全程皆以英文進行。

☑ TOEIC 基本資訊

考試時間

原則上每個月會舉辦一次 TOEIC 考試。不過各地舉辦時程不同，詳情請至官方網站確認。

如何報名

目前報名方式有三種：網路報名、APP 報名、通訊報名。最新辦法以官網公告為主。

報名費用

一般考生報名費為 1,700 元，另有特殊身分優惠，請至官網查詢。

成績通知

依正常情況，ETS 預定於測驗結束後 12 個工作日（不含假日）寄出該場次成績單。考生可視個別需求自行申請證書。

TOEIC 台灣區總代理公司聯繫資訊
- 客服電話：02-2701-7333
- 客服信箱：service@examservice.com.tw
- 官方網站：https://www.toeic.com.tw

☑ TOEIC 題型架構

ETS 為確保多益測驗與時俱進，並如實檢驗應試者是否具備在真實生活情境中所需之英語溝通技巧，不定期針對考試內容進行更新。以下為現行題型內容說明。

多益分為下列七大題型，共有 200 題，考試時間共兩小時。

聽力部分（45 分鐘 / 100 題）

PART	題數	測驗方式
1 照片題	6	聽取語音播放四個選項，從中選出最符合題本上照片的敘述。選項只播放一次，且不會印在題本上。
2 應答題	25	每道題目配有三個應答句選項，從中選出最符合題目的答案。題目與選項都不會印在題本上，而語音只播放選項一次。
3 簡短對話題	39 （13 組對話 ×3 題）	聽取二～三人之間的對話，回答與該內容相關的三道題目。題目與選項皆印在題本上，而題目會在對話之後播放。對話和題目都只播放一次。
4 簡短獨白題	30 （10 段獨白 ×3 題）	聽取廣播、旁白等人物的談話，回答與該段談話相關的三道題目。與 PART 3 相同，題目也會播放。談話內容與題目同樣也僅播放一次。

閱讀部分（75 分鐘 / 100 題）

PART	題數	測驗方式
5 單句填空題	30	從四個選項中，選出最適合填入句子的字詞。每道題目裡有一個空格。
6 短文填空題	16 （4 篇文章 ×4 題）	從四個選項中，選出最適合填入文章的字詞或句子。每篇文章裡共有四個空格。
7 文章理解題 ·單篇文章 ·多篇文章	29 25	閱讀各種內容，回答相關題目。包括單篇文章題、雙篇文章題、三篇文章題等三種類型。

☑ TOEIC 分數與能力分級

PROFICIENCY SCALE

--TOEIC 分數與溝通能力分級的關係表--

分級	多益分數	評價（能力指標）
A	860	☞ 充分具備非母語者所需之溝通能力 可根據自身經驗理解非專業領域的話題，並做出適當的回應。 雖與母語者仍有一小段差距，但已能正確掌握字彙、文法及句構，整體而言英語對答如流。
B	730	☞ 可於各種情況下以英文進行溝通 完全理解一般對話，也能快速應答。即便是特定領域的話題，也能適當回應。應付職務所需基本上沒有太大問題。 此級學習者在使用英文的正確性與流暢性因人而異，有時也會出現文法或句構上的錯誤，但不至於影響溝通。
C	470	☞ 英文能力足以應付日常生活所需，可於特定範圍內進行業務溝通 只要是一般對話，都能理解重點，應答也沒問題。於複雜情況下的對應與溝通，則有巧拙程度之差。 具備基本文法・句構知識，即便表達能力稍嫌不足，至少能以英文詞彙傳達自身想法。
D	220	☞ 可進行最低程度的日常對話 只要對方放慢說話速度，或是重述一次，就能理解簡單的對話內容。對於熟悉的話題，也能做出適當的回應。 雖然字彙、文法、句構仍有許多不足之處，但在對方考慮此級學習者為非母語者之下，仍可順利地溝通。
E		☞ 無法進行溝通 即便對方以簡單的字彙進行對話，也只能理解隻字片語。 只能以拼湊單字的方式使用英語，因此實際上並無法幫助溝通。

資料提供：日本（一財）國際商業溝通協會

☑ Speaking and Writing Test / Speaking Test 是什麼？

多益也有口說與寫作測驗，與聽力・閱讀測驗分別實施。另，考生亦可單獨選考口說測驗。以上相關資訊請參照官方網站。

七大題型答題指示與應考要領

　　參加 TOEIC 測驗時有兩個重點必須先了解。第一個是熟悉 TOEIC 獨特的出題趨勢，並學習簡中解題技巧；另一個是強化商英用語。TOEIC 測驗對沒有商務經驗者或商英字彙量薄弱者而言，或許會感覺相當困難。然而相反地，只要掌握頻出用語和固定的書寫形式，便十分有望考取高分。TOEIC 測驗的試題說明全為英文，以下依各大題彙整開頭答題指示 (direction) 的中文翻譯幫助讀者事先掌握指示內容，並提供「奪分攻略」、「解題技巧」、「試題範例」，只要用心研讀必能輕鬆掌握奪高分之要領。

☑ 聽力測驗

　　聽力測驗的目的在於檢測考生理解英語口說對話的程度，考試時間為四十五分鐘，共分成四個 PART，並皆附有答題指示。答案須填在答案卡裡，不可寫在題本上。

Part 1

答題
指示

此部分的每道問題都將播放四個與題本照片有關的句子，考生須從四個句子中，選出最符合照片內容的描述，並依題號在答案卡上劃記答案。問題不會印在題本上，且只會播放一次。

以下為參考用的例題。
請聽下列四個句子：

(A) 她們正在移動家具。
(B) 她們正要進入會議室。
(C) 她們坐在桌子附近。
(D) 她們正在清潔地毯。

選項 (C)「她們坐在桌子附近。」最符合照片內容，因此請將答案卡裡的 (C) 塗黑。
接下來 Part 1 的試題即將開始。

❶ 在播放答題指示時，先快速地瀏覽前兩張照片

當語音在敘述答題指示 (direction) 時，首先觀察第一頁 No. 1 和 No. 2 的這兩張照片，根據圖中物品、人物的位置和動作等，推測題目將出現什麼單字。No. 1 基本上固定會出 He's/She's ... 此題型，解題關鍵在於動作（動詞或受詞）。

❷ 快速地答題，別浪費每道題目之間的空白時間

一聽到正確答案就立刻劃答案卡，然後看下一張照片準備作答。若遇到聽不懂的題目也不要糾結在原處，應趁下一題語音播放前趕緊轉換心情，集中注意力。

解題
技巧

TIP 1 注意發音類似的單字

work 與 walk、coffee 與 copy、fold 與 hold 這種發音相似的單字常出現在考題中作為陷阱，千萬別上當。

TIP 2 熟記表位置關係的介系詞和片語

在照片描述中，表位置關係的語句出現的頻率很高，例如 on the wall（掛在牆上）、side by side（並排地）等。另，關於介系詞，利用「畫面」記憶十分重要。比方說，看到 into 就要想到「人或物進入某場所」之動作。

TIP 3 確實掌握以「人」做主詞時的動詞和受詞

當主詞是「人」時，該人物的動作通常以現在進行式〈be ＋動詞 ing〉表示。不過，有時也會出現動詞部分的描述正確但受詞不正確的情形，因此要格外仔細聽。

TIP 4 以「物」為主詞時句子多為被動式

當主詞是「物」時，動詞多為被動語態，包括兩種形式：〈is/are being ＋過去分詞〉或〈have/has been ＋過去分詞〉，關鍵在於聽取過去分詞。

TIP 5 注意與照片中未出現或不確定之人・物有關的描述

照片並未照到人，若選項出現與人相關的描述，即為錯誤答案。唯有照片中明顯出現的人・物和客觀的事實，才有可能是正解。假如選項提及看不清楚的物品或難以判斷的動作，也大多是錯誤的。不過要注意的是，有時答案會用 something、someone 來表示曖昧不明的人或物。

1

(A) He's making some coffee.
(B) He's walking into a room.
(C) He's looking at a computer screen.
(D) He's putting on a pair of glasses.

技巧 **1**
技巧 **2**
技巧 **3**

譯 (A) 他正在泡咖啡。　　　　(B) 他正走進房間。
　 (C) 他正看著電腦螢幕。　　(D) 他正戴上眼鏡。

正解：**(C)**

照片中男子的確正在看著電腦螢幕，因此 (C) 為正解。若說男子在喝咖啡還有點可能，但是他並非正在 making（泡）咖啡，故可判斷 (A) 為錯誤選項。選項 (B) 利用 working 和 walking 這兩個發音類似的單字引誘誤答。選項 (D) 的 be putting on 指「正在」戴眼鏡，所以也不正確。假如是描述狀態 He's wearing some glasses.（他戴著眼鏡。）的話則可選為正確答案。

2

(A) The woman is talking on the phone.
(B) The woman is holding something.
(C) One of the men is waving his hands.
(D) The men are seated across from each other.

技巧 **2**
技巧 **3**
技巧 **5**

譯 (A) 女子正在講電話。　　　(B) 女子手中拿著東西。
　 (C) 其中一名男子正在揮手。　(D) 男子們面對面坐著。

正解：**(B)**

女子手上的確拿著某樣東西，因此 (B) 為正解。而女子並未使用電話談論事情 (talking on the phone)，選項 (A) 明顯錯誤；照片中沒有人在揮手 (waving)，故選項 (C) 也不對。假如是說 The two men are shaking hands.（兩位男士正在「握手」。）的話則為正確答案。這兩名男子是面對面「站著」，而非「坐著」，所以描述成 seated 的選項 (D) 亦不正確。注意，以 are seated 為例，針對主詞「人」的狀態未使用現在進行式的說法，以及當照片中有兩名以上的同性人物時，One of ...「其中一位……」的敘述皆須特別留意。

3

(A) An entrance floor is being cleaned.
(B) A man is watering some plants.
(C) Some pots have been placed around the pond.
(D) The fountain is surrounded by plants.

技巧 **2**
技巧 **4**
技巧 **5**

譯 (A) 入口地板正在被清潔中。　(B) 男子正在給植物澆水。
　 (C) 有一些壺被放在池塘周圍。　(D) 噴泉被一些植物包圍著。

正解：**(D)**

聚焦於照片中央的噴泉之選項 (D) 爲本題正解。照片中並沒有人在掃地，故選項 (A) 不正確，且 floor 是指室內的「地板」，而非地面。另，因爲〈is being＋過去分詞〉爲被動式，表「某人正在進行該動作」，所以在未照到人物的照片中，若選項出現此被動式則可視爲錯誤。而光聽到 man 這個字即可刪去選項 (B)；water（澆水）爲 PART 1 經常考的動詞。最後，照片中並未看見池塘，故選項 (C) 亦非正解。注意，例如 have been placed（被放置）、be surrounded by ...（被……包圍）這種表「物品」之位置或狀態的說法須多多熟記。

Part 2

答題指示

此部分各題將播放一個疑問或敘述，以及三個回答選項。問題與選項都不會印在題本上，且只會播放一次。請從答案卡的 (A)、(B)、(C) 裡，選出一個最符合問題的回應。

奪分攻略

全神貫注聆聽語音，有節奏地作答
新制考題的 PART 2 從 30 題減少爲 25 題，並且難度有稍微提高的趨勢。這個 PART 不必看題目紙，單憑聽力作答，所以就需要持續的注意力。當恍神時，即使只是漏聽開頭的疑問詞，也有可能因此選不出正解。萬一整個題目沒聽清楚也不要慌張、沮喪，姑且先在答案卡上劃記一個選項，然後轉換心情準備回答下一題。

解題技巧

TIP 1 聽懂開頭疑問詞等於答對了一半
若是以疑問詞起始的疑問句，有些題目僅須聽懂疑問詞就能答對了。此外，以疑問詞爲首的疑問句不會以 Yes-No 來回答，因此聽到 Yes-No 開頭的選項即可不予理會。

TIP 2 內含和題目文一樣或發音類似的單字的選項須多加留意
遇到使用題目裡出現的單字，或者選用如 lunch 和 launch、riding 和 writing 等發音類似的單字之選項時，須小心作答。

TIP ③ 注意利用易使人與題目產生聯想之詞彙的選項

例如 restaurant → reservation / meal 或 meeting → schedule / agenda，像這樣選項為從題目單字聯想而來之字彙常為吸引誤答的陷阱，小心不要上當。

TIP ④ 即使題目問 **Why** 也不代表答案一定會是理由

Why don't you ...?「你要不要……？」此說法表提議、邀請，並不是在詢問理由。此外，針對以 Why ...? 詢問「理由」的問句，回答句不見得都是 Because ....，有時也會改用一個句子或〈To ＋動詞原形〉來表達目的。

TIP ⑤ 語帶保留的選項正是答案

面對提問，回答「我不知道」、「請去問……」、「隨便你」這種不清楚講明自身意思的選項反而是答案的情形也不在少數。

TIP ⑥ 遇到附加問句或否定問句時不要執著於 **Yes-No**

對於 You ..., don't you? 或 Hasn't Jane sent ...? 此類附加問句或否定問句，不能因為看到選項裡有 Yes-No 就作答，重要的是之後接續的敘述。

試題範例　　　　　　　　　　　　　　　　　　　　　　　　　MP3 ex04 – ex06

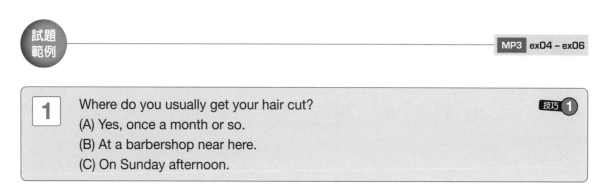

1　Where do you usually get your hair cut?　　　　　　　　　　技巧 ①
(A) Yes, once a month or so.
(B) At a barbershop near here.
(C) On Sunday afternoon.

譯 你通常都去哪裡剪頭髮？

　(A) 是的，差不多一個月剪一次。　　(B) 附近的理髮店。　　(C) 星期日的下午。

正解：**(B)**

題目用疑問詞 Where 詢問，具體回答了「地點」的選項 (B) 為正解。選項 (A) 以 Yes 回答以疑問詞開頭的疑問句，可立即判斷為錯誤。而選項 (C) 回答了時間，所以不正確。

2　Mr. Wilson looks tired, doesn't he?　　　　　　　　　　　技巧 ②
(A) He's been busy recently.　　　　　　　　　　　　　　　　技巧 ⑥
(B) No, I've got a flat tire.
(C) We saw him last week.

譯 威爾森先生看起來很累，不是嗎？

　(A) 他最近很忙。　　(B) 不，我的輪胎爆胎了。　　(C) 我們上禮拜有看到他。

正解：**(A)**

選項 (A) 回答了威爾森先生疲倦的理由，故為正解。選項 (B) 試圖以和 tired 發音類似的 tire 設下陷阱，小心別上當。遇到附加問句的題目，不要認為 Yes-No 開頭的選項就一定是答案，還是要仔細聽取之後的內容才能決定。選項 (C) 並未針對問題回應，故不可選。

> **3** Why don't you come to the party tonight?
> (A) Because I have a cold.
> (B) Let me think about it.
> (C) The dinner was great.

 技巧 **3**
 技巧 **4**
技巧 **5**

譯 你今天晚上何不來參加派對？

　(A) 因為我感冒了。　　(B) 讓我考慮一下。　　(C) 那頓晚餐很棒。

正解：**(B)**

對於 Why don't you ...?「你何不……？」的邀請疑問句，「讓我考慮一下。」這種未講明要去或不去、語帶「保留」的選項 (B) 才是正確答案。因題目問的不是理由，所以一聽到 (A) Because 即可先刪去。而選項 (C) 只是利用容易使人與題目的 party 產生聯想的 dinner 作為陷阱，故不可選。

Part 3 & Part 4

 答題指示

Part 3 此部分將播放二人以上的對話，考生須回答與該內容相關的三道題目。請從答案卡的 (A)、(B)、(C)、(D) 裡，選出一個最符合問題的敘述。對話不會印在題本上，且只會播放一次。

Part 4 此部分將播放單人口述的談話，每段談話皆附有三道考題，考生須從答案卡的 (A)、(B)、(C)、(D) 裡選出最符合問題的敘述。談話不會印在題本上，且只會播放一次。

 奪分攻略

❶ 在語音播放前，先將題目（試題和選項）大致看過一遍

趁播放答題指示時，先掃瞄接下來的問題，掌握一下問的是什麼，以便有效答題。而在聆聽題目對話或獨白時，也會因此較能夠專心尋找相關段落或關鍵字。此外，事先瀏覽問題，某種程度上也具有預測題目內容的好處。

❷ 回答 PART 4 的題目時，仔細聽 direction

獨白開始前會先播放如 Questions 1 through 3 refer ... telephone message 之類的說明以提示語音內容的種類，可藉此預測題目的走向。

14

TIP 1 提高對「換句話說」的熟悉度

許多選項是題目文內的詞彙之「同義表達」(paraphrase)，也就是「換句話說」，而其常為解題關鍵。這一點也適用於閱讀部分的 PART 7。

TIP 2 習慣發語詞或不完整的口語說法

多益測驗題型更新後，聽力部分 PART 2, 3, 4 的新趨勢包括考題融入 Hmm ...、Uh ... 等發語詞，不過對此無須特別準備對策，因為這在實際的對話當中，是很自然的現象，放輕鬆去聽就好了。此外，PART 3 新增三人或一來一往較長的對話，甚至也有像 Could you? 這樣簡短而不完整的應答，考生須由上下文思考其為何字句之省略。

TIP 3 針對問說話者為何提及某單字之問題，預先判斷考點效率高

PART 3, 4 新增問說話者於對話或獨白中發表某字之意圖的問題，例如 What does the man mean when he says, "..."?。預先弄清楚引號裡詞彙的涵義，再仔細聽取題目中該部分，便不難找到答案。這類考題大致可分為兩種。第一種是問該詞彙本身是什麼意思，例如 Why not? → 表示「同意」。另一種則引用比較長的段落，測驗考生對前後文脈的理解。

TIP 4 使用圖表的題目要提前快速掌握

PART 3, 4 還增加了圖表 (graphic) 問題。此題型的破解關鍵在於事先快速掃瞄圖表內容。注意，沒必要讀完所有的文字，將焦點集中在「這是關於什麼的圖表」就好，然後再依此推測對話或獨白的主旨。

試題
範例
MP3 ex07

Questions 1 through 3 refer to the following conversation.

M : Good afternoon. My name is Gabriel Sanchez. Can I speak with Mr. Joel Matthews, please?

W : I'm sorry, but he's out of the country on business this week. This is his assistant, Janice Taylor. Can I give him a message?

M : Oh, would you mind? I'm interested in the position of head chef that was advertised in last Friday's paper and I was wondering if he had received my résumé yet. I sent it last Saturday.

W : Hmm. Well, he left on ... uhh, Tuesday — Tuesday afternoon, so he probably hasn't seen it yet.

M : Ah, I see.

W : But he should be back in the restaurant the day after tomorrow. I'll let him know then.

譯 第 1 到 3 題請參照下面這段對話。

男：午安，我叫加百列・桑契斯。可以請約爾・麥修思先生聽電話嗎？

女：抱歉，這禮拜他因為出差不在國內。我是他的助理珍妮絲・泰勒。需要我為您轉達訊息給他嗎？

男：噢，您介意嗎？我對上星期五報紙廣告上所徵求的主廚職位有興趣，我在想不知道麥修思先生是不是已經收到了我的履歷表。我是上星期六寄的。

女：嗯，他是……呃，星期二、星期二下午出發的，所以可能還沒看。

男：啊，了解。

女：不過他後天應該會來餐廳，到時候我會轉告他。

---

1 Where does the woman most likely work?
(A) At a restaurant
(B) At a travel company
(C) At an advertising company
(D) At a newspaper

譯 女子最有可能是在哪裡工作？
(A) 餐廳　(B) 旅行社　(C) 廣告公司　(D) 報社

正解：**(A)**

關於基本事項的問題，必須從整段對話找關鍵字。男子提及 I'm interested in the position of <u>head chef ...</u>，表示欲應徵主廚一職，再由女子的最後一句話 ... he should be back in the <u>restaurant</u> ... 可知，正解為 (A)。

---

2 What did the man do last week?　
(A) He advertised a job.
(B) He applied for a job.
(C) He went on a business trip.
(D) He met with Mr. Matthews.

譯 男子上星期做了什麼事？
(A) 他刊登了徵才廣告。
(B) 他應徵了工作。
(C) 他去出差了。
(D) 他與麥修思先生見了面。

正解：**(B)**

預先掃瞄過問題之後，就知道要仔細聽取關於上星期發生的事情。男子提到 I sent it last Saturday.，表示他上週「寄了履歷表」，換句話說即他「應徵了工作」，所以正確答案是 (B) He applied for a job.。

---

3 Why does the man say, "Oh, would you mind"?　
(A) To decline a request
(B) To make a complaint
(C) To accept an offer
(D) To consider a question

譯 男子為什麼說 "Oh, would you mind"？
(A) 為了婉拒一項請求
(B) 為了抱怨
(C) 為了接受提議
(D) 為了考慮一個問題

正解：**(C)**

Would you mind ...ing? 此句型的涵義是「可以請你……嗎？」，用以表達請求。女子詢問 Can I give him a message?，提議自己可協助轉達訊息，而男子接著說的 would you mind 是 would you mind giving him a message 之省略，表示接受該提議，並認為女子若能幫忙就太好了。因此，選項 (C) 為正解。注意，題型更新後 PART 3 新增如本例題般長度較長的對話，並融入如 Hmm、uhh 之類的發語詞，以及類似 Ah, I see. 這種簡短應答，考生應多加熟悉。

Questions 1 through 3 refer to the following telephone message and schedule.
Hi John, it's Carly. Listen, it's around noon, and I'm here at the conference venue. I just got a call from the office. It looks like we'll have to cut out of the conference early. We've been asked to go meet a client this afternoon at the downtown convention center at five. It takes a little under an hour to get there from here by taxi. Could you meet me in the lobby after Stephanie Almarro's seminar? It's too bad we have to leave early, but at least we'll get to hear Kenji Endo. I hear he's really good. Thanks John, see you soon.

Conference Schedule	
Session Time	Speakers
1:00 – 1:50	Kenji Endo
2:00 – 2:50	Jack Winters
3:00 – 3:50	Stephanie Almarro
4:00 – 4:50	Kareem Singh

譯 第 1 到 3 題請參照下列電話留言和時程表。
嗨，約翰，我是卡莉。我跟你說，現在時間大概是中午，我人在會議舉辦場所這裡。我剛接到一通辦公室打來的電話。看來我們得提早從會議離開。他們要我們今天下午五點去城區會議中心和一位客戶碰面。從這裡搭計程車到那裡將近要一小時。史黛芬妮‧愛瑪羅的研討會之後，你能不能在大廳和我會合？我們必須提早離開實在太令人遺憾了，不過至少我們能聽到遠藤健二的場次。我聽說他真的很棒。謝啦約翰，待會見。

會議預定時程表	
會議時間	演講者
1:00 – 1:50	遠藤健二
2:00 – 2:50	傑克‧溫特斯
3:00 – 3:50	史黛芬妮‧愛瑪羅
4:00 – 4:50	卡里姆‧辛格

1 Where is the woman now?
(A) At a conference venue
(B) At her company
(C) At a convention center
(D) In a taxi

譯 女子現在在哪裡？
(A) 在會議舉辦場所 (B) 在她的公司 (C) 在會議中心 (D) 在計程車裡

正解：**(A)**

本題問說話者之目前所在地。從第二句 ... I'm here at the conference venue. 即可知，選項 (A) 為正解。像「說話者是誰」、「說話者的對象是誰」這類基本資訊，通常在最前面幾句話裡就能找到線索。

2 Why is the woman calling?
(A) A meeting has been canceled.
(B) A conference has been rescheduled.
(C) Plans have been changed.
(D) Travel plans have been delayed.

譯 女子為何來電？
(A) 會議被取消了。 (B) 會議被改時間了。 (C) 計畫有所變更。 (D) 旅行計畫被遲延。

正解：**(C)**

本題問這通電話的目的。根據 ... we'll have to cut out of the conference early. We've been asked ... at five. 這段話可知，說話者和聽者約翰兩人原本都要出席會議，但因為五點與客戶有約，所以不得不提早離開。選項 (C) 將此狀況做了簡潔的詮釋，故為正解。

---

3 Look at the graphic. What time will the man meet the woman in the lobby? 技巧 **4**
(A) Around 1:00 P.M.
(B) Around 2:00 P.M.
(C) Around 3:00 P.M.
(D) Around 4:00 P.M.

譯 請看圖表。男子將於幾點和女子在大廳碰面？
(A) 下午一點左右　　　　(B) 下午二點左右
(C) 下午三點左右　　　　(D) 下午四點左右

正解：**(D)**

遇到圖表題時，首先掃瞄一下是關於什麼的圖表能提高解題效率。本題是會議預定時間表，只要知道上面寫著幾點誰要演講就能應付大部分的問題了。女子詢問 Could you meet me in the lobby after Stephanie Almarro's seminar?，對照時程表，史黛芬妮・愛瑪羅的演講為 3:00 – 3:50，因此以兩人會合時間來說，最適當的是選項 (D) 下午四點左右。注意，圖表題必須綜合分析對話或獨白以及圖表資訊方可正確解答。

☑ 閱讀測驗

閱讀測驗將以各種不同類型的文章測試考生的理解能力。考試時間為七十五分鐘，分成三個 PART，並皆附有答題指示。請於考試時間之內，儘可能地作答。答案須填在答案卡裡，不可寫在題本上。

Part 5 & Part 6

答題指示

Part 5 下列句子中都缺少了部分的單字或片語，請從句子下方的四個選項中，選出最能使句意完整的字詞，並將答案卡裡的 (A)、(B)、(C)、(D) 其中一個塗黑。

Part 6 請閱讀下列文章。文章裡，有些地方缺少了某個字詞或句子，請從下方四個選項中，選出最能使語意完整的字句，並將答案卡裡的 (A)、(B)、(C)、(D) 其中一個塗黑。

❶ 察看選項和空格前後的內容，判斷可否不看完全文就作答

閱讀英文時應隨時記得一件事：注意看主詞和謂語動詞。但是，若為僅看空格前後即知解答的問題，則無須將全文看完，應趕緊劃記答案卡。

❷ 目標以 PART 5 一題 20 秒、PART 6 一篇文章 2 分鐘的速度作答

由於 PART 7 的閱讀分量增加，因此作答完後一般不太有足夠的時間重頭檢查。建議考生將答題時間的目標設成 PART 5 一題約 20 秒、總共 10 分鐘，PART 6 一篇文章（四道題目）約 2 分鐘、總共 8 分鐘，確保 PART 7 有 57 分鐘的時間可解題。

TIP 1 仔細觀察句型結構

許多「詞性題」只要看空格前後就能解答，例如「冠詞與名詞之間須填入形容詞」、「介系詞之後接名詞相當字（而不接主詞、動詞）」，以及當空格落在句首時，若之後有逗號區隔開來的話，空格內應填入副詞；而之後的構造若為〈子句，子句〉，空格內則應填入從屬連接詞。諸如此類之「句型構造」，考生應大量記憶。

TIP 2 注意具多種詞性的單字

弄清非單一詞性的單字在句中是什麼意思、什麼用法，也是解題重點之一。比方說，to 用作不定詞或介系詞，that 是作代名詞、形容詞（指示詞）、連接詞還是關係代名詞用等。

TIP 3 讀完整篇文章再選擇適當的語彙

觀察選項後發現問題屬於字彙題時，應立即設法理解上下文。

TIP 4 鎖定慣用語和片語

快速察覺空格為慣用語或片語的一部分，有助提高得分效率。

TIP 5 PART 6 插入句問題之重點在於上下文

多益題型更新後於 PART 6 新增了一題插入句問題。不過，此變革僅是將一直以來的判斷文脈題改成一整個句子而已，考生無須將之想得太困難。舉例來說，this 等指示詞、they 等代名詞係作指稱用，若要連接上下文作為補充內容是否合適？插入句是否表逆接關係？插入句是作為具體例子？整段話的涵義是正面的還是負面的……諸如此類對於文脈走向之理解就是這類問題的解題關鍵。

1 After the company's losses were announced last Tuesday, the _____ of its stock fell dramatically.
(A) valued
(B) value
(C) valuate
(D) valuable

技巧 1

譯 在上星期二公布虧損後，該公司的股價就急遽下滑。

正解：**(B)**

看題目之前先看選項得知，這是一道「詞性題」。首先觀察空格前後，適合填入〈the _____ of〉此構造的應為名詞，因此本題選 (B) value（價值；價格）。另注意，the 之後必定接名詞，就〈the _____ 名詞〉而言，在大多數的情形下空格內皆應為形容詞，作答時不能只看前面，後面也應仔細確認。本題選項 (A) 為動詞 value（評價）的過去式‧過去分詞，(C) 為動詞（對……估價），(D) 為形容詞（貴重的）。

2 Speaking _____ behalf of all the employees, Alan Lee thanked the departing CEO for all he had done for the company.
(A) on
(B) at
(C) for
(D) by

技巧 4

譯 李艾倫代表全體員工向即將離開的執行長表達謝意，感謝他為公司所做的一切。

正解：**(A)**

Speaking ... employees 此部分為分詞構句，不過本題考的不是分詞，而是測驗考生是否認識 on behalf of ...（代表……）此片語。和第一題一樣，本題只要知道 on behalf of 此用法就能快速解答，而無須將整個句子全部看完。

3 We have no option but to _____ halt production of our new sport utility model due to a downturn in global markets and lack of consumer demand.
(A) temporarily
(B) formerly
(C) initially
(D) consecutively

技巧 3

譯 由於全球市場的不景氣和消費者需求不足，我們公司除了暫停生產休旅車之外別無選擇。

正解：**(A)**

四個選項都是副詞，本題是必須看完整句再根據上下文選出答案的「字彙題」。景氣下滑與消費者需求不足而導致汽車的生產必須「暫時地」中止。最符合文脈之正解為 (A) temporarily。其他選項的意思分別為 (B)「先前地」、(C)「最初地」、(D)「連續地」。

Questions 1-4 refer to the following letter.

Timothy Mann
116, Bay Drive
San Francisco
California 94106
January 15

Dear Mr. Mann,

We'd like to remind you that your subscription to *Best Car* is due to _____ at the end
                                                                    1.
of March. We would also like to make you a special offer, if you renew by the end of

February: _____ two free copies, we'll also send you a Best Car family card. This card
          2.
entitles you to many benefits, _____ discounts on car rentals nationwide.
                               3.
All you need to do is fill out the enclosed renewal card, and drop it in the nearest

mailbox. Postage has been prepaid. _____.
                                    4.
We look forward to hearing from you.

Sincerely,

The Customer Service Team
Dominic Boules, Manager

1 (A) expires   技巧 1
  (B) expire
  (C) expiring   技巧 2
  (D) expiration

2 (A) In order to   技巧 1
  (B) As for
  (C) In addition to 技巧 2
  (D) As long as

3 (A) including   技巧 1
  (B) inclusive
  (C) included
  (D) includes

4 (A) Please send this letter back to us as soon as possible.   技巧 5
  (B) Your subscription will then be discontinued.
  (C) Please include necessary postage with this card.
  (D) We sincerely hope you will take full advantage of this offer.

譯 第 1 到 4 題請參照下面這封信件。

提摩西‧曼恩
加州三藩市 94106 海灣徑 116 號
1 月 15 日

曼恩先生您好：

我們想提醒您，您《貝斯特車誌》的訂閱將於三月底到期。假如您在二月底之前續訂的話，我們也想提供您一個特別方案：除了免費獲得兩本雜誌外，我們還會寄給您一張貝斯特車誌家族卡。持有該卡您可以享受許多優惠，包括全國適用的租車折扣。

您只須填妥隨附的續訂卡並就近投入郵筒。郵資已預付。我們誠摯希望您能多加利用本特惠方案。

期待您的回覆。

客服部經理
多明尼克‧布爾敬上

1 正解：**(B)**
本題考動詞 expire 的變化。句中 that 子句的主詞是 your subscription，動詞是 is。而解題關鍵在於察覺 be due to *do* 在此指「預定將……」，不定詞 to 之後的空格應填入原形動詞，故本題選 (B)。另注意，due to ... 則是指「起因於……」，這裡的 to 是介系詞，因此之後須接名詞結構。例如：The accident was due to their carelessness.（該起車禍肇因於他們的粗心大意。）勿將二者混淆。

2 正解：**(C)**
本題須選出適合填入句首之片語。由於 two free copies 為名詞結構，空格內需要的是能夠扮演介系詞角色的詞彙。觀察到空格後有 also，以「除了兩本免費雜誌之外，還要送出……」最符合前後文意，故選項 (C) In addition to 為正解。注意，這裡的 to 是介系詞，而選項 (A) In order to「為了……」的 to 則屬不定詞，其後須接原形動詞。其他選項的意思分別為 (B) As for「關於……」，後接名詞、(D) As long as「只要」，後接 SV（主詞＋動詞）。

3 正解：**(A)**
本題為詞性題。空格前一直到 benefits 是一個完整的句子，空格後屬一名詞結構，所以空格內應填入介系詞。正確答案是 (A) including「包括」。此類問題即使不甚理解整篇、整句內容，也可藉由觀察空格前後的字詞選出正解。

4 正解：**(D)**
本題考哪一個句子插入文章最合理，解題須由上下文思考何者適合作為文章最後的總結。這封信的主要目的是通知客戶其所訂閱的雜誌即將到期，並介紹一個特惠方案。四個選項當中，以選項 (D)「我們誠摯希望您能多加利用本特惠方案。」最符合文意。注意，this offer 即前面所介紹的特惠方案。由於續訂卡已附回郵，故選項 (C) 不正確。
其他選項的意思分別為：
(A)「請儘快將此信函寄回給我們。」
(B)「您的訂閱就將會被中止。」
(C)「請連同本卡附上所需郵資。」

Part 7

答題
指示

此部分的考題包括雜誌、新聞報導、電子郵件、即時通訊息等文章，每篇文章皆附有幾道問題，請選出最適當的答案，並將答案卡裡的 (A)、(B)、(C)、(D) 其中一個塗黑。

奪分
攻略

❶ 困難或不拿手的題目放棄也沒關係

比起單篇文章或長篇信件，應該會有人覺得雙篇、三篇文章題還比較容易作答吧？優先作答對自己而言較簡單的或較拿手之文件類型的題目，也是奪分的攻略之一。

❷ 作完所有題目直到最後一刻

在測驗結束前，即便是沒時間解答的題目，也務必挑個選項將答案卡劃滿。

解題
技巧

TIP❶ 快速察覺「同義表達」

和 PART 3&4 一樣，要仔細觀察文章與選項的「換句話說」。

TIP❷ 利用 Skimming「略讀」和 Scanning「掃瞄」兩大技巧

由於閱讀分量相當多，沒時間精讀所有的文章。做閱讀題目時，應活用 Skimming（指迅速讀完全文以掌握大意）和 Scanning（指瀏覽問題內容之後再從文章中找出相關處）這兩種技巧，其中「掃瞄」技巧對關於具體人名的問題，以及像是列表、表單這類文件特別有效。

TIP❸ 習慣手機・通訊軟體訊息和線上聊天對話等類型之題目

在題型更新後導入的行動載具訊息和線上聊天對話當中，相對於正式文件的一板一眼，取而代之的是較自然的口吻，考生應多多習慣閱讀這種較輕鬆的英文。

TIP❹ 對於問文件中某語句之意圖的問題，應先看試題再回看文章

更新後的多益測驗新增了問文件中某語句之意圖的問題。解答時應先確認問題問什麼，再一邊尋找該語句所在處，一邊閱讀文章（Scanning 技巧），找到後再徹底理解其上下文內容。

TIP❺ 對於插入句問題，應鎖定上下文語意不通順之處

新題型還包括問某個句子應插入文章何處最適當。首先確認插入句，然後利用 Skimming 略讀技巧，檢查出上下文中因缺漏句子而導致語意不流暢的地方。

試題範例 ────────────────────────── **單篇文章 (Single Passage)**

Questions 1-2 refer to the following text message chain.

Abdul Jazareh 5:56 P.M.
Donna, could you e-mail me a copy of the Donworth Inc. portfolio?

Donna Hastings   5:58 P.M.
Donworth? I don't think it's been digitized yet. We only have a printed version.

Abdul Jazareh   5:59 P.M.
Do you know where it is?

Donna Hastings   6:01 P.M.
You mean it's not at the Lexington branch?

Abdul Jazareh   6:02 P.M.
Nope, I've been looking all over for it.

Donna Hastings   6:05 P.M.
Then it's got to be at the downtown office. Hang on, OK?

Abdul Jazareh   6:07 P.M.
Don't they close at 6:00?

Donna Hastings   6:12 P.M.
I just talked to Cynthia Stride. She says it's there. She just locked up, but she said she will drop back in, scan it, and send it to you. I gave her your e-mail address.

Abdul Jazareh   6:14 P.M.
Oh, thanks so much, Donna!

譯 第 1 到 2 題請參照下面這段手機訊息。

阿卜杜爾‧賈札勒　　下午 **5:56**
唐娜,妳可以用電子郵件寄一份丹沃斯公司的卷宗給我嗎?
唐娜‧海斯廷斯　　　下午 **5:58**
丹沃斯?我想那些資料還沒做成電子檔案。我們只有影印版。
阿卜杜爾‧賈札勒　　下午 **5:59**
妳知道東西在哪裡嗎?
唐娜‧海斯廷斯　　　下午 **6:01**
你的意思是它不在萊辛頓分公司嗎?

阿卜杜爾・賈札勒　　下午 **6:02**

沒，我一直到處在找它。

唐娜・海斯廷斯　　下午 **6:05**

那它一定是在城區辦事處。等一下，好嗎？

阿卜杜爾・賈札勒　　下午 **6:07**

他們不是六點關門嗎？

唐娜・海斯廷斯　　下午 **6:12**

我剛跟辛希雅・史特德通過電話了。她說資料在那裡。她才剛鎖門離開，不過她說她會回辦公室一趟，掃描好就傳給你。我有給她你的電子郵件地址。

阿卜杜爾・賈札勒　　下午 **6:14**

噢，太感謝了，唐娜！

---

1 Where most likely does Ms. Stride work?
　(A) At Donworth Inc.
　(B) At the Lexington branch
　(C) At the downtown office
　(D) At a printing company

技巧❷　技巧❸

譯 史特德小姐最有可能在哪裡工作？
　(A) 丹沃斯公司　　(B) 萊辛頓分公司　　(C) 城區辦事處　　(D) 印刷公司

正解：**(C)**

通常手機訊息為兩人對話，線上聊天則為三人以上的對話。本題和史特德小姐有關，所以要掃瞄對話中出現此人名的地方。6:05 時海斯廷斯小姐說 Then it's got to be at the downtown office.「那它（客戶資料）一定是在城區辦事處。」之後於 6:12 時表示 I just talked to Cynthia Stride.「我剛跟辛希雅・史特德通過電話了。」由以上線索可推測史特德小姐應該就是城區辦事處的人員，因此本題選 (C)。

---

2 At 6:05 P.M., what does Ms. Hastings most likely mean when she writes, "Hang on, OK"?
　(A) She wants to get a printed portfolio.
　(B) She intends to visit the downtown office.
　(C) She is too busy to call Mr. Jazareh.
　(D) She needs a short amount of time.

技巧❷　技巧❸　技巧❹

譯 六點零五分時，海斯廷斯小姐打的 "Hang on, OK?" 最有可能是什麼意思？
　(A) 她想要一份影印的客戶卷宗資料。　　(B) 她打算去拜訪城區辦事處。
　(C) 她太忙沒時間打電話給賈札勒先生。　　(D) 她需要一點時間。

正解：**(D)**

本題問對話中某語句之意思。首先看試題，然後掃瞄文中出現 Hang on, OK? 的地方。只要知道 hang on 有「等待（回應）」的意思，應該就不難選出正確答案是 (D)。另，藉由確認上下文也可知 (D) 為正解，因為海斯廷斯小姐打完 Hang on, OK? 七分鐘之後接著表示自己剛才已經和辛希雅・史特德通話，也就是說，她要對方 Hang on 就是要對方在她與史特德小姐聯絡的這段時間稍待片刻。

Questions 1-3 refer to the following letter.

Patrick Slater
President
Garden International
394 Selby Ave.
St. Paul, MN 55104

Dear Mr. Slater,

I am writing with regard to the industrial grade lawnmower model X900 that we purchased from your company half a year ago. －[1]－.

As you may recall, at the time of purchase, I spoke with you at length about our requirements. I explained that our country club is located in a highly wooded area and that we needed a model that can cope with this. －[2]－.

However, in the last two months, I have had to contact your maintenance department a total of six times due to twigs and other small pieces of wood becoming jammed in the blades, causing the machine to short circuit. －[3]－. On his last visit Andy Hart confirmed there is nothing wrong with the machine itself but that it is simply not up to the task required.

I would appreciate it if you would either replace the lawnmower with a more dependable model or refund the full purchase price. －[4]－.

As ours is a high-class establishment and the upkeep of our estate is of the greatest importance to us, we are keen to sort this matter out as soon as possible.

An early reply in regard to this matter would be appreciated.

Sincerely yours,

Brian Beatty
Maintenance Manager
Mountain View Country Club

譯 第 1 到 3 題請參照下面這封信件。

派翠克・史萊特
花園國際董事長
明尼蘇達州聖保羅市 55104
塞爾比大道 394 號

史萊特先生您好：

我寫這封信與敝公司半年前向貴公司購買的工業級除草機 X900 有關。— [1] —。

您可能還記得，在購買該除草機時，我曾詳述過敝公司的需求。我向您說明敝公司的鄉村俱樂部位於樹木茂盛的地區，必須購買能應付此情況的機型。— [2] —。

但是在過去的兩個月間，由於小樹枝和其他小木片會卡在刀片裡面，導致除草機短路，我不得不與貴公司的維修部門聯絡一共多達六次。— [3] —。安迪・哈特最後一次來的時候，他確認機械本身沒什麼問題，但就是無法執行我們要求的工作。

如果貴公司願意用一台比較可靠的機型來換這台除草機或全額退費的話，本人將會很感激。— [4] —。

由於敝公司屬高級俱樂部，一切設施的維護至為重要，因此我們熱切希望能儘快解決這個問題。

期待此事能早日得到您的回覆，謝謝您。

山景鄉村俱樂部
維修部經理
布萊恩・比提敬上

---

1 Who is Andy Hart?
(A) An employee of Garden International
(B) A colleague of Brian Beatty
(C) A gardener at Mountain View Country Club
(D) A machine salesman

譯 安迪・哈特是誰？
(A) 花園國際的員工 　　　　(B) 布萊恩・比提的同事
(C) 山景鄉村俱樂部的園丁　　(D) 機具業務員

正解：**(A)**

看到試題問 Andy Hart（安迪・哈特）這個人，就直接鎖定文章中出現此名字的段落。由信函第三段中提到的 On his last visit, Andy Hart confirmed there is nothing wrong with the machine itself ... 可知，比提先生聯絡花園國際的維修部門後，安迪・哈特曾為了檢查機器而拜訪比提先生。由此可推測安迪・哈特應是花園國際裡負責修理機具的員工，故本題選 (A)。

---

2 What does Mr. Beatty ask Mr. Slater to do?
(A) Repair the lawnmower
(B) Replace the broken parts
(C) Provide them with a more reliable machine
(D) Pay for the cost of repairs

譯 比提先生要求史萊特先生做什麼？
(A) 修理除草機 　　　　　(B) 更換壞掉的零件
(C) 提供他們較可靠的機型　(D) 支付修理費用

正解：**(C)**

先看試題，閱讀文章時再將焦點放在「比提先生對史萊特先生的要求」上。信中第四段提及 ... replace the lawnmower with a more dependable model or refund the full purchase price，意即比提先生希望「更換一台較可靠的機型或全額退費」，所以正確答案是選項 (C)。注意，(C) 中以 reliable 代換文中的 dependable。

3 In which of the positions marked [1], [2], [3] and [4] does the following sentence best belong?

技巧 **2**

技巧 **5**

"At that time you gave me every assurance that this particular model was the right one for the job."

(A) [1]
(B) [2]
(C) [3]
(D) [4]

譯 下面這個句子插入文中標示的 [1]、[2]、[3]、[4] 四處當中的何處最符合文意？

「當時您保證這台特別機型恰恰能勝任這項工作。」

(A) [1]　　　(B) [2]　　　(C) [3]　　　(D) [4]

正解：**(B)**

本題屬插入句題。首先，請確認試題中所列出的句子。注意，At that time 是解答線索。合理推測「當時您 (= Garden International) 保證這台特別機型恰恰能勝任這項工作」應該是指比提先生購買除草機的時候，而第二段內容寫的正是購買當下的事情，因此本題正解為選項 (B)。第一段為開場白、第三段描述的是使用後的狀況，第四段則要求解決問題，三處明顯皆不適合插入該句。

試題
範例

雙篇文章 **(Double Passage)**

Questions 1-5 refer to the following advertisement and e-mail.

Junior Advertising Executive Wanted For Prominent Fashion Publication Aimed At Young Women

A college degree in a related subject is required as is familiarity with publishing. At least two years' comparable work experience is essential. Successful applicants will also be able to demonstrate a knowledge of current trends in fashion. Those interested should e-mail a résumé with a cover letter to arrive no later than April 21 to Melanie Marshall at the following address: Mmarshall@stargroup.com

---

From: abigailFNY@hotmail.com
To: Mmarshall@stargroup.com
Date: April 15th
Subject: Application for Junior Advertising Executive position

Dear Ms. Marshall,

I would like to apply for the position advertised in last week's edition of *The Evening Herald*. I have attached my résumé for your consideration. I believe I have the experience and skills that you are looking for and that I am the right person for the job.

I was born in England, where I studied Communications and Media at the University of East Anglia. After leaving college, I worked for a department store in London, as a trainee fashion buyer for a year, before relocating to New York two years ago. Since last September, I have been working on a temporary basis as an advertising assistant for a trade publication *Trends In Fashion Today*. I feel that my unique background could add value to your Advertising Executive position.

Thank you very much for your time and consideration.

Sincerely,

Abigail Fraser

譯 第 1 到 5 題請參照下列廣告和電子郵件。

目標族群為年輕女子的知名時尚雜誌
徵求廣告宣傳 AE 助理

須具備相關科系的大學學位並熟悉出版業。至少須兩年相關產業的工作經驗。錄取者也必須能夠展現本身對當今流行趨勢的了解。意者請於 4 月 21 日之前以電子郵件將履歷和求職信寄至：Mmarshall@stargroup.com，梅蘭妮・馬歇爾收。

寄件者：abigailFNY@hotmail.com
收件者：Mmarshall@stargroup.com
日　期：4 月 15 日
主　旨：應徵廣告宣傳 AE 助理一職

馬歇爾小姐您好：

我想應徵上週刊登於《先驅晚報》之廣告中的職位。本信已附上履歷表，煩請參閱。我認為我擁有貴公司所要求的經驗與技能，而且我相信我是最適合這個職位的人選。

我出生於英國，在東安格里亞的大學主修大眾傳播與媒體。畢業之後，我先在倫敦的一家百貨公司擔任一年的時尚商品採購實習生，之後被調任至紐約工作兩年。從去年九月開始，我在業界雜誌《今日時尚潮流》擔任臨時廣告宣傳助理。我認為我的獨特經歷背景能為貴公司的廣告宣傳 AE 職位加分。

非常感謝您撥冗審查我的應徵。

艾比蓋兒・弗雷澤
敬上

1 Where does Melanie Marshall most likely work?
(A) For a magazine
(B) For an advertising agency
(C) For a fashion store
(D) For a design office

譯 梅蘭妮‧馬歇爾最有可能在哪裡工作？
(A) 雜誌社　　　　　　(B) 廣告公司
(C) 時尚精品店　　　　(D) 設計事務所

正解：**(A)**

由廣告標題 Wanted for Prominent Fashion Publication 可知，這是一篇時尚出版品的徵人啓事，而 Melanie Marshall 此人名出現在最後，明顯是職位的聯絡窗口。由此合理推測其所服務的公司應爲 (A) 雜誌社。注意，選項中以 magazine 將文中的 publication 做另一種詮釋。

2 Where did Abigail Fraser attend college?
(A) London
(B) East Anglia
(C) New York
(D) Northern England

譯 艾比蓋兒‧弗雷澤曾在哪裡就讀大學？
(A) 倫敦　　　　　　　(B) 東安格里亞
(C) 紐約　　　　　　　(D) 英國北部

正解：**(B)**

Abigail Fraser 即電子郵件的寄件者。觀察文中提及大學的段落，由第二段的 I studied ... at the University of East Anglia 即可知，正確答案就是選項 (B)。注意，選項中的 attend 和文中的 study 同義。

3 What requirement does Abigail Fraser most likely NOT meet?
(A) Knowledge of publishing
(B) A relevant college degree
(C) Amount of similar work experience
(D) Familiarity with current trends in advertising

譯 艾比蓋兒‧弗雷澤最有可能「不」符合哪一項條件？
(A) 出版業的知識　　　　(B) 相關科系的大學學位
(C) 類似工作的經驗量　　(D) 當今廣告業流行趨勢的熟悉度

正解：**(C)**

廣告中所詳述的應徵必備條件包含選項 (A)、(B)、(C)。而電子郵件中寫道 I worked for a department store in London, as a trainee fashion buyer for a year，亦即應徵者艾比蓋兒‧弗雷澤曾有一年的百貨公司工作經驗；又說，從 Since last September, I have been working ...，也就是她自去年九月起曾做過業界刊物的助理，但由於電子郵件的日期爲 4 月，因此還不滿一年。綜合以上線索可

知其總工作經驗少於兩年，換言之，並不符合應徵條件中的 At least two years' comparable work experience is essential.（至少須兩年相關產業的工作經驗。）故本題選 (C)。注意，雙篇文章題與三篇文章題的特色之一就是必須跨文件尋找資訊，並將資訊做連結方可正確解答。

---

4 What is indicated about Abigail Fraser?
(A) Her present job is not permanent.
(B) She graduated from university two years ago.
(C) She is currently out of the country.
(D) Her present job is not challenging enough.

譯 關於艾比蓋兒‧弗雷澤的敘述何者正確？
(A) 她目前的工作並非長期正職。　　(B) 她兩年前從大學畢業。
(C) 她目前人在國外。　　　　　　　(D) 她現在的工作內容不具挑戰性。

正解：**(A)**

像「下列敘述何者正確」這種不是問單一資訊的題型，必須根據整篇文章來判斷。電子郵件第二段後半提到 I have been working on a temporary basis as an advertising assistant ...，表示艾比蓋兒‧弗雷澤目前擔任的是「臨時廣告宣傳助理」，故正解為選項 (A)。not permanent 是 on a temporary basis 的另一種說法。

---

5 In the e-mail, the word "unique" in paragraph 2, line 5, is closest in meaning to
(A) special
(B) single
(C) affluent
(D) strange

譯 電子郵件第二段第五行的 "unique" 這個字的意思最接近
(A) 特別的　　　　　　　　(B) 單一的
(C) 富裕的　　　　　　　　(D) 奇怪的

正解：**(A)**

unique 這個字具有「唯一的；獨特的；極好的；無與倫比的」等意思，而由於電子郵件為艾比蓋兒‧弗雷澤突顯自身經歷的文件，因此依上下文判斷，在此 unique 應是指選項 (A) special（特別的）之意。（PART 7 的字彙題經常會考多義字的使用，考生須加留意。）

Business
Vocabulary

高頻商英字彙 200

公司・組織

- □ **company** [ˈkʌmpənɪ] 名 公司；企業　　相關 corporation 法人；股份（有限）公司
- □ **firm** [fɜm] 名 商號；商店；公司　　用法 law firm 法律事務所
- □ **organization** [ˌɔrgənəˈzeʃən] 名 團體；組織　　動 organize 組織化；安排
- □ **institute** [ˈɪnstətjut] 名 協會；研究所；專科學校
- □ **establish** [əˈstæblɪʃ] 動 設立；創辦　　用法 establish a company 創辦一家公司
- □ **head office** 本店；總公司
- □ **headquarters** [ˈhɛdˈkwɔrtəz] 名 總公司；總部
- □ **branch** [bræntʃ] 名 分公司；分店　　用法 overseas branch 海外分店
- □ **department** [dɪˈpartmənt] 名（公司等的）部門；課、（行政組織的）省、（學校機構的）學系；科
- □ **division** [dəˈvɪʒən] 名（公司等的）事業分部；局；課、（學校機構的）學系
- □ **human resources (HR) department** 人資部　　類 personnel department 人事部
- □ **research and development (R&D) department** 研究開發部

職稱

- □ **CEO** 名 執行長（chief executive officer 的縮寫）
- □ **president** [ˈprɛzədənt] 名 會長；董事長　　相關 director 董事；主任
- □ **vice president** 副會長；副董事長
- □ **employer** [ɪmˈplɔɪə] 名 老闆；雇主　　反 employee 雇員；員工
- □ **board** [bord] 名 董事會；委員會　　用法 board of directors 董事會
- □ **executive** [ɪgˈzɛkjʊtɪv] 名 主管；重要幹部
- □ **administration** [ədˌmɪnəˈstreʃən] 名 管理；經營　　用法 the administration 行政部門；管理團隊
- □ **manager** [ˈmænɪdʒə] 名 經理；主任；店長　　動 manage 經營　　名 management 管理（團隊）
- □ **staff** [stæf] 名 員工；工作人員　　相關 worker 勞工
- □ **boss** [bɔs] 名 上司；老闆
- □ **supervisor** [ˈsupəˌvaɪzə] 名 主管；上司
- □ **subordinate** [səˈbɔrdnɪt] 名 部下；部屬
- □ **colleague** [ˈkɑlig] 名 同事　　類 co-worker 同事；工作夥伴

2 客戶・職業・職務

客戶・職業

- □ **client** [ˈklaɪənt] 名 客戶

- □ **contract** [ˈkɑntrækt] 名 合約（書）　相關 agreement 協議；契約

- □ **manufacturer** [ˌmænjəˈfæktʃərə] 名 製造業者　動 manufacture 製造

- □ **retailer** [ˈritelə] 名 零售業者

- □ **agency** [ˈedʒənsɪ] 名 代理機構；仲介　相關 agent 代理人　travel agency 旅行社　real estate agency 不動產仲介商

- □ **publisher** [ˈpʌblɪʃə] 名 出版社　類 publishing company 出版公司

- □ **architect** [ˈɑrkəˌtɛkt] 名 建築師

- □ **secretary** [ˈsɛkrəˌtɛrɪ] 名 祕書

- □ **editor** [ˈɛdɪtə] 名 編輯

- □ **accountant** [əˈkaʊntənt] 名 會計師

- □ **lawyer** [ˈlɔjə] 名 律師　相關 attorney【美】律師

- □ **salesclerk** [ˈselzˌklɜk] 名 店員　類 shop assistant 銷售員

- □ **professor** [prəˈfɛsə] 名 教授　相關 instructor（運動或大學的）講師

職務

- □ **duties** [ˈdjutɪz] 名 職務；責任〔複數形〕

- □ **operation** [ˌɑpəˈreʃən] 名 操作；運轉；經營　動 operate 經營；操作

- □ **performance** [pəˈfɔrməns] 名 業績　類 achievement, accomplishment 成績　用法 sales performance 銷售成績

- □ **campaign** [kæmˈpen] 名 行銷活動

- □ **strategy** [ˈstrætədʒɪ] 名 策略

- □ **publicity** [pʌbˈlɪsətɪ] 名 廣告；宣傳

- □ **proposal** [prəˈpozl] 名 提案；提議書

- □ **submit** [səbˈmɪt] 動 提出；提交　類 hand in 繳交　名 submission 提交（物）

- □ **expire** [ɪkˈspaɪr] 動 滿期；（期限）終止　相關 due〔形容詞〕到期的

- □ **deadline** [ˈdɛdˌlaɪn] 名 截止期限；最後限期　用法 meet the deadline 在期限內把事情做完

- □ **schedule** [ˈskɛdʒʊl] 動 安排；預定　相關 reschedule 重新安排日期、時間

- □ **be in charge of ...** 負責……；管理……　相關 be responsible for ... 負責……

3 會議・出差

☐ **conference** [ˈkɑnfərəns] 名 會議

☐ **board meeting** 董事會議　　　　　　　用法 executive board meeting 執行董事會

☐ **committee** [kəˈmɪtɪ] 名 委員會

☐ **attend** [əˈtɛnd] 動 出席

☐ **venue** [ˈvɛnju] 名（活動）場所

☐ **exhibition** [ˌɛksəˈbɪʃən] 名 展覽；展示會；博覽會

☐ **agenda** [əˈdʒɛndə] 名 議程

☐ **discussion** [dɪˈskʌʃən] 名 討論　　　　動 discuss 討論（≒ talk about）

☐ **handout** [ˈhændaʊt] 名（在會議等分發的）講義；發放的資料

☐ **projector** [prəˈdʒɛktə] 名 投影機

☐ **minutes** [ˈmɪnɪts] 名 會議記錄〔複數形〕　　用法 take the minutes 做會議記錄

☐ **chairperson** [ˈtʃɛrˌpɝsn̩] 名 主席；董事長

☐ **representative** [ˌrɛprɪˈzɛntətɪv] 名 代表；代理人

☐ **passenger** [ˈpæsn̩dʒə] 名 乘客

☐ **departure** [dɪˈpɑrtʃə] 名 出發　　　　動 depart 出發　　反 arrive 到達

☐ **bound for ...** 往……

☐ **round-trip ticket** 來回票　　　　　　相關 one-way ticket 單程票

☐ **boarding** [ˈbordɪŋ] 名 登機、船、火車等　　用法 boarding pass 登機證

☐ **aisle seat** 靠走道座位　　　　　　　　反 window seat 靠窗座位

☐ **destination** [ˌdɛstəˈneʃən] 名 目的地　　用法 final destination 終點

☐ **take off** 起飛　　　　　　　　　　　反 land 著陸

☐ **delay** [dɪˈle] 名 延遲　動 耽擱；延誤

☐ **itinerary** [aɪˈtɪnəˌrɛrɪ] 名 旅遊行程表

☐ **fare** [fɛr] 名 車費

☐ **accommodations** [əˌkɑməˈdeʃənz] 名 旅館等住宿之處〔複數形〕

□ **apply for ...** 應徵……　　　　　用法 apply for a position 應徵某項職務

□ **hire** [haɪr] 動 雇用

□ **résumé** ['rɛzu,me] 名 履歷　　　　類 CV 簡歷表, cover letter 求職信

□ **job opening** 職缺

□ **recruit** [rɪ'krut] 動 招募　名 新進員工

□ **trainee** [tre'ni] 名 實習生　　　　動 train 培訓　名 trainer 訓練者

□ **orientation** [,orɪɛn'teʃən] 名 職前訓練

□ **part time** 兼職　　　　　　　　反 full time 全職

□ **employment** [ɪm'plɔɪmənt] 名 雇用；在職　　反 unemployment 失業

□ **temporary** ['tɛmpə,rɛrɪ] 形 暫時的　　副 temporarily 暫時地　反 permanent 永久的

□ **shift** [ʃɪft] 名 輪班（制）

□ **requirement** [rɪ'kwaɪrmənt] 名（職務的）必備條件

□ **condition** [kən'dɪʃən] 名（協議、合約等的）條件

□ **terms** [tɜmz] 名（付款、合約等的）條件〔複數形〕

□ **certificate** [sə'tɪfəkɪt] 動 認證；發給證書　名 證明書；執照　名 certification 證照

□ **qualification** [,kwaləfə'keʃən] 名 資格　　相關 be qualified for ... 具有……的資格

□ **skill** ['skɪl] 名 技術；技能

□ **knowledge** ['nalɪdʒ] 名 知識

□ **background** ['bæk,graund] 名 背景；經歷

□ **degree** [dɪ'gri] 名 學位　　　　用法 graduate degree 研究所學位

□ **retire** [rɪ'taɪr] 動（因屆齡或生病等的）退休　名 retirement 退休

□ **resign** [rɪ'zaɪn] 動（自願提出的、正式的）辭職　類 quit, leave 離職

□ **reorganization** [,riɔrgənə'zeʃən] 名 改組；重新制定

□ **layoff** ['le,ɔf] 名 臨時解雇；裁員；資遣

□ **fire** [faɪr] 動 解雇　　　　　　類 dismiss 遣散（語氣比 fire 弱）

5 薪資・福利・人事異動

□ **salary** [ˈsælərɪ] 名（通常指每月領取的固定）薪水

□ **income** [ˈɪnˌkʌm] 名（定期的）收入；（特指一年內）所得

□ **fee** [fi] 名（支付給專業人士一次性的）酬金

□ **wage** [wedʒ] 名（特指支付給勞動者的）日・時・週薪

□ **payment** [ˈpemənt] 名 支付；付款

□ **payroll** [ˈpeˌrol] 名（公司的）薪水冊；（員工的）薪金總額

□ **paycheck** [ˈpeˌtʃɛk] 名 薪水；薪資支票

□ **remuneration** [rɪˌmjunəˈreʃən] 名（勞動工作方面的）報酬；薪水

□ **compensation** [ˌkampənˈseʃən] 名 賠償；報酬

□ **raise** [rez] 名 加薪

□ **welfare** [ˈwɛlˌfɛr] 名 福利

□ **benefit** [ˈbɛnəfɪt] 名 津貼；福利

□ **allowance** [əˈlauəns] 名（定期的）津貼　　用法 monthly allowance 每月津貼

□ **pension** [ˈpɛnʃən] 名 退休金；養老金

□ **health insurance** 健康保險

□ **paid holiday** 有薪假

□ **vacation** [veˈkeʃən] 名 假期

□ **incentive** [ɪnˈsɛntɪv] 名 獎金

□ **award** [əˈword] 名 獎金；獎品

□ **commission** [kəˈmɪʃən] 名 佣金

□ **promotion** [prəˈmoʃən] 名 升遷　　動 promote 使晉升；拔擢

□ **appoint A as [to be] B** 任命 A 為 B　　名 appointment 任命；指名

□ **allocate A to B** 將 A 分派至 B

□ **transfer** [ˈtrænsfɜ] 名 人事異動；調職　動 轉調　用法 transfer him to Tokyo office 將他轉調至東京分處

□ **relocate A to B** 將 A 調任至 B

☐ **product** [`prɑdəkt] 名 產品	相關 produce 製作、production 生產	
☐ **item** [`aɪtəm] 名 項目；品項	用法 damaged item 損傷品	
☐ **goods** [gʊdz] 名 商品		
☐ **defective** [dɪ`fɛktɪv] 形 有缺陷的		
☐ **replacement** [rɪ`plesmənt] 名 替換（品）	動 replace A with B 用 B 替換 A	
☐ **factory** [`fæktərɪ] 名 工廠		
☐ **plant** [plænt] 名 工廠；機器設備		
☐ **warehouse** [`wɛr͵haʊs] 名 倉庫	相關 storeroom 貯藏室；置物間	
☐ **stock** [stɑk] 名 貯藏；儲藏	用法 out of stock 沒有庫存、in stock 有庫存	
☐ **shortage** [`ʃɔrtɪdʒ] 名 短缺	用法 be short of... ⋯⋯不足 run out of ... ⋯⋯用盡	
☐ **facility** [fə`sɪlətɪ] 名（醫院、圖書館等）設施〔通常複數形〕	用法 medical facilities 醫療設施	
☐ **equipment** [ɪ`kwɪpmənt] 名 設備；裝置	用法 electrical equipment 電器設備	
☐ **supplies** [sə`plaɪz] 名 生活必需品〔複數形〕	用法 office supplies 辦公事務用品	
☐ **appliance** [ə`plaɪəns] 名 電子產品；電器設備	相關 home appliance 家電製品	
☐ **device** [dɪ`vaɪs] 名 裝置；儀器	相關 tool 工具；（專業人士使用的）道具	
☐ **supply** [sə`plaɪ] 動 名 供給	反 demand 需要　名 supplier 供應商	
☐ **package** [`pækɪdʒ] 名 包裹		
☐ **envelope** [`ɛnvə͵lop] 名 信封		
☐ **delivery** [dɪ`lɪvərɪ] 名 遞送	用法 delivery charge 運費　動 deliver 配送	
☐ **shipment** [`ʃɪpmənt] 名 運送；出貨	動 ship 運送	
☐ **distribute** [dɪ`strɪbjut] 動 配送；分布	名 distribution 分配；配送	
☐ **loading** [`lodɪŋ] 名 裝載貨物	動 load 裝載（貨品等）	
☐ **cargo** [`kɑrgo] 名 貨物	用法 unload cargo 卸下貨物	
☐ **courier** [`kʊrɪə] 名 快遞業者		
☐ **invoice** [`ɪnvɔɪs] 名 發票；出貨單	相關 bill 請款單	

7 金融・收支・投資・景氣

金融・收支

☐ **market** [`markɪt] 名 市場

☐ **tax** [tæks] 名 稅金 　　　　　　　　　用法 tax included 含稅

☐ **debt** [dɛt] 名 債務；欠款

☐ **profit** [`prafɪt] 名 利潤

☐ **loss** [lɔs] 名 虧損

☐ **revenue** [`rɛvə.nju] 名 稅入；收益

☐ **earnings** [`ɜnɪŋz] 名（投資）盈餘；（工作）所得

☐ **sales** [selz] 名 銷售額〔複數形〕

☐ **turnover** [`tɜn.ovə] 名（一定期間的）營業額

☐ **expenses** [ɪk`spɛnsɪz] 名 經費〔複數形〕 　用法 travel expenses 旅費

投資

☐ **shareholder** [`ʃɛr.holdə] 名 股東 　　　用法 shareholders' meeting 股東大會

☐ **stock** [stak] 名 股票 　　　　　　　　用法 stock market 股票市場

☐ **investment** [ɪn`vɛstmənt] 名 投資 　　動 invest 投資

☐ **dividend** [`dɪvə.dɛnd] 名 紅利；股息

☐ **interest rate** 利率 　　　　　　　　注意 此處 interest 指「利息」

☐ **statement** [`stetmənt] 名 報告書；交易明細表 用法 bank statement 銀行對帳單

☐ **merger** [mɜdʒə] 名 合併 　　　　　　動 merge 合併

☐ **take over ...** 收購……；接管…… 　　類 acquire 獲取

景氣

☐ **economy** [ɪ`kanəmɪ] 名 經濟；景氣 　注意 economic 經濟上的、economical 節省的 economics 經濟學

☐ **recession** [rɪ`sɛʃən] 名（暫時性的）不景氣

☐ **depression** [dɪ`prɛʃən] 名 蕭條

☐ **slowdown** [`slo.daʊn] 名 衰退

☐ **sluggish** [`slʌgɪʃ] 形 緩慢的；停滯的

☐ **bankruptcy** [`bæŋkrəptsɪ] 名 破產；倒閉 　動 bankrupt 使破產

☐ **turnaround** [`tɜnə.raʊnd] 名 好轉

電話

□ **mobile phone** 行動電話 　　　　　　 注意 單以 phone 一字表「手機」也經常可見

□ **text message**（手機上的）文字訊息 　 相關 text 傳送手機訊息

□ **leave a message** 留言 　　　　　　　 反 take a message 替人留言

□ **disconnect** [͵dɪskəˋnɛkt] 動 切斷（電話等） 　用法 disconnect the line 掛電話

□ **hang up** 掛電話

□ **answering machine** 電話答錄機

□ **extension** [ɪkˋstɛnʃən] 名（電話）分機 　用法 extension number 分機號碼

□ **line** [laɪn] 名 電話線 　　　　　　　 用法 hold the line 稍等、別掛斷電話

□ **area code** 區碼

□ **customer service** 客服

網路

□ **online** [ˋɑn͵laɪn] 形 線上的；網路的　 副 在網路上 　用法 online chat 網路聊天

□ **install** [ɪnˋstɔl] 動 安裝

□ **Web site** 網站 　　　　　　　　　　 類 Web page 網頁

□ **access** [ˋæksɛs] 動【電腦】存取（資料）；進入；連接

E-mail · 信件

□ **sender** [ˋsɛndɚ] 名 寄件者

□ **recipient** [rɪˋsɪpɪənt] 名 收件者

□ **subject** [ˋsʌbdʒɪkt] 名 主旨

□ **attach** [əˋtætʃ] 動 附加 　　　　　　 名 attachment 附加檔案；附件

□ **enclose** [ɪnˋkloz] 動 封入；隨信（包裹）寄送

□ **forward** [ˋfɔrwəd] 動 轉寄；傳送

□ **reply** [rɪˋplaɪ] 名 回信　 動 回覆 　　　用法 reply to an inquiry 答覆詢問

□ **regarding** [rɪˋgardɪŋ] 介 與……有關

□ **including** [ɪnˋkludɪŋ] 介 包括 　　　　 反 excluding 除……之外

□ **hear from ...** 得到……的回覆

□ **look forward to ...** 期待

解答一覽表

題號	正解	題號	正解	題號	正解	題號	正解	題號	正解
1	B	41	C	81	B	121	C	161	D
2	B	42	B	82	B	122	B	162	A
3	A	43	D	83	D	123	C	163	B
4	A	44	B	84	B	124	B	164	C
5	D	45	A	85	B	125	D	165	D
6	B	46	C	86	C	126	C	166	B
7	A	47	D	87	C	127	B	167	A
8	C	48	D	88	D	128	A	168	A
9	B	49	C	89	B	129	C	169	D
10	C	50	B	90	D	130	B	170	A
11	A	51	C	91	B	131	D	171	D
12	B	52	A	92	C	132	B	172	D
13	A	53	B	93	B	133	B	173	A
14	B	54	A	94	D	134	D	174	D
15	A	55	A	95	C	135	C	175	C
16	A	56	A	96	D	136	D	176	A
17	B	57	C	97	C	137	A	177	A
18	C	58	D	98	D	138	B	178	C
19	A	59	A	99	C	139	A	179	B
20	B	60	D	100	C	140	C	180	C
21	A	61	B	101	D	141	D	181	C
22	C	62	B	102	B	142	B	182	D
23	A	63	C	103	D	143	D	183	A
24	B	64	B	104	B	144	C	184	D
25	B	65	C	105	D	145	C	185	A
26	A	66	D	106	C	146	B	186	D
27	C	67	A	107	B	147	D	187	C
28	A	68	A	108	D	148	B	188	A
29	B	69	C	109	A	149	A	189	C
30	A	70	C	110	B	150	B	190	B
31	A	71	A	111	B	151	A	191	B
32	B	72	B	112	D	152	A	192	C
33	D	73	A	113	C	153	B	193	A
34	C	74	C	114	A	154	D	194	D
35	B	75	B	115	D	155	C	195	C
36	A	76	C	116	C	156	C	196	A
37	A	77	B	117	B	157	D	197	D
38	D	78	B	118	C	158	A	198	D
39	D	79	A	119	C	159	C	199	C
40	B	80	A	120	A	160	D	200	B

PART 1 MP3 001-004

1

(A) They're looking out the window.
(B) They're examining the documents.
(C) They're polishing the table.
(D) They're writing on the paper.

(A) 她們正在看窗外。
(B) 她們正在檢查文件。
(C) 她們正在把桌子擦亮。
(D) 她們正在紙上寫東西。

正解 (B) 人物動作

照片為兩位女子對著文件討論的情景，最符合此情景的選項為 (B)。不要被照片裡的 window、table、paper 所迷惑，其他選項的「動作」皆與照片內容不一致，因此並不恰當。

☐ **examine** [ɪgˋzæmɪn] 動 檢查；考核
☐ **polish** [ˋpɑlɪʃ] 動 擦亮

2

(A) He's pointing at himself.
(B) He's wearing a tie.
(C) He's moving the computer.
(D) He's taking off his glasses.

(A) 他正指著自己。
(B) 他打著領帶。
(C) 他正在移動電腦。
(D) 他正把眼鏡摘下來。

正解 (B) 人物動作

照片中男子的手指向空中，並非指著自己，故選項 (A) 不正確。他的右手雖然摸著滑鼠，但並未移動電腦，也沒有在脫眼鏡，所以 (C) 與 (D) 也都不適合。(B)「打著領帶」的描述為正解。

☐ **point at** 指著某人‧事‧物
☐ **take off** 脫掉（衣物等）

3

(A) The wheels are on the pavement.
(B) The cart is tipped over.
(C) The store window is broken.
(D) The shopping bag is empty.

(A) 輪子在人行道上。
(B) 推車翻倒了。
(C) 商店的窗子破了。
(D) 購物袋是空的。

正解 (A) 事物狀態

人行道上有一台購物車，選項 (A) 正確描述此情景。購物車並未翻倒，一旁商店的窗戶也沒有破掉，故選項 (B)、(C) 都不對。如果沒有聽出選項 (D) 裡的 bag，可能會誤以為 (D) 就是正解，所以答題時須仔細聆聽細節。

☐ **wheel** [hwil] 名 車輪
☐ **pavement** [ˋpevmənt] 名 人行道〔英〕
☐ **tip over** 翻倒

試題與翻譯	答案與解析

4

(A) She's viewing the screen.
(B) She's touching the monitor.
(C) She's holding the handset.
(D) She's typing on the keyboard.

(A) 她正在看螢幕。
(B) 她正在觸摸顯示器。
(C) 她正拿著電話聽筒。
(D) 她正在用鍵盤打字。

正解 (A) 人物動作

照片中一位女子正看著電腦螢幕，故正解為 (A)。這位女子右手扶著滑鼠，可是並未觸摸其他物品，因此其他的選項都是錯的。

□ **view** [vju] 動 觀看
□ **handset** ['hænd.sɛt] 名（電話的）話筒

5

(A) Some buildings are being built.
(B) Some employees are working in the office.
(C) Some shops are being cleaned.
(D) Some people are walking along the avenue.

(A) 有幾棟大樓正在興建中。
(B) 有幾個員工們正在辦公室裡工作。
(C) 有幾家商店正在被清理。
(D) 有些人正沿著大馬路在步行。

正解 (D) 人物與環境關係

照片中的人正走在大樓之間的馬路上，因此答案為 (D)。注意，別被照片裡的 buildings 和 shops 誤導，要仔細聽出題目裡以現在進行式描述的「動作」。

6

(A) The woman is at a table.
(B) The woman is in a corner.
(C) The woman is behind the screen.
(D) The woman is under the window.

(A) 女子在桌邊。
(B) 女子在角落裡。
(C) 女子在螢幕後。
(D) 女子在窗戶下。

正解 (B) 人物與環境關係

女子站在房間裡的角落，故正解為 (B)。本題目的在於測驗考生對 at、behind、under 這些表示位置相對關係的介系詞是否理解透徹。一看到這類照片就要迅速掌握人物的位置，方能選出正確答案。

□ **in a corner** 在角落裡
□ **behind** [bɪˈhaɪnd] 介 在……後面

PART 2 MP3 008-013

7　M🇦🇺　W🇬🇧

M : Could you review these figures for me?
W : (A) I've already done that twice.
　　　(B) From the accounting office.
　　　(C) Yes, these figs are tasty.

M：妳能不能幫我檢查一下這些數字？
W：(A) 我已經看過兩次了。
　　(B) 會計事務所給的。
　　(C) 是的，這些無花果很可口。

正解 (A)　請求、提議

Could you ...?「能否請你……？」是禮貌地請求幫忙的問句。以 I've already done that twice.（我已經看過兩次了。）來拒絕對方的選項 (A) 為正解。選項 (B) 利用容易讓人聯想到 figures 的 accounting office 設下陷阱，選項 (C) 則以近似於 figures 發音的 figs 來混淆考生。
□ **review** [rɪˋvju] 動 檢閱
□ **figure** [ˋfɪgjɚ] 名 數字
□ **accounting office**　會計事務所
□ **fig** [fɪg] 名 無花果

8　W🇺🇸　M🇨🇦

W : How many weeks are left in this quarter?
M : (A) Two dimes and a nickel.
　　　(B) Yes, our main headquarters.
　　　(C) Only one.

W：本季還剩下幾週？
M：(A) 2.5 角。
　　(B) 是的，我們的總公司。
　　(C) 只剩一週。

正解 (C)　How 疑問句

How many ...? 是詢問「數量」的說法。選項 (A) 回答的是「硬幣的數量」，與問題所問無關，故不適當。選項 (B) 故意用 headquarters 來造成與 quarter 之混淆，且本題是疑問詞開頭的問句，看到用 Yes 回應就可以知道並不正確。明確地回答「（剩下）一週」的選項 (C) 才是正解。
□ **quarter** [ˋkwɔrtɚ] 名 季
□ **dime** [daɪm] 名 一角硬幣
□ **nickel** [ˋnɪkl] 名 五分鎳幣
□ **headquarters** [ˋhɛdˋkwɔrtɚz] 名 總部；總公司

9　W🇺🇸　M🇨🇦

W : Where is Mr. Chen going on vacation?
M : (A) Two weeks.
　　　(B) No one knows.
　　　(C) He went to Peru last year.

W：陳先生要去哪裡度假？
M：(A) 兩個星期。
　　(B) 沒有人知道。
　　(C) 他去年去了秘魯。

正解 (B)　Where 疑問句

Where ...? 是詢問「地點」的問句。選項 (A) 回答的是「期間」，故不適當。選項 (C) 雖然回答了「場所」，但題目的 is ... going 指「未來」的事情，以「過去式」回答時態不合，因此不正確。回答「沒人曉得」的選項 (B) 為正解。

10　M🇨🇦　W🇬🇧

M : Why are you leaving so early?
W : (A) I love autumn leaves.
　　　(B) About 2:00 P.M.
　　　(C) I'm not feeling well.

M：妳為什麼要這麼早下班？
W：(A) 我愛秋葉。
　　(B) 下午兩點左右。
　　(C) 我覺得不太舒服。

正解 (C)　Why 疑問句

Why ...? 是詢問「理由」的問句。題目問的是「為什麼早退？」，所以說明了「早退」理由的選項才是正解。選項 (A) 利用 leaves 來造成與 leaving 之混淆。選項 (B) 回答的是「時間」，故非正解。只有回答「身體不適」的選項 (C) 才是最適當的解答。

□ **autumn leaves**　秋葉（leaves 為 leaf 的複數形）
□ **feel well**　身體覺得舒適

11　W🇬🇧　W🇺🇸

W : Did Ms. Shibata ask Tom about his new client?
W : (A) Yes, in an e-mail.
　　　(B) They're called West Pacific Industries.
　　　(C) I'll ask her for advice.

W：柴田小姐有沒有問湯姆有關他的新客戶的事？
W：(A) 有，在電子郵件裡問了。
　　(B) 他們叫「西太平洋工業」。
　　(C) 我會詢問她的建議。

正解 (A)　Yes-No 問句

Did Ms. Shibata ask Tom about ...? 的意思是「柴田小姐問了湯姆有關……嗎？」，因此回答 Yes, in an e-mail.（有，在電子郵件裡問了。）的選項 (A) 是正解。題目並沒有問「公司名稱」，所以選項 (B) 不適當。選項 (C) 則是利用題目中也有出現的 ask 當作陷阱，小心不要上當。

□ **client** [ˋklaɪənt] 名 顧客
□ **ask A for B**　向 A 要求 B

試題與翻譯	答案與解析

12 W 🇬🇧 M 🇦🇺

W : You haven't resigned your position, have you?
M : (A) I have read the sign, in fact.
　　(B) No, that's just a rumor.
　　(C) For personal reasons.

W：你還沒有辭去職務，對吧？
M：(A) 其實我看過標誌了。
　　(B) 沒有，那只是謠傳。
　　(C) 基於私人理由。

正解 (B) 附加問句

本題為提出問題加以確認的附加問句題。問對方「尚未請辭，對吧？」，回答 No, that's just a rumor.（沒有，那只是謠傳。）的選項 (B) 為正解。選項 (A) 利用 read the sign 的發音與題目中的 resigned 製造混淆。而題目問的不是「辭職的理由」，故選項 (C) 也不適當。
☐ **resign** [rɪˋzaɪn] 動 辭職
☐ **position** [pəˋzɪʃən] 名 職位
☐ **in fact** 實際上　☐ **rumor** [ˋrumɚ] 名 謠言
☐ **personal reason** 個人理由

---

13 M 🇨🇦 W 🇺🇸

M : How much do I have to pay for express bus tickets?
W : (A) Check the board.
　　(B) I bought them online.
　　(C) For two adults, please.

M：買快捷客運票要多少錢？
W：(A) 請看一下價目板。
　　(B) 我是上網買的。
　　(C) 兩張成人票，麻煩你。

正解 (A) How 疑問句

How much ...? 是詢問「價錢」的問句。此句並非用 How 詢問「方法、手段」，故選項 (B) 答非所問。選項 (C) 雖然出現了數字，但回答的是「車票的張數」，而不是「車票的價錢」，所以也不對。只有回答「請看一下價目板」的選項 (A) 才是正解。

☐ **express** [ɪkˋsprɛs] 名 特快車
☐ **board** [bord] 名 佈告板

---

14 M 🇨🇦 W 🇺🇸

M : What ideas are you bringing to the morning meeting?
W : (A) After breakfast.
　　(B) I haven't given it a thought.
　　(C) Of course I'll be there.

M：妳在晨會上要提出什麼想法？
W：(A) 早餐之後。
　　(B) 我還沒去想它。
　　(C) 我當然會去。

正解 (B) What 疑問句

What ...? 是詢問「何物」的問句，因此回答「時間」的選項 (A) 不適當，而且也要注意容易讓人與題目中 morning 產生聯想的 breakfast。選項 (C) 並未針對所問回應。只有選項 (B) I haven't given it a thought.（我還沒去想它。）才是合理的回應。

☐ **bring** [brɪŋ] 動 帶出（話題等）
☐ **give ... a thought** 思考（某事）

---

15 W 🇬🇧 M 🇦🇺

W : I think you should resend that scan.
M : (A) Didn't it go through?
　　(B) Yes, they can send it then.
　　(C) I'll buy butter and raisins.

W：我想你應該重寄那份掃描。
M：(A) 它沒有傳出去嗎？
　　(B) 對，他們可以那時候再傳。
　　(C) 我會買奶油和葡萄乾。

正解 (A) 直述句

就「我想你該重寄那份掃描」的敘述句而言，以詢問 Didn't it go through?（它沒有傳出去嗎？）回應的選項 (A) 是正解。注意，選項 (B) 試圖以 can 製造與題目的 resend、scan 在發音上的混淆；選項 (C) 用 raisins 來與 resend 混淆。

☐ **resend** [riˋsɛnd] 動 重新發送
☐ **scan** [skæn] 名 掃描圖像
☐ **go through** 順利完成
☐ **raisin** [ˋrezn] 名 葡萄乾

---

16 M 🇦🇺 W 🇺🇸

M : When's the presentation due to start?
W : (A) I've no idea.
　　(B) Yes, it's a beautiful present.
　　(C) Jenna will be speaking.

M：簡報預定什麼時候開始？
W：(A) 我不曉得。
　　(B) 是的，那是件漂亮的禮物。
　　(C) 珍娜將會發言。

正解 (A) When 疑問句

When ...? 是詢問「時間」的問句，所以回答「人」的選項 (C) 不適當。要小心不要因 presentation 而誤選含有 present 的選項 (B)。對於「預定何時開始」的問句，以 I've no idea.（我不知道。）作為回應的選項 (A) 為正解。

☐ **presentation** [ˌprizɛnˋteʃən] 名 簡報
☐ **be due to** 預定（進行某事）

試題與翻譯	答案與解析

17 M🇦🇺 W🇬🇧

M: How are negotiations proceeding to date on the merger with that overseas company?
W: (A) I'll accompany you to the sea.
    (B) Could be better.
    (C) The due date is July 19.

M：跟那家海外公司合併的談判目前進行得怎麼樣？
W：(A) 我會陪你去海邊。   (B) 原本可以更順利。
    (C) 截止日期是 7 月 19 日。

正解 (B) How 疑問句

How ...? 是詢問「狀態」的問句。選項 (A) 以 accompany 與 company、sea 與 overseas 的發音讓人產生混淆。選項 (C) 則是以 date 引誘考生上當。只有回答「談判進行狀況」的選項 (B) 才是正解。

☐ **negotiation** [nɪˌgoʃɪˈeʃən] 名 談判
☐ **proceed** [prəˈsid] 動 進展
☐ **to date** 到目前為止
☐ **merger** [ˈmɝdʒə] 名 併購
☐ **accompany** [əˈkʌmpənɪ] 動 陪同；伴隨

18 M🇦🇺 W🇬🇧

M: How about moving your desk over there?
W: (A) The movie was quite exciting.
    (B) Because of the computer on it.
    (C) Okay, but could you help me?

M：把桌子搬到那邊怎麼樣？
W：(A) 這部電影相當刺激。
    (B) 因為上面的電腦。
    (C) 好啊，可是你能不能幫我？

正解 (C) How 疑問句

How about ...ing? 是詢問對方「要不要做某事」的問句，所以回答 Okay, but could you help me?（好啊，可是你能不能幫我？）的選項 (C) 為正解。選項 (A) 以 movie 的發音來與題目裡的 moving 混淆。選項 (B) 回答了某種「理由」，但與題目風馬牛不相及。

☐ **quite** [kwaɪt] 副 相當地
☐ **exciting** [ɪkˈsaɪtɪŋ] 形 令人興奮的

19 W🇺🇸 M🇦🇺

W: Would you mind leading the planning session today instead of Rick?
M: (A) No, if I can make time for it.
    (B) That's what he said.
    (C) I didn't mind at all.

W：你介不介意代替瑞克主持今天的企劃會議？
M：(A) 不介意，假如我撥得出時間的話。
    (B) 他是這麼說的。
    (C) 我完全不介意。

正解 (A) 請求、提議

Would you mind ...ing? 意指「你介不介意……？」，是一種詢求對方同意的禮貌性問句。以 No, if I can make time for it.（不介意，假如我撥得出時間的話。）來回應的選項 (A) 為正解。〔另，要注意，如果允許對方的請求，必須以 No 來回答。〕選項 (B) 所敘述的與題目毫無關係。題目問的是「現在」，但選項 (C) 卻以「過去式」回答，因此不可選。

☐ **lead** [lid] 動 領導；指揮
☐ **instead of** 取……而代之
☐ **make time** 騰出時間

20 W🇺🇸 M🇨🇦

W: Where is the building maintenance being carried out?
M: (A) Jack's team is doing it.
    (B) On the third floor.
    (C) No, it will carry on.

W：大樓維修保養在哪裡進行？
M：(A) 傑克的團隊正在做。
    (B) 在三樓。
    (C) 不，它會繼續下去。

正解 (B) Where 疑問句

Where ...? 是詢問「地點」的問句，因此應選回答出地點的 (B) On the third floor.（在三樓。）注意，不要被選項 (C) 中的 carry on 與題目裡的 carried out 給搞混了。

☐ **maintenance** [ˈmentənəns] 名 維修；保養
☐ **carry out** 執行
☐ **carry on** 繼續

21 W🇺🇸 M🇦🇺

W: Why don't you ask for a raise?
M: (A) It'd be of no use.
    (B) Sorry, I can't give you one.
    (C) It's 15 percent higher.

W：你何不要求加薪？
M：(A) 那不會有用的。
    (B) 抱歉，我沒辦法給你加薪。
    (C) 調高了 15%。

正解 (A) Why 疑問句

對於 Why don't you ask for a raise?（你何不要求加薪？）這個「提出建議」的問句，以 It'd be no use.（那不會有用的。）回應的選項 (A) 為正解。選項 (B) 回答的內容與題目不符；題目問的不是「加薪幅度」，因此選項 (C) 亦不適當。

☐ **raise** [rez] 名 加薪

試題與翻譯	答案與解析

22 W 🇬🇧 M 🇨🇦

W：Isn't this package supposed to go to Mike?
M：(A) Four stamps, please.
　　(B) He won't oppose you.
　　(C) Not as far as I know.

W：這個包裹不是應該交給麥克嗎？
M：(A) 四張郵票，麻煩你。
　　(B) 他不會反對你。
　　(C) 就我所知不是。

正解 (C) 否定疑問句

Isn't ...? 是向對方確認的否定問句，意指「不是……嗎？」。回答 Not as far as I know.（就我所知不是。）的選項 (C) 為正解。選項 (A) 利用 stamps 這個容易與 package 聯想在一起的單字來誤導考生。選項 (B) 則以近似於 supposed 發音的 oppose 製造混淆。

☐ **be supposed to** 應該（做某事）
☐ **oppose** [ə`poz] 動 反對
☐ **as far as I know** 就我所知

23 W 🇺🇸 M 🇦🇺

W：Are you going to the fitness center, or straight home?
M：(A) I guess I'll work out.
　　(B) Thanks, I've been exercising.
　　(C) Running machines and weights.

W：你要去健身中心，還是直接回家？
M：(A) 我想我會去運動。
　　(B) 謝謝，我一直都在運動。
　　(C) 跑步機和槓鈴。

正解 (A) 選擇疑問句

本題為 TOEIC 測驗常見的 A or B 二選一題型。以 work out 代替 go to the fitness center 的選項 (A) 是正確答案。選項 (B) 以 exercising，選項 (C) 也以 Running machines、weights 來引誘考生誤答，但是二者皆答非所問。

☐ **work out**（在健身房等）運動
☐ **weight** [wet] 名 槓鈴

24 W 🇬🇧 W 🇺🇸

W：Would you like to apply for a store membership?
W：(A) I can't remember it.
　　(B) Sure, why not?
　　(C) Place it in storage.

W：您要不要申請成為本店會員？
W：(A) 我記不起來。
　　(B) 好啊，有何不可？
　　(C) 把它放在倉庫裡。

正解 (B) 邀請、提議

Would you like to ...? 意指「您要……嗎？」，是一種客氣的邀請，因此回答 Sure, why not?（好啊，有何不可？）的選項 (B) 為正解。選項 (A) 以 remember 來與題目中的 membership 混淆，選項 (C) 則利用 storage 與題目中的 store 混淆。

☐ **apply for** 申請
☐ **membership** [`mɛmbəʃɪp] 名 會員資格
☐ **place in storage** 放在倉庫裡

25 M 🇨🇦 M 🇦🇺

M：Who's that talking to Mr. Wong?
M：(A) They've been talking for 20 minutes.
　　(B) Our in-house lawyer.
　　(C) No, I missed his talk.

M：那位在跟王先生講話的人是誰？
M：(A) 他們已經聊二十分鐘了。
　　(B) 我們的內聘律師。
　　(C) 沒有，我錯過了他的談話。

正解 (B) Who 疑問句

Who ...? 是詢問「誰」的問句。選項 (A) 利用出現在題目裡的 talking 來誤導考生。而以疑問詞起始的問句不可用 Yes-No 來回答，因此選項 (C) 錯誤。選項 (B) 以「內聘律師」回應了問題，所以是正確答案。

☐ **in-house lawyer** 公司內聘律師
☐ **miss** [mɪs] 動 錯過

26 M 🇨🇦 W 🇬🇧

M：Isn't that your briefcase sitting in the corner there?
W：(A) Looks like it.
　　(B) At Watson Office Supplies.
　　(C) No, leave it at the office.

M：擺在角落那裡的那個不是妳的公事包嗎？
W：(A) 看起來像是。
　　(B) 在華森辦公用品店。
　　(C) 不，把它留在辦公室。

正解 (A) 否定疑問句

Isn't ...?（不是……嗎？）是向對方確認的否定問句。回答 Looks like it.（看起來像是。）的選項 (A) 即為正解。題目問的並非「地點」，故選項 (B) 不對。選項 (C) 所敘述的內容與題目牛頭不對馬嘴，因此也不可選。

☐ **briefcase** [`brif.kes] 名 公事包
☐ **sit** [sɪt] 動 處於某位置（不動）
☐ **office supplies** 辦公室用品

第1回完全解析

PART 2

試題與翻譯	答案與解析

27 M🇦🇺 W🇺🇸

M：Are you ready for the product launch?
W：(A) It's a new type of mobile phone.
　　(B) Thanks, but I've had lunch.
　　(C) We need another week.

M：你們準備要推出產品了嗎？
W：(A) 那是一款新的行動電話。
　　(B) 謝謝，我吃過午飯了。
　　(C) 我們還需要一星期。

正解 (C) be 動詞疑問句

Are you ready for ...? 意指「準備好……了嗎？」，因此回答 We need another week. 的選項 (C) 是恰當的回應。選項 (A) 利用 new type of mobile phone 試圖讓考生與題目裡的 product launch 產生聯想，而導致誤答。選項 (B) 中的 launch 則易與 lunch 在發音上產生混淆。

☐ **be ready for ...** 準備好做……
☐ **launch** [lɔntʃ] 名（新商品等的）推出

28 W🇬🇧 M🇨🇦

W：Do you want to speak first, or should I?
M：(A) After you.
　　(B) Miranda is the speaker.
　　(C) We both spoke well, I think.

W：你要先發言嗎，還是我該先說？
M：(A) 您先請。
　　(B) 米蘭達是演講者。
　　(C) 我想我們兩個都說得不錯。

正解 (A) 選擇疑問句

本題為 A or B 二選一的題目，作答時須選出有明確回答出其中一方的選項。(A) After you.（您先請。）為禮讓對方的說法，所以是正確答案。選項 (B) 的 speaker 和選項 (C) 的 spoke 則都是引誘誤選的陷阱。

☐ **both** [boθ] 副 兩者皆

29 W🇺🇸 W🇬🇧

W：What do I need to enter the convention?
W：(A) Indeed, it's quite conventional.
　　(B) Any piece of photo ID will do.
　　(C) This year in Shanghai, last year Singapore.

W：參加代表大會需要什麼？
W：(A) 的確，那相當常見。
　　(B) 任何一種有照片的身分證件都行。
　　(C) 今年在上海，去年在新加坡。

正解 (B) What 疑問句

題目問的是「需要什麼」，所以答出「任何一種有照片的身分證件」的選項 (B) 為正解。選項 (A) 企圖以 conventional「慣例的；常見的」來與題目裡的 convention「大會」混淆。選項 (C) 提到的是「地點」，答非所問，故不可選。

☐ **enter** [ˈɛntə] 動 參加
☐ **convention** [kənˈvɛnʃən] 名 代表大會
☐ **indeed** [ɪnˈdid] 副 的確
☐ **conventional** [kənˈvɛnʃənl] 形 慣例的；常見的
☐ **do** [du] 動 足夠；適合

30 M🇨🇦 M🇦🇺

M：I heard the 8:00 train will be delayed.
M：(A) No, here it comes now.
　　(B) Yes, it will arrive at 7:00.
　　(C) Yes, an eight-layer cake.

M：我聽說八點的班車會誤點。
M：(A) 不會，它現在進站了。
　　(B) 對，它七點會到。
　　(C) 對，是一個八層的蛋糕。

正解 (A) 直述句

針對「我聽說八點的班車會誤點。」這個直述句，回答 No, here it comes now.（不會，它現在進站了。）的選項 (A) 即為正解。選項 (B) 以未來式回答七點，與題目的八點情境不符。選項 (C) 則利用 eight 來混淆考生。

☐ **delay** [dɪˈle] 動 使……延遲
☐ **eight-layer** [ˈetˈleə] 形 八層的

31 W🇺🇸 M🇨🇦

W：Could you tell me how to get to Denby Street?
M：(A) You're on it.
　　(B) Yes, for 5 or 6 blocks.
　　(C) She took a different route.

W：能不能請你告訴我到丹比街要怎麼走？
M：(A) 妳已經在丹比街了。
　　(B) 對，過五、六個街區。
　　(C) 她走了不同的路線。

正解 (A) How 的間接問句

Could you tell me how to ...?（能否請您告訴我如何……？）是禮貌地請教他人「方法」的問句。本題問的是到丹比街怎麼走，回答「妳已經在那條街上了。」的選項 (A) 為正解。選項 (B) 回答的是「距離」而不是「方法」，所以不適當。選項 (C) 則利用 route 這個容易與 street 產生聯想的單字來誤導答題。

☐ **block** [blɑk] 名 街區
☐ **route** [rut] 名 路線

PART 3 MP3 034-035 M 🇦🇺 W 🇬🇧

題目	題目翻譯
Questions 32 through 34 refer to the following conversation.	第 32 到 34 題請參照下面這段對話。
M：What's wrong, Cindy? You look worried.	M：怎麼了，辛蒂？妳看起來憂心忡忡的。
W：I need to e-mail these files to the design engineer at Durant Piper Corporation by 5:00 P.M. and my computer isn't working!	W：我得在下午五點前把這些檔案用電子郵件寄給杜蘭特派伯公司的設計工程師，而我的電腦卻掛了！
M：Don't worry. It's only 3:00 now. You still have two hours left. I'm sure IT will be able to fix it soon. Just to be sure, though, why don't you send the files from my computer?	M：別擔心。現在才三點，妳還有兩個小時。我相信資訊人員很快就能修好。不過為了保險起見，妳要不用我的電腦寄那些檔案？
W：Oh yes, I hadn't thought of that. Thanks, Randy!	W：喔，對耶，我沒想到這點。謝了，藍迪！

Vocabulary

☐ **be able to ...** 能夠　　☐ **fix** [fɪks] **動** 修理　　☐ **just to be sure** 為了保險起見　　☐ **think of ...** 想到……

試題	試題翻譯	答案與解析
32 What is the woman's problem? (A) Her document is missing. (B) Her computer is not functioning. (C) An e-mail address is incorrect. (D) A file is not complete.	女子的問題是什麼？ (A) 她的文件不見了。 (B) 她的電腦不能運作。 (C) 有一個電郵地址不對。 (D) 有一個檔案不完整。	**正解 (B)** 由女子在第一句的對白裡說的 I need to e-mail these files ... and my computer isn't working!，就知道她遇到了電腦無法正常運作的問題，所以將 working 換成 functioning 的選項 (B) 為正解。 ☐ **incorrect** [ˌɪnkəˈrɛkt] **形** 不正確的
33 When should the files be sent? (A) By 2:00 P.M. (B) By 3:00 P.M. (C) By 4:00 P.M. (D) By 5:00 P.M.	檔案應該在什麼時候寄出？ (A) 下午兩點前 (B) 下午三點前 (C) 下午四點前 (D) 下午五點前	**正解 (D)** 從女子所說的 I need to e-mail these files to the design engineer at Durant Piper Corporation by 5:00 P.M.，就知本題應選 (D)。
34 What does the man suggest the woman do? (A) Call the design engineer (B) Revise the file (C) Log onto a different computer (D) Use a delivery service	男子建議女子怎麼做？ (A) 打電話給設計工程師 (B) 修改檔案 (C) 登入別台電腦 (D) 使用快遞服務	**正解 (C)** 男子雖說 IT 部門應該會立刻修好電腦，不過為了以防萬一，又提議 why don't you send the files from my computer?，也就是登入他的電腦來發信，所以正確答案是選項 (C)。 ☐ **revise** [rɪˈvaɪz] **動** 修正

題目	題目翻譯

Questions 35 through 37 refer to the following conversation.

第 35 到 37 題請參照下面這段對話。

W：Hello, I bought this purse here two days ago but the zipper broke yesterday. Can I exchange it for another one, please?

W：你好，我兩天前在這裡買了這個包包，可是拉鏈昨天壞了。請問我能換一個嗎？

M：I'm sorry, ma'am, but I think this was the last one we had in the store. That style was very popular and sold out almost immediately.

M：抱歉，小姐，我想這是我們店裡的最後一個了。那款非常受歡迎，幾乎立刻就賣光了。

W：Oh no! I love the shape and color. I've received so many compliments on it already.

W：噢，真糟糕！我很喜歡它的形狀和顏色。我已經得到一堆人的讚美。

M：Well, in that case, they may have them in our other outlet on Rushmore Street. I can give them a call to check if you like.

M：嗯，如果是那樣，我們在拉許莫街上的另一家店面可能還有。假如您要的話，我可以打個電話去問問看。

Vocabulary

- □ **purse** [pɝs] 名（女用）手提包
- □ **exchange A for B** 用 A 和 B 交換
- □ **ma'am** [mæm] 名 女士（= madam，對女子的尊稱）
- □ **sell out** 賣光
- □ **immediately** [ɪ'midɪtlɪ] 副 立即；馬上
- □ **shape** [ʃep] 名 形狀；外形
- □ **compliment** [`kɑmpləmənt] 名 讚美
- □ **outlet** [`aʊtlɛt] 名 銷路；商店；暢貨中心

試題	試題翻譯	答案與解析
35 What does the woman ask the man to do? (A) Send her a refund (B) Give her a new purse (C) Repair her purse (D) Offer her a discount	女子要求男子做什麼？ (A) 把錢退給她 (B) 給她一個新的包包 (C) 修理她的包包 (D) 給她一個折扣	**正解 (B)** 女子在一開始的對白裡提到她所購買的手提包拉鏈壞掉了，於是向男子要求換貨（Can I exchange it for another one, please?），所以正確答案是 (B)。 □ **refund** [rɪ'fʌnd] 名 退錢
36 What does the woman like about her purse? (A) Its design (B) Its size (C) Its price (D) Its texture	女子喜歡包包的哪一點？ (A) 設計 (B) 尺寸 (C) 價格 (D) 質地	**正解 (A)** 女子說 I love the shape and color.（我很喜歡它的形狀和顏色。）也就是說，她喜歡包包的設計，故選 (A)。 □ **texture** ['tɛkstʃə] 名 質地；素材的質感
37 What will the man probably do next? (A) Make a telephone call (B) Choose a different purse (C) Visit another branch (D) Pay by check	男子接下來大概會做什麼？ (A) 打一通電話 (B) 選一款不同的包包 (C) 去另一家分店看看 (D) 開支票付錢	**正解 (A)** 根據男子在最後說的 I can give them a call to check if you like. 可知，由於女子想要相同款式的包包，男子接下來應該會打電話給其他店面確認是否仍有庫存，因此正解為 (A)。

題目	題目翻譯
Questions 38 through 40 refer to the following conversation.	第 38 到 40 題請參照下面這段對話。
M : Good morning, Goldstar Bank. How may I help you?	M：金星銀行，您早。有什麼可以為您效勞的嗎？
W : My daughter told me you're offering new customers 0% interest on Goldstar Credit Cards. Is that correct?	W：我女兒跟我說，你們正在提供零利率優惠給金星信用卡的新客戶。對嗎？
M : Yes, it is. But I should say that this offer only lasts for a period of 3 months. After that time, the interest rises to 18 percent.	M：是的，沒錯。但是我應該說明一下，這項優惠只為期三個月。過了那段時間，利率就會調升到 18%。
W : Oh, I see. Well, yes, even so, I would be interested in getting one. If I give you my e-mail address, could you send me a form so I could sign up?	W：噢，我明白了。嗯，好，就算是這樣，我還是想辦一張。假如我給你我的電子郵件地址，你能不能把表格寄給我，好讓我申辦？

Vocabulary

☐ **interest** [ˈɪntrɪst] 名 利息　　☐ **correct** [kəˈrɛkt] 形 正確的　　☐ **last** [læst] 動 持續　　☐ **rise** [raɪz] 動 提升　　☐ **form** [fɔrm] 名 表格
☐ **sign up** 報名登記

試題	試題翻譯	答案與解析
38 Why is the woman calling? (A) To ask for her account balance (B) To make a payment (C) To renew a contract (D) To apply for a card	女子為何來電？ (A) 為了詢問她的帳戶餘額 (B) 為了繳費 (C) 為了續約 (D) 為了辦卡	**正解 (D)** 女子在詢問零利率優惠的相關事宜之後，說 ... could you send me a form so I could sign up?，請對方寄送信用卡的申辦表格給她，因此本題選 (D)。 ☐ **account balance**（存款的）餘額 ☐ **renew** [rɪˈnju] 動 更新 ☐ **apply for** 申請
39 What condition does the man mention? (A) The minimum balance for an account (B) Credit scores to open an account (C) Qualifications to be new members (D) The time limit of the interest rate	男子提到了什麼條件？ (A) 帳戶的最低餘額 (B) 開立帳戶所需的信用評分 (C) 成為新會員的資格 (D) 利率的期限	**正解 (D)** 由男子提到的 this offer only lasts for a period of 3 months 可知，該優惠僅適用三個月，所以正確答案是選項 (D)。 ☐ **balance** [ˈbæləns] 名 存款餘額 ☐ **credit score** 信用評分 ☐ **qualification** [ˌkwɑləfəˈkeʃən] 名 資格 ☐ **interest rate** 利率
40 What does the woman ask the man to do? (A) Review a charge (B) Send her a document (C) Increase her credit limit (D) Confirm receipt of her e-mail	女子要男子做什麼？ (A) 重新檢視一項收費 (B) 寄文件給她 (C) 提高她的信用額度 (D) 確認收到了她的電子郵件	**正解 (B)** 由女子在對話的最後提出 could you send me a form ...? 可知正解為選項 (B)。 ☐ **increase** [ɪnˈkris] 動 增加 ☐ **credit limit** 信用額度 ☐ **confirm** [kənˈfɝm] 動 確認

題目	題目翻譯
Questions 41 through 43 refer to the following conversation.	第 41 到 43 題請參照下面這段對話。

M : Hello, this is Rowan Mortimer. Could I speak to Angela Shen, please?

W : I'm sorry, Ms. Shen hasn't come into work yet. I'm her assistant, Jenny Franks.

M : Do you know when she will be in?

W : I'm afraid I have no idea. Would you like me to take a message for you?

M : Yes, please. I was wondering if I could see her today about some copiers she is interested in. I was planning on showing her some brochures about our equipment.

W : Oh yes, she told me she wouldn't have any time today because she has department meetings scheduled all day. She said she would probably have time tomorrow. I'll let her know you called.

M : That'd be great. I appreciate it. Good-bye.

M：妳好，我是羅安‧莫蒂默。能不能麻煩請安琪拉‧沈聽電話？

W：抱歉，沈小姐還沒有來上班。我是她的助理珍妮‧法蘭克斯。

M：妳知道她什麼時候會進公司嗎？

W：不好意思，我不清楚。需要我幫您留言嗎？

M：好的，麻煩妳。我原本在想不知道我能不能今天和她見個面談談她有興趣的幾款影印機。我打算拿一些關於我們設備的文宣給她看。

W：噢對，她跟我說她今天不會有空，因為她有一整天的部門會議要開。她說她明天或許會有空。我會轉告她您有來電。

M：那太好了。謝謝。再見。

Vocabulary

☐ **copier** [ˈkɑpɪə] 名 影印機　☐ **brochure** [broˈʃʊr] 名 文宣；小冊子　☐ **equipment** [ɪˈkwɪpmənt] 名 設備；機器

試題	試題翻譯	答案與解析
41 Who most likely is the man? (A) A customer (B) A technician (C) A salesperson (D) A receptionist	男子最有可能是誰？ (A) 一位客戶 (B) 一名技師 (C) 一個業務員 (D) 一位接待人員	**正解 (C)** 由男子說的 ... if I could see her today about some copiers she is interested in. I was planning on showing her some brochures about our equipment. 可知，他打算向沈小姐推銷影印機，故本題選 (C)。
42 What does the man want to talk to Ms. Shen about? (A) Late documents (B) Office equipment (C) Computer repairs (D) Brochure design	男子想跟沈小姐談什麼事？ (A) 遲交的文件 (B) 辦公室設備 (C) 電腦維修 (D) 文宣的設計	**正解 (B)** 男子在第三次的發言中提及，沈小姐對男子公司的影印機有興趣，男子打算向沈小姐展示文宣手冊，由此可知男子希望能進一步說明自家產品，選項 (B) Office equipment（辦公室設備）即代表他提到的 some copiers 和 our equipment 等，故為正解。
43 What is Ms. Shen's plan for today? (A) Meeting customers (B) Dealing with shareholders (C) Reorganizing schedules (D) Talking with staff	沈小姐今天有什麼計畫？ (A) 拜會客戶 (B) 應付股東 (C) 重新安排日程 (D) 與員工談話	**正解 (D)** 由女子在對白裡提到的 ... because she has department meetings scheduled all day 可知，沈小姐今天一整天都忙於部門會議，而部門會議屬於公司內部會議，所以正確答案是 (D) Talking with staff。 ☐ **deal with** 處理；應對 ☐ **reorganize** [riˈɔrgəˌnaɪz] 動 重新安排

題目	題目翻譯

Questions 44 through 46 refer to the following conversation.

第 44 到 46 題請參照下面這段對話。

M : Hello, it's John. Have you heard from Kareem Adjani at Monroe Development Corporation yet? I need to know when the heavy equipment for the Schreiber Apartment Complex will arrive.

M：喂，我是約翰。孟羅開發公司的柯里姆‧阿傑尼給妳回覆了沒？我得知道薛瑞伯複合式公寓的重型設備什麼時候會到。

W : I just received an e-mail from Mr. Adjani's secretary.

W：我剛收到阿傑尼先生秘書的電子郵件。

M : Oh. What did she say in it?

M：噢。她信裡說了什麼？

W : She said he's supervising progress at the construction area this afternoon.

W：她說他今天下午會在建築工地盯進度。

M : Is there any way to reach him before I go into my next meeting?

M：在我開下一個會之前，有沒有什麼辦法可以聯絡到他？

W : Yes, his phone is probably in silent mode, but you can always text him. I'll get his address for you.

W：有，他的手機八成會調成靜音模式，但是你可以隨時傳簡訊給他。我會幫你問他的電子郵件地址。

M : It'd be a great help if you could do that.

M：假如妳能那麼做真是幫大忙了。

Vocabulary

- □ **secretary** [ˋsɛkrəˌtɛrɪ] 名 秘書
- □ **supervise** [ˋsupəˌvaɪz] 動 監督；管理
- □ **progress** [ˋprɑgrɛs] 名 進展
- □ **construction** [kənˋstrʌkʃən] 名 建設；建築物
- □ **reach** [ritʃ] 動 與……取得聯繫
- □ **text** [tɛkst] 動（利用手機等）傳送訊息

試題	試題翻譯	答案與解析
44 What is the purpose of the man's call? (A) To submit a progress report (B) To confirm a delivery time (C) To revise technical information (D) To prepare a presentation	男子來電的目的為何？ (A) 為了交進度報告 (B) 為了確認交貨時間 (C) 為了修改技術資訊 (D) 為了準備簡報	**正解 (B)** 從男子第一次發言時說的 I need to know when the heavy equipment for the Schreiber Apartment complex will arrive. 就可以知道，他想確認重型機具何時會送達，故本題選 (B)。 □ **delivery time** 送達時間
45 Where is Mr. Adjani now? (A) At a building site (B) At his desk (C) In his apartment (D) In a meeting	阿傑尼先生此刻在哪裡？ (A) 在建築工地 (B) 在辦公桌前 (C) 在自家公寓 (D) 在開會	**正解 (A)** 女子在第一次對話裡提到 She said he's supervising progress at the construction area this afternoon.，也就是說 Mr. Adjani 目前人在建築工地，而 building site 是 construction area 的另一種說法，因此選項 (A) 為正解。
46 What will the woman do next? (A) Start a meeting (B) Phone Mr. Adjani (C) Get contact information (D) Read a text message	女子接下來會做什麼？ (A) 召開會議 (B) 打電話給阿傑尼先生 (C) 取得聯絡資訊 (D) 讀取手機簡訊	**正解 (C)** 女子在最後提到 I'll get his address for you.，表示她接下來會設法取得阿傑尼先生手機的電郵地址然後告知男子，而電郵地址是一種「資訊」，故正解為選項 (C)。因為要用手機電郵聯繫阿傑尼先生，而不是打電話，所以選項 (B) 不正確。注意，在多益測驗中，經常以 "phone" 一字指行動電話，例如本段對話中的 his phone is ...。

第 1 回完全解析

PART 3

題目	題目翻譯
Questions 47 through 49 refer to the following conversation.	第 47 到 49 題請參照下面這段對話。
W: I was wondering if you have any TZ inkjet cartridges in stock. I can't find any in the office supplies section of your Web site.	W：我在想不知道你們 TZ 噴墨墨水匣有沒有任何存貨。我在你們網站的辦公用品區裡都找不到。
M: I'm afraid we don't sell those anymore.	M：不好意思，我們已經不再賣那款墨水匣了。
W: Is that right? Does that mean I can't use my printer anymore?	W：這樣啊？那是不是表示我的印表機再也不能用了？
M: Oh, not at all. We still sell the newer VX cartridges. They're just as good. Scroll over to the "printer and cartridges" part of the office supplies tab, and you'll see them.	M：噢，完全不會。我們還是有賣比較新款的 VX 墨水匣。它們一樣好用。把頁面下拉到辦公用品標籤中的「印表機與墨水匣」部分，您就會看到了。
W: Okay I'm scrolling ... I do see them. Umm ... I really wanted the TZ because I've used them for so long. But I guess I'll have to go with the VX.	W：好，我正在下拉網頁……我看到了。嗯……我真的很想要 TZ，因為這款墨水匣我已經用很久了，不過，我想我也只能選 VX 了。
M: Good. You won't be disappointed with the VX ones.	M：太好了。您不會對 VX 墨水匣失望的。

Vocabulary

☐ **in stock** 有現貨　　☐ **not ... anymore** 不會再……　　☐ **scroll** [skrol] 動（電腦螢幕上）從上到下捲動（資料等）　　☐ **go with ...** 選擇……

試題	試題翻譯	答案與解析
47 Where most likely is the man? (A) In a printer factory (B) In a product warehouse (C) In an engineering office (D) In a customer service center	男子最有可能在哪裡？ (A) 印表機工廠 (B) 產品倉庫 (C) 工程辦公室 (D) 客服中心	**正解 (D)** 依對話內容可知，男子正對一名邊瀏覽其產品網站邊詢問的女性顧客給予答覆。因此，男子最有可能的所在地即為選項 (D) 客服中心。 ☐ **warehouse** [ˈwɛr.haʊs] 名 倉庫
48 What does the woman prefer about TZ inkjet cartridges? (A) Availability (B) Functionality (C) Quality (D) Familiarity	女子喜歡 TZ 噴墨墨水匣的哪一點？ (A) 可得性 (B) 功能性 (C) 品質 (D) 熟悉度	**正解 (D)** 女子在最後一次發言裡提到 I really wanted the TZ because I've used them for so long，由此可知，TZ 是她長久以來愛用的產品，所以 (D) Familiarity（熟悉度）是最適當的選項。
49 What does the woman decide to do? (A) Track a delivery online (B) Look at a different Web site (C) Accept the man's suggestion (D) Sell the office supplies	女子決定怎麼做？ (A) 在網路上追蹤送貨狀況 (B) 查看不同的網站 (C) 接受男子的建議 (D) 賣掉辦公用品	**正解 (C)** 女子雖然一開始指定要 TZ，但是在最後說 I guess I'll have to go with the VX，表示她接受了男子的提議，故正解為選項 (C)。 ☐ **track** [træk] 動 追蹤

題目	題目翻譯
Questions 50 through 52 refer to the following conversation.	第 50 到 52 題請參照下面這段對話。

W: Hi, I'll be checking out tomorrow, since my trip is just about over. I noticed there's always a line at the front desk here in the mornings. Is there any way to avoid that?

M: Yes, ma'am. You can use your room computer to check out. Just go to our Web site, enter your room number and your credit card information. You will find a list of all your charges there, including any from our room service. It only takes a few minutes.

W: Thanks, you've been very helpful.

W：嗨，我明天要退房，因為我的旅行差不多要結束了。我注意到櫃台這裡早上總是有人在排隊。有沒有什麼辦法可以避開人潮？

M：有的，小姐。您可以用您房裡的電腦來退房。只要上我們的網站，輸入您的房間號碼和信用卡資料，您就會看到一張列出您所有費用的清單，包括客房服務的收費。只要花幾分鐘的時間。

W：謝謝，你真是幫了大忙。

第1回完全解析

PART 3

Vocabulary

- [ ] **check out** 結帳（退房）
- [ ] **just about** 差不多；幾乎
- [ ] **avoid** [əˋvɔɪd] 勔 避開
- [ ] **charge** [tʃɑrdʒ] 名 費用
- [ ] **including** [ɪnˋkludɪŋ] 介 包括

試題	試題翻譯	答案與解析
50 Where most likely are the speakers? (A) At an airport (B) At a hotel (C) At a travel agency (D) At a restaurant	說話者最有可能在哪裡？ (A) 在機場 (B) 在飯店 (C) 在旅行社 (D) 在餐廳	**正解 (B)** 本題須從出現於通篇各段的關鍵字來做綜合判斷。由女子提到的 I'll be checking out tomorrow 和 front desk，以及男子提到的 room number 和 room service 等就知道對話的地點為「飯店」，故選項 (B) At hotel 為正解。 □ **travel agency** 旅行社
51 What problem does the woman mention? (A) Attitude of staff (B) High prices (C) Long waiting lines (D) Lack of room service	女子提及什麼問題？ (A) 員工的態度 (B) 高昂的價格 (C) 排隊人潮多 (D) 缺乏客房服務	**正解 (C)** 女子注意到早上櫃台前總是有房客大排長龍要退房，正在向一名男性員工詢問避開排隊人潮的方法。line 在這裡指的是「排隊的隊伍」，因此本題選 (C)。 □ **attitude** [ˋætətjud] 名 態度 □ **lack** [læk] 名 欠缺；不足
52 What does the man recommend the woman do? (A) Settle her bill online (B) Line up early (C) Change rooms (D) Wait a few minutes	男子建議女子做什麼？ (A) 在網路上結算房費 (B) 提早排隊 (C) 更換房間 (D) 稍等幾分鐘	**正解 (A)** 男子表示 You can use your room computer to check out.，也就是建議女子利用客房電腦進行退房。另，他還提到只要在飯店網站上輸入資訊，就能顯示出全部的住宿費用 (all your charges)，所以正解為選項 (A) Settle her bill online。 □ **settle (hotel) bill** 結算住宿費用 □ **line up** 排隊

題目	題目翻譯

Questions 53 through 55 refer to the following conversation.

M : Are you going to Margaret Kang's going-away party? It's next Friday at the Charles Lake Hotel.

W : What? You've got to be kidding! I had no idea she was quitting the company.

M : She's not, but she's transferring to the Melbourne branch. We got a memo on it last week.

W : I must have missed it. I'll certainly be there, however. It's the least I can do, considering all the help she's given us on past projects.

第 53 到 55 題請參照下面這段對話。

M：妳會不會去瑪格麗特‧康的歡送會？下星期五在查爾斯湖飯店。

W：什麼？你一定是在開玩笑吧！我不曉得她要辭職。

M：她並沒有要辭職，她是要轉調到墨爾本的分公司。我們上星期有收到內部通知。

W：我一定是漏看了，不過我一定會到場。這是我最起碼能做的，畢竟她在之前的案子上幫了我們那麼多忙。

Vocabulary

- ☐ **going-away party** 歡送會　☐ **quit** [kwɪt] 動 辭職　☐ **transfer** [trænsˋfɝ] 動 調換　☐ **branch** [bræntʃ] 名 分公司
- ☐ **memo** [ˋmɛmo] 名 公司內部通知　☐ **considering** [kənˋsɪdərɪŋ] 介 考慮到；就……而論

試題	試題翻譯	答案與解析

53

What are the speakers discussing?

(A) A recruiting program
(B) An upcoming event
(C) Employee benefits
(D) Office schedules

說話者在討論什麼？

(A) 徵才方案
(B) 即將到來的活動
(C) 員工福利
(D) 辦公室的時程表

正解 (B)

一開始男子就提到 Are you going to Margaret Kang's going-away party?，也就是在詢問關於即將要舉行的「歡送會」一事，故正解為選項 (B)。

☐ **upcoming** [ˋʌp͵kʌmɪŋ] 形 即將發生的
☐ **benefit** [ˋbɛnəfɪt] 名 津貼；福利

54

What does the woman mean when she says, "You've got to be kidding"?

(A) She is surprised by what the man said.
(B) She disagrees with the man's opinion.
(C) She sympathizes with Margaret's situation.
(D) She appreciates the man's humor.

女子所說的 "You've got to be kidding" 是什麼意思？

(A) 她很驚訝於男子所言。
(B) 她不同意男子的意見。
(C) 她很同情瑪格麗特的處境。
(D) 她很欣賞男子的幽默。

正解 (A)

由前一句的 What? 的反應，以及之後的 I had no idea she was quitting the company. 可知，女子以為康小姐要辭職而感到十分驚訝，故本題選 (A)。kid 作動詞時指「開玩笑」。You've got to be kidding! 或 You must be kidding! 皆指「你一定是在開玩笑！」。

55

What is mentioned about Ms. Kang?

(A) She commonly assisted colleagues.
(B) She frequently went to Chicago.
(C) She usually provided funding for projects.
(D) She often helped at parties.

對話中提及了康小姐如何？

(A) 她常協助同事。
(B) 她常去芝加哥。
(C) 她通常為企劃案提供資金。
(D) 她經常在派對上幫忙。

正解 (A)

由女子最後提到的 considering all the help she's given us on past projects 可推測，康小姐常常幫同事的忙，所以正確答案是選項 (A) She commonly assisted colleagues.。

☐ **commonly** [ˋkɑmənlɪ] 副 通常地
☐ **colleague** [ˋkɑlig] 名 同事
☐ **frequently** [ˋfrikwəntlɪ] 副 頻繁地
☐ **funding** [ˋfʌndɪŋ] 名 資金

題目	題目翻譯
Questions 56 through 58 refer to the following conversation.	第 56 到 58 題請參照下面這段對話。

W：Hi Phil, I'm on my way out. Let Mr. Howell know I'll be in Pretoria today, then Kimberley until Monday, Johannesburg on Tuesday and back here in Cape Town by noon the following day.

W：嗨，菲爾，我要出門了。跟豪爾先生說一聲，我今天會到普利托里亞，然後在金伯利待到星期一，星期二到約翰尼斯堡，並在隔天中午前回到開敦普這裡。

M：Okay, Ms. Lind, but he'll still be able to get hold of you on your phone, right?

M：好的，琳德小姐，但他還是能打妳的手機找到妳，對吧？

W：Yes, by all means. But as I'll be touring quite a few factories, it would be better if he called after 6:00 P.M. instead of in the afternoon.

W：對，當然可以。不過因為我會參觀好幾家工廠，所以在下午六點以後打會比較好，不要在下午打。

M：Okay, I'll let him know.

M：好的，我會轉告他。

Vocabulary

- ☐ **on one's way out** 在外出途中
- ☐ **the following day** 隔天
- ☐ **get hold of ...** 與……取得聯繫；獲得
- ☐ **quite a few** 相當多的
- ☐ **factory** ['fæktərɪ] 名 工廠

試題	試題翻譯	答案與解析
56 What does the woman ask the man to do? (A) Inform Mr. Howell of her schedule (B) Give Mr. Howell her phone number (C) Confirm her schedule (D) Get hold of some documents	女子要男子做什麼？ (A) 把她的行程告知豪爾先生 (B) 把她的手機號碼給豪爾先生 (C) 確認她的行程 (D) 取得一些文件	**正解 (A)** 女子在一開始就提到 Let Mr. Howell know I'll be in Pretoria ....，請男子向豪爾先生傳達自己接下來幾天的行程，故正解為選項 (A)。注意，由男子說的 ... he'll still be able to get hold of you on your phone, right? 可知，豪爾先生已經有女子的電話號碼，因此選項 (B) 錯誤。
57 What does the woman mean when she says, "by all means"? (A) She needs to buy a new file for the trip. (B) She cannot be contacted if there is an emergency. (C) She will be able to receive telephone calls. (D) She has to think carefully before making a decision.	女子所說的 "by all means" 是什麼意思？ (A) 她需要買一個新的資料夾以便出差時使用。 (B) 如有緊急事件時無法聯絡到她。 (C) 她將能夠接到電話。 (D) 在做決定之前她必須仔細思考。	**正解 (C)** by all means 的意思是「當然 (certainly)」，選項 (C) 即為正解。另，由女子先回答的 Yes 亦可推論出本題答案。注意，get hold of you on your phone 在選項 (C) 當中改以 receive telephone calls 描述。
58 When does the woman prefer to be contacted? (A) At noon (B) In the afternoon (C) At any time (D) In the evening	女子認為在什麼時候跟她聯絡比較好？ (A) 中午 (B) 下午 (C) 隨時 (D) 晚上	**正解 (D)** 女子在最後的對話裡提到 it would be better if he called after 6:00 P.M. instead of in the afternoon，由此可知女子希望豪爾先生在晚上六點以後再跟她聯絡，故選項 (D) In the evening 為正解。

題目	題目翻譯
Questions 59 through 61 refer to the following conversation with three speakers.	第 59 到 61 題請參照下面這段三人對話。
W-1 : Hi, Marcel and Vicki. Are you guys ready for your new responsibilities as manager and vice-manager of the Santiago branch? It's bound to be different from working here.	W-1：嗨，馬賽爾、薇琪。你們準備好接任聖地牙哥分公司經理和副理的新職務了嗎？在那工作一定會和在這裡不一樣喔。
M : I don't know if I'm ready, to be honest. I'm getting more and more nervous.	M ：老實說，我不曉得自己是不是已經準備好了。我覺得愈來愈緊張。
W-2 : I feel the same way. I've never worked in South America before, and I've only just begun to learn Spanish.	W-2：我也是。我以前從來沒在南美工作過，而且我才剛開始學西班牙語。
W-1 : Don't worry too much about that. All the office staff there are pretty fluent in English.	W-1：這一點你不用太擔心。分公司那裡的人員英語都說得相當流利。
W-2 : Maybe you're right. Still, I want to learn Spanish as quickly as possible.	W-2：也許妳說得對。但我還是想儘快學好西班牙語。
M : That's why we've enrolled in an online university course, right? I don't know about you, Vicki, but I try to log on at work every lunch hour.	M ：所以我們才報名參加了線上大學課程，不是嗎？我不知道薇琪妳怎麼樣，不過我現在試著每天上班午休的時候都登入學習。

Vocabulary

☐ **responsibility** [rɪ.spɑnsəˈbɪlətɪ] 名 責任　　☐ **be bound to ...** 一定會……　　☐ **to be honest** 老實說　　☐ **pretty** [ˈprɪtɪ] 副 相當
☐ **fluent** [ˈfluənt] 形 流利的　　☐ **enroll** [ɪnˈrol] 動 登記；註冊　　☐ **lunch hour** 午休時間

試題	試題翻譯	答案與解析
59 What are the speakers talking about? (A) Upcoming promotions (B) Hiring strategies (C) Overseas expansion (D) Regional markets	說話者在談論什麼？ (A) 即將發生的升遷 (B) 雇用策略 (C) 海外擴張 (D) 區域市場	**正解 (A)** 從開頭第一位女子 (W-1) 對另外兩人說的 Are you guys ready for your new responsibilities as manager and vice-manager ...? 來推斷，他們應該是在討論兩人晉升新職之事，所以正確答案是選項 (A)。 ☐ **promotion** [prəˈmoʃən] 名 升遷 ☐ **strategy** [ˈstrætədʒɪ] 名 策略 ☐ **expansion** [ɪkˈspænʃən] 名 拓展；展開
60 What is a stated goal of Marcel and Vicki? (A) Getting local experience (B) Recruiting more staff (C) Enrolling in a university (D) Learning a language	馬賽爾和薇琪明確的目標是什麼？ (A) 吸取地方經驗 (B) 擴大徵才 (C) 到一所大學登記入學 (D) 學好一個語言	**正解 (D)** 薇琪 (W-2) 在第二次的發言中表示 I want to learn Spanish as quickly as possible，而馬賽爾 (M) 在最後則提到他報名了大學的線上課程並於午休時登入學習。由此可知，兩人明確的目標為選項 (D)。 ☐ **recruit** [rɪˈkrut] 動 募集人才
61 How is the man using his lunch hours nowadays? (A) To prepare for a trip (B) To improve his skills (C) To contact universities (D) To do research on South America	男子最近如何利用午休時間？ (A) 籌備一趟旅行 (B) 增進他的技能 (C) 與大學接洽 (D) 針對南美做研究	**正解 (B)** 由男子最後一次的談話可知，他在午休時透過大學線上課程學習西班牙語，換言之，他想增進自己的技能，因此正解為選項 (B)。 ☐ **do research on** 研究、調查（某事物）

題目	題目翻譯

Questions 62 through 64 refer to the following conversation and coupon.

M : I'd like to buy these three bags of coffee. These were all highly rated in a consumer magazine, so I'd like to try them out. Here ... I've brought this coupon with me.

W : Let me take a look … uh … sorry … but you can only use that for one of the bags.

M : Oh, I see … Since that's the case ... um ... I'll just buy one bag instead of three. Let me use it for this one, Bright Hills Coffee.

W : OK, that bag is 20 dollars, minus the coupon value. Also, if you have time, please go to our Web site to fill out a customer survey. That will make you eligible for future discounts.

第 62 到 64 題請參照下列對話和折價券。

M：我要買這三包咖啡。這些在消費者雜誌上都受到相當高的評價，所以我想要試試看。這兒……我有帶這張折價券來。

W：請讓我看一下。啊……很抱歉，這三包裡只有一包能使用折價券。

M：噢，這樣啊……既然如此……嗯……我不買三包了，就只買一包。我要用這張折價券來買這款明山咖啡。

W：好的，那包是二十美元，再減掉折價券上的面額。而且假如您有時間的話，請上我們的網站填寫顧客問卷。填問卷可讓您日後享折扣優惠。

```
折價券
Axton 食品公司
在清爽氛圍中甦醒！

店內各品牌咖啡
全品項 95 折

10 月 31 日前有效
```

Vocabulary

□ **rate** [ret] 動 評價	□ **coupon** [ˈkupɑn] 名 折價券	□ **fill out** 填寫	□ **survey** [səˈve] 名 調查	□ **eligible for ...** 具……資格

試題	試題翻譯	答案與解析

62

Why is the man looking for a certain product?
(A) He wants to try healthy foods.
(B) He read about it in a publication.
(C) He has tried it out before a few times.
(D) He needs to rate it for his blog.

男子為何在尋找某項特定商品？

(A) 他想嘗試健康食品。
(B) 他在一本刊物上看過它的介紹。
(C) 他以前試過了幾次。
(D) 他需要為自己的部落格評價它。

正解 (B)

男子在對話開頭說想買三包咖啡，並接著提出理由為 These were all highly rated in a consumer magazine，故選項 (B)「他在一本刊物上看過它的介紹」為正解。

□ **publication** [ˌpʌblɪˈkeʃən] 名 出版品；刊物

63

Look at the graphic. How much will the man pay?
(A) 5 dollars
(B) 10 dollars
(C) 15 dollars
(D) 20 dollars

請看圖表。男子將支付多少錢？

(A) 五美元
(B) 十美元
(C) 十五美元
(D) 二十美元

正解 (C)

男子表示要用折價券購買明山咖啡，女性店員回應 that bag is 20 dollars, minus the coupon value。對照折價券上寫著 Take $5 off coffee, any brand in store，男子須支付定價二十美元減五美元等於十五美元。(C) 為正解。

64

What does the woman encourage the man to do?
(A) Purchase an additional bag
(B) Go to a Web site
(C) Fill out a membership card
(D) Apply for a new account

女子鼓勵男子做什麼？

(A) 再多買一包
(B) 上一個網站
(C) 填寫一張會員卡
(D) 申請一個新帳戶

正解 (B)

由女子第二次發言提到的 ... please go to our Web site to fill out a customer survey 可知，選項 (B) 為正解。注意，不要被 fill out 誤導而錯選了 (C)。

題目	題目翻譯

Questions 65 through 67 refer to the following conversation and sign.

W : Hi … um … I'm a bit lost. I've got a job interview at Stephens and Vale Law ... um ... but when I got to their office, I saw a different company nameplate on the door.

M : That's because they've relocated to the same floor as Bilo Investments.

W : Thanks a lot. I didn't see that marked anywhere on the information displays.

M : It's not, because the move just took place. The updated location will be posted around the building soon. In the meantime, you should use Elevator 3. It'll take you to where you want to go.

第 65 到 67 題請參照下列對話和標示牌。

W：嗨……嗯……我有點迷路了。我要去 Stephens and Vale 法律事務所面試……嗯……但是當我到達他們的辦公室時，我看到的是別家公司的名牌。

M：那是因為他們的辦公室已經搬到和 Bilo 投資信託同一層樓的關係。

W：謝謝。我在標示牌上沒看到任何搬遷的資訊。

M：是還沒有標示，因為他們才剛搬。最新的樓層資訊很快就會在這棟樓各處張貼。這會兒，妳應該搭三號電梯，它會載妳到妳要去的地方。

Floor	Tenants
5	Bilo Investments / Jowon Media, Inc.
4	Wannable Textiles / Deni Biomedical
3	Aril Publishing / Somtio Engineering
2	Cimin Lighting, Inc. / Rea Catering
1	Gillo Realty, Inc. / Ashik Software Co.

樓	承租人
5	· Bilo 投資信託 / · Jowon 媒體
4	· Wannable 紡織 / · Deni 生物醫療
3	· Aril 出版 / · Somtio 工程
2	· Cimin 照明 / · Rea 酒席宴客
1	· Gillo 不動產 / · Ashik 軟體

Vocabulary

☐ **interview** [ˈɪntə.vju] 名 面試　☐ **relocate** [riˈloket] 動 搬遷　☐ **mark** [mɑrk] 動 做記號；標明　☐ **display** [dɪˈsple] 名 展示；陳列
☐ **take place** 發生；舉行　☐ **in the meanwhile** 在此同時

試題	試題翻譯	答案與解析

65

Why did the woman come to the building?
(A) To visit an apartment
(B) To retrieve a lost item
(C) To go to an interview
(D) To rent an office

女子為何來到這棟大樓？
(A) 為了參觀一間公寓
(B) 為了取回遺失物品
(C) 為了前往面試
(D) 為了租一間辦公室

正解 **(C)**

女子在一開始時說她迷路了，接著就提到 I've got a job interview at Stephens and Vale Law，所以她來到這棟建築物的目的就是要參加求職面試，故正確答案是選項 (C)。

☐ **retrieve** [rɪˈtriv] 動 取回（遺失物等）

66

Look at the graphic. What floor does the woman have to go to?
(A) Floor 2
(B) Floor 3
(C) Floor 4
(D) Floor 5

請看圖表。女子必須前往幾樓？
(A) 二樓
(B) 三樓
(C) 四樓
(D) 五樓

正解 **(D)**

關於 Stephens and Vale Law 的所在地，男子提到 they've relocated to the same floor as Bilo Investments，這裡的 they 指的就是 Stephens and Vale Law，而對照圖表即可知 Bilo 投資信託在五樓，故本題正解為 (D)。

67

What does the man recommend the woman do?
(A) Take an elevator
(B) Change a nameplate
(C) Check the information displays again
(D) Update her online profile

男子建議女子做什麼？
(A) 搭電梯
(B) 換名牌
(C) 再次確認標示牌上的資訊
(D) 更新她的線上簡介

正解 **(A)**

關於如何前往 Stephens and Vale 法律事務所，男子表示 you should use Elevator 3，所以選項 (A) 是正確答案。

題目	題目翻譯
Questions 68 through 70 refer to the following conversation and card.	第 68 到 70 題請參照下列對話和卡片。

W : Hi, my name is Nancy Katz. It's my first day at the firm, but I still don't have a photo ID card. How can I get one?

M : I'll be happy to help you. It'll only take me a minute to print one out. After I do, you'll see that each card has a large capital letter printed on it. Letters A through D are for staff in Administration. The other ones are for employees in IT, Operations, Marketing or Research.

W : Got it. And, of course, I'll try not to, but what should I do if I lose it?

M : If that happens, please report it right away. We'll deactivate your old card and give you a new one. Just be sure to keep the card visible at all times.

W：嗨，我叫南希·卡斯，今天第一天上班，但是我還沒有拿到照片識別證。請問我該怎麼做？

M：我很樂意協助妳。列印一張只要花我一分鐘的時間。在我印出來之後，妳會發現每張卡片上都印有一個大大的大寫英文字母。A 到 D 代表行政管理部人員。其他字母則代表資訊部、營運部、行銷部或研究中心的員工。

W：了解。另外，當然我會儘量不讓它發生，不過萬一識別證弄丟的話該怎麼辦？

M：如果妳遺失識別證，請立即回報。我們會註銷舊卡，再給妳一張新的。記得識別證務必隨時放在看得到的地方。

Halon 科技股份有限公司

Nancy Katz
總部門禁管制等級 C

Vocabulary

- ☐ **print out** 印刷
- ☐ **capital letter** 大寫字母
- ☐ **Administration** [əd.mɪnə'streʃən] 名 行政管理部
- ☐ **report** [rɪ'port] 動 報告
- ☐ **right away** 立即；馬上
- ☐ **deactivate** [di'æktə.vet] 動 撤銷；使無效
- ☐ **be sure to ...** 一定要……
- ☐ **visible** ['vɪzəbl] 形 可看見的
- ☐ **at all times** 隨時

試題	試題翻譯	答案與解析
68 What is the woman asking about? (A) How to obtain an ID (B) How to pay a bill (C) How to get to a branch office (D) How to apply for a job	女子在詢問什麼事？ (A) 如何獲得識別證 (B) 如何付帳 (C) 如何前往分公司 (D) 如何應徵工作	**正解 (A)** 女子的問題就在一開始的談話當中：I still don't have a photo ID card. How can I get one?。photo ID card 即「照片識別證」，故選項 (A) 為正解。注意，答案中將 get 改用 obtain 表示，而將 a photo ID card 簡略為 an ID。
69 Look at the graphic. What area does the woman work in? (A) Operations (B) IT (C) Administration (D) Research	請看圖表。女子在什麼部門工作？ (A) 營運部 (B) 資訊部 (C) 行政管理部 (D) 研究中心	**正解 (C)** 女子的識別證上印的大寫字母為「C」，而根據男子所言 Letters A through D are for staff in Administration. 可知，女子隸屬部門為 (C) Administration。
70 According to the man, what should the woman do after she gets an employee card? (A) Take another photo (B) Deactivate her old card (C) Carry it with her at all times (D) Report to the marketing department	根據男子的發言，女子取得員工識別證之後應該做什麼？ (A) 再拍一張照片 (B) 註銷她的舊卡 (C) 隨身攜帶識別證 (D) 向行銷部報告	**正解 (C)** 由男子最後說的 Just be sure to keep the card visible at all times. 即可知，正確答案是 (C)。注意，選項 (B) 敘述的乃當遺失識別證時的處理辦法。

PART 4

題目	題目翻譯
Questions 71 through 73 refer to the following telephone message. Hi Michael, it's Carla McIntyre from Lowlands Construction's personnel department. We received your application for Quality Controller and would like to offer you an interview on either January 11 or January 12. Please let me know which date is most convenient. After that, I'll send you confirmation of the date by express letter. I left a message two or three days ago about this, but got no response. If I don't hear from you within 24 hours, I'll assume you're no longer interested in the job. Please call me at 845-976-2389 extension 14 or on my phone 721-716-667. Or you can e-mail me at cmcintyre@lowlandsonline.co.uk. Unfortunately, our office fax machine is currently being repaired.	第 71 到 73 題請參照下面這段電話留言。 嗨，麥可，我是 Lowlands 建設人事部的卡拉·麥因泰。我們收到了你的品管員應徵資料，想請你在 1 月 11 日或 1 月 12 日來面試。請告知我哪一天最方便。然後我會用快捷郵件將日期確認的結果寄給你。兩三天前我有為這件事給你留了話，但沒有得到回音。假如在 24 小時內再沒有收到你的回覆，我就會認定你對這個職務不再感興趣。請撥個電話給我，845-976-2389，分機 14，或是打我的手機 721-716-667。或者你可以寄電子郵件給我：cmcintyre@lowlandsonline.co.uk。很不巧，我們辦公室的傳真機目前正在維修。

Vocabulary

- **personnel department** 人事部
- **convenient** [kən'vinjənt] 形 方便的
- **confirmation** [.kɑnfə'meʃən] 名 確認
- **express letter** 快捷郵件
- **response** [rɪ'spɑns] 名 回覆；回答
- **hear from ...** 得到（某人的）消息
- **assume** [ə'sjum] 動 以為；認定
- **unfortunately** [ʌn'fɔrtʃənɪtlɪ] 副 遺憾地；可惜
- **currently** ['kɜəntlɪ] 副 目前

試題	試題翻譯	答案與解析
71 What is the speaker calling about? (A) A job interview (B) An interview result (C) A schedule change (D) A job description	說話者為了什麼事來電？ (A) 職缺的面試 (B) 面試結果 (C) 行程的變更 (D) 職務說明	**正解 (A)** 由說話者提到的 We received your application for Quality Controller and would like to offer you an interview ... 可知，她收到麥可的應徵資料，並要提供面試的機會。換句話說，這段留言和「職缺的面試」有關。正確答案是 (A)。
72 What did the speaker do a few days ago? (A) Talked with Michael on the phone (B) Left a message about an interview (C) Sent a letter with an application (D) Transferred to the personnel department	說話者前幾天做了什麼事？ (A) 和麥可通了電話 (B) 留下了關於面試的訊息 (C) 寄了一封附應徵資料的信 (D) 轉調到了人事部	**正解 (B)** 關於說話者幾天前所做的事情，由留言中段的 I left a message two or three days ago about this 可見端倪，其中 this 指的就是確認面試日期這件事，因此選項 (B) 為正解。針對詢問過去行為的題目須多留意。
73 How long does Michael have to respond? (A) One day (B) Two days (C) Three days (D) Four days	麥可必須在多久之內回覆？ (A) 一天 (B) 兩天 (C) 三天 (D) 四天	**正解 (A)** 說話者在後段提到 If I don't hear from you within 24 hours, I'll assume you're no longer interested in the job.，意思是「如果在 24 小時內不回應，就表示對這份工作沒興趣」，而 24 小時的另一個說法就是選項 (A) One day。

題目	題目翻譯
Questions 74 through 76 refer to the following announcement.	第 74 到 76 題請參照下面這段廣播。

Good afternoon ladies and gentlemen, this is flight attendant Jennifer Hollings. On behalf of the airline, I'd like to apologize for our late departure. Planes ahead of us have taken off, but we are having our wings inspected by ground crews. The procedure should take approximately 20 more minutes and is an essential mechanical safety process before we can be cleared for takeoff. We should now touch down in Toronto at 10:00 P.M., 45 minutes later than scheduled. Passengers for connecting Flight GO-899 to Mexico City should proceed directly upon disembarkation to Gate 10, not Gate 11 as previously stated. I'd like to thank you again for joining us on Scotts Airways.

各位女士、各位先生,午安,我是空服員潔西卡．霍玲斯。在此謹代表本航空公司針對起飛誤點向您致歉。本航班之前的班機已經起飛,但是地勤維修人員正在檢查本機的機翼。本程序預估還需 20 分鐘左右,這是獲准起飛前不可或缺的基本機械安全流程。本航班目前應會於晚間十點在多倫多降落,比預定時刻晚 45 分鐘。需要轉乘 GO-899 班機前往墨西哥市的乘客下機後請直接前往 10 號登機門,而非原本指定的 11 號登機門。再次感謝您搭乘史考特航空。

Vocabulary

- [ ] **on behalf of ...** 代表……
- [ ] **apologize for ...** 為……道歉
- [ ] **ahead of ...** 在……之前
- [ ] **take off** 起飛
- [ ] **inspect** [ɪnˈspɛkt] 動 檢查
- [ ] **crew** [kru] 名 全體機組人員
- [ ] **procedure** [prəˈsidʒə] 名 程序
- [ ] **approximately** [əˈprɑksəmɪtlɪ] 副 大約
- [ ] **essential** [ɪˈsɛnʃəl] 形 基本的;必須的
- [ ] **touch down** 降落
- [ ] **connecting flight** 轉接班機
- [ ] **disembarkation** [ˌdɪsɛmbarˈkeʃən] 名 下飛機;下車(等交通工具)
- [ ] **previously** [ˈpriviəslɪ] 副 先前地
- [ ] **state** [stet] 動 陳述;聲明;指定

試題	試題翻譯	答案與解析
74 What has delayed the aircraft? (A) Planes ahead of it (B) Obstacles on the runway (C) Mechanical safety check (D) Bad weather	是什麼造成了飛機的延誤? (A) 之前的班機 (B) 跑道上的障礙物 (C) 機械安全檢查 (D) 天候不良	**正解 (C)** 本篇為關於起飛誤點的機內廣播。說話者在中段提到,地勤維修人員正在檢查機翼……此乃「不可或缺的機械安全流程」(an essential mechanical safety process),因此正解為 (C)。 ☐ **obstacle** [ˈɑbstəkl] 名 障礙(物)
75 How much longer will the plane have to wait? (A) 10 minutes (B) 20 minutes (C) 40 minutes (D) 45 minutes	該班機還要等多久? (A) 10 分鐘 (B) 20 分鐘 (C) 40 分鐘 (D) 45 分鐘	**正解 (B)** 答案線索同樣在中段:The procedure should take approximately 20 more minutes ...,故正解為選項 (B)。由於本篇廣播出現多個數字,建議先掃瞄一遍選項,如此有助聽懂題目。
76 What are passengers traveling to Mexico City advised to do? (A) Follow previously stated information (B) Get a travel update at their destination (C) Board from a different gate (D) Contact airline staff upon disembarkation	要前往墨西哥市的乘客被建議做什麼? (A) 遵照原來指定的資訊 (B) 在目的地獲取最新旅遊訊息 (C) 從另一個登機門登機 (D) 下機後聯絡航空公司的工作人員	**正解 (C)** 根據廣播後半段的 Passengers for connecting Flight GO-899 to Mexico City should proceed ... to Gate 10, not Gate 11 as previously stated. 可知,預定轉機至墨西哥的旅客下機後應前往 10 號登門機,而非之前通知的 11 號門,故選項 (C) Board from a different gate(從另一個登機門登機)的敘述正確。

題目	題目翻譯

Questions 77 through 79 refer to the following report.

Global fashion corporation Orient Mist Incorporated has announced a 4 percent rise in profits as of the last fiscal quarter. Analysts predict profits for the year will rise further to 6 percent. This is in contrast to last year, when the company posted a 12 percent loss. Recently-appointed CEO Alexander Chou said he expected this trend to continue, helped by the company's new clothing line *Secret Fire*. Mr. Chou said the line has done especially well among college-aged women. He stated the company's future will be further improved by large numbers of customers switching to the Internet to make their purchases instead of going into stores. He noted the company's online sales have risen substantially following an upgrade of its Web site, with visitors up by 16 percent for the year.

第 77 到 79 題請參照下面這則報導。

全球知名的時裝公司 Orient Mist 宣布，截至上個會計季度為止他們的獲利增加了 4%。分析師預測，他們今年的獲利將增加到 6%。這和去年該公司宣布的 12% 虧損形成了對比。最近才被任命的執行長亞歷山大‧周說，在公司新服裝系列「祕密之火」的推波助瀾下，他預期這股趨勢會持續下去。周先生說該系列尤其受到女大生的青睞。他表示，由於有大量的顧客不到店面而是改到網路上消費，公司的前景還會更好。他提到，在他們的網站升級而年度的訪客多了 16% 之後，公司的網購銷售大有斬獲。

Vocabulary

- **global** ['globl] 形 全世界的
- **profit** ['prɑfɪt] 名 收益
- **as of ...** 截至……
- **fiscal quarter** 會計季度
- **predict** [prɪ'dɪkt] 動 預測
- **in contrast to ...** 與……對照
- **post** [post] 動 發表；宣告
- **loss** [lɔs] 名 虧損
- **do well** 進展良好
- **switch to ...** 改變；轉移
- **substantially** [səb'stænʃəlɪ] 副 大幅地

試題	試題翻譯	答案與解析

77

What is the report mainly about?

(A) Luxury markets
(B) Corporate performance
(C) Economic trends
(D) Business investments

本篇報導主要與什麼有關？

(A) 精品市場
(B) 公司業績
(C) 經濟趨勢
(D) 商業投資

正解 (B)

由於整篇報導主要在敘述一時裝公司的收益成長與年度收益預測，因此正解為選項 (B) Corporate performance。

- **luxury** ['lʌkʃərɪ] 名 奢侈（品）
- **performance** [pə'fɔrməns] 名 成果；業績

78

How much do analysts expect profits to rise for the year?
(A) 4 percent
(B) 6 percent
(C) 12 percent
(D) 16 percent

分析師預期今年的獲利會增加多少？

(A) 4%
(B) 6%
(C) 12%
(D) 16%

正解 (B)

根據報導的第二句 Analysts predict profits for the year will rise further to 6 percent.，即可知本題應選 (B)。

79

What does the report imply?

(A) Shopping trends are changing.
(B) CEO policies are failing.
(C) More customers are coming into stores.
(D) Online sales are decreasing.

本篇報導暗示什麼？

(A) 消費趨勢正在改變。
(B) 執行長的政策失敗。
(C) 有較多的顧客進到商店裡。
(D) 線上銷售在減少中。

正解 (A)

報導後段提到 ... large numbers of customers switching to the Internet to make their purchases instead of going into stores，這說明有愈來愈多消費者不在實體店面而改在網路上購買商品，換句話說，「消費趨勢正在改變」，所以正確答案是 (A)。

題目	題目翻譯

Questions 80 through 82 refer to the following advertisement.

It's hard to clean all the different surfaces in your home, isn't it? Usually, you need one cleaner for the kitchen, one for the bathroom, and one for the furniture. *SteadyClean* is different. Its powerful yet gentle chemicals allow you to clean any area of your home. Just spray it on a wet cloth and wipe it over any surface: it'll be spotless in seconds! Now, I'm going to invite some of you from the audience to join me on stage. You're going to have the chance to use this product on some of the items I have up here with me. Then, you'll see just how great this cleaner really is!

第 80 到 82 題請參照下面這則廣告。

家裡各種不同的表面很難清理，不是嗎？通常廚房需要一種清潔劑，浴室也需要一種，家具還需要另外一種。「穩淨」就不一樣了。它強效卻溫和的化學成分讓您能清潔家中的任何地方。只要把它噴在濕布上擦拭表面，污漬在幾秒內就會消失！現在，我要從現場觀眾中邀請幾位朋友到台上來。各位將有機會用一些我擺在這裡的物品來試試這項產品。之後您就會看到這款清潔劑到底有多棒！

Vocabulary

□ **surface** [ˈsɜfɪs] 名 表面 　　□ **chemical** [ˈkɛmɪkl] 名 化學成分 　　□ **wipe** [waɪp] 動 擦拭 　　□ **spotless** [ˈspɑtlɪs] 形 沒有汙點的
□ **in seconds** 幾秒內

試題	試題翻譯	答案與解析

80

What is the speaker doing?

(A) Introducing a product
(B) Cleaning a house
(C) Helping a customer
(D) Arranging a program

說話者在做什麼？

(A) 介紹產品
(B) 清理房子
(C) 協助顧客
(D) 安排節目

正解 (A)

本題須聽完整段語音才能做出判斷。從說話者說明商品優點的部分即可得到答題線索。此外，由於說話者具體提到了 *SteadyClean* 這個商品名稱，因此正解為 (A)。

81

What does the man imply when he says, "it'll be spotless in seconds"?
(A) The cloth will dry fast.
(B) The surface will be clean quickly.
(C) The chemicals need time to mix.
(D) The cleaner cannot remove all dirt.

當男子說 "it'll be spotless in seconds" 時，他暗示了什麼？
(A) 布料會乾得很快。
(B) 表面會很快變乾淨。
(C) 那些化學成分需要花時間攪拌。
(D) 清潔劑無法去除所有髒汙。

正解 (B)

劃線部分的主詞 it 指其前提到的 surface「表面」；spotless 是「乾淨；無塵」之意；in seconds 則是「數秒內；轉眼間」的意思。選項 (B) 中的 clean 是 spotless 的另一種說法，而 quickly 又等於 in seconds，故 (B) 為正解。

82

What are some listeners invited to do?

(A) Ask the speaker questions
(B) Participate in a demonstration
(C) Talk about their experiences
(D) Receive product samples

部分聽眾受邀做什麼？

(A) 對說話者提問
(B) 參與一項示範
(C) 講述自身經驗
(D) 領取產品樣品

正解 (B)

在談話的最後，說話者提到 I'm going to invite some of you from the audience to join me on stage, 也就是，他要邀請現場觀眾上台體驗該產品的功效，所以正確答案是 (B)。

□ **participate in ...** 參與……

題目	題目翻譯

Questions 83 through 85 refer to the following talk.

Good evening. At Centennial Tools Incorporated, we want the best for all our employees. That includes providing special benefits for those who are parents. We are therefore proud to announce the opening of our Centennial Headquarters Daycare Center. The center includes a playground, outdoor water fountain, and 3-meter fence to safeguard your children. Shortly, Jessica Langdon, head teacher at the center, will be telling us about how it will be run on a daily basis, the curriculum involved and the activities children there will be able to enjoy. After that, Aaron Cummings will talk about our plans for the long-term future of the center before Betsy Chung and Brian Masoud from human resources give you details of how you can enroll your child in the center.

第 83 到 85 題請參照下面這段談話。

晚安。我們百年工具有限公司希望給全體員工最好的，其中包括提供身為父母的員工特別的福利。因此，我們很榮幸地宣布，我們的百年總部托兒中心開幕了。園內設有遊樂場、戶外噴水池，還有可以保護幼童的三公尺圍牆。稍後，園長潔西卡·藍登會告訴我們本園每天的運作模式，以及它的相關課程和園內小朋友會很喜歡的活動。接著，亞倫·康明斯會談到我們對於中心未來長遠的計畫。之後則是由人事部的貝琪·鍾和布萊恩·馬蘇迪來詳細說明如何為您的子女登記入學。

Vocabulary

- [ ] **special benefit** 特別福利
- [ ] **therefore** [ˋðɛr.for] 副 因此；因而
- [ ] **daycare center** 托兒中心
- [ ] **playground** [ˋple.graʊnd] 名 遊樂場
- [ ] **water fountain** 噴水池
- [ ] **safeguard** [ˋsef.gɑrd] 動 保護
- [ ] **shortly** [ˋʃɔrtlɪ] 副 馬上；不久
- [ ] **run** [rʌn] 動 運作
- [ ] **on a daily basis** 按每天……
- [ ] **long-term** [ˋlɔŋˋtɜm] 形 長遠的

試題	試題翻譯	答案與解析

83

What is the main purpose of the talk?

(A) To develop a curriculum
(B) To explain the existing service
(C) To ask for donations
(D) To inform parents about a new facility

這段談話的主要目的是什麼？

(A) 開發課程
(B) 解說現有的服務
(C) 募捐
(D) 告知父母們一項新設施

正解 (D)

談話一開始就提到要提供全體員工最好的，特別是提供身為父母的人特別的福利，且根據之後所說的 We are therefore proud to announce the opening of our Centennial Headquarters Daycare Center. 來判斷，選項 (D) 為本題正解。注意，facility 指的就是該公司的 Daycare Center。

84

What is a feature of the center?

(A) Child computers
(B) Protective enclosures
(C) Special teachers
(D) Expanded curriculums

下列何者為該中心的特色？

(A) 兒童電腦
(B) 保護用的圍欄
(C) 特別教師
(D) 廣泛的課程

正解 (B)

解答線索在於談話中段提到的 The Center includes ..., and 3-meter fence to safeguard your children. ，而 fence to safeguard 的另一種說法就是選項 (B) Protective enclosures。

- [ ] **protective** [prəˋtɛktɪv] 形 保護的
- [ ] **enclosure** [ɪnˋkloʒə] 名 柵欄；圍牆

85

What will Aaron Cummings talk about?

(A) The history of the center
(B) Future plans
(C) The details of activities
(D) Ways to sign up

亞倫·康明斯將談論什麼？

(A) 中心的歷史
(B) 將來的計畫
(C) 活動詳情
(D) 註冊辦法

正解 (B)

由 Aaron Cummings will talk about our plans for the long-term future of the center 即可知，正解為選項 (B)。注意，像這種關於特定人物的問題，解題技巧在於先掃瞄一遍題目，當聆聽語音時將注意力放在該名字所出現的段落上就能聽出答案。

題目	題目翻譯
Questions 86 through 88 refer to the following excerpt from a meeting. We have had a very successful fiscal year. Our sales rose by 14 percent and our market share by 12 percent. Many of you have worked long hours under tight deadlines and difficult conditions to achieve that, and I believe you should get credit. So, in order to show our appreciation, the company is creating a profit-sharing program. Five percent of our total net income will be distributed among all staff who have worked here for at least nine months. You can get details on this on the company Intranet. This is our small way of thanking you for all you've done.	第 86 到 88 題請參照下面這段會議摘錄。 本公司在去年的會計年度表現得非常優秀。我們的營業額增加了 14%，市占率提高了 12%。在座有不少人都是在緊迫的期限與困難的條件下長時間工作，才有了這樣的成績，而我認為你們應該獲得表揚。為了表示感謝之意，公司正在設計一個分紅機制。總淨利的 5% 將分配給所有在這裡服務了九個月以上的人員。詳情可上公司的內部網路查閱。對於各位所做的一切，這是我們表達感謝的小小心意。

Vocabulary

- **deadline** [ˋdɛdˏlaɪn] 名 截止期限
- **achieve** [əˋtʃiv] 動 完成；實現
- **get credit** 獲得表揚
- **appreciation** [əˏpriʃɪˋeʃən] 名 感謝
- **net income** 淨利
- **distribute** [dɪˋstrɪbjut] 動 分配
- **Intranet** [ˋɪntrənɛt] 名 （企業的）內部網路

試題	試題翻譯	答案與解析
86 Who is the talk most likely intended for? (A) Corporate shareholders (B) Financial reporters (C) Company employees (D) Market researchers	這段談話最有可能的對象是誰？ (A) 企業股東 (B) 財金記者 (C) 公司員工 (D) 市調人員	**正解 (C)** 說話者口中的 you 明顯指的是公司員工；換言之，此番談話的對象即為 (C) Company employees。
87 What success is mentioned by the speaker? (A) A reduction in production costs (B) An increase in stock prices (C) An increase in revenue (D) A reduction in working hours	說話者所提到的成功是什麼？ (A) 生產成本的降低 (B) 股價的走高 (C) 營收的增加 (D) 工時的縮短	**正解 (C)** 從談話開頭提到的 Our sales rose by 14 percent and our market share by 12 percent. 這句話即可知，選項 (C) An increase in revenue 為正解。 ☐ **stock price** 股價 ☐ **revenue** [ˋrɛvəˏnju] 名 收益
88 What does the speaker mean when she says, "I believe you should get credit"? (A) She considers sales to be adequate. (B) She hopes higher goals will be achieved. (C) She owes money to her staff. (D) She thinks her employees deserve a reward.	當說話者說 "I believe you should get credit" 時，她是什麼意思？ (A) 她認為業績尚可。 (B) 她希望能達成更高的目標。 (C) 她積欠員工金錢。 (D) 她認為員工應得一份獎賞。	**正解 (D)** 這段談話前半段敘述了員工所達成的業績，再從 So, ... 開始感謝員工，並表示將透過利潤分享機制給予報酬。credit 是「功勞；讚揚」的意思，所以正確答案為 (D)。注意，deserve「應受（賞罰）」是 get credit 的另一種說法，而 a reward 則指前面提到的酬金、獎賞。

題目	題目翻譯

Questions 89 through 91 refer to the following excerpt from a meeting.

Before we begin, I'd like to make a short announcement. As some of you already know, Maria Lopez, the head of our Operations Department, is currently away sick and will not be returning for at least another six weeks. As a result, we have decided to move Richard Slater from IT to her position until she returns. Personnel from both Consumer Finance and Planning will also help as required during this period. I know this is an added burden for us. However, we need to make sure our service continues to be first-class — at the same level that *Corporate Review Magazine* praised us for. Now, as there seem to be no questions, I'd like to proceed with a look at the monthly report as planned. Please look at the first of these slides.

第 89 到 91 題請參照下面這段會議摘錄。

在開始前,我想先簡短地宣布一下。在座有些人已經知道,我們營運部的主管瑪麗亞‧羅培茲目前請病假,至少還要六個星期之後才會回來。因此,我們決定把理查‧史雷特從資訊部調任到她的位置,直到她回來為止。在這段期間,消費金融和企劃部的人員在必要時也都要幫忙。我知道這是我們的額外負擔,但是我們必須確保能持續一流的服務品質,也就是維持住《企業評論雜誌》讚揚我們的那種水準。現在,既然各位似乎都沒有問題,我就照原訂的計畫接著來看月報。請看第一張投影片。

Vocabulary

□ **head** [hɛd] 名 主管　　□ **added** [ˈædɪd] 形 額外的　　□ **burden** [ˈbɜdn̩] 名 負擔;重擔　　□ **make sure (that)** 確定(某事)
□ **first-class** [ˈfɜstˈklæs] 形 一流的　　□ **praise** [prez] 動 稱讚　　□ **monthly report** 月報

試題	試題翻譯	答案與解析

89

Which department does Richard Slater normally work in?
(A) Accounting
(B) IT
(C) Consumer Finance
(D) Planning

理查‧史雷特平常在哪個部門工作?

(A) 會計部
(B) 資訊部
(C) 消費金融部
(D) 企劃部

正解 (B)

從 we have decided to move Richard Slater from IT to her position until she returns 可知,平常服務於資訊部的理查‧史雷特暫時被調部門,正解為 (B)。注意,由於試題裡包含具體的人名,因此當語音播放出該人名時就要特別仔細聽。

90

What does the man mean when he says, "I know this is an added burden for us"?
(A) He wants to have more staff.
(B) There will be another position available.
(C) A department will be divided into two.
(D) The company will face some hardship.

當男子說 "I know this is an added burden for us" 時,他是什麼意思?

(A) 他想要更多員工。
(B) 將會有另一個職缺。
(C) 某部門將被一分為二。
(D) 公司將面臨一些難關。

正解 (D)

解題線索在於表「負擔;重擔」的 burden,而即使不了解這個字,從 added「額外的;附加的」的字意和前後文脈去思考也能找出答案。這段話的話題是在主管瑪麗亞‧羅培茲請病假的期間,理查‧史雷特將從別的部門調過來協助。之後,說話者又提到「但仍須維持一流品質的服務」,在人手不足時要做到這點並不容易,意即,員工們必須努力突破此難關,因此本題應選 (D)。

91

What will the listeners do next?

(A) Offer opinions
(B) View a presentation
(C) Ask questions
(D) Write monthly reports

聽講的人接下來會做什麼?

(A) 發表意見
(B) 看簡報
(C) 問問題
(D) 寫月報

正解 (B)

說話者在表示接下來請看月報之後又說了 Please look at the first of these slides.(請看第一張投影片。)這句話,換言之,聽講者將觀看一場簡報發表,所以正確答案是 (B)。注意,問「接下來要做什麼」這類的題目,答案線索通常會出現在語音的最後。

題目	題目翻譯
Questions 92 through 94 refer to the following broadcast. I'm Jason Kim with all your business news. A report by expert, Kate Smith of Lake University, has found that the key to communicating effectively in front of groups is preparation. While relaxation exercises or advanced speaking techniques can help with nervousness, there is no alternative to having a thorough knowledge of a subject. In an experiment, speakers who were thoroughly prepared for a presentation were found to be 20-30% more persuasive than those who were not. The difference was particularly clear when speakers had to face audience questions at the end of their presentations. At that point, well-prepared speakers did an especially good job with their topics. Now, here's Alicia Hernandez with the weather.	第 92 到 94 題請參照下面這段廣播。 我是傑森‧金，為您報導商業新聞。雷克大學的專家凱特‧史密斯在她的報告中指出，在群眾面前有效傳達的關鍵在於準備。雖然舒展運動或高明的說話技巧有助於消除緊張，但是對主題有透徹的了解卻是無可替代的。實驗發現，充分準備報告的講者比準備不充分的講者多了兩到三成的說服力。當講者在簡報最後必須面對聽眾的提問時，差別尤其明顯。此時有好好準備的講者特別能針對他們的題目侃侃而談。接下來將由艾莉西亞‧賀南德茲為您播報氣象。

第 1 回完全解析

PART 4

Vocabulary

- **expert** [ˈɛkspət] 名 專家
- **effectively** [ɪˈfɛktɪvlɪ] 副 有效地
- **nervousness** [ˈnɝvəsnɪs] 名 緊張
- **alternative** [ɔlˈtɝnətɪv] 名 選擇；二選一
- **subject** [ˈsʌbdʒɪkt] 名 主題；題目
- **experiment** [ɪkˈspɛrəmənt] 名 實驗
- **thoroughly** [ˈθɝolɪ] 副 徹底地
- **persuasive** [pəˈswesɪv] 形 勸說的
- **particularly** [pəˈtɪkjələlɪ] 副 尤其地
- **face** [fes] 動 面對

試題	試題翻譯	答案與解析
92 Who most likely is the speaker? (A) A business expert (B) A company president (C) A news reporter (D) A communication specialist	說話者最有可能是誰？ (A) 商業專家 (B) 公司總裁 (C) 新聞記者 (D) 溝通專家	**正解 (C)** 從題目指示中的 ... following broadcast 就能得知本篇為（電視或電台的）一則報導。在說話者一開始以 I'm Jason Kim with all your business news. 自我介紹之後，緊接著就轉述一位專家的報告。除此之外，也可由最後的 Now, here's Alicia Hernandez with the weather. 這句話來判斷，答案是 (C)。
93 According to the speaker, what does the report say is necessary for a good presentation? (A) Practice while in university (B) Substantial mastery of material (C) Thorough relaxation exercises (D) Advanced speaking techniques	根據說話者，報導指出一場出色的簡報什麼不可或缺？ (A) 在讀大學時練習 (B) 對資料瞭若指掌 (C) 徹底的放鬆運動 (D) 高明的說話技巧	**正解 (B)** 報導中段提及 ... there is no alternative to having a thorough knowledge of a subject，意思是「對主題透徹的了解是無可替代的」，選項 (B) 用另一種說法表示，正是本題最適切的答案。 ☐ **substantial** [səbˈstænʃəl] 形 實在的；相當的
94 What is preparation particularly effective for? (A) Making points clear (B) Choosing a topic (C) Facing the public (D) Replying to inquiries	準備對哪方面特別有成效？ (A) 清楚陳述論點 (B) 挑選主題 (C) 面對群眾 (D) 回答提問	**正解 (D)** 根據報導，充分準備者比未充分準備的人員具說服力，而 The difference was particularly clear when speakers had to face audience questions ...，也就是說，「在面對聽眾的提問時差異尤其明顯」，因此正解為選項 (D) Relying to inquiries。

題目	題目翻譯

Questions 95 through 97 refer to the following talk and map.

Now that everyone's here, I'd like to say a few words about the company picnic next month. This year, it's going to be bigger than ever — partly as a reward for the record profits that we earned last fiscal year. It will be at Naden Park and organized by the Human Resources Department. It's a public space, so we can't reserve any section of the area. However, Human Resources will arrive early to find a spot for us just south of Basto Lake. There's a bicycle path that cuts that area into two sections. We'll be in the southwest section. Travel directions have already been e-mailed companywide, so all staff should know how to get there — by car or public transportation. Festivities will begin at 11:00 A.M., but our staff will begin setting up everything — including unpacking food and drinks — at around 9:00 A.M.

第 95 到 97 題請參照下列談話和地圖。

既然大家都到了，關於公司下個月的野餐，我想說幾句話。今年，這個活動將辦得比以往更盛大——部分是為了犒賞各位在去年度贏得破紀錄的營收。本次活動將於那登公園舉行，並由人資部規劃。活動場地是一個公開的空間，因此我們沒辦法預訂場內的任何區域。不過，人資部同仁會提早抵達幫我們在巴斯托湖南側找塊空地。那裡有一條自行車道將該區切割成兩邊，而我們將會在西南邊。交通指南已經用電子郵件寄給全公司的人了，所以各位應該都知道如何前往——開車或搭乘大眾交通工具。慶祝活動將於上午 11 點開始，但是我們的工作人員會在上午 9 點左右開始準備所有的東西，包括把食物和飲料打開拿出來。

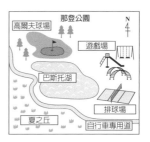

Vocabulary

- [ ] **record profit** 破紀錄的營收
- [ ] **cut ... into ... sections** 將⋯⋯切割為⋯⋯區
- [ ] **companywide** [`kʌmpənɪˌwaɪd] 副 全公司地
- [ ] **festivity** [fɛsˈtɪvətɪ] 名 慶祝活動
- [ ] **unpack** [ʌnˈpæk] 動 從（箱、包等）中取出

試題	試題翻譯	答案與解析

95

What type of event is being prepared?

(A) A talent contest
(B) A marathon
(C) An outdoor gathering
(D) A local tour

何種類型的活動正在籌備中？

(A) 才藝比賽
(B) 馬拉松
(C) 戶外聚會
(D) 地方旅行

正解 (C)

說話者在一開始就說 I'd like to say a few words about the company picnic next month，而整段談話是在詳細說明該 company picnic（公司野餐）。選項 (C) outdoor gathering 用另一種說法表達出 picnic 之意，故為正解。

96

Look at the graphic. Where will the company staff meet?
(A) At the golf course
(B) At the volleyball court
(C) At the playground
(D) At Summer Hill

請看圖表。這家公司的員工將於何處會合？

(A) 高爾夫球場
(B) 排球場
(C) 遊戲場
(D) 夏之丘

正解 (D)

首先從中段的 Human Resources will arrive ... just south of Basto Lake. 可知，野餐場地位於巴斯托湖的南側。接著再由 There's a bicycle path that cuts that area into two sections. We'll be in the southwest section. 這兩句話對照地圖判斷，答案應該是被自行車專用道貫穿之區域當中的西南方，故選 (D)。

97

What has already been sent companywide?
(A) Travel coupons
(B) Public transportation passes
(C) Directions to the venue
(D) A list of festivities organizers

下列何者已全公司發送？

(A) 旅遊折價券
(B) 大眾交通工具乘車券
(C) 會場交通指引
(D) 活動籌備者一覽表

正解 (C)

根據接近中段的談話 Travel directions have already been e-mailed companywide ... 即可確定，換句話說的選項 (C) 為正解。directions to ... 指「前往某場所的方向、方法」，而 venue 則是「場地」的意思。

- [ ] **organizer** [`ɔrgəˌnaɪzə] 名 組織者；規劃者

第1回完全解析

PART 4

題目	題目翻譯

Questions 98 through 100 refer to the following telephone message and order form.

John, this is Stella Gomez from headquarters. I turned in an order for office supplies this morning, but I hope that you haven't processed it yet. We have to add another three laptops to our order. I was just informed that we'll be having six new employees arriving on March 21, and we need to have all the necessary office equipment set up for them before that date. The rest of the order seems fine as it is. I sent you an e-mail with this same request, but I'm not sure whether you've had a chance to read it. When you get a moment, please call me back to confirm whether you can make these adjustments. Thanks.

第 98 到 100 題請參照下列電話留言和訂購單。

約翰,我是總公司的史黛拉·戈梅茲。我今天早上提交了一份訂購辦公室用品的訂單,但是我希望你還沒處理它。我們得再加訂三台筆記型電腦。我剛才被告知說 3 月 21 日將會有六位新員工報到,我們需要在那天之前幫他們把所有的辦公室必需設備就定位。訂單上的其他物品看起來沒問題,維持不變。我有寄電子郵件給你拜託這同一件事,我不確定你是不是已經有機會看到信。有空時請回電話給我,跟我確認一下你能不能調整訂單。謝謝。

KASIK PAINT CO.
Office Supplies Order Form
Order Number: 903H2

Item	Units ordered
Desk lamps	8
Photocopier ink	6
Laptops	4
Fax machine	1

KASIK 塗料公司
辦公用品訂購單
訂單編號:903H2

品項	訂購數量
檯燈	8
影印機墨水	6
筆電	4
傳真機	1

Vocabulary

☐ **turn in** 提出　　☐ **process** [`prɑsɛs] 動 處理　　☐ **as it is** 照現狀　　☐ **adjustment** [ə`dʒʌstmənt] 動 調整

試題	試題翻譯	答案與解析

98

Look at the graphic. How many laptops does the company need in total?
(A) 3
(B) 5
(C) 6
(D) 7

請看圖表。這家公司總共需要幾台筆電?

(A) 三台
(B) 五台
(C) 六台
(D) 七台

正解 (D)

這通電話留言的目的是要請對方更改辦公用品的訂單。從 We have to add another three laptops to our order. 這句話得知要追加 3 台筆記型電腦,再看訂單上記載著筆電的訂購數量為 4,所以總共需要 4 + 3 = 7 台。本題正確答案是 (D)。

99

According to the telephone message, what has the company recently done?
(A) Improved its headquarters
(B) Processed a claim
(C) Hired some staff
(D) Changed a launch date

根據電話留言,這家公司最近進行了什麼事?
(A) 改善總公司
(B) 處理一項請求
(C) 招募一些員工
(D) 更改上市日期

正解 (C)

從 I was just informed that we'll be having six new employees arriving on March 21 即可知,公司新聘了六個人,故 (C) 為正解。

☐ **claim** [klem] 名 請求
☐ **launch date**(活動等的)開始日;(新商品等的)推出日

100

What is the listener asked to do?

(A) Train recruits
(B) Adjust a price
(C) Make a phone call
(D) Wait for a text

聽者被要求做什麼?

(A) 訓練新進員工
(B) 調整一個價格
(C) 打一通電話
(D) 等一則手機簡訊

正解 (C)

詢問聽者被要求做什麼的這種題型,絕大部分的答題線索都在語音的結尾處。從這通留言的最後一句話的 ... please call me back to confirm .... 可知,選項 (C) 就是正確答案。注意,關於聽者應該做什麼或被要求做什麼的題目,在談話中通常是以命令句或 Could you ...? 之類的句型來表達請求。

☐ **text (message)**(手機上的)簡訊

PART 5

試題與翻譯	答案與解析

101

Mr. Krishna informed the company of _____ plan to visit several important clients on the West Coast the following week.

(A) its
(B) it
(C) he
(D) his

克里希納先生向公司報告了他的計畫，下週他將要去拜訪西岸的幾家重要客戶。

正解 (D) 代名詞的所有格

本題問何者為適切的代名詞。空格後面是名詞 plan，所以前面應該接所有格。而由於此句主詞為 Mr. Krishna，故選項 (D) his 為正解。注意，若不小心將空格前的 the company 當作主詞，就會誤選 (A) its。

□ **inform A of B** 向 A 通知 B

102

Genetic advances at Warsaw Pharmaceuticals mean it may soon be possible to protect people from a _____ variety of diseases.

(A) long
(B) wide
(C) thick
(D) high

華沙製藥在遺傳學上的進展意謂著，它或許很快就能使人遠離多種各式各樣的疾病。

正解 (B) 字彙

a variety of ... 的意思是「各式各樣；五花八門的……」，而最適合用來修飾 variety 的形容詞為 "wide"。正解為選項 (B)。

□ **genetic** [dʒəˈnɛtɪk] 形 遺傳學的
□ **advance** [ədˈvæns] 名 進步
□ **pharmaceuticals** [ˌfɑrməˈsjutɪk|z] 名 藥廠
□ **disease** [dɪˈziz] 名 疾病

103

Director Rao convinced the board to begin export sales to Europe this year, _____ at least lay the groundwork for doing so.

(A) while
(B) since
(C) but
(D) or

饒主任說服了董事會今年開始應外銷到歐洲，或至少要在這方面打下基礎。

正解 (D) 連接詞

根據文意推敲，以表「抑或」、「或是」的連接詞 or 來接續另一個動詞最為恰當。正確答案是選項 (D)。

□ **convince** [kənˈvɪns] 動 說服
□ **groundwork** [ˈɡraʊndˌwɜk] 名 基礎

104

Alistair Properties Co. _____ to closing most deals in dollars, but due to client demand began accepting euros and yen as well.

(A) accustomed
(B) had been accustomed
(C) will accustom
(D) will have been accustomed

阿里斯戴爾房地產公司已習慣於用美金來敲定大部分的買賣，但由於客戶的要求，他們也開始接受歐元和日圓。

正解 (B) 動詞

只要知道被動形式的 be accustomed to ...ing 的意思是「習慣於……」，就能先刪去 (A)（過去式）與 (C)（未來式），留下選項 (B)（過去完成被動式）與 (D)（未來完成被動式）。而依文意，該公司在開始接受歐元和日圓之前就已習慣使用美金，也就是，應該使用過去完成式來表達「過去的過去」，因此本題選 (B)。

□ **close a deal** 完成交易
□ **demand** [dɪˈmænd] 名 要求；需求

105

First Harbor Pharmaceutical Inc. is one of the top private caregivers in the province and _____ is a leader in advanced medical research.

(A) since
(B) whichever
(C) although
(D) moreover

首港製藥公司是該省一家頂尖的私人照護業者，而且也是高端醫療研究的領導者。

正解 (D) 連接副詞

根據前後文脈，因空格前已有連接詞 "and"，故填入具有「此外」意思的連接副詞 (D) moreover 才正確。

□ **caregiver** [ˈkɛrˌɡɪvə] 名 看護人員；管理人員
□ **province** [ˈprɑvɪns] 名 省；州

106

CEO Brian Greene stated at the meeting that an increase in sales of 13% by the end of the year was quite _____.

(A) attains
(B) attaining
(C) attainable
(D) attainably

執行長布萊恩‧葛林於會議上表示，在年底前增加 13% 的銷售量是相當可行的。

正解 (C) 詞性

空格前出現了 be 動詞的過去式 was 和副詞 quite。由於已有動詞 was，因此選項 (A)（動詞第三人稱單數現在式）不恰當。而因主詞為 an increase 不可能做動作，所以 (B)（現在分詞或動名詞）亦不合適。另外，因 be 動詞為不完全不及物動詞，故其後需要主詞補語，因此選項 (D)（副詞）也不恰當。最合適做主詞補語的只有選項 (C) 的形容詞 attainable。

□ **attain** [ə`ten] 動 達到

107

Sun Lady bath soap is certainly _____ than any similar product in fine stores today.

(A) fragrant
(B) more fragrant
(C) most fragrant
(D) fragrance

陽光女郎浴皂肯定比現今精品商店裡任何類似的產品更香。

正解 (B) 比較

因為空格之後出現了 than，所以選項 (B) 的比較級形容詞 more fragrant 為正解。注意，選項 (C) 最高級 most fragrant 不可選，因為空格前必須要有 the，且其後也不接 than。

□ **certainly** [`sɝtənlɪ] 副 確定地
□ **similar** [`sɪmələ] 形 類似的
□ **fragrant** [`fregrənt] 形 芳香的
□ **fragrance** [`fregrəns] 名 芳香；香氣

108

Mr. Ephron wished there _____ more funds for the company picnic, but the employees seemed satisfied with the snacks and beverages provided.

(A) is
(B) are
(C) would
(D) were

艾福隆先生希望公司野餐能有更多的經費，但是員工似乎對公司提供的零食和飲料已感到滿足。

正解 (D) 假設語氣

本題是表達願望的假設用法，wish 之後的動詞必須使用過去式以表示「與現在事實相反」。而 there is/are 句型當中的 be 動詞在假設語氣中之過去式為 were，故本題應選 (D)。

□ **fund** [fʌnd] 名 資金
□ **(be) satisfied with ...** 對……感到滿足；滿意
□ **beverage** [`bɛvərɪdʒ] 名 飲料

109

News reports indicate that some corporations are preparing _____ an economic upturn by making large investments now.

(A) for
(B) and
(C) to
(D) but

新聞報導指出，有些企業現正大舉投資以為經濟好轉預做準備。

正解 (A) 介系詞

prepare for 為一片語，是「為……做準備」之意，故本題選 (A)。

□ **indicate** [`ɪndə͵ket] 動 指示
□ **upturn** [ʌp`tɝn] 名 好轉
□ **investment** [ɪn`vɛstmənt] 名 投資

110

Ms. Singh made it her personal _____ to track the company's profit margins in each of the major regions it operated in.

(A) interesting
(B) interest
(C) interestingly
(D) interested

辛小姐把追蹤該公司在各主要經營地區的毛潤率當成個人的興趣。

正解 (B) 詞性

空格前出現了所有格 her 及形容詞 personal，因此空格內應填入名詞。正解為選項 (B) interest。另注意，made it 當中的 it 是虛受詞，to 後面的敘述才是真正的受詞。

□ **profit margin** 利潤率
□ **interestingly** [`ɪntrəstɪŋlɪ] 副 有趣地

試題與翻譯	答案與解析

111

Evertrue Media Corporation is _____ the number one firm in the entertainment industry in terms of market share.

(A) responsively
(B) undoubtedly
(C) mutually
(D) compassionately

就市占率而言，極真媒體公司無庸置疑地是娛樂圈的第一大公司。

正解 (B) 字彙

四個選項皆為副詞，但最能用來修飾空格後的 the number one firm 且最符合文意的應是選項 (B) undoubtedly（無庸置疑地）。

☐ **firm** [fʒm] 名 公司；企業
☐ **in terms of** 從……的角度來看
☐ **responsively** [rɪˋspɑnsɪvlɪ] 副 積極回應地
☐ **mutually** [ˋmjutʃʊəlɪ] 副 互相地
☐ **compassionately** [kəmˋpæʃənɪtlɪ] 副 有同情心地

112

Greater Vancouver, particularly during times of economic slowdowns, is _____ many Canadian IT companies locate their offices.

(A) how
(B) why
(C) when
(D) where

大溫哥華地區是加拿大許多資訊科技公司現在設點的地方，尤其是在經濟衰退的時候。

正解 (D) 關係副詞

就句構而言，本句主詞為 Greater Vancourver，is 是謂語動詞，故空格之後須填入補語。而由於主詞指「地方」，空格的關係副詞以選項 (D) 的 where 最適切，修飾先行詞 the place。

☐ **slowdown** [ˋslo͵daʊn] 名 減速；衰退
☐ **locate** [loˋket] 動 把……設置在

113

Mr. Anwar's design team was _____ on time with all its projects, causing the company to rely on it a great deal.

(A) invariable
(B) invariant
(C) invariably
(D) invariability

安瓦先生的設計團隊在所有的案子上始終如一地準時，使得該公司對它倚賴甚深。

正解 (C) 詞性

空格之前出現了 be 動詞過去式 was，之後出現副詞片語 on time（準時），所以必須選擇能修飾副詞的副詞。選項 (C) invariably（不變地；總是）為唯一副詞，故為正解。

☐ **rely on** 依賴……
☐ **a great deal** 大量地
☐ **invariable** [ɪnˋvɛrɪəbl] 形 不變的
☐ **invariant** [ɪnˋvɛrɪənt] 形 無變化的
☐ **invariability** [ɪn͵vɛrɪəˋbɪlətɪ] 名 不變性

114

Trainor Inc. maintains a competitive bonus system _____ order to motivate staff in all of its departments.

(A) in
(B) by
(C) from
(D) at

崔納公司維持一個競賽獎金制度，藉此激勵各部門的人員。

正解 (A) 字彙

in order to ... 的意思是「為了……」，為固定用法。正確答案是 (A)。

☐ **maintain** [menˋten] 動 維持
☐ **competitive** [kəmˋpɛtətɪv] 形 能與他人競爭的
☐ **motivate** [ˋmotə͵vet] 動 激發

115

Five cents of every dollar _____ on goods in the Tyler Department Store goes toward local charities that help children.

(A) credited
(B) cashed
(C) paid
(D) spent

在泰勒百貨公司的商品上所花的每一塊錢都有五分會捐給當地幫助幼童的慈善機構。

正解 (D) 字彙

本題選項皆為動詞的過去分詞，置於名詞之後有修飾作用。選項 (A) credited（賒）和 (B) cashed（兌現）皆與文意不符。如果要填入的意思是「付費」，則 pay 之後須用介系詞 for，所以選項 (C) 也不對。只有 spent（花費）後適合用介系詞 on，因此選項 (D) 為正解。句型 spend A on B「花費 A 金額在 B 上」，在此句將 A 提前變成 A spent on B「在 B 上花費的 A 金額」。

☐ **goods** [gʊdz] 名 商品（複數形）
☐ **charity** [ˋtʃærətɪ] 名 慈善事業
☐ **credit** [ˋkrɛdɪt] 動 借貸；賒欠

試題與翻譯	答案與解析

116

Mr. M'Krumah is in _____ of the company's Lagos branch, operating all its major business activities in West Africa.

(A) responsibility
(B) touch
(C) charge
(D) engaged

姆克魯馬先生掌管公司的拉哥斯分處，經營公司在西非所有主要的商業活動。

正解 (C) 字彙

片語 in charge of ... 是「管理……；負責……」的意思，(C) 即為正解。選項 (B) be in touch with 指「與某人聯繫」，選項 (D) be engaged in 指「忙於某事」。

☐ **responsibility** [rɪˌspɑnsəˈbɪlətɪ] 名 責任

117

_____ a sensation among teenagers, the Jumping Box online game rapidly became popular throughout East Asia.

(A) Creates
(B) Creating
(C) Created
(D) Create

在青少年之間造成轟動，「跳箱」線上遊戲迅速紅遍了東亞。

正解 (B) 分詞構句

本題須選出置於句首的分詞構句，關鍵在於判斷意義上的主詞是「主動」還是「被動」。這句話的意思是主詞 the Jumping Box online game「造成……」，屬於主動，所以用現在分詞選項 (B) Creating。

☐ **teenager** [ˈtinˌedʒɚ] 名 十幾歲的青少年男女
☐ **rapidly** [ˈræpɪdlɪ] 副 快速地
☐ **throughout** [θruˈaʊt] 介 遍及

118

Director Kim is an _____ fine scholar in the field of robotics, as well as being a good businessman.

(A) intrusively
(B) oppositely
(C) exceptionally
(D) affordably

金主任在機器人學方面是格外優秀的學者，同時也是一名很好的生意人。

正解 (C) 字彙

要加強修飾空格後的形容詞 fine（優秀的），填入 (C) exceptionally（格外地）最為恰當。

☐ **scholar** [ˈskɑlɚ] 名 學者
☐ **intrusively** [ɪnˈtrusɪvlɪ] 副 干擾地
☐ **oppositely** [ˈɑpəzɪtlɪ] 副 相反地
☐ **affordably** [əˈfɔrdəblɪ] 副 負擔得起地

119

Real estate prices in Hanoi are expected to rise by as much as 15% _____ the local business boom continues.

(A) and
(B) but
(C) as
(D) or

隨著當地的商業榮景持續下去，河內的不動產價格可望上漲多達 15%。

正解 (C) 連接詞

空格前後皆有＜主詞＋動詞＞的結構，也就是本句有兩個子句，因此空格須填入連接詞，而表「隨著……」的選項 (C) as 最符合文意，故為正解。

☐ **real estate** 不動產
☐ **boom** [bum] 名 蓬勃發展；激增

120

Mr. Armatelli feels that _____ is certainly the best way to resolve any problems among co-workers.

(A) talking
(B) has talked
(C) talks
(D) will talk

阿瑪泰利先生覺得，要解決同事間的任何問題，談話肯定是最好的方式。

正解 (A) 動名詞

空格應為由 that 引導的名詞子句之主詞，而根據其後出現 be 動詞 is 可知，空格內須填入名詞或相當字詞。四個選項中只有可作名詞用的動名詞 (A) talking 符合條件。

☐ **resolve** [rɪˈzɑlv] 動 解決

121

Mr. Larson used to work for the Imperial Builders, but he found a new job with Central Constructions three years _____.

(A) else
(B) soon
(C) ago
(D) already

拉森先生以前在帝國建設公司上班，但是他三年前在中央營造公司找到了新工作。

正解 (C) 副詞

本題考適合填入句尾的副詞。but 之後接「三年前找到新工作」的語意最合理，故 (C) 為正解。其實，光看到 three years 應該也能正確選出 ago。

122

The marketing department came up with an excellent plan, but relied on local salespeople for proper _____ of it.

(A) execute
(B) execution
(C) executed
(D) executively

行銷部提出了絕佳的企劃，但是要靠當地的銷售人員來妥善執行。

正解 (B) 詞性

空格前為形容詞，因此空格內應填入名詞。四個選項中，只有 (B) execution 是名詞，故為正解。

☐ **came up with ...** 想出……
☐ **rely on** 依靠……
☐ **execute** [ˈɛksɪˌkjut] 動 執行
☐ **executively** [ɪgˈzɛkjuˈtɪvlɪ] 副 執行上地

123

Passengers must show the boarding passes _____ were given to them in the ticketing area prior to boarding the aircraft.

(A) what
(B) whose
(C) that
(D) who

乘客在登機前必須出示在售票區發給的登機證。

正解 (C) 關係代名詞

空格前指「事物」的名詞 boarding passes（登機證）為先行詞，而其後出現動詞 were given，所以應選可代替 boarding passes 的選項 (C) that。

☐ **passenger** [ˈpæsṇdʒə] 名 乘客
☐ **boarding pass** 登機證
☐ **prior to ...** 在……之前

124

Umagi Corporation's new steel _____ its shape and strength even when exposed to very high temperatures or pressures.

(A) sustenance
(B) sustains
(C) sustainably
(D) sustainable

烏瑪基公司的新鋼材能維持它的形狀與硬度，即使遇到非常高的溫度或壓力也不會變。

正解 (B) 詞性

空格前的 Umagi Corporation's new steel 為主詞，空格後的 its shape and strength 則為受詞，因此應於空格內填入動詞才適當。正解為選項 (B) sustains（動詞第三人稱單數現在式）。

☐ **expose A to B** 使 A 暴露於 B
☐ **sustenance** [ˈsʌstənəns] 名 維持
☐ **sustain** [səˈsten] 動 維持
☐ **sustainably** [səˈstenəblɪ] 副 能持續地
☐ **sustainable** [səˈstenəbl] 形 能維持的

125

This MP3 player is guaranteed against breakdowns caused by the manufacturer's _____ during shipping.

(A) warranty
(B) mindset
(C) default
(D) negligence

這台 MP3 播放器對於廠商在運送期間因疏失所造成的損壞有提供保固。

正解 (D) 字彙

整個句子以「廠商因 negligence（疏忽）而造成損壞」最符合文意，故本題選 (D)。

☐ **be guaranteed against ...** 對……提供保固
☐ **breakdown** [ˈbrekˌdaʊn] 名 損壞；故障
☐ **warranty** [ˈwɔrəntɪ] 名 保證
☐ **mindset** [ˈmaɪndˌsɛt] 名 心態
☐ **default** [dɪˈfɔlt] 名 (約定等的) 不履行

126

Mr. Nagy always brought a keen _____ perspective to trends in global manufacturing.

(A) analysis
(B) analyze
(C) analytic
(D) analytically

納吉先生總能以犀利的分析角度切入全球製造業的趨勢。

正解 (C) 詞性

空格前出現了不定冠詞 a 和形容詞 keen，而空格後為名詞 perspective（觀點；角度），所以空格內必須填入另一個能修飾名詞 perspective 的形容詞。正解為選項 (C) analytic（分析的）。

☐ **keen** [kin] 形 銳利的
☐ **analysis** [ə`næləsɪs] 名 分析
☐ **analyze** [`ænḷˏaɪz] 動 分析
☐ **analytically** [ˏænə`lɪtɪkəlɪ] 副 分析地

127

After successfully producing 20,000 units last year, the Rabo Corporation's Brazil subsidiary was able _____ on its own as a manufacturer.

(A) had stood
(B) to stand
(C) standing
(D) stood

在去年成功地生產了兩萬套組件之後，羅柏公司的巴西子公司作為一家製造商已能獨當一面。

正解 (B) 不定詞

be able to ... 是「能夠做……」的意思，為固定用法，故空格內應填入不定詞。正確答案是選項 (B) to stand。

☐ **subsidiary** [səb`sɪdɪˏɛrɪ] 名 子公司
☐ **stand on one's own** 自立；獨當一面

128

Connor Furniture Inc. has been selling top brands for over 21 _____ years in major cities across the country.

(A) straight
(B) direct
(C) connected
(D) totaled

康納家具公司已經連續在全國各大城市銷售頂尖品牌超過 21 年。

正解 (A) 字彙

空格之前是數字 21，之後出現 years，中間填入選項 (A) straight（連續的），使句意變成「連續 21 年」最合理。

☐ **direct** [də`rɛkt] 形 直接的
☐ **connected** [kə`nɛktɪd] 形 有關聯的
☐ **totaled** [`totḷd] 形 合計的

129

Passengers _____ internationally must go to Terminal D, which houses all gates for overseas flights.

(A) travel
(B) to travel
(C) traveling
(D) traveled

搭乘國際線的旅客必須前往 D 航廈，國外班機的登機門都在那裡。

正解 (C) 現在分詞

最適合用來修飾空格前的名詞 passengers 的應為現在分詞 traveling。由於「旅行」乃「主動」之行為，因此不能選表被動的過去分詞 traveled，而不定詞 to travel 也不符合語意。正解為 (C)。

☐ **internationally** [ˏɪntɚ`næʃənḷɪ] 副 國際地
☐ **house** [haʊs] 動 設在……之內
☐ **overseas flight** 國際航線

130

Packages that _____ from Los Angeles may take up to five days to arrive in Cairo using Interprize Express Service.

(A) original
(B) originate
(C) originally
(D) originating

使用英特普來斯快遞服務，從洛杉磯寄出的包裹可能需要到五天的時間送達開羅。

正解 (B) 詞性

空格前為關係代名詞 that，而為了完成該關係子句，須於空格內填入動詞，故本題選 (B) originate（源自）。

☐ **up to ...** 高達……
☐ **original** [ə`rɪdʒənḷ] 形 原本的
☐ **originally** [ə`rɪdʒənḷɪ] 副 原本地

PART 6

Questions 131-134 refer to the following letter.

January 14
Marie-Therese Deneuve
34 Rue de la Croce
Marseilles

Dear Ms. Deneuve,

We are pleased to present you with a business loan of up to €250,000. We are offering this _____ because you are one of our most valued customers with an
131.
excellent credit history.

_____. You only have to pay an interest rate of 6.7%. This is a rate you are
132.
unlikely to find _____ else. This special rate is available _____ to a selected
133.   134.
group of valuable customers such as yourself. If you would like to discuss this offer further, please call me at 008-7745-3009 ext. 19.

Sincerely,

Xavier Bayer
Senior Customer Service Representative
Bank of West Marseilles
The Bank to France, the Bank to Europe, the Bank to the World

131. (A) requirement
    (B) inquiry
    (C) request
    (D) opportunity

132. (A) Your loan application is
        incomplete as it is.
    (B) We would also like to inform you
        of another positive aspect.
    (C) We cannot help you any further
        at this point.
    (D) Interest rates are not favorable
        in today's economy.

133. (A) somewhere
    (B) anywhere
    (C) everywhere
    (D) nowhere

134. (A) according
    (B) close
    (C) thanks
    (D) only

答案與解析

131

正解 (D) 字彙

本題考的是哪一個名詞可與空格前的動詞 offer「提供」搭配。選項 (A) requirement（要求）、選項 (B) inquiry（詢問）、選項 (C) request（請求）都不符文意。最合理的選項為 (D) opportunity。offer this opportunity 指「提供這個機會」。

132

正解 (B) 插入句

本題考四個選項當中何者插入文章中最合理。第一段的目的是提供總額 25 萬歐元的商業貸款，第二段則提出此貸款的低利率，對閱讀此信的顧客而言，接連都是令人高興的訊息。由於除了 (B) 以外，其他選項都是否定的內容，因此插入 (B) 最符合文脈。

(A) 您的貸款申請書就目前而言並不完整。
(B) 我們還要再通知您另一項好康。
(C) 本行現階段無法繼續再協助您。
(D) 此利率在現今的經濟狀況中並不有利。

☐ **positive** [`pɑzətɪv] 形 正面的；有助益的
☐ **aspect** [`æspɛkt] 名 方面

133

正解 (B) 副詞

本題考字尾為 –where 的副詞何者正確。主詞 This special rate 指的是 an interest rate of 6.7%，此利率是相當低的，所以接「在其他任何地方找不到」的文意較適當。再注意到前面是否定字 unlikely，故可確定選項 (B) 為正解。但假如文句是 you are likely to find 的話就要選 (D) nowhere。

134

正解 (D) 字彙

available 是「可獲得的」之意，而空格內須填入可修飾 to a selected group of valuable customers such as yourself「給像您這樣的精選貴賓」的字，只有 (D) only 最適切。其他選項如 according to（根據……）、close to（靠近……）、thanks to（感謝……），皆與文意不符。

試題翻譯

第 131 到 134 題請參照下面這封信。

1 月 14 日
瑪麗·特蕾澤·丹妮芙
馬賽市克羅齊街 34 號

丹妮芙女士您好：

本行很榮幸將總額 25 萬歐元的商業貸款介紹給您。本行之所以提供這個機會是因為您是本行的貴賓客戶，並有絕佳的信用紀錄。

我們還要再通知您另一項好康。您只須支付 6.7% 的利率。這樣的利率您在別的地方是找不到的。此特別利率只提供給像您這樣的精選貴賓。如果您想進一步討論此優惠，請來電 008-7745-3009 轉分機 19。

敬祝　商祺
資深客服代表
薩維爾·拜爾
西馬賽銀行
法國的銀行·歐洲的銀行·世界的銀行

Vocabulary

☐ **valued** [`væljud] 形 受重視的
☐ **excellent** [`ɛkslənt] 形 優等的
☐ **credit history** 信用紀錄
☐ **interest rate** 利率

Questions 135-138 refer to the following e-mail.

To: Michael Chen <michael.chen@goldcrestbanking.ca>
From: Orianne Durand <orianne.Durand@tzdesign.com>
Subject: Update
Date: Wednesday, February 23

Dear Mr. Chen,

We _____ the revised visuals for the design of your company's new gym shoe,
135.
Street Tiger.

Please see the PDF files attached _____ the composition of the materials and
136.
the internal structure. Our apologies for the extra time necessary to complete
the revisions.

Our art directors are still _____ your suggestions from last week's meeting into
137.
the logo you want as well. _____.
138.

Thanks again for choosing us to create this very important new product for you.

Sincerely,

Orianne Durand
Chief Designer
TZ Design Ltd.

135. (A) will complete
(B) would have completed
(C) have completed
(D) have been completing

136. (A) show
(B) shows
(C) shown
(D) showing

137. (A) integrating
(B) articulating
(C) evaluating
(D) asserting

138. (A) Please make sure to keep it in a safe place.
(B) We hope to show you the selections during Monday's presentation.
(C) You might already have noticed some necessary changes.
(D) Apart from that, they were considered acceptable.

第 135 到 138 題請參照下面這封電子郵件。

收件者：麥可‧陳 <michael.chen@goldcrestbanking.ca>
寄件者：歐瑞安‧杜蘭德 <orianne.Durand@tzdesign.com>
主旨：最新進展
日期：2 月 23 日星期三

陳先生您好：

我們已經完成貴公司新運動鞋「街虎」的設計圖稿修改。請參照隨附的 PDF 檔，其中顯示了材質的成分和內部結構。非常抱歉在修改上多花了一些時間。

本公司的藝術總監們也還在將您上星期開會的建議整合到您所需要的商標裡。我們希望在星期一簡報時，能將幾個備選呈現給您。

再次感謝您選擇我們為您製作這樣重要的新產品。

敬祝　商祺

首席設計師
歐瑞安‧杜蘭德
TZ 設計公司

135

正解 **(C)** 動詞

由下一個句子提到 the PDF files attached（隨附的 PDF 檔）即可推知，「目前已經完成修改」，故選現在完成式的選項 (C) have completed。

136

正解 **(D)** 動詞

本題考正確之動詞形態。Please see the PDF files attached（請參照隨附的 PDF 檔）為止已是一個完整的句子，空格後的部分要能修飾前面的名詞 the PDF files attached。而因為該 PDF 檔是「主動」顯示材質成分和內部結構，故現在分詞選項 (D) showing 為正解。

137

正解 **(A)** 字彙

請注意文中的介系詞 into。integrate A into B 是「將 A 整合至 B 中」的意思。正解為 (A)。其他選項皆與文意不符。

□ **articulate** [ɑr'tɪkjəˌlet] 動 清楚地表達
□ **evaluate** [ɪ'væljuˌet] 動 評估
□ **assert** [ə'sɝt] 動 斷言

138

正解 **(B)** 插入句

寄件者向對方報告進度「……還在將您上星期開會的建議整合到您所需要的商標裡」，按此文脈，後面接選項 (B) 最適當。suggestions 在此指商標 (logo)。

(A) 請務必將其保管於安全的場所。
(B) 我們希望在星期一簡報時，能將幾個備選呈現給您。
(C) 您或許已經注意到幾個必要的變更。
(D) 除此之外，它們被視為可接受的。

Vocabulary

□ **revised** [rɪ'vaɪzd] 形 經過修訂的
□ **visual** ['vɪʒuəl] 名（照片或設計等）宣傳用展示資料
□ **attached** [ə'tætʃt] 形 隨附的
□ **composition** [ˌkɑmpə'zɪʃən] 名 成分
□ **material** [mə'tɪrɪəl] 名 材料；原料
□ **internal structure** 內部結構
□ **create** [krɪ'et] 動 創造；製造

第 1 回完全解析

PART 6

Questions 139-142 refer to the following article.

According to the latest research, more and more employees are suffering from stress in the workplace. _____. In one study, 43% of employees _____ as
139.   **140.**
being under heavy stress had weak concentration and poor work performance. Corporations operating in highly competitive environments commonly prefer to extend current employee work hours _____ hire new staff, but such long hours
141.
invariably lower employee productivity.

Women combining motherhood with careers were found to be at particular risk; _____, reports from workplaces imply that working mothers may experience
142.
exhaustion from the responsibility of balancing both homes and jobs. Experts recommend corporations expand the number of daycare centers to reduce their burdens.

139. (A) Reports suggest it is a serious problem among all levels of workers.
(B) It has become of great importance to a successful job search.
(C) Both men and women have been found to be unaffected by such difficulties.
(D) Research shows that many employees are confused by this concept.

140. (A) are described
(B) will describe
(C) described
(D) to describe

141. (A) more than
(B) less than
(C) than not
(D) rather than

142. (A) specific
(B) specifically
(C) specify
(D) specification

第 139 到 142 題請參照下面這篇文章。

根據最新的研究，有愈來愈多的上班族為職場壓力所苦。報告顯示，對於各階層的勞工而言這都是個嚴重的問題。在一項調查中，被形容為壓力沉重的勞工中有 43% 專注力低落，工作表現也欠佳。在競爭激烈的環境中運作的公司通常都傾向延長員工現有的工時，而不雇用新人，但這麼長的工時勢必會降低員工的生產力。

身兼母職的職業婦女被發現風險尤其大；明確地說，來自職場的報告指出，身兼母職的上班族可能會為了要兼顧家庭與工作上的責任而身心俱疲。專家們建議，企業應該增設托兒中心，以減輕她們的負擔。

139

正解 (A) 　插入句

前一句提到「根據最新的研究，有愈來愈多的上班族為職場壓力所苦」，空格後接著繼續描述研究結果最合理，因此選項 (A) 最適合填入空格。

(A) 報告顯示，對於各階層的勞工而言這都是個嚴重的問題。
(B) 這對成功的求職已變得非常重要。
(C) 男女皆被發現不受此類困難影響。
(D) 調查顯示，許多員工皆對此概念感到困惑。

140

正解 (C) 　過去分詞

本題考分詞的後位修飾。employees 是「被」形容，故應以表「被動」的過去分詞選項 (C) described 來修飾。注意，由於句中已有動詞 had，因此動詞形式的 (A) 或 (B) 皆不可選。

141

正解 (D) 　字彙

本題須選出能適當地連接上下文的字詞。注意看到動詞為 prefer 即可判斷，選項 (D) 為正解，prefer A rather than B 是「偏好 A 多過於 B」的意思。在此篇文章中 A 指 to extend current employee work hours，B 指 (to) hire new staff。

142

正解 (B) 　詞性

要注意的是空格前的分號和空格後的逗號。能完成句子的應該是能替前一子句補充資訊的副詞，所以正確答案是 (B)。

Vocabulary

☐ **according to ...** 根據……
☐ **suffer from ...** 受……之苦
☐ **concentration** [ˌkɑnsɛnˈtreʃən] 名 專注
☐ **environment** [ɪnˈvaɪrənmənt] 名 環境
☐ **extend** [ɪkˈstɛnd] 動 延長
☐ **invariably** [ɪnˈvɛrɪəblɪ] 副 一定；總是
☐ **productivity** [ˌprodʌkˈtɪvətɪ] 名 生產力
☐ **imply** [ɪmˈplaɪ] 動 暗示
☐ **exhaustion** [ɪgˈzɔstʃən] 名 耗盡
☐ **recommend** [ˌrɛkəˈmɛnd] 動 建議
☐ **burden** [ˈbɝdn] 名 負擔

Questions 143-146 refer to the following notice.

Travel and Weather Update
EuroLine Bus Corporation

*************** Update for the Eastern European Region ***************

Bus service on the Prague to Sofia route is currently experiencing severe delays due to sudden and heavy rainstorms. The _____ flooding has affected
143.
many places. Roads in such areas have become impassable because of these high waters, _____ have closed them to vehicle travel of any kind.
144.

Travelers are advised to check the main terminal board for the latest information on arrival and departure times. Passengers preparing _____ on any
145.
buses at the gates are advised to wait. Buses there will leave only when the weather clears enough for them to do so.

_____.
146.

---

143. (A) innocuous
(B) anticipated
(C) interrupted
(D) consequent

144. (A) what
(B) that
(C) which
(D) those

145. (A) departing
(B) will depart
(C) to depart
(D) departed

146. (A) Finally, the scheduled departure times have now been posted.
(B) Please continue to watch this board for further updates.
(C) Thank you to all who have participated in our bus tour.
(D) We hope you will continue to enjoy the weather during your trip.

第 143 到 146 題請參照下面這則公告。

最新旅遊及氣象資訊
歐洲線客運公司

*************** 東歐地區最新消息 ***************

由於突如其來的強烈暴風雨，布拉格至索非亞路線的客運服務目前嚴重誤點。有多處受到了隨之發生的水災所影響。大水使這些地區的道路無法通行，並阻斷了各種車輛的進出。

建議旅客查看主站公告版以獲得到站及發車時間的最新資訊。在發車處準備搭乘任一班次客運出發的旅客敬請稍候。當天氣好轉到可以發車時，客運才會開出。

有關進一步的最新消息，請持續注意本公告版。

143

正解 (D) 字彙

空格內須填入能修飾 flooding（洪水）的形容詞。從前一句提及的暴風雨來看，選項 (D) consequent（隨之發生的）較符合文意。

☐ **innocuous** [ɪˋnɑkjuəs] 形 無害的
☐ **anticipated** [ænˋtɪsəˏpetɪd] 形 被預期的
☐ **interrupted** [ˏɪntəˋrʌptɪd] 形 中斷的

144

正解 (C) 關係代名詞

空格出現在逗號後面，而逗號前為先行名詞 these high waters，這表示其後應為「非限定用法」之關係子句，所以 that 立刻被排除。能為先行詞加以說明且又為「非限定用法」的關係代名詞只有選項 (C) which。注意，which 承接了前面的 these high waters，表示「是因為這些洪水才使道路不通」。

145

正解 (C) 動詞

空格前的現在分詞 preparing 由動詞 prepare 變化而來，而 prepare 須搭配不定詞使用：prepare to *do*（準備做某事）。選項 (A) 為現在分詞或動名詞、選項 (D) 為過去分詞，都無法接在 preparing 之後。而選項 (B) 為動詞結構，故亦非正解。

146

正解 (B) 插入句

本題考何者最適合作為此公告之結尾。由文章主旨為「因天候不佳導致客運誤點」即可判斷，建議乘客確認最新資訊的選項 (B) 最適當。

(A) 發車預定時刻表現在終於公布了。
(B) 有關進一步的最新消息，請持續注意本公告版。
(C) 感謝各位參加本公司的巴士旅遊。
(D) 我們希望旅途中各位能持續享有好天氣。

Vocabulary

☐ **update** [ʌpˋdet] 名 最新的情況
☐ **currently** [ˋkɝntlɪ] 副 當前；目前
☐ **severe** [səˋvɪr] 形 嚴重的；劇烈的
☐ **sudden** [ˋsʌdn] 形 突然的；出其不意的
☐ **rainstorm** [ˋrenˏstɔrm] 名 暴風雨
☐ **affect** [əˋfɛkt] 動 影響
☐ **impassable** [ɪmˋpæsəbl] 形 不能通行的
☐ **arrival** [əˋraɪvl] 名 抵達；到來
☐ **departure** [dɪˋpɑrtʃə] 名 出發

題目	題目翻譯

Questions 147-148 refer to the following table.

第 147 到 148 題請參照下面這個表格。

Travel information for The Irish Princess

Destinations (from Cork)	Gibraltar	Tenerife	Antigua	Aruba
Estimated arrival date	17th	20th	22nd	24th
Present Travel Status	Arrival on Schedule	Updating	Updating	Two days late
Medical Certificate required	No	Yes	No	No
Visa Requirements	Not required for EU residents	Necessary for stays over 30 days	See Passenger Service for Updates	Not required for EU residents

IRELAND-CARIBBEAN CRUISE LINES INC.

愛爾蘭公主號旅遊資訊

目的地 (自科克啟程)	直布羅陀	特內里費	安地卡	阿魯巴
預估到達日期	17 日	20 日	22 日	24 日
目前航行狀態	準時抵達	更新中	更新中	延遲兩天
所需醫療證明	無	有	無	無
簽證要求	歐盟居民不需要	停留超過 30 天者需要	最新消息參見旅客服務處	歐盟居民不需要

愛爾蘭－加勒比海船運公司

Vocabulary

- **estimated** [ˈɛstəˌmetɪd] 形 預估的
- **travel status** 航行狀態
- **medical certificate** 醫療證明；診斷書
- **requirement** [rɪˈkwaɪrmənt] 名 要求；必備條件
- **resident** [ˈrɛzədənt] 名 居民

試題	試題翻譯	答案與解析

147

On what date will passengers on The Irish Princess most likely arrive in Aruba?

(A) 20th
(B) 22nd
(C) 24th
(D) 26th

愛爾蘭公主號的乘客最有可能在哪一天抵達阿魯巴？

(A) 20 日
(B) 22 日
(C) 24 日
(D) 26 日

正解 (D)

看表格可知，預定的到達日期為 24 日，但受航運狀況影響，將晚兩天抵達，所以正確答案是選項 (D) 26th。做這種表格題時，必須先判斷有沒有陷阱，最好連細節都注意，才不致於上當。

- **passenger** [ˈpæsṇdʒɚ] 名 乘客；旅客

148

Which destination requires a visa for stays over a month?

(A) Gibraltar
(B) Tenerife
(C) Antigua
(D) Aruba

在哪個目的地停留超過一個月就需要簽證？

(A) 直布羅陀
(B) 特內里費
(C) 安地卡
(D) 阿魯巴

正解 (B)

從表格裡的「簽證要求欄」可知，要在特內里費停留超過 30 天（即一個月），就需要簽證。正解為選項 (B) Tenerife。

題目	題目翻譯

Questions 149-150 refer to the following text message chain.

第 149 到 150 題請參照下面這段手機簡訊。

山姆・波特　　　　　　　　　上午 9:00
國隆塗料公司的客戶打電話來說他們的飛機剛剛已經著陸。他們還要再一個小時才會到，我會請提姆到正門接他們。

張英莉　　　　　　　　　　　上午 9:02
好。我現在正在出地鐵，大概 15 分鐘後到辦公室。記得準備好塗料樣本好讓他們確認。

山姆・波特　　　　　　　　　上午 9:04
我已經在展示桌上擺設好 30 款我們公司最受歡迎的顏色。

張英莉　　　　　　　　　　　上午 9:06
正如我所料。你總是把任何事情都掌控得很好。做得好。

山姆・波特　　　　　　　　　上午 9:07
然後，會議室也都已經安排好了，有充足的咖啡和茶。

(Text message content:)

Sam Porter　　　9:00 A.M.
Our clients from Gron Paint Co. called to say that their plane has just touched down. They won't be here for another hour, but I'll have Tim meet them at the front door.

Chang Ying Li　　　9:02 A.M.
Okay. I'm getting out of the subway now. I'll be in the office in about 15 minutes. Make sure that we have paint samples set up for them to review.

Sam Porter　　　9:04 A.M.
I've laid out 30 of our most popular colors on a demonstration table.

Chang Ying Li　　　9:06 A.M.
I should have guessed. You always have a handle on things. Good job.

Sam Porter　　　9:07 A.M.
Also, the conference room is already arranged, with plenty of coffee and tea.

Vocabulary

☐ **lay out** 展示；擺出　　☐ **plenty of ...** 許多的……

試題	試題翻譯	答案與解析

149

At 9:06 A.M., what does Chang Ying Li mean when she writes, "I should have guessed"?

(A) Mr. Porter often anticipates needs.
(B) Mr. Porter must make a decision.
(C) Mr. Porter requires further advice.
(D) Mr. Porter usually follows instructions.

九點零六分時，張英莉打的 "I should have guessed" 是什麼意思？

(A) 波特先生經常預先考慮到需求。
(B) 波特先生必須做出決定。
(C) 波特先生需要進一步的建議。
(D) 波特先生通常都會遵守指示。

正解 (A)

＜ should have ＋過去分詞＞此句型表示對過去某事感到後悔或提出檢討，I should have guessed. 直譯為「我早應該猜到的」。由後面接續的內容可判斷，張英莉認為波特先生平常辦事就很周到，不用問也知道都準備好了。正解為 (A)。

150

What does Mr. Porter indicate that he will do?

(A) Call some clients
(B) Have someone meet a group
(C) Wait by a door
(D) Get some samples tested

波特先生表示他將會做什麼？

(A) 打電話給幾位客戶
(B) 請某人和一個團體碰面
(C) 在門邊等候
(D) 請人檢查一些樣本

正解 (B)

解題線索就在對話一開始的 I'll have Tim meet them at the front door。them 指搭飛機抵達的客戶，正確答案就是 (B)，其中以 a group 代表 clients。＜ have ＋某人＋原形不定詞＞的意思是「叫某人做某事」。注意，選項 (D) 用的句型＜ get ＋某事物＋過去分詞＞是類似的用法。

Questions 151-152 refer to the following memo.

MEMORANDUM

To: All Staff
From: Sven Bjorg
Time: 10:45 A.M., Wednesday
RE: Christian Jonson

Dear Staff,

As you already know, Christian is leaving us this Friday after more than 30 years with the firm. Before taking his present job as head of Research, he worked in various areas, including Production—both here and in Oslo—Design, and IT. Over the last 18 months, he has been overseeing the highly successful Z45-t drug trials in Zurich.

He has been an invaluable member of Lind Technologies and I know he will be sorely missed by his colleagues and friends. However, I am happy to say he has agreed to stay with us for the next four weeks in a part-time capacity so we will benefit from his expertise.

I hope you will join me and the rest of the Board of Directors for a Bread and Cheese Reception in the Premier Boardroom this Friday afternoon from 4:30 P.M. to formally congratulate Christian on his retirement and wish him every success in his new life!

Thank you,

Sven Bjorg
Managing Director
Lind Technologies

備忘錄
收件者：全體員工
寄件者：思凡‧柏格
時間：星期三上午 10:45
主旨：克里斯汀‧強森

大家好：

誠如各位已經知道的，於公司服務了超過三十年後，克里斯汀即將在本週五離職。在擔任現職研究主管前，他在多個不同的單位工作過，包括生產（本地和奧斯陸）、設計和資訊部門。在過去的十八個月，他一直在蘇黎世監督十分成功的 Z45-t 藥物試驗。

他是林德科技的無價之寶，我相信他的同事和朋友都將對他深感懷念。不過我要很高興地宣布，他已經答應在接下來的四個星期內以兼職的方式留任，所以我們將可以受惠於他的專長。

希望各位能跟我和董事會的其他董事一起於本週五下午四點半在第一會議室參加簡單茶點的歡送會，以正式恭賀克里斯汀榮退，並祝福他的新生活一切順利！

謝謝。

常務董事
思凡‧柏格
林德科技

Vocabulary

- [ ] **oversee** [ˏovɚˋsi] 動 監督
- [ ] **drug trial** 藥物試驗
- [ ] **invaluable** [ɪnˋvæljəbl] 形 無價的
- [ ] **sorely** [ˋsorlɪ] 副 非常地
- [ ] **colleague** [ˋkɑlig] 名 同事
- [ ] **capacity** [kəˋpæsətɪ] 名 職位
- [ ] **expertise** [ˏɛkspɚˋtiz] 名 專門技術 / 知識
- [ ] **bread and cheese** 簡單的餐食
- [ ] **formally** [ˋfɔrmlɪ] 副 正式地
- [ ] **congratulate A on B** 為 B 事祝賀 A

151

Which department is Mr. Jonson working in now?

(A) Research
(B) Production
(C) Design
(D) IT

強森先生目前在哪個部門工作？

(A) 研究
(B) 生產
(C) 設計
(D) 資訊

正解 (A)

從第一段第二句提到的 his present job as head of Research 即可知，選項 (A) Research 為正解。選項 (B) Production、(C) Design、(D) IT 都是他「過去」服務的部門。

152

What will Mr. Jonson do over the coming month?

(A) Contribute personal knowledge
(B) Conduct a job search
(C) Hire part-time workers
(D) Attend a board meeting

強森先生在接下來的一整個月會做什麼？

(A) 貢獻個人所知
(B) 做求職研究
(C) 雇用兼職員工
(D) 出席董事會議

正解 (A)

由第二段 he has agreed to stay with us for the next four weeks ... so we will benefit from his expertise. 這句可判斷，強森先生會在之後的四週內留在公司指導後進，因此本題選 (A) Contribute personal knowledge。注意，是強森先生以兼職方式續留，而不是他將雇用兼職員工。不可誤選 (C)。

- [ ] **contribute** [kənˋtrɪbjut] 動 捐助；貢獻
- [ ] **board meeting** 董事會議

題目	題目翻譯

Questions 153-154 refer to the following label.

第 153 到 154 題請參照下面這張標籤。

Installation Guide for your Sparkle White Dishwasher
Wonder Electronics Co.

Install the appliance in accordance with the instructions below.

- Ensure that the appliance is not connected to any power outlets during installation.

- Do not remove any of the metal plates covering electronic components or wiring inside.

- Confirm the power supply of the residence is compatible with this appliance. If it is not, a converter will be necessary (sold separately).

- Install this appliance on a flat surface. Failure to do so could severely affect its stability.

- Connect the appliance's water tubes to the main pipes beneath your sink. Check the diagram on the back of the appliance for the correct procedure.

- Following installation, please dispose of the packaging in an environmentally friendly way.

For more information on this and other fine appliances made by Wonder Electronics Co., go to www.wonderelectronicsonthenet.com.

亮白洗碗機安裝指南
驚奇電子公司

請依照下列指示安裝電器。

● 請確定本電器在安裝時未連接任何插座。
● 請勿拆除覆蓋電子元件或內部線路的任何金屬板。
● 請確認住處的電源與本電器相容。如不相容，則須使用變壓器（另售）。
● 請於平坦的表面上安裝本電器。若不如此做，可能會嚴重影響到穩定性。
● 請將本電器的水管接至水槽底下的主要排水管。正確程序請見電器背面的圖示。
● 安裝後請以符合環保的方式丟棄包裝。

欲知更多關於本電器和驚奇電子公司所製造的其他優質電器的資訊，請上 www.wonderelectronicsonthenet.com 查詢。

Vocabulary

- installation [ˌɪnstəˈleʃən] 名 安裝；設置
- appliance [əˈplaɪəns] 名 器具
- in accordance with ... 依照⋯⋯；根據⋯⋯
- instruction [ɪnˈstrʌkʃən] 名 指示
- ensure [ɪnˈʃʊr] 動 保證；擔保
- power outlet 電源插座
- remove [rɪˈmuv] 動 去除
- component [kəmˈponənt] 名 零件
- residence [ˈrɛzədəns] 名 住所
- compatible [kəmˈpætəbl] 形 相容的
- converter [kənˈvɝtɚ] 名 變流器
- stability [stəˈbɪlətɪ] 名 穩定性
- sink [sɪŋk] 名 水槽
- diagram [ˈdaɪəˌɡræm] 名 圖表
- dispose of ... 處理⋯⋯
- environmentally friendly 對環境友善的；符合環保的

試題	試題翻譯	答案與解析

153

What is NOT listed as an installation step for the appliance?

(A) Checking that the electrical supply is suitable
(B) Contacting company technicians
(C) Ensuring positioning is on a surface that is level
(D) Referring to graphs on the device

下列何者「未」列於電器的安裝步驟中？

(A) 檢查電源供應是否適當
(B) 聯絡公司的技師
(C) 確定有將電器擺放在水平的表面
(D) 參考裝置上的圖例

正解 (B)

內文中分別提到選項 (A)、(C)、(D)，只有選項 (B) 沒有提到，故本題選 (B)。

- electrical supply 電源供應
- refer to ... 參考⋯⋯
- device [dɪˈvaɪs] 名 裝置

154

What are users suggested to do?

(A) Test the appliance when installation is complete
(B) Replace the water pipes beneath the sink if necessary
(C) Disconnect the power supply when not in use
(D) Consider the environment when discarding items

使用者被建議要做什麼？

(A) 安裝完成後測試電器
(B) 必要時更換水槽底下的水管
(C) 不使用的時候切斷電源
(D) 丟棄廢物時要考慮到環境

正解 (D)

安裝指示的最後一點提到 ... please dispose of the packaging in an environmentally friendly way.，選項 (D) Consider the environment when discarding items 以同義的另一種說法描述，故為正解。

- disconnect [ˌdɪskəˈnɛkt] 動 切斷（電源等）
- discard [dɪsˈkɑrd] 動 丟棄

Questions 155-157 refer to the following e-mail.

	* E-mail * ✕
From:	Thiago de Silva <tdesilva@ozatmail.net>
To:	Lucia Morais <lucia.morais@olivehotel.fr> Manager, Olive Hotel
Date:	Wednesday, October 7
Subject:	My room

Dear Ms. Morais,

Two weeks ago I e-mailed you to reserve accommodations, along with an online deposit to secure them. — [1] —. I was scheduled to check in tomorrow, so that I can attend the European Manufacturing Conference there in Lyons.

However, I have recently been accepted into a 1-week international management development course in Switzerland, so I would like to cancel my reservation. — [2] —. One of the original team members has had to drop out for health reasons and I have been offered his spot. — [3] —. I realize this is extremely short notice, but considering these circumstances I am hoping I can still get my money back.

Please e-mail as soon as possible to let me know. — [4] —. I hope to hear from you before then.

Kind regards,
Thiago de Silva

第 155 到 157 題請參照下面這封電子郵件。

寄件者：堤亞哥·德席瓦 <tdesilva@ozatmail. net>
收件者：露西亞·摩拉斯 <lucia.morais@ olivehotel.fr> 橄欖飯店經理
日期：10 月 7 日星期三
主旨：我的訂房

摩拉斯女士您好：

兩個星期前，我寄了一封預約住宿的電子郵件給您，並在線上付了訂金以確認訂房。— [1] —。我原本預定明天入住，以便參加在里昂所舉行的歐洲製造業大會。

不過，我最近錄取了瑞士為期一週的國際管理發展課程，所以我想取消訂房。— [2] —。有一位原本的團員因健康因素必須退出，於是我就遞補了他的位置。— [3] —。我明白這是十分緊急的通知，但是考慮到這些情況，我希望還是能獲得退費。

煩請儘快以電子郵件通知我。— [4] —。希望在那之前就能收到您的回覆。

堤亞哥·德席瓦敬上

Vocabulary

- **accommodation** [ə.kɑmə'deʃən] 名 住宿（通常複數形）
- **along with ...** 與……一起
- **deposit** [dɪ'pɑzɪt] 名 保證金
- **secure** [sɪ'kjʊr] 動 確保
- **drop out** 脫離；退出（學校等）
- **spot** [spɑt] 名 職位；職務
- **short notice** 緊急通知
- **considering** [kən'sɪdərɪŋ] 介 考慮到
- **circumstance** ['sɝkəm.stæns] 名 情況；環境（通常複數形）

試題	試題翻譯	答案與解析

155

What is the purpose of the e-mail?

(A) To schedule an arrival
(B) To confirm a transaction
(C) To state a change
(D) To make a payment

這封電子郵件的目的是什麼？

(A) 為了排定抵達時間
(B) 為了確認一筆交易
(C) 為了陳述一項變更
(D) 為了支付一筆款項

正解 (C)

寄件者原本為了出席會議而預約了飯店，但後來無法出席會議而寫信取消訂房，也就是通知事情有所變更，所以正確答案是 (C)。

- **transaction** [træn'zækʃən] 名 交易
- **make a payment** 支付一筆款項

156

What is a stated concern of Mr. de Silva?

(A) Room availability
(B) Hotel amenities
(C) Refund policy
(D) Cancellation deadlines

文中提及德席瓦先生擔憂的事是什麼？

(A) 有沒有房間
(B) 飯店的設施
(C) 退費規定
(D) 取消的截止期限

正解 (C)

由於是緊急取消飯店，從第二段最後面 ... I am hoping I can still get my money back. 可知，德席瓦先生煩惱的是能否退費這件事，正解為選項 (C)。

- **amenity** [ə'mɪnɪti] 名 設施；設備（通常複數形）
- **refund** ['riˌfʌnd] 名 退費

157

In which of the positions marked [1], [2], [3] and [4] does the following sentence best belong?
"I have to leave for the training program within the next 12 hours."

(A) [1]　　　(B) [2]
(C) [3]　　　(D) [4]

下面這個句子插入文中標示的 [1]、[2]、[3]、[4] 四處當中的何處最符合文意？

「我必須在現在之後的 12 個小時內出發去上研修課程。」

(A) [1]　　　(B) [2]
(C) [3]　　　(D) [4]

正解 (D)

注意看到空格 [4] 後之句子中的 before then。德席瓦先生提及「希望對方在那之前與其聯絡」，而對照空格前所說的 Please e-mail as soon as possible to let me know.，可發現該句並未完整做出敘述。故題目所問的句子插入空格 [4] 最符合該段文意。

題目	題目翻譯

Questions 158-160 refer to the following instructions.

第 158 到 160 題請參照下面這篇使用說明。

How to use Eazee Breeze in your washing machine

Measure out Eazee Breeze Detergent concentrate (1 scoop per medium load of clothes) into a cup of lukewarm water and allow it to dissolve completely for about 5-10 minutes or until it can no longer be seen. Turn on your washing machine, choosing the shortest cycle and making sure your soiled clothes are fully immersed in water. Next, pour the Eazee Breeze mixture onto the clothes. Let clothes soak for at least 15 minutes to allow Eazee Breeze's fast-penetrating formula to work on grime, stains and odors.* Next, close the lid and continue the cycle. With Eazee Breeze you can say goodbye to scrubbing, cut down on wash time and save on electricity.

* Eazee Breeze is safe for all types of fabrics, but as a precaution do not soak dark clothes and whites together.

如何在洗衣機中使用清爽微風

酌量將清爽微風濃縮洗衣粉（每中等衣量一匙）倒進一杯溫水裡，並讓它完全溶解五到十分鐘左右，或是到完全看不見為止。啟動洗衣機，選擇最短行程，並確定髒衣服完全浸在水裡。接著將清爽微風混合液倒在衣物上，為使清爽微風的快速滲透配方對污垢、斑點和異味產生作用，將衣物浸泡至少十五分鐘。* 接著關閉上蓋，使其繼續運轉。有了清爽微風，您就可以對搓揉說再見、縮短洗衣時間，並節省用電。

* 清爽微風對各種衣料都很安全，但為以防萬一，請勿將深色和白色衣物浸泡在一起。

Vocabulary

- **measure out** 酌量
- **detergent** [dɪˋtɝdʒənt] 名 洗潔劑；洗衣粉
- **concentrate** [ˋkɑnsɛnˌtret] 名 濃縮物；濃縮液
- **scoop** [skup] 名 一匙
- **load** [lod] 名 一次的量
- **lukewarm** [ˋlukˋwɔrm] 形 （液體）微溫的
- **dissolve** [dɪˋzɑlv] 動 分解
- **soiled** [sɔɪld] 形 髒的
- **immerse** [ɪˋmɝs] 動 使浸沒
- **soak** [sok] 動 浸泡
- **fast-penetrating** [fæstˋpɛnəˌtretɪŋ] 形 快速滲透的
- **formula** [ˋfɔrmjələ] 名 配方
- **grime** [graɪm] 名 污垢
- **stain** [sten] 名 斑點
- **odor** [ˋodə] 名 異味；臭味
- **precaution** [prɪˋkɔʃən] 名 謹慎；預防措施

試題	試題翻譯	答案與解析

158

What is the first step in using Eazee Breeze?

(A) Letting the substance melt
(B) Soaking clothes in water
(C) Letting water sit for 15 minutes
(D) Washing clothes for 5 minutes

使用清爽微風的第一個步驟是什麼？

(A) 讓顆粒溶化
(B) 將衣物浸泡於水中
(C) 將水靜置十五分鐘
(D) 讓衣物洗五分鐘

正解 (A)

從第一句就知道第一階段該做的事就是讓定量的濃縮洗衣精在溫水裡充分溶解，所以正確答案是 (A)。

- **substance** [ˋsʌbstəns] 名 物質

159

The word "soiled" in line 5 is closest in meaning to

(A) rough
(B) shabby
(C) dirty
(D) old

第五行的 "soiled" 這個字的意思最接近

(A) 粗糙的
(B) 破爛的
(C) 髒污的
(D) 老舊的

正解 (C)

與 soiled（髒污的）意思最接近的單字是 dirty。正解為選項 (C)。

160

What are people using Eazee Breeze advised NOT to do?

(A) Add extra concentrate
(B) Scrub items before washing
(C) Use together with other products
(D) Combine colors and whites

使用清爽微風的人「不」建議做什麼？

(A) 添加額外的濃縮劑
(B) 洗衣前先搓揉
(C) 和其他的產品一起使用
(D) 將其他顏色和白色混在一起

正解 (D)

根據最後的 * 部分提及 but as a precaution do not soak dark clothes and whites together（勿將深色衣服與白衣服浸泡在一起），故本題選 (D)。題目中雖然寫到「使用清爽微風洗衣粉就可以不用再用力搓揉衣物」，但是並沒有說「不能搓洗」，所以選項 (B) 不適當。

Questions 161-164 refer to the following online chat discussion.

Alvarez, Hector [11:05 A.M.]
Hi everyone. I went over the last report on our sales. They are still too low. Give me your thoughts.

Terao, Katsuya [11:06 A.M.]
Our sales staff needs more training in how to approach customers—especially because many of them are new.

Dean, Andrew [11:10 A.M.]
We could focus more on online sales. With big upgrades to our Web site, we could generate more revenue online. Elisa Smythe has shown me several revenue projections that seem to indicate that.

Alvarez, Hector [11:13 A.M.]
I can see that. We're not getting the level of sales online that our competitors are.

Rao, Manisha [11:15 A.M.]
I have to caution you that changes to our Web site wouldn't be cheap. It would impact my teams the most, because we'd have to devote a lot of IT resources to that.

Baldwin, Veronica [11:17 A.M.]
We might also have to adjust our product line. Rick Jones has plenty of data showing that online shoppers and in-store shoppers sometimes have different preferences.

Alvarez, Hector [11:20 A.M.]
Nevertheless, I'd like to explore that option. Have Elisa share her information with Rick. Then I want both of them—and all of you—to join me in my office tomorrow at 2:00 P.M.

第 161 到 164 題請參照下面這段線上聊天討論。

赫克特・阿爾瓦雷茲 [上午 11:05]
大家好。我仔細看過我們最終的業績報告。業績還是太低了。我想知道你們的想法。

寺尾勝哉 [上午 11:06]
我們的販售員需要更多如何招呼客人的訓練，尤其是因為他們很多人都是新手。

安德魯・狄恩 [上午 11:10]
我們可以集中更多心力在網路銷售上。只要大幅升級我們的網站，我們就能靠網路創造更多利潤。艾莉莎・史麥絲曾經給我看過一些營收預測，似乎都指出這點。

赫克特・阿爾瓦雷茲 [上午 11:13]
這我懂。我們的網路銷售業績不及我們競爭對手的水準。

瑪妮莎・饒 [上午 11:15]
我必須提醒各位，網站變更並不便宜。我的團隊將受到最多的影響，因為那樣我們將必須投入許多資訊科技資源。

薇羅妮卡・鮑德溫 [上午 11:17]
或許我們的產品線也必須調整一下。瑞克・瓊斯有很多資料顯示，網購消費者和進店消費者的偏好有時並不相同。

赫克特・阿爾瓦雷茲 [上午 11:20]
不管怎麼樣，我想探討一下那個辦法。請叫艾莉莎把她的資訊分享給瑞克，然後我想請他們兩位，還有你們大家，明天下午兩點來我辦公室。

Vocabulary

☐ **focus on ...** 把重點放在……上　　☐ **generate** [ˈdʒɛnəˌret] 動 產生；引起　　☐ **projection** [prəˈdʒɛkʃən] 名 預測
☐ **caution** [ˈkɔʃən] 動 警告；提醒　　☐ **devote A to B** 把 A 專用於 B　　☐ **preference** [ˈprɛfərəns] 名 偏好
☐ **nevertheless** [ˌnɛvəðəˈlɛs] 副 儘管如此

161

At 11:05 A.M., what does Mr. Alvarez mean when he writes, "Give me your thoughts"?

(A) He has to meet a deadline.
(B) He needs to update an account.
(C) He hopes to persuade a supervisor.
(D) He wants to gather some opinions.

十一點零五分時，阿爾瓦雷茲先生打的 "Give me your thoughts" 是什麼意思？

(A) 他必須趕上截止期限。
(B) 他必須更新一個帳戶。
(C) 他希望能說服一位上司。
(D) 他想收集一些意見。

正解 (D)

thought 是 think 的名詞形，意思是「想法；意見」，換言之，正解為選項 (D)。

☐ **meet a deadline** 趕上截止期限
☐ **persuade** [pə`swed] 動 說服
☐ **supervisor** [ˌsupə`vaɪzə] 名 主管；上司
☐ **gather** [`gæðə] 動 收集

162

For what type of company do these people most likely work?

(A) A retail outlet
(B) A consulting agency
(C) A cyber security firm
(D) An event planning company

這些人最有可能在何種類型的公司上班？

(A) 零售店
(B) 顧問公司
(C) 網路安全公司
(D) 活動策畫公司

正解 (A)

由五人的對話內容可推測，他們所在的職場應為店鋪兼在網路上販賣商品。根據寺尾先生的 Our sales staff needs more training in how to approach customers ... 和狄恩先生的 We could focus more on online sales. 之發言可知，本題選 (A)。

163

According to the discussion, whose department would be most affected by Mr. Dean's suggestion?

(A) Mr. Terao's department
(B) Ms. Rao's department
(C) Ms. Baldwin's department
(D) Mr. Jones' department

根據這段討論，誰的部門會因狄恩先生的提議而受到最多影響？

(A) 寺尾先生的部門
(B) 饒小姐的部門
(C) 鮑德溫小姐的部門
(D) 瓊斯先生的部門

正解 (B)

針對狄恩先生提出應加強發展網路銷售之建議，饒小姐說 I have to caution .... It would impact my teams the most ...，由此可知最受影響的就是饒小姐的部門。

☐ **impact** [ɪm`pækt] 動 產生影響

164

What information will Ms. Smythe most likely share with Mr. Jones?

(A) Training methods
(B) Customer profiles
(C) Financial statistics
(D) Team organization

史麥絲小姐最有可能和瓊斯先生分享什麼資訊？

(A) 研修方法
(B) 客戶資料
(C) 財務統計數字
(D) 團隊組織

正解 (C)

阿爾瓦雷茲先生最後給了一個指示：Have Elisa share her information with Rick.，而艾莉莎·史麥絲小姐手上握有網路銷售的營收預測，故她將告訴瑞克。瓊斯先生的資料應為選項 (C) Financial statistics。

☐ **statistics** [stə`tɪstɪks] 名 統計數字；統計資料

Questions 165-168 refer to the following advertisement.

Shanghai Romance

MUSICAL LOVERS WILL LOVE THIS NEW PRODUCTION FROM THE RED BALLOON PERFORMANCE COMPANY.

◆

Chosen Best Musical by the Evening Star Monthly!

Set in China in the 1920s, this lavish extravaganza will thrill and excite you!

Read what people are saying about it:

"I'm not much of a theatergoer, but I loved it!"
–Amy Winters, university student, Edinburgh

"If you want lighthearted entertainment for the whole family, this show is for you. We and the kids had a grand time seeing it."
–Frank Coswell, business owner, London

Don't miss out on Helen McTavish's performance as Eleanor Gantry. Also starring Richard Mace as Ewan Lockhart.

Tickets are available at the box office from May 18, with online sales starting the day before. Reserve yours anytime until June 20. Seats can otherwise be obtained at the door. The final performance will be on June 27 unless extended.

Discounted matinee performances are held at 2:00 P.M. every Saturday and Wednesday for £35-£40. These cannot be purchased online or used in combination with group discounts or season passes.
For more details, call the Box Office (9:30 A.M. – 11:00 P.M., Monday through Saturday), at 0845-671-1200 or visit us online at www.thamestheater.co.uk.

*Refunds available up to half an hour before each performance begins, less fees.

第 165 到 168 題請參照下面這則廣告。

上海羅曼史
音樂愛好者將愛上這齣由紅氣球演藝
公司所推出的新作。

獲《夜星月刊》選為最佳歌舞劇！

以 1920 年代的中國為背景，這齣華麗的大戲
將帶給您震撼與刺激！

看看觀眾的評語：

「我並不常看戲，但我非常喜歡這齣戲！」
——艾美‧溫特斯，大學生，愛丁堡
「假如你要找適合全家觀賞的輕鬆娛樂，這
場表演正適合你。我們和孩子們都看得很開
心。」
——法蘭克‧柯斯威爾，企業主，倫敦

別錯過海倫‧麥克塔維許所飾演的艾蓮娜‧甘
崔，以及由理查‧梅斯所主演的伊旺‧洛克哈
特。

5 月 18 日起可於售票處購票，網路售票則早
一天開始。至 6 月 20 日止，隨時都可訂票。
您也可於入口處劃位。除非有加演，否則最後
一場將於 6 月 27 日演出。

有折扣的日場演出訂於每週六及週三下午兩
點，票價 35 到 40 英鎊。這些場次無法上網購
票或搭配團體折扣或季票使用。
詳情請電洽售票處（週一至週六早上九點半到
晚上十一點），電話 0845-671-1200，或上網查
閱 www.thanestheater.co.uk。

* 各場次開演半小時前皆可退費，但須酌收手
續費。

Vocabulary

- **lavish** ['lævɪʃ] 形 奢華的；華麗的
- **extravaganza** [ɪkˌstrævəˈgænzə] 名 華麗的娛樂表演
- **theatergoer** ['θɪətəˌgoə] 名 戲迷
- **lighthearted** ['laɪtˌhɑrtɪd] 形 輕鬆愉快的
- **grand** [grænd] 形【口】極好的；快樂的
- **miss out on ...** 錯過……
- **star** [stɑr] 動 主演
- **box office** 售票處
- **obtain** [əb'ten] 動 得到；獲得
- **matinee** [ˌmætən'e] 名 日場；午後的演出

試題	試題翻譯	答案與解析

165

What is indicated about Shanghai Romance?

(A) It has an international cast.
(B) It is a show for adults.
(C) It is a long running show.
(D) It has received favorable reviews.

廣告中指出《上海羅曼史》如何？

(A) 它有國際級的卡司。
(B) 它是一齣給大人看的戲。
(C) 它是一齣長期演出的戲。
(D) 它受到了好評。

正解 (D)

文中並未提及演員陣容的國籍，因此選項 (A) 不適當；根據觀眾的評語，小孩也很喜歡這齣戲，故選項 (B) 也不正確；而由這齣戲是新作品判斷，因此選項 (C) 也不適當。廣告之次標題提到月刊將這齣戲選為最佳音樂劇，文中也強調這齣劇佳評如潮，所以正解應為選項 (D) It has received favorable reviews.。

☐ **favorable** [ˈfevərəbl] 形 懷抱好意的
☐ **review** [rɪˈvju] 名 評論

166

Who has praised Shanghai Romance?

(A) The theater owner
(B) Audience members
(C) Play writers
(D) Stage actors

《上海羅曼史》受到誰的稱讚？

(A) 劇場老闆
(B) 觀眾們
(C) 劇作家
(D) 舞台劇演員

正解 (B)

廣告中列出了大學生與企業主，也就是所謂「一般人」而非「專業人士」的讚詞，由此可知答案應選 (B)。

☐ **praise** [prez] 動 讚美

167

When can the earliest tickets be purchased?

(A) May 17
(B) May 18
(C) June 20
(D) June 27

票最早可以在什麼時候買到？

(A) 5 月 17 日
(B) 5 月 18 日
(C) 6 月 20 日
(D) 6 月 27 日

正解 (A)

廣告中第三段提到 Tickets are available at the box office from May 18, with online sales starting the day before.，也就是說，雖然售票處於 5 月 18 日起售票，但網路訂票提早一天開始，因此正解為選項 (A)。注意，6 月 20 日為預約訂票的最後一天，6 月 27 日則為最後公演預定日。

168

How can guests get lower prices?

(A) By attending afternoon performances
(B) By purchasing tickets online
(C) By seeing the performance twice
(D) By contacting the performers

觀眾如何獲得較低的票價？

(A) 看下午的場次
(B) 上網買票
(C) 看兩次表演
(D) 和表演者聯絡

正解 (A)

由廣告最後一段中提到的 Discounted matinee performances（有折扣的日場演出）即可知，選項 (A) By attending afternoon performances 為正解。即使不懂 matinee 此單字的意思，也可從下午演出之票價有折扣這件事推知答案。

Questions 169-171 refer to the following e-mail.

第 169 到 171 題請參照下面這封電子郵件。

＊ E-mail ＊	✕
From:	Joseph Mooresville <joseph@gentryparts.au> President & CEO Gentry Car Parts Inc.
To:	Emiko Takeda <emiko.takeda@ichigoauto.co.jp> Purchasing Director Ichigo Automobile Corporation
Date:	September 4
Subject:	Your visit

Dear Ms. Takeda,

Here are the directions you requested. They should bring you directly to our main factory outside Melbourne.

As you drive out of the airport, get onto Highway Nine going west. Take that for about 15 kilometers, until you reach the Pettigrew Overpass. Continue on for an additional 3 kilometers to Exit 3. Take that exit and it will lead you to Coldicote Road. Turn right there, and head north for about 4 more kilometers.

After you pass the Herald Hotel on your right, you'll only be a minute or two away from us. If you see Blake Stadium, you'll know you've gone too far, so make a U-turn at Carlton Park or East Pacific Bank and come back toward us.

Guest parking inside the facility is free, but please be sure to enter one of the spaces marked for visitors. My assistants, Marsha Jensen and William Marsden, will meet you at the gate and see you through security. You'll be able to see them as soon as you pull up.

If you have any questions at any time, please e-mail me at the address above. Or you are welcome to contact me by phone. I look forward to seeing you soon.

Sincerely,

Joseph Mooresville

World Specialists in Car Parts Design

寄件者：約瑟夫・摩斯維爾
<joseph@gentryparts.au>
詹崔汽車零件公司總裁暨執行長
收件者：武田惠美子
<emiko.takeda@ichigoauto.co.jp>
一護汽車公司採購部長
日期：9 月 4 日
主旨：您的光臨

親愛的武田女士：

您所要求的路線說明如下。這些說明應該能直接引導您到我們位於墨爾本市外的主廠。

您開車出機場後，就上九號公路往西走。開大約十五公里左右，一直到抵達佩堤格魯高架道。繼續再開三公里，就會到三號出口。從那裡出去，會接到柯帝柯特路。在那裡右轉，再往北開個四公里左右。

在您經過您右手邊的哈洛德飯店之後，離我們這裡就只剩一、兩分鐘了。假如您看到了布雷克球場，就表示您過頭了，您必須在卡爾頓公園或東太平洋銀行迴轉，以回到我們這裡。

訪客在廠內停車不用付費，但是請一定要停到標有訪客專用的位置上。我的助理瑪莎・簡森和威廉・馬斯登會在大門口迎接您，並帶您通過安全檢查。您一靠邊停，就會看到他們。

若您任何時候有任何問題，請寄電子郵件到上面的地址給我。或者也歡迎您打電話到我的手機。期待很快與您見面。

約瑟夫・摩斯維爾敬上

汽車零件設計的世界級專家

Vocabulary

☐ **directions** [dəˈrɛkʃənz] **名** 指示（用複數形）　　☐ **directly** [dəˈrɛktlɪ] **副** 直接地　　☐ **pull up** （靠路邊）停車

試題	試題翻譯	答案與解析
169 How far is Ms. Takeda instructed to drive down Highway Nine? (A) Three kilometers (B) Four kilometers (C) Fifteen kilometers (D) Eighteen kilometers	依照指示，武田女士在九號公路上要開多遠？ (A) 三公里 (B) 四公里 (C) 十五公里 (D) 十八公里	**正解 (D)** 這是一道需要計算的問題。首先，從九號公路開往佩堤格魯高架道約 15 公里，而佩堤格魯高架道又與三號出口相距 3 公里，所以總行程為 15 + 3 = 18 公里。正解為 (D)。
170 What landmark will Ms. Takeda see before she reaches the Melbourne factory? (A) Herald Hotel (B) Blake Stadium (C) Carlton Park (D) East Pacific Bank	武田女士到達墨爾本廠之前會看到什麼地標？ (A) 哈洛德飯店 (B) 布雷克球場 (C) 卡爾頓公園 (D) 東太平洋銀行	**正解 (A)** 電子郵件第三段第一句提到，經過哈洛德飯店之後，只需要再開一至兩分鐘就可抵達目的地，因此正解為選項 (A)。注意，布雷克球場為若開過頭會見到之指標，卡爾頓公園和東太平洋銀行銀行則都是迴轉的指標，因此 (B)、(C)、(D) 皆非正解。 □ **landmark** [ˈlænd͵mɑrk] 名 地標
171 What should Ms. Takeda do upon arriving? (A) Park outside the facility (B) Show her guest pass (C) Contact security (D) Look for Mr. Mooresville's staff	武田女士抵達時該做什麼？ (A) 把車停在廠外 (B) 出示訪客通行證 (C) 聯絡保全人員 (D) 尋找摩斯維爾先生的員工	**正解 (D)** 第四段提及瑪莎‧簡森和威廉‧馬斯登會在大門口等候，所以武田女士必須先找到他們，而這兩人皆為摩斯維爾先生的助理，所以正確答案是 (D)。注意，郵件中寫道「訪客在廠內停車不用付費」，意思就是武田女士可於廠內停車，因此選項 (A) 並不適當。 □ **facility** [fəˈsɪlətɪ] 名 （供特定用途的）場所 □ **guest pass** 訪客證

Questions 172-175 refer to the following newspaper article.

Big Changes at Diaz Motors

Diaz Motors yesterday announced substantial changes at the company's assembly plants in Guadalajara, where it employs 3,200 people, and Veracruz, where it employs 1,200. From April 1, staff will work four-day weeks and take 20% reductions in base salaries. — [1] —. This policy will be subject to a 12-month review, at which time it will be decided whether to continue it.

CEO Felipe Kahlo said the move was designed to secure the long-term competitiveness of the company. — [2] —. Earlier this month, Diaz introduced a voluntary layoff program and eliminated 300 part-time jobs at its subsidiary component plant just outside of Mexico City. Diaz's board of directors has also reportedly discussed outsourcing some processes to lower-cost Guatemala.

— [3] —. According to the latest statistics, car purchases from Diaz and other South American automakers have fallen by 63% over the past three months. This decline is despite a $US 200 million investment the company made recently in advanced production technologies. Diaz stock held steady in light trading on the announcement.

Union officials are reported to be in negotiations with company representatives over ways to avoid further layoffs or outsourcing. — [4] —. Senior union director Miguel Hayek said he was willing to work with management to safeguard jobs in the face of current uncertainty in the market.

第 172 到 175 題請參照下面這則新聞報導。

迪亞茲汽車的重大變革

迪亞茲汽車昨日宣布，其位於瓜達拉哈拉和韋拉克魯斯之組裝工廠有重大的變革。該公司於瓜達拉哈拉雇用了 3,200 人，在韋拉克魯斯則雇用了 1,200 人。四月一日起，員工將每週上班四天，並削減兩成底薪。— [1] —。此政策將於 12 個月後檢討，屆時將再決定是否繼續下去。

執行長菲力普·卡羅表示，這項措施的目的在於確保公司的長期競爭力。— [2] —。在本月稍早時，迪亞茲實施了自願離職方案，並於旗下位於墨西哥市外圍的零組件廠裁撤了三百份兼職工作。據報導，迪亞茲的董事會還討論到要將部分的製程外包到成本較低的瓜地馬拉。

— [3] —。根據最新的統計資料，過去三個月來，向迪亞茲和其他南美車廠所購買的車輛數量減少了 63%。儘管該公司最近投資了兩億美元在高端生產技術上，但情況仍無起色。消息宣布後，迪亞茲的股價持穩，交易量清淡。

據報導，工會將派員與公司的代表談判，設法避免進一步的裁員或外包。— [4] —。資深工會會長米格爾·海耶克說，面對目前市場上的不確定性，他願意和資方合作以保障工作機會。

Vocabulary

- **substantial** [səb'stænʃəl] 形 實質的；大量的
- **assembly plant** 組裝廠
- **reduction** [rɪ'dʌkʃən] 名 減少；削減
- **base salary** 基本薪水
- **be subject to ...** 受⋯⋯支配的
- **competitiveness** [kəm'pɛtətɪvnɪs] 名 競爭力
- **voluntary** ['vɑlən.tɛrɪ] 形 自願的
- **layoff** ['le.ɔf] 名 臨時解雇；裁員
- **eliminate** [ɪ'lɪmə.net] 動 排除；消除
- **subsidiary** [səb'sɪdɪ.ɛrɪ] 形 附屬的；附帶的
- **component plant** 零組件廠
- **reportedly** [rɪ'portɪdlɪ] 副 據報導
- **outsource** ['aʊt.sɔrs] 動 委外代工
- **statistics** [stə'tɪstɪks] 名 統計數字
- **despite** [dɪ'spaɪt] 介 儘管；不管
- **light trading** （股票）交易清淡
- **union** ['junjən] 名 工會
- **in negotiations with ...** 與⋯⋯談判；協商
- **representative** [rɛprɪ'zɛntətɪv] 名 代表；代理人
- **be willing to do ...** 願意做⋯⋯
- **safeguard** ['sef.gɑrd] 動 保護；防衛
- **in the face of ...** 面對⋯⋯
- **uncertainty** [ʌn'sɜtntɪ] 名 不確定性

試題	試題翻譯	答案與解析

172

What is the article mainly about?

(A) Economic trends in South America
(B) Labor relations at auto companies
(C) Productivity changes in car factories
(D) Ongoing corporate reorganizations

這則報導主要在講什麼？

(A) 南美的經濟趨勢
(B) 汽車公司的勞資關係
(C) 車廠的生產力變化
(D) 正在進行的公司重組

正解 (D)

本篇報導一開始就提到 Diaz Motors yesterday announced substantial changes at the company's assembly plants ...，說明該公司將進行「大幅度改革」，因此正解為 (D)。注意，雖然報導中提到南美的景氣下滑和裁員、外包等，但本文最主要還是在說明該公司重組的策略，故選項 (A) 並不正確。

☐ **ongoing** [ˈɑn͵goɪŋ] 形 正在進行中的
☐ **reorganization** [͵riɔrgənəˋzeʃən] 名 重組

173

The word "subsidiary" in paragraph 2, line 6, is closest in meaning to

(A) divisional
(B) remaining
(C) partial
(D) sequential

第二段第六行的 "subsidiary" 這個字的意思最接近

(A) 分支的
(B) 剩餘的
(C) 部分的
(D) 連續的

正解 (A)

文中的 subsidiary 指「附屬的」而最接近此單字意思的則為選項 (A) divisional（分支的）。注意，subsidiary 作名詞用時可指「子公司」。

174

What problem is Diaz Motors facing?

(A) A lack of competitive technologies
(B) Sharp decreases in stock prices
(C) A reduction of market share
(D) A slump in consumer demand

迪亞茲汽車面臨了什麼問題？

(A) 缺乏有競爭力的技術
(B) 股價重挫
(C) 市占率下滑
(D) 消費需求銳減

正解 (D)

報導第三段提及 ... car purchases from Diaz and other South American automakers have fallen by 63% ...，這說明迪亞茲汽車正面臨「消費者需求不振」的問題，故正解為選項 (D)。注意，報導中提到 Diaz stock held steady ...，也就是說該公司股價仍維持穩定，所以選項 (B) 並不正確。

☐ **slump** [slʌmp] 名 暴跌；劇降

175

In which of the positions marked [1], [2], [3] and [4] does the following sentence best belong?

"The news comes as the Mexican car manufacturer battles a regional recession."

(A) [1]
(B) [2]
(C) [3]
(D) [4]

下面這個句子插入文中標示的 [1]、[2]、[3]、[4] 四處當中的何處最符合文意？

「在這家墨西哥車廠對抗當地的不景氣的同時傳出此消息。」

(A) [1]
(B) [2]
(C) [3]
(D) [4]

正解 (C)

由上下文可推測迪亞茲是墨西哥的一家汽車製造商，而根據各段內容的涵義，可知空格 [3] 之前提到的是關於迪亞茲公司的重組、裁員、委外代工的話題，之後則是在說明迪亞茲和其他南美的汽車廠商營運正遭逢不景氣。而著眼於題目所問插入句中的 a regional recession 即可判斷該句置於 [3] 之處最為恰當。

☐ **regional** [ˈridʒən!] 形 （整個）地區的
☐ **recession** [rɪˋsɛʃən] 名 （經濟的）衰退

Questions 176-180 refer to the following survey and e-mail.

Car4U Inc.

Customer Survey

Customer Name: (Mr.)/Ms.) Ibrahim Rafsanjani

Address: 17 Rue De Mons, Lyons, France 90A-E7K

E-mail: Rafsanjani2947@francotel.com

Date of Car Rental: From 8 June to 15 June

Applicable rules, fees or other information regarding your rental: N/A

Please indicate your level of service satisfaction with Car4U Inc. by rating us in each of the categories below, from 1 to 5.   1= Very unsatisfied   5 = Very satisfied

Category	Condition of car at time of rental	Cost per day	Service Staff Helpfulness	Car Model Options	Drop-off and Pick-up convenience
Rating	4	3	3	1	3

Comments: I think my responses above show my opinion about renting from you. I have also rented from Falcon Rental Co., and frankly I believe they do a better job. It's easy to see why they're the number one car rental agency in Europe. I would recommend that you work to improve your service if you want to compete with them.

Thank you for taking the time to fill out our survey. Fully completed surveys earn 200 Frequent Flier Miles on World Wings Airlines. Let World Wings fly you across the globe—and choose Car4U when you land.

---

* E-mail *

From:	eva.veblen@car4u.net
To:	robert.heller@car4u.net
Date:	18 July
Subject:	Survey

Dear Mr. Heller,

We completed a survey of customer satisfaction last month: over 3,000 respondents were included. I have a broad statistical analysis of the results I will send later. However, I have attached this particular response because the scores are representative of many of the surveys we collected. Furthermore, the respondent offered a succinct written summary of what other customers might also feel.

As you can see, it indicates that we have varying levels of performance in different areas. I spoke with some analysts in the company who said it is "impossible" to perform well in all areas.

However, I don't accept this as necessarily true. Instead, I would like to suggest that we try to make improvements in our worst area of performance, clearly shown in the survey, by expanding our budget in that area. I know that it's not easy to increase expenses, but in my opinion it would be a very positive move that would result in the long-term success of our company.

Yours truly,

Eva Veblen
Director of Operations

顧客姓名：(先生)／女士）伊布拉辛·拉夫桑雅尼
地址：90A-E7K 法國里昂市芒斯街 17 號
電子郵件：Rafsanjani2947@francotel.com
租車日期：自 6 月 8 日至 6 月 15 日
關於所租車輛的適用規定、費用或其他資訊：無

請指出您對 Car4U 公司的服務滿意度。請利用下列各欄評分，從 1 分到 5 分。
1＝非常不滿意 5＝非常滿意

類別	租用時的車況	每日費用	服務人員的協助性	車款選擇性	取還車的方便性
評分	4	3	3	1	3

意見：我想上述的回應說明了我跟你們租車的感想。我也跟獵鷹租車公司租過車，而老實說我深深覺得他們做得比較好。很容易就看得出來他們為什麼是歐洲第一名的租車公司。如果你們想跟他們競爭的話，那我建議你們要努力改善服務。

感謝您撥冗填寫調查問卷。完整填寫問卷可獲得世翼航空 200 哩的常客里程數。讓世翼帶您飛遍全球，並在降落時選擇 Car4U。

寄件者：eva.veblen@car4u.net
收件者：robert.heller@car4u.net
日期：7 月 18 日
主旨：意見調查

親愛的海勒先生：

我們上個月完成了顧客滿意度調查，受訪者超過三千位。我把結果做了廣泛的統計分析，稍後將寄出。不過，我特別附上這份調查回覆，因為它的得分可代表我們收到的許多份問卷。除此之外，這位受訪者簡短地填寫了一段或許其他顧客也有同感的感想。

正如您可以看到的，調查顯示我們在不同方面的表現有好有壞。我請教過公司的一些分析人員，他們說要在各方面全都表現很好是「不可能的」。

不過，我並不認為必然是如此。相反地，我想建議增加預算努力改善在調查中清楚顯示我們表現最差的那個部分。我知道要增加經費不容易，但是依我看，這將會是非常正面的舉措，並能為公司帶來長遠的成功。

營運主任
伊娃·威卜蘭敬上

Vocabulary

- **customer survey** 顧客意見調查
- **applicable** [ˋæplɪkəbl] 形 可應用的
- **regarding** [rɪˋgɑrdɪŋ] 介 關於
- **category** [ˋkætə.gorɪ] 名 種類；範疇
- **frankly** [ˋfræŋklɪ] 副 坦白地（說）
- **compete with ...** 與……競爭
- **respondent** [rɪˋspɑndənt] 名 應答者
- **broad** [brɔd] 形 概括的
- **statistical** [stəˋtɪstɪk!] 形 統計的
- **representative of ...** 代表……
- **succinct** [səkˋsɪŋkt] 形 簡潔的
- **varying** [ˋvɛrɪŋ] 形 不同的
- **budget** [ˋbʌdʒɪt] 名 預算
- **positive** [ˋpɑzətɪv] 形 正面的；積極的

試題	試題翻譯	答案與解析

176

What is Mr. Rafsanjani most satisfied with?

(A) The state of the cars
(B) Rental fees
(C) The quality of customer service
(D) Car models available

拉夫桑雅尼先生最滿意什麼？

(A) 車況
(B) 租車費用
(C) 客服品質
(D) 可租用車款

正解 (A)

拉夫桑雅尼先生在滿意度調查表裡的 Condition of car at time of rental 一欄中填入「4」，所以他對車況感到最滿意，選項 (A) 為正解。注意，state 是 condition 的另一種說法。

□ **state** [stet] 图 狀態

177

Why does Mr. Rafsanjani mention Falcon Rental Co.?

(A) To provide a comparison
(B) To comment on a car he rented
(C) To support his comments on price
(D) To complain about the company's service

拉夫桑雅尼先生為什麼提到獵鷹租車公司？

(A) 為了提供一個比較
(B) 為了評論他所租的車
(C) 為了佐證他對價格的意見
(D) 為了抱怨公司的服務

正解 (A)

拉夫桑雅尼先生在意見欄提到競爭公司的等級，他舉這個例子來表達他所要求的水準，正確答案就是選項 (A)。

178

What do people who answer the survey get?

(A) Lower rental prices
(B) Complimentary airline upgrades
(C) Frequent flier miles
(D) Discounted accommodations

回答調查問卷的人會獲得什麼？

(A) 較低的租車價格
(B) 免費的航空升等
(C) 常客哩程數
(D) 折扣住宿

正解 (C)

由問卷最下方的 Fully completed surveys earn 200 Frequent Flier Miles on World Wings Airlines. 可知，本題應選 (C)。（Frequent flier miles 是航空公司所實施的集點優惠措施，依搭機距離給予哩程點數。）注意，如本題欄位外的小字常會是考點，千萬不要看漏。

□ **complimentary** [ˌkɑmpləˈmɛntərɪ] 形 免費的；贈送的

179

Why did Ms. Veblen attach the single response?

(A) It answers her boss' request.
(B) It is a good example of the overall survey results.
(C) It corrects a previous statistical error.
(D) It solicits approval for more responses.

威卜蘭小姐為什麼單獨附上一則調查回答？

(A) 為了回應她老闆的要求。
(B) 因為它是一個顯示整體調查結果的好例子。
(C) 因為它修正了之前的一個統計錯誤。
(D) 為了請求批准更多回應。

正解 (B)

題目的 the single response 是指拉夫桑雅尼先生所填寫的問卷。威卜蘭小姐之所以將其附上郵件，理由就在第一段的 I have attached this particular response because the scores are representative of many of the surveys we collected.。也就是說，她認為這份評價相當具有代表性，故正解為選項 (B)。

180

What does Ms. Veblen suggest doing to improve the company's performance?

(A) Conducting market research
(B) Cutting down on labor expenses
(C) Increasing the variety of cars
(D) Analyzing the results of the survey

為了改善公司的業績，威卜蘭小姐提議做什麼？

(A) 做市調
(B) 削減人事費用
(C) 增加車輛種類
(D) 分析調查結果

正解 (C)

威卜蘭小姐在電子郵件第三段第二句提出具體的提案，其中 our worst area of performance, clearly shown in the survey「我們表現最差的部分，清楚地顯示於問卷中」是解題關鍵。對照滿意度調查表，Car Model Options（車款選擇性）得分最低，所以正確答案是選項 (C)。

Questions 181-185 refer to the following Web page and e-mail.

第 181 到 185 題請參照下列網頁和電子郵件。

---

www.cheshirefoods.com/raspberryleaftea/

Thank you for visiting Cheshire Foods. See our main Internet homepage for exciting links to other great Cheshire products.

 Recommended! *Raspberry Leaf Tea*

A delicate blend of raspberry leaf, natural flavor and real pieces of apple comes together to make this deliciously fragrant tea.
Completely organic, without artificial flavorings, colors or preservatives.

What's inside?

Raspberry Leaves, Hibiscus, Blackberry Leaves, Natural Raspberry Flavor, Tartaric Acid, Rosehips, Raspberries, Apple pieces.
CAFFEINE-FREE

How to enjoy it?

Place the teabag in a cup or teapot of boiled water (one bag per person). Immerse for 3-5 minutes to bring out the full flavor. Best drunk without adding milk, cream or any other liquids or condiments.

Unfortunately, we are unable to make direct sales.
Please pick up some at your local grocery store.

www.cheshirefoods.com/raspberryleaftea/
感謝您造訪赤郡食品。赤郡其他優良產品的驚喜連結請見網站首頁。

強力推薦！ 覆盆子葉茶
將覆盆子葉、天然香料與真蘋果片巧妙融合在一起，製作成這款美味又芳香的茶。
完全有機，不含人工香料、色劑或防腐劑。

成分為何？
覆盆子葉、木槿、黑莓葉、天然覆盆子香料、酒石酸、玫瑰果、覆盆子、蘋果片。
不含咖啡因

如何享用？
將茶包放進裝有滾水的杯子或茶壺裡（每包一人份），浸泡三到五分鐘，以便讓香味充分散發出來。飲用時最好不要添加牛奶、奶油，或其他任何液體或調味料。

本站恕不直接銷售。
請於您住家附近的雜貨店選購。

To:	CustomerService@Cheshirefoods.com
From:	gloria7902@laketel.com
Date:	Wednesday, May 3
Subject:	Ordering raspberry tea

Dear Cheshire Foods,

I have enjoyed your Raspberry Leaf Tea for many years. I usually take mine with a bit of Korean or Chinese ginseng, and find it delicious. I even check for product updates regularly on your Web site.

Indeed, I think it would be ideal if I were able to buy it there directly. That's because I sometimes forget to pick it up when I'm out shopping. At other times, your tea may not be available at a particular store I go to. In such cases, I purchase other products, though they are not as enjoyable as yours.

Is there any way that I could order directly from your company—perhaps by catalog or phone? If you have no way for customers to do so at this time, I suggest you consider making such an option available. You would certainly benefit through increased sales, and customers like me would benefit through the convenience of the product being brought right to our doors. I should tell you that Longfellow Grey Tea does provide such a service already.

Sincerely,

Gloria Han

收件者：CustomerService@Cheshirefoods.com
寄件者：gloria7902@laketel.com
日期：5 月 3 日星期三
主旨：訂購覆盆子茶

赤郡食品您好：

多年來我一直很喜歡喝貴公司的覆盆子葉茶。我喝的時候，通常會加一點韓國或中國人蔘，我發現這樣很好喝。我甚至會固定到你們的網站上查閱最新的產品消息。

的確，我想要是能從網站上直接購買的話，那就太好了，因為我外出購物時，有時會忘了買。有時則是在我去的那家店裡買不到你們的茶。如此一來，我只好買別家的產品，雖然它們沒你們的好喝。

有沒有什麼辦法可以讓我直接跟貴公司訂購？也許利用型錄或電話？假如你們目前沒辦法讓顧客這麼做，我建議你們不妨把這個方式列入考慮。銷售量增加一定對你們有利，而將產品直接送到家門口的便利性則對像我這樣的顧客有利。我應該告訴你們，朗費羅伯爵茶已經提供這項服務了。

葛洛莉亞‧韓敬上

Vocabulary

- **delicate** [ˈdɛləkət] 形 精巧的
- **blend** [blɛnd] 名 混合物
- **flavor** [ˈfleva] 名 味道；風味
- **organic** [ɔrˈgænɪk] 形 施用有機肥料的
- **artificial** [ˌɑrtəˈfɪʃəl] 形 人工的
- **preservative** [prɪˈzɜvətɪv] 名 防腐劑
- **immerse** [ɪˈmɜs] 動 使浸沒
- **bring out ...** 帶出……
- **liquid** [ˈlɪkwɪd] 名 液體
- **condiment** [ˈkɑndəmənt] 名 調味料
- **pick up** 買
- **grocery store** 食品雜貨店
- **ginseng** [ˈdʒɪnsɛŋ] 名 人蔘
- **indeed** [ɪnˈdid] 副 真正地；的確
- **benefit** [ˈbɛnəfɪt] 動 得益；受惠

試題	試題翻譯	答案與解析

181

What is a stated feature of Cheshire Foods Raspberry Leaf Tea?

(A) Low price
(B) New flavors
(C) Natural ingredients
(D) Wide popularity

文中描述赤郡食品的覆盆子葉茶有什麼特色？

(A) 廉價
(B) 新口味
(C) 天然成分
(D) 廣受歡迎

正解 (C)

從網站上提到的 Completely organic, without artificial flavorings, colors or preservatives. 可知，使用「自然材料」為此茶之特徵，因此正解為選項 (C)。其他選項皆未記載於文中，故不可選。

□ **ingredient** [ɪnˈgridɪənt] 名 原料；成分

182

What suggestion does the Web site offer?

(A) To add apple pieces to the tea
(B) To allow to cool before consuming
(C) To use the appropriate type of teapot
(D) To avoid adding any dairy products

網站給了什麼建議？

(A) 把蘋果片加進茶裡
(B) 飲用前先讓茶冷卻
(C) 使用種類合適的茶壺
(D) 避免添加任何乳製品

正解 (D)

網站文章底下提到 Best drunk without adding milk, cream ...，建議不要加入牛奶、奶油等，所以正確答案是選項 (D)。蘋果片是原本就含在產品當中，小心不要誤選 (A)。

□ **appropriate** [əˈproprɪɪt] 形 適當的
□ **dairy product** 乳製品

183

What is indicated about Ms. Han?

(A) She enjoys tea in a different way from the producer's instructions.
(B) She prefers ginseng to raspberry leaf tea.
(C) She purchases tea in large quantities.
(D) She goes shopping for tea at a certain store.

關於韓小姐，下列敘述何者正確？

(A) 她喜歡以有別於業者所指示的方式喝茶。
(B) 她喜歡人蔘勝過覆盆子葉茶。
(C) 她大量買茶。
(D) 她都去特定的店買茶。

正解 (A)

韓小姐在電子郵件的第一段當中提到 I usually take mine with a bit of Korean or Chinese ginseng，從這段敘述可知韓小姐喝茶有她獨到的方式，與網站建議的「如何享用？」有所不同，故本題選 (A)。注意，她只說她有時到一家特定的商店買不到茶，而不是一直在那家店購買，所以選項 (D) 並不正確。

□ **prefer A to B** 比起 B 而言，更喜歡 A
□ **in large quantities** 大量地

184

What does Ms. Han ask Cheshire Foods to do?

(A) Post product updates on their Web site
(B) Provide product details
(C) Use larger tea boxes
(D) Increase their products' availability

韓小姐要求赤郡食品做什麼？

(A) 將最新的產品訊息公布在網站上
(B) 提供產品詳情
(C) 使用較大的茶盒
(D) 增加產品的可得性

正解 (D)

由於韓小姐在店面常買不到茶，因此寫道 Is there any way that I could order directly from your company ...?，詢問是否有直接購得產品的方法。換言之，也就是希望能增加購買產品的管道，故選項 (D) 為正解。

□ **post** [post] 動（在網路上）張貼訊息

185

How does Ms. Han try to persuade Cheshire Foods to consider her suggestion?

(A) By mentioning a competitor
(B) By threatening to shop elsewhere
(C) By illustrating a business mistake
(D) By showing past losses

韓小姐試圖用什麼方式說服赤郡食品考慮她的建議？

(A) 提及競爭對手
(B) 威脅要到別家購物
(C) 說明經營上的錯誤
(D) 指出過去的虧損

正解 (A)

郵件最後提到 I should tell you that Longfellow Grey Tea does provide such a service already.，表示有其他公司已經開始直接銷售，因此正解為選項 (A)。注意，韓小姐上面提及她無法購得覆盆子葉茶時會改買其他茶，並非藉由告知購買其他公司產品來威脅對方一定要接受她的建議，故選項 (B) 並不適當。

□ **competitor** [kəmˈpɛtətə] 名 競爭者
□ **threaten to do** 威脅做（某事）

Questions 186-190 refer to the following list, schedule, and memo.

第 186 到 190 題請參照下列表單、日程和備忘錄。

Starden Foods, Inc.

Created by Consumer Research Department
June 29

Comparison of marketing expenses on food categories with sales changes

Study covered all 637 stores in the European Union. A comparison next quarter will focus on stores in the Americas and the Asia Pacific.

Department	Amount spent on marketing (in millions)	Change in unit sales from last year
Fruits and Vegetables	€4.3	+4.2%
Breads	€12.8	+3.8%
Dry Goods	€26.6	-1.9%
Meats	€18.2	+0.5%
Dairy	€31.4	-2.2%
Seafood	€12.6	+0.1%

Note: Scheduled for discussion at the Marketing Plans Meeting on July 25. There will be an updated schedule soon.

史塔丹食品公司

消費者調查部製表
6 月 29 日

食品類行銷費用之比較與業績

本調查涵蓋歐盟內全部的 637 間店。下一季的比較將聚焦於美國和亞太地區的店鋪。

類別	行銷支出額（單位：百萬）	單位銷售量去年比
蔬果類	€4.3	+4.2%
麵包類	€12.8	+3.8%
乾貨類	€26.6	-1.9%
肉類	€18.2	+0.5%
乳製品	€31.4	-2.2%
海鮮類	€12.6	+0.1%

備註：預定 7 月 25 日開會討論行銷計畫。最新日程即將公布。

Starden Foods, Inc.

Division Manager Committee Meetings for the Month of July

Final agendas for each meeting will be issued at least 3 days ahead of time. Attendance at all meetings is mandatory, unless urgent client-related or other business arises.

Date	Topic
July 4	Supplier Review
July 11	Marketing Plans
July 18	Store Maintenance Issues
July 25	Quality Control
July 31	Human Resources

Board directors may attend any meeting with little or no advance notice.

史塔丹食品公司
7 月份部門經理委員會會議

各會議的最終議程最晚將於三天前發布。除非有緊急的客戶相關事務或發生其他業務須處理，否則所有會議皆必須參加。

日期	議題
7 月 4 日	供應商審查
7 月 11 日	行銷計畫
7 月 18 日	店鋪維修問題
7 月 25 日	品質管理
7 月 31 日	人事問題

董事們有可能僅通知少數人或不事前通知就出席任一會議。

題目	題目翻譯

MEMO

To: Division Managers
From: Brenda Phan, COO
Date: July 12
Subject: Business Report

Colleagues,

In yesterday's meeting, we discussed whether there is a correlation between the amount of money spent on marketing certain products and the revenue generated from those products. Currently, we can say that the connection is not very clear. We reviewed the list that compares shopper spending traits, and found some surprises. Helen Smith had to miss the meeting, but we talked afterwards. She pointed out products that experienced high sales growth.

You might intuitively feel that we have to spend more money on our products experiencing the lowest sales. However, I think it would be better instead to increase marketing support for our products experiencing the highest sales.

If a product category is experiencing weak sales, I do not think that more advertising alone can improve the situation. Instead, we have to look at other factors, such as quality or price. That is what I tried to stress to Evan Lee, who unexpectedly but fortunately was able to join the meeting. He seemed to agree with my analysis. In any event, I have attached a report detailing this idea, which I'd like to discuss at our next meeting. I don't think that we should put it off until the last gathering of the month.

Thank you,

Brenda Phan

備忘錄

收件者：部門經理
寄件者：營運長布蘭達・潘
日期：7 月 12 日
主旨：業務報告

各位同事：

在昨天的會議上，我們討論了特定產品的行銷支出金額與其營收之間是否有關聯。目前，我們可以說當中的關係並不太明顯。在審閱過消費者的消費特徵比較表之後，我們發現有幾點令人相當出乎意料。雖然海倫・史密斯不克前來會議，但是我們之後有討論了一下。她指出了幾項業績大幅成長的產品。

或許各位會直覺地認為我們應該在銷售最差的品項上投入更多經費，不過我反倒認為對銷售最好的品項增加行銷支援更妥當。

假如某一類產品的業績不佳，我不認為單純靠加強宣傳能改善狀況。我們反而必須檢視其他因素，例如品質或價格。這就是我對李伊帆試圖強調的一點。我沒想到他會出席會議，但很慶幸他能來。他似乎也同意我的分析。無論如何，我已經附上一個報告詳細說明這個想法，我希望我們下次開會時討論。我想我們不應該把這件事拖到本月最後的會議。

謝謝
布蘭達・潘

Vocabulary

- **comparison** [kəmˋpærɪsn] 名 比較
- **agenda** [əˋdʒɛndə] 名 議程
- **issue** [ˋɪʃju] 動 發布
- **... ahead of time** 在某時間之前
- **attendance** [əˋtɛndəns] 名 出席
- **mandatory** [ˋmændəˏtorɪ] 形 義務的；強制的
- **urgent** [ˋɝdʒənt] 形 緊急的
- **correlation** [ˏkɔrəˋleʃən] 名 相互關係
- **trait** [tret] 名 特徵；特點
- **afterwards** [ˋæftəˏwədz] 副 後來
- **intuitively** [ɪnˋtjuɪtɪvlɪ] 副 直覺地
- **unexpectedly** [ˏʌnɪkˋspɛktɪdlɪ] 副 出乎意料地；意外地
- **in any event** 無論如何
- **put off** 延遲；拖延

試題	試題翻譯	答案與解析

186

According to the list, what is true about the research?

(A) It compares different shopper categories.
(B) It spans several quarters.
(C) It includes many Asian stores.
(D) It covers a single region.

根據表單，關於調查何者正確？

(A) 它針對不同的消費者分類做比較。
(B) 它涵括數個季度。
(C) 它包括許多亞洲店鋪。
(D) 它涵蓋單一地區。

正解 (D)

從表單中的 Study covered all 637 stores in the European Union. 可知，選項 (D) 為正解，其中的 a single region 指的就是「歐盟區」。由於該表單是針對食品做比較而非消費者，故選項 (A) 錯誤。另，由 A comparison of next quarter will focus on stores in the Americas and the Asia Pacific. 可判斷選項 (B)、(C) 也不對。

☐ **span** [spæn] 動 橫跨；包括

187

What is suggested about the list?

(A) It was created by an outside firm.
(B) It will be distributed at a meeting.
(C) A meeting about it was rescheduled.
(D) A report about it has been written.

關於這份表單顯示了什麼？

(A) 它是由外部公司所製作。
(B) 它將被派發於一個會議上。
(C) 關於表單的會議被改期了。
(D) 有人寫了一份關於表單的報告。

正解 (C)

根據表單下的備註，7 月 25 日的行銷計畫會議將討論此表單。但是對照日程，行銷計畫會議定於 7 月 11 日，因此可推論會議的預定日期有變更。正解為選項 (C)。注意，備忘錄的日期 7 月 12 日，以及本文開頭的 In yesterday's meeting, ... 也都是解題的線索。

188

What is indicated about the July 11 meeting?

(A) A member had urgent business.
(B) A rule was revised.
(C) A maintenance issue was solved.
(D) An important client was invited.

關於 7 月 11 日的會議指出了什麼訊息？

(A) 有一名與會者有緊急業務。
(B) 有一條規則被修改。
(C) 有一個維修問題被解決了。
(D) 有一位重要的客戶受邀參加。

正解 (A)

由日期寫 7 月 12 日和本文一開始提及 In yesterday's meeting, ... 可知，備忘錄的內容與 7 月 11 日的會議有關。從第一段的 Helen Smith had to miss the meeting, but ... 得知海倫·史密斯缺席會議，對照日程提及 Attendance at all meetings is mandatory, unless urgent client-related or other business arises. 可推測，此人應有緊急業務才無法參加會議。故正解為選項 (A)。

189

In the memo, the word "connection" in paragraph 1, line 3, is closest in meaning to

(A) termination
(B) wire
(C) relationship
(D) payment

備忘錄第一段第三行的 "connection" 這個字的意思最接近

(A) 結束
(B) 電線
(C) 關係
(D) 付款

正解 (C)

根據之前的內容可知，此處的 connection 是指 a "correlation" between the amount of money spent on marketing certain products and the revenue generated from those products（特定產品的行銷支出金額與其獲利之間的關聯）。四個選項當中，(C) relationship 的意思最接近。

190

Who most likely is Evan Lee?

(A) A marketing expert
(B) A senior executive
(C) A consumer analyst
(D) A dairy manufacturer

李伊帆最有可能是誰？

(A) 行銷專家
(B) 資深主管
(C) 消費者分析師
(D) 乳製品廠商

正解 (B)

從備忘錄第三段當中的 Evan Lee, who unexpectedly but fortunately was able to join the meeting. 得知，李伊帆並非原本必須出席的人。再對照日程下方所寫的 Board directors may attend any meeting with little or no advance notice. 來判斷，李伊帆最有可能是位董事，故選項 (B) 資深主管最符合推論。

Questions 191-195 refer to the following product information, online review, and response.

H-3000 Mobile Phone

Karn Telecom

This best-selling device is easy to use to surf the Web, download apps, talk, text, and perform many other functions. Its most valuable feature is its ability to link to wireless systems even in remote locations.

The device is only compatible with Karn Telecom hardware. This extends to chargers, power cords, and batteries.

A product warranty is enclosed, covering all internal components for 3 years. External surfaces and damage from dropping or ordinary wear and tear are excluded.

---

www.electronicshopper.net/reviews/892361/

Customer comment

Product: The H-3000 Mobile Phone
Customer: Blake Woods
Verified Purchase:

I can say that the device is basically good. I enjoy it in most respects. The price is a little high, and the design isn't particularly elegant, but it does have excellent reception, just as advertised. I am very pleased with that.

I was disappointed, however, because the screen scratched too easily—after only a month of use. I took it to a Karn Telecom store, but the Customer Service representative there only cited the warranty information. In my opinion, the company should reevaluate what "ordinary wear and tear" means.

第 191 到 195 題請參照下列產品資訊、網路評鑑和回應。

卡恩電信
H-3000 行動電話

這款銷售最佳的裝置能讓您輕鬆上網、下載應用程式、通話、傳簡訊,以及執行其他多項功能。它最有用的特色是能夠連結無線系統,即使您身處偏遠地區。

此款手機僅與卡恩電信的硬體相容,包括充電器、電源線和電池等。

隨貨附三年保固,涵蓋所有內部零件,但不包括外層表面和因掉落所造成的損壞或自然磨損。

www.electronicshopper.net/reviews/892361/
顧客意見

產品:H-3000 行動電話
顧客:布雷克‧伍茲
認證購入:

基本上我可以說這支手機還不錯,大部分方面我都蠻喜歡的。價格稍貴,設計也並非特別漂亮,但是它的收訊確實很棒,正如同廣告中所言。這點我非常滿意。

不過,我很失望,因為螢幕太容易刮到了──我才用了一個月。我把手機帶到卡恩電信門市,但是那裡的客服人員只是跟我傳達了保固內容。我認為,這家公司應該重新評估「自然磨損」的定義。

www.electronicshopper.net/reviews/892361/

Customer comment

Product: The H-3000 Mobile Phone
Customer: Blake Woods
Response from: Karn Telecom Customer Service

Thank you very much for your review. Your feedback is very important to us. Unfortunately, our 3-year warranty is explicit on the subject of surface wear, and the response given to you by the Customer Service representative you spoke with is consistent with that. However, if you do opt for a replacement, we recommend our Z-1X model, which has a stronger screen and is more scratch-resistant. Additionally, we would suggest enrolling in our Extended Care Program. This will warranty your internal components for 2 additional years. The cost for this program is only $175. We want to make sure that you receive the very best support for your product, and we look forward to your continued patronage and feedback.

www.electronicshopper.net/reviews/892361/
顧客意見

產品：H-3000 行動電話
顧客：布雷克‧伍茲
回覆自：卡恩電信客服

非常感謝您的評鑑。您的反饋對我們而言十分重要。很遺憾地，本公司的三年保固已載明關於手機外表磨損的問題，而與您交談的該位客服人員所給您的回覆也符合內容規定。然而，假如您選擇換機，我們推薦本公司的 Z-1X 型號，這款手機的螢幕硬度較強，並且更加耐刮。此外，建議您登錄我們的延長保固專案。此專案提供額外兩年的內部零件保固，價格僅須 175 美元。我們希望確保您所購買的產品受到最完善的支援，並且期待您繼續給予惠顧和意見。

Vocabulary

- [ ] **app** [æp] 名 應用程式（application program 之簡略）
- [ ] **function** [ˈfʌŋkʃən] 名 功能
- [ ] **remote** [rɪˈmot] 形 遙遠的；偏僻的
- [ ] **compatible** [kəmˈpætəbl] 形 相容的
- [ ] **extend to ...** 延伸至⋯⋯
- [ ] **product warranty** 產品保證（書）
- [ ] **internal** [ɪnˈtɜnl] 形 內部的
- [ ] **external** [ɪkˈstɜnəl] 形 外部的
- [ ] **surface** [ˈsɜfɪs] 名 表面
- [ ] **exclude** [ɪkˈsklud] 動 排除在外；不包括
- [ ] **cite** [saɪt] 動 引用；舉出
- [ ] **reevaluate** [riˈvæljuˌet] 動 重新評估
- [ ] **feedback** [ˈfidˌbæk] 名 反饋的意見
- [ ] **explicit** [ɪkˈsplɪsɪt] 形 明確的
- [ ] **be consistent with ...** 與⋯⋯一致
- [ ] **opt for ...** 選擇／決定⋯⋯
- [ ] **replacement** [rɪˈplesmənt] 名 替代品
- [ ] **scratch-resistant** [ˈskrætʃrɪˌzɪstənt] 形 耐刮的
- [ ] **enroll in** 參加；登錄
- [ ] **patronage** [ˈpætrənɪdʒ] 名 惠顧

191

What is NOT mentioned in the product information?

(A) Internet use
(B) Access security
(C) Battery components
(D) Sales ranking

下列何者在產品資訊中「未」被提及？

(A) 上網用途
(B) 存取安全性
(C) 電池零件
(D) 銷售排行榜

正解 (B)

題目問的 product 是指第一篇文章所描述的 H-3000 行動電話。第一段的 This best-selling device 與選項 (D) 呼應，surf the Web 即選項 (A)，第二段的 ..., and batteries 與選項 (C) 有關，唯有選項 (B) 並未被提及，故為正解。

192

In the online review, the word "respects" in paragraph 1, line 1, is closest in meaning to

(A) predictions
(B) transmissions
(C) aspects
(D) patterns

網路評鑑第一段第一行的 "respects" 這個字的意思最接近

(A) 預測
(B) 傳送
(C) 方面
(D) 樣式

正解 (C)

I enjoy it in most respects. 的意思是「大部分方面我都蠻喜歡的。」四個選項當中，只有 (C) aspects 與 "respects" 同義，所以是正確答案。

193

What is Mr. Woods particularly pleased with about the mobile phone?

(A) Its connectivity
(B) Its compatibility
(C) Its design
(D) Its price

伍茲先生特別滿意這台手機的哪一點？

(A) 通訊網路連接性
(B) 相容性
(C) 設計
(D) 價格

正解 (A)

本題解答線索就在評鑑第一段的 ... it does have excellent reception, just as advertised. I am very pleased with that. 這部分。而第一篇文章第一段提到的 Its most valuable feature is its ability to link to wireless systems even in remote locations. 即伍茲先生說的 excellent reception。換句話說，選項 (A) Its connectivity 為正解。

194

What is the total warranty length Karn Telecom can offer?

(A) 1 year
(B) 3 years
(C) 4 years
(D) 5 years

卡恩電信總共最長能提供多久的保固？

(A) 一年
(B) 三年
(C) 四年
(D) 五年

正解 (D)

根據第一篇文章的第三段，產品的基本保固期為三年。此外，客服人員在收到伍茲先生的評鑑之後，於第三篇文章中段表示 Additionally, we would suggest enrolling in our Extended Care Program. This will warranty ... for 2 additional years.，也就是說，登錄延長保固專案可追加兩年。因此，保固期最長可達 3 + 2 = 5 年。

195

What was the Customer Service representative correct about?

(A) The method to avoid scratches
(B) The need for program enrollment
(C) The coverage for a device
(D) The best kind of mobile phone screen

客服人員哪一點是正確的？

(A) 避免刮損的方法
(B) 登錄方案的必要性
(C) 手機保固的涵蓋範圍
(D) 手機螢幕最好的種類

正解 (C)

本題的關鍵在於第三篇文章當中的「本公司的三年保固已載明關於手機外表磨損的問題，而與您交談的該位客服人員所給您的回覆也符合內容規定。」根據第二篇文章，伍茲先生表示他帶著手機到門市表明螢幕受損，客服人員雖提供了服務，但是「客服人員只是跟我傳達了保固內容。我認為，這家公司應該重新評估『自然磨損』的定義」。然而，從第一篇文章產品資訊的最後得知「保固並不包括自然磨損」。綜合以上訊息推論，關於保固範圍，客服人員的回覆並沒有錯，因此正解為 (C)。

Questions 196-200 refer to the following notice, e-mail, and article.

Jowel Community Center
17 Lakeland Street
www.jowelccenter.org

Special Event: Building Your Wealth — Tips for Ordinary People

Speaker: Joseph Steinz, Personal Financial Consultant

April 23

Free and open to the public

Learn: **Home budget management skills**

Choosing the right bank or financial institution

The basics of stocks, bonds, and other investing or reinvesting options

30-Minute Question and Answer Session to follow the talk

Tea, coffee and snacks provided

While the event is free and open to the public, space is limited, and guaranteed seating can be assured only to the first 75 people who register. Please visit the Web site above to register. For more information, contact Bozena Kovac, special event organizer: bozena@jowelccenter.org.

* E-mail *	✕
To:	bozena@jowelccenter.org
From:	joseph.steinz@zoneumail.net
Date:	April 11
Subject:	Second Reminder: Certification

Dear Ms. Kovac,

I regret to inform you that I will not be able to speak at your April 23 Community Center event on finance management. I have an urgent business matter that I have to attend to on that day. I do not want to let down your attendees, so I have arranged a colleague of mine to take my place. I can guarantee that he is more than qualified to do so as he has both taught and written extensively on this topic. Details are in the attachment.

I apologize for this situation, and trust the event will work out well. If I can help in any other way, please do not hesitate to let me know.

Yours sincerely,

Joseph Steinz

喬維爾社區中心
萊克蘭街 17 號
www.jowelccenter.org

特別活動:創造財富——給平凡人的訣竅
講師:個人理財顧問喬瑟夫・史汀茲
4 月 23 日

免費且開放給一般民眾

學習:家庭預算管理技巧
選擇正確的銀行或理財機構
股票、債券和其他投資或再投資
選擇之基本原則
演講後將進行 30 分鐘問答時間
備有茶、咖啡和點心

雖然本活動免費且開放給大眾,但空間有限,預訂座位只提供給前 75 名註冊者。註冊請登入上面網站。欲知更多資訊,請與特別活動主辦人波潔娜・柯維克聯繫:bozena@jowelccenter.org。

收件者:bozena@jowelccenter.org
寄件者:joseph.steinz@zoneumail.net
日期:4 月 11 日
主旨:第二次提醒:證明信

柯維克小姐您好:

我很遺憾要通知您我將無法在您 4 月 23 日的社區中心活動上做理財管理的演講。那天我有緊急的公務必須出席。我不想讓您的參加者失望,所以我已經安排了我的同事代替我。我可以保證他非常有資格擔任此事,因為他在這個主題上所教授的課程和著述相當豐富。詳情如附件。

我很抱歉造成此情況。我確信這個活動一定會辦成功。如果還有其他任何方面我能幫得上忙的話,請不要客氣,儘管告訴我。

喬瑟夫・史汀茲
敬上

NEWS DAILY

Special Event at Jowel Community Center

By Eve Sanders, Special Correspondent

It was a pleasure to hear Wazir Sanjrani speak at the April 23 financial planning event at the Jowel Community Center. This highly accomplished investor took complex topics such as stocks, bonds, and mutual funds, and simplified them so that everyone could understand. He did this repeatedly and in a friendly way, making the talk not only informative but pleasant.

He also explained clearly how people could slowly grow their money starting with just a low sum. This was encouraging, since most of the attendees were simple working men and women. I think all of the attendees also appreciated the fact that Mr. Sanjrani allowed a full one-hour question and answer session.

However, I believe the audiovisual system of the center could benefit from renovation. Several times, it faded out and it was difficult to understand what the speaker was saying.

每日新聞
喬維爾社區中心特別活動
特派記者依芙‧桑德絲報導

4 月 23 日我很榮幸地於喬維爾社區所舉辦的理財計畫活動上聆聽了華茲爾‧桑拉尼的演講。這位傑出的投資家將股票、債券、共同基金等複雜的主題化繁為簡,因此每一個人都能理解。他以不厭其煩而又親切的態度進行,使得這場演講不僅極具教育性,同時也令人十分愉快。

他也清楚地解釋民眾如何能以小額的金錢開始慢慢地增加財富。這相當激勵人心,因為在場大多數的與會者都只是普通的上班族。我想現場的聽眾們也都非常感謝桑拉尼先生保留了整整一小時開放問答互動。

然而,我認為該中心的視聽系統若能加以修繕會更好。有好幾次系統逐漸地沒有聲音,以至於很難聽懂講者在說什麼。

Vocabulary

- [ ] **tip** [tɪp] 名 提示;訣竅
- [ ] **public** [`pʌblɪk] 名(前加 the)民眾
- [ ] **institution** [ˌɪnstə`tjuʃən] 名 機構
- [ ] **stock** [stɑk] 名 股票;股份
- [ ] **bond** [bɑnd] 名 債券
- [ ] **option** [`ɑpʃən] 名 選擇(的自由)
- [ ] **assure** [ə`ʃur] 動 保證
- [ ] **I regret to inform you (that) ...** 我很遺憾要通知你……
- [ ] **matter** [`mætə] 名 事情;問題
- [ ] **let down ...** 使……失望
- [ ] **attendee** [əˈtɛndi] 名 出席者
- [ ] **colleague** [`kɑlig] 名 同事
- [ ] **take someone's place** 代替某人
- [ ] **qualified** [`kwɑlə.faɪd] 形 合格的
- [ ] **extensively** [ɪk`stɛnsɪvlɪ] 副 廣泛地
- [ ] **attachment** [ə`tætʃmənt] 名 附件
- [ ] **work out** 順利進行
- [ ] **Please do not hesitate to do ...** 別客氣,請儘管做……
- [ ] **correspondent** [ˌkɔrɪ`spɑndənt] 名 特派記者
- [ ] **accomplished** [ə`kɑmplɪʃt] 形 熟練的
- [ ] **complex** [`kɑmplɛks] 形 複雜的
- [ ] **simplify** [`sɪmplə.faɪ] 動 簡化
- [ ] **so that S can ...** 好讓 S 可以……
- [ ] **repeatedly** [rɪ`pitɪdlɪ] 副 一再地
- [ ] **informative** [ɪn`fɔrmətɪv] 形 教育性的;有益的
- [ ] **sum** [sʌm] 名 金額
- [ ] **appreciate** [ə`priʃɪ.et] 動 感謝
- [ ] **the fact that ...** ……的事實
- [ ] **audiovisual** [`ɔdɪo`vɪʒuəl] 形 視聽的
- [ ] **renovation** [ˌrɛnə`veʃən] 名 修繕

試題	試題翻譯	答案與解析

196

What information is NOT mentioned in the notice?

(A) Photo IDs
(B) Participant registration
(C) Refreshment items
(D) Event location

下列哪一項資訊在通知中「未」被提及？

(A) 附照片的身分證
(B) 參加者註冊事宜
(C) 茶點項目
(D) 活動地點

正解 **(A)**

面對「NOT 題」就用刪去法解。通知裡標題的 17 Lakeland Street 為選項 (D)，Tea, coffee and snacks provided 為選項 (C)，Please visit the Web site above to register. 則為選項 (B)。文中未被提及的只有選項 (A)。

197

What is indicated about Wazir Sanjrani?

(A) He updated a Web site.
(B) He earned speaker fees.
(C) He works at a bank.
(D) He replaced a presenter.

關於華茲爾‧桑拉尼，下列何者為正確敘述？

(A) 他更新了網站。
(B) 他賺取了講演費。
(C) 他在銀行工作。
(D) 他代替了一位演講人。

正解 **(D)**

從新聞報導開頭的 It was a pleasure to hear Wazir Sanjrani speak 得知，華茲爾‧桑拉尼是在活動上講演的人物。然而通知裡寫道講師為喬瑟夫‧史汀茲，且由電子郵件第一段的 I have arranged a colleague of mine to take my place. 可知，原本預定由喬瑟夫‧史汀茲出任講演，但是後來華茲爾‧桑拉尼代替他上場，故本題選 (D)。

198

What is indicated about the event?

(A) The main topic of the session was changed.
(B) The payment to sign up was increased.
(C) Entrance to the location was unrestricted.
(D) The question and answer time was extended.

關於此活動，下列何者為正確敘述？

(A) 會議主題有變更。
(B) 報名費增加了。
(C) 入場未設限制。
(D) 問答時間延長了。

正解 **(D)**

根據活動通知中提到的 30-Minute Question and Answer Session to follow the talk，問答時間原訂三十分鐘，但對照新聞報導 ... allowed a full one-hour question and answer session.，實際上則延長進行了一小時。故正解為 (D)。

☐ **unrestricted** [ˌʌnrɪˈstrɪktɪd] 形 不受限制的

199

In the article, what does Ms. Sanders say the speaker did well?

(A) He summarized his financial accomplishments.
(B) He reviewed the best financial markets.
(C) He put difficult topics into plain terms.
(D) He made individual investment portfolios.

在文章中，桑德絲小姐說講者哪一點做得很好？

(A) 他總結了他的理財成就。
(B) 他針對最好的金融市場做出評論。
(C) 他用簡易的話來說明艱深的主題。
(D) 他做了個人的投資組合。

正解 **(C)**

桑德絲小姐為新聞的撰文者。從報導第一段的 This highly accomplished investor took complex topics ...，and simplified them so that everyone could understand. 即可知，選項 (C) 是正確答案。

☐ **summarize** [ˈsʌməˌraɪz] 動 總結；概括
☐ **accomplishment** [əˈkɑmplɪʃmənt] 名 成就
☐ **put A into B** 將 A 改變成 B 狀態
☐ **term** [tɜm] 名 措詞；說話的方式
☐ **investment portfolio** 投資組合

200

What problem is mentioned in the article?

(A) Attendees were fewer than expected.
(B) Some equipment was defective.
(C) Some topics were omitted.
(D) Financial analyses were unclear.

文章中提到了什麼問題？

(A) 參加者比預期的少。
(B) 有些設備出現瑕疵。
(C) 有些主題被遺漏。
(D) 財務分析不清楚。

正解 **(B)**

關於活動上發生的問題記述在報導的第三段，其中提到視聽設備不甚理想，因此選項 (B) 為正解。注意，some equipment 就是指文中的 audiovisual system，而 defective 則是「有缺陷的；不完美的」之意。

☐ **omit** [oˈmɪt] 動 遺漏；省略

解答一覽表

題號	正解	題號	正解	題號	正解	題號	正解	題號	正解
1	D	41	C	81	D	121	C	161	C
2	A	42	D	82	C	122	B	162	B
3	A	43	B	83	C	123	D	163	C
4	D	44	B	84	B	124	B	164	B
5	B	45	A	85	D	125	C	165	D
6	C	46	B	86	A	126	C	166	C
7	B	47	C	87	A	127	A	167	C
8	B	48	B	88	B	128	A	168	D
9	A	49	D	89	B	129	C	169	A
10	C	50	B	90	A	130	A	170	A
11	B	51	C	91	C	131	A	171	D
12	A	52	A	92	B	132	D	172	D
13	C	53	C	93	A	133	B	173	D
14	A	54	A	94	A	134	B	174	A
15	A	55	D	95	B	135	C	175	B
16	C	56	B	96	A	136	D	176	A
17	B	57	C	97	B	137	C	177	B
18	B	58	A	98	B	138	A	178	D
19	C	59	B	99	C	139	D	179	A
20	C	60	B	100	D	140	C	180	D
21	B	61	D	101	B	141	B	181	C
22	C	62	C	102	D	142	D	182	D
23	A	63	B	103	A	143	B	183	B
24	C	64	D	104	D	144	B	184	C
25	A	65	C	105	B	145	D	185	A
26	C	66	A	106	D	146	A	186	D
27	A	67	D	107	D	147	B	187	B
28	B	68	C	108	A	148	B	188	A
29	C	69	B	109	B	149	D	189	C
30	A	70	D	110	C	150	A	190	D
31	C	71	C	111	A	151	D	191	B
32	B	72	B	112	D	152	C	192	C
33	D	73	D	113	B	153	C	193	A
34	A	74	A	114	C	154	D	194	A
35	C	75	C	115	A	155	C	195	A
36	A	76	B	116	D	156	C	196	D
37	C	77	A	117	B	157	B	197	A
38	D	78	C	118	C	158	D	198	A
39	D	79	A	119	B	159	D	199	B
40	B	80	A	120	B	160	C	200	D

試題與翻譯	答案與解析

1

(A) The man is entering a building.
(B) The man is using a vending machine.
(C) The man is looking for a parking lot.
(D) The man is standing beside the road.

(A) 男子正進入大樓。
(B) 男子在使用販賣機。
(C) 男子在找停車場。
(D) 男子站在路旁。

正解 (D) 人物動作

男子正將硬幣投入停車計時錶裡，但是他並非在使用選項 (B) vending machine。他也不是在找 parking lot，因此選項 (C) 亦不恰當。圖中的男子正站在路旁並非正進入大樓，故選項 (A) 亦錯誤。本題正確答案是 (D)。注意，多益測驗的考點通常不會落在像「投幣」般細微的「動作」，而大多會問如「站立著」般簡單的「狀態」。

□ **vending machine** 自動販賣機
□ **parking lot** 停車場

2

(A) A clock is attached to the building.
(B) A clock is lying on its face.
(C) An alarm clock's hands are turning.
(D) A clock hand has been taken off the wall.

(A) 時鐘安裝在建築物上。
(B) 時鐘正面向下平擺著。
(C) 鬧鐘的指針在轉。
(D) 時鐘的指針從牆上被拿掉了。

正解 (A) 事物狀態

照片中的時鐘掛在建築物的牆壁上，正確說明此狀態的選項 (A) 為正解。而時鐘並非平擺，因此選項 (B) 不恰當。另，一聽到 alarm clock（時鐘）這個主詞時，就知道選項 (C) 錯誤。最後，照片裡的時鐘仍有時針，所以選項 (D) 也不正確。

□ **attach** [əˋtætʃ] 動 附上；貼上
□ **hand** [hænd] 名（鐘錶等的）指針

3

(A) They're by a post.
(B) They're under a tree.
(C) They're in a building.
(D) They're in a driveway.

(A) 她們在柱子旁。
(B) 她們在樹下。
(C) 她們在大樓裡。
(D) 她們在車道上。

正解 (A) 人物與環境關係

照片中兩位女子站在看起來像是路燈的「柱子」旁，故選項 (A) 正確。注意，post 除了指「崗位」、「職位」之外，也有「柱子」的意思。而兩位女子並非站在樹下，而且也身處屋外，因此選項 (B) 與 (C) 皆非正解。此外，她們也不是站在車道上，所以選項 (D) 也不適當。

□ **driveway** [ˋdraɪv͵we] 名 私人車道

試題與翻譯	答案與解析

4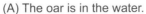

(A) The oar is in the water.
(B) Water is being drained from the boat.
(C) A hole is being drilled.
(D) The boat is tied up.

(A) 船槳在水裡。
(B) 水正從船裡被排出。
(C) 有人正在鑽洞。
(D) 船是綁著固定住的。

正解 (D) 事物狀態

照片中的小船被纜繩綁住，所以正確答案是 (D)。船槳是在小船上，而即便船中有一個看起來像是洞的構造，也沒有正在排水，故 (A) 與 (B) 皆不適當。另，並沒有人在鑿洞，因此 (C) 亦不正確。

- □ **oar** [or] 名 船槳
- □ **drain** [dren] 動 排出（液體）；使流出
- □ **tie up** 繫住；使停泊

5

(A) The woman is opening a cabinet drawer.
(B) The woman is taking out a file.
(C) The woman is folding paper.
(D) The woman is crossing her fingers.

(A) 女子正在打開櫃子的抽屜。
(B) 女子正在取出檔案。
(C) 女子正在折紙。
(D) 女子正在祈求幸運。

正解 (B) 人物動作

照片中的女子正從抽屜裡取出文件，故正解為選項 (B)。圖中抽屜已經打開，而並非她「正在」打開抽屜，故選項 (A) 並不適當。選項 (C) 與 (D) 則是利用照片裡看得到的 paper 和 fingers 來誤導答題。

- □ **cabinet** [ˋkæbənɪt] 名 櫃子
- □ **drawer** [ˋdrɔə] 名 抽屜
- □ **fold** [fold] 動 折疊
- □ **cross one's fingers** 交叉手指（祈求幸運；祈禱成功）

6

(A) They're operating an oven.
(B) They're selling baked goods.
(C) They're working opposite each other.
(D) They're putting bread on shelves.

(A) 他們正在操作烤箱。
(B) 他們在賣烘焙食品。
(C) 他們面對面在工作。
(D) 他們正在將麵包上架。

正解 (C) 人物動作

照片中的兩人面對著面正在工作中，所以正確答案是選項 (C)。注意，千萬不要被相關的字眼 oven、baked goods、putting bread on shelves 等誤導，只要不是照片裡人物所做的「動作」都不是正解。

- □ **baked goods** 烘焙食品
- □ **opposite** [ˋɑpəzɪt] 介 在對面

第 2 回完全解析

PART 1

066-071

試題與翻譯	答案與解析

7 M 🇨🇦 W 🇬🇧

M：Where is the film showing?
W：(A) Yes, I really like that show.
(B) At the Roxy Theater downtown.
(C) Tomorrow evening at 7:30.

M：電影在哪裡上映？
W：(A) 對，我真的很喜歡那個節目。
(B) 在市中心的羅克西戲院。
(C) 明天晚上七點半。

正解 (B) Where 疑問句

5W1H 問句不能以 Yes 回答，所以選項 (A) 一開始就應排除。回答「時間」的選項 (C) 也不恰當。只有具體回答「電影上映之處」的選項 (B) 才是正解。

□ **downtown** [ˌdaʊnˈtaʊn] 名 鬧區

---

8 M 🇨🇦 M 🇦🇺

M：You're from the local office, aren't you?
M：(A) I'll locate the officer.
(B) No, headquarters.
(C) Great, it does look official.

M：你是從地方分處來的，不是嗎？
M：(A) 我會找到幹事。
(B) 不是，是從總部。
(C) 好極了，看起來的確很正式。

正解 (B) 附加問句

這是「……，不是嗎？」，再次確認疑問的「附加問句」。選項 (A) 試圖以 officer 與 office 混淆，而選項 (C) 則以 official 來混淆 office。只有回答 No, headquarters.（不，是從總部。）的選項 (B) 最適當。

□ **locate** [loˈket] 動 找出
□ **official** [əˈfɪʃəl] 形 官方的；正式的

---

9 M 🇦🇺 W 🇺🇸

M：What did Mr. Kamal talk with Barbara about?
W：(A) Our year-end report.
(B) They met for about an hour.
(C) Yes, I talked to them about it.

M：卡馬先生和芭芭拉談了些什麼？
W：(A) 我們的年終報告。
(B) 他們會面了大約一個小時。
(C) 是的，我跟他們談過了。

正解 (A) What 疑問句

題目問「談了些什麼？」，選項 (B) 雖然與題目一樣，都用了 about，但卻不是回答「談話內容」，故非正解。選項 (C) 雖然出現了 talk 此動詞，但以 Yes 回答 5W1H 問句並不恰當。只有明確回答「談話內容」的選項 (A) 為正解。

□ **year-end** [ˈjɪrˌɛnd] 形 年終會計結算的；年底的

---

10 W 🇺🇸 M 🇦🇺

W：When is the summer sale supposed to begin?
M：(A) Yes, it's some kind of sale, isn't it?
(B) 17 percent off everything.
(C) It's still being decided.

W：夏季拍賣應該會在什麼時候展開？
M：(A) 是的，那是某種拍賣，不是嗎？
(B) 全面降價 17%。
(C) 還在決定中。

正解 (C) When 疑問句

題目問的是「時間」。選項 (A) 雖然和題目一樣也包含了 sale 此單字，但是答非所問。另，題目問的不是「折扣數」，因此選項 (B) 亦非正解。只有回答「還在決定中」的選項 (C) 為正解。

□ **be supposed to do** 應該要……
□ **decide** [dɪˈsaɪd] 動 決定

---

11 M 🇨🇦 W 🇬🇧

M：Was Marla given the new supervisory position?
W：(A) She's worked here about a year.
(B) Yes, hadn't you heard?
(C) Because of the higher pay.

M：瑪拉有沒有獲得新的主管職位？
W：(A) 她已經在這裡工作了一年左右。
(B) 有，你沒聽說嗎？
(C) 因為薪水比較高。

正解 (B) be 動詞疑問句

就「瑪拉有沒有獲得新的主管職位？」的問句而言，以 Yes, hadn't you heard?（有，你沒聽說嗎？）反問的選項 (B) 最適當。選項 (A) 利用容易與 new supervisory position 產生聯想的 work 來誤導，不可選；而題目問的並不是「理由」，所以選項 (C) 也不正確。

□ **supervisory** [ˌsupɚˈvaɪzərɪ] 形 管理的；監督的

試題與翻譯	答案與解析

12 M 🇦🇺 W 🇬🇧

M : Has Bill asked you about your new job?
W : (A) Not yet.
   (B) It's in Sales.
   (C) I'll start next week.

M：比爾有沒有問過妳新工作的事？
W：(A) 還沒。
   (B) 是在業務部。
   (C) 我將從下星期開始。

正解 (A) 一般動詞疑問句

針對 Has Bill asked you about ...? 這種現在完成式的題目，回答 Not yet. 的選項 (A) 即為正解。由於問的不是「在哪個部門服務」，故選項 (B) 不適當。此外，也不是在問「什麼時候開始」，因此選項 (C) 亦非正解。

13 W 🇺🇸 M 🇦🇺

W : Do you want me to have Mr. Jackson call you when he returns later today?
M : (A) I'd like to return the item.
   (B) Yes, I'll be back tomorrow.
   (C) No thanks, I'll call again tomorrow.

W：你要不要我請傑克森先生今天稍晚回來時打電話給你？
M：(A) 我想退貨。
   (B) 是的，我明天將會回來。
   (C) 不用了，謝謝。我明天會再打來。

正解 (C) 邀請、提議

Do you want me to ...? 這個句型用以表達提議，就「是否需要請傑克森先生打電話」此問句，以「不用了……我明天會再來電。」婉拒的選項 (C) 即為正解。其他選項全都牛頭不對馬嘴。

14 M 🇨🇦 W 🇬🇧

M : Why are you skipping your break to stay in the office?
W : (A) I have to finish this report.
   (B) I stayed for breakfast.
   (C) Yes, he's still at the office.

M：妳為什麼不休息要留在辦公室？
W：(A) 我得把這份報告做完。
   (B) 我留下來吃早餐。
   (C) 對，他還在辦公室。

正解 (A) Why 疑問句

本題的 Why 是在問「理由」。選項 (B) 利用 breakfast、選項 (C) 利用 office 來引誘誤答。另，選項 (C) 以 Yes 來回答 Why 問句，也是選項 (C) 不正確的原因之一。「必須完成報告」可視為「不休息」的一種「理由」，所以正確答案是選項 (A)。

□ **skip** [skɪp] 動 略過

15 W 🇬🇧 M 🇨🇦

W : Would you like to stop and rest for a while?
M : (A) Good idea.
   (B) She's in the restroom.
   (C) The next stop's mine.

W：你要不要停下來休息一下？
M：(A) 好主意。
   (B) 她在洗手間。
   (C) 我下一站就到了。

正解 (A) 邀請、提議

Would you like to ...? 意指「你要不要做某件事？」，是一種客氣地提出建議的詢問句。回答 Good idea.（好主意。）表示同意的選項 (A) 為正解。選項 B 以 restroom 來混淆 rest，選項 (C) 則以 stop's 來混淆 stop。

□ **rest** [rɛst] 動 休息
□ **for a while** 暫時；一會兒
□ **restroom** ['rɛst.rum] 名 洗手間
□ **stop** [stɑp] 名 停車站牌

16 W 🇬🇧 M 🇦🇺

W : I got my accounting certification yesterday.
M : (A) After I did well on the test.
   (B) Yes, you can count on it.
   (C) Congratulations!

W：我昨天拿到我的會計證照了。
M：(A) 在我考試拿了高分之後。
   (B) 是的，你可以指望它。
   (C) 恭喜！

正解 (C) 直述句

對於對方說的「取得會計師資格」，回以 Congratulations!（恭喜！）給予祝賀的 (C) 即為正解。選項 (B) 試圖利用 count 的發音讓考生與 accounting 產生混淆。

□ **certification** [.sɝtɪfə'keʃən] 名 資格；證明
□ **count on** 依賴；指望

試題與翻譯	答案與解析

17 W🇬🇧 M🇦🇺

W：How can we reduce costs?
M：(A) It costs 32 dollars.
　　(B) Let's discuss that later.
　　(C) By about 18 percent.

W：我們要怎麼降低成本？
M：(A) 這要 32 元。
　　(B) 我們等下再討論那件事。
　　(C) 大概是 18%。

正解 (B) How 疑問句

本題是以 How 詢問如何降低成本 (costs) 的「方法」。選項 (A) 以動詞 costs 為陷阱，試圖混淆考生。題目不是在問「數量」，所以選項 (C) 的 By about ... 亦不正確。只有回答「我們等下再討論那件事。」的選項 (B) 才是正解。

☐ **reduce** [rɪˋdjus] 動 減少
☐ **cost** [kɔst] 名 費用
　　　　　　動 花費（多少金額）

18 M🇨🇦 W🇬🇧

M：How about something cool to drink?
W：(A) It's only 4 degrees Celsius.
　　(B) Sounds nice.
　　(C) Thanks, it was refreshing.

M：喝點冷飲怎麼樣？
W：(A) 只有攝氏四度。
　　(B) 聽起來不錯。
　　(C) 謝謝，很提神。

正解 (B) How 疑問句

這是以 How about ...?（你覺得……如何？）提出「建議」的問句。對於「來點冷飲如何？」的建議，以 Sounds nice.（聽起來不錯。）來表示贊同的選項 (B) 為正解。注意，不要因為聽到選項 (A) 的 4 degrees 就與 cool 產生混淆而誤答。選項 (C) Thanks 之後的內容與題目不符，因此亦不正確。

☐ **degree** [dɪˋgri] 名 度數；程度
☐ **refreshing** [rɪˋfrɛʃɪŋ] 形 清涼的；提神的

19 W🇺🇸 M🇦🇺

W：Who put all these papers on my desk?
M：(A) Oh, did you?
　　(B) No, they're hard to describe.
　　(C) Probably Beth.

W：是誰把這一大堆文件放在我桌上的？
M：(A) 噢，你有嗎？
　　(B) 不，它們難以形容。
　　(C) 八成是貝絲。

正解 (C) Who 疑問句

Who ...? 是詢問「誰」的句型。以疑問詞開頭的問句不能以 Yes-No 回答，所以選項 (B) 可先排除。選項 (A) 的附加問句亦不知所云。只有回答出「人名」的選項 (C) 才是正解。

☐ **describe** [dɪˋskraɪb] 動 描述；形容

20 W🇬🇧 M🇨🇦

W：Aren't you going to take the shuttle bus back to the hotel?
M：(A) It only takes about 10 minutes.
　　(B) I reserved a suite.
　　(C) No, I'll just walk.

W：你不搭接駁車回飯店嗎？
M：(A) 只要十分鐘左右。
　　(B) 我訂了一間套房。
　　(C) 不了，我用走的就可以了。

正解 (C) 否定疑問句

本題是以 Aren't you ...?（你不……嗎？）向對方確認行動的否定疑問句。由於問的是「你不搭接駁車嗎？」，因此回答「不，我用走的。」的選項 (C) 為正解。選項 (A) 以 take 的另一用法、選項 (B) 以容易與 hotel 產生聯想的 reserved 和 suite 來引誘誤答。

☐ **shuttle bus** 接駁車
☐ **reserve** [rɪˋzɜv] 動 預約；預定
☐ **suite** [swit] 名 套房

21 M🇦🇺 W🇺🇸

M：How soon can I get an update on our sales this month?
W：(A) It went well.
　　(B) Give me an hour.
　　(C) Uh ... it's not for sale.

M：我多快才可以知道我們這個月業績的最新數字？
W：(A) 進行得很順利。
　　(B) 給我一個小時。
　　(C) 呃……那是非賣品。

正解 (B) How 疑問句

這是以 How soon ...? 詢問「多快」的題目。選項 (A) 不知所云；選項 (C) 試圖以 sale 造成與題目中的 sales 混淆。選項 (B) Give me an hour. 意指「只要給我一小時，我就能給您最新資訊」，是最適當的回應。

☐ **update** [ʌpˋdet] 名 最新資訊

| 試題與翻譯 | 答案與解析 |

22　M🇦🇺　W🇬🇧

M: Who will take over the research and development division during Mr. Jang's absence next month?
W: (A) I haven't asked about any takeover.
　　(B) He's been in charge for three years.
　　(C) Ashley Garner would be ideal.

M：簡先生下個月不在的時候，由誰來帶研發部？
W：(A) 我沒有問有關收購的事。　　　　(B) 他已經執掌三年了。
　　(C) 艾希莉．嘉納會是理想的人選。

正解 (C)　Who 疑問句

選項 (A) 試圖利用名詞 takeover 與題目裡的動詞 take over 來魚目混珠。選項 (B) 則利用 be in charge 這個容易與題目裡的 take over 產生聯想的片語誘導誤答。只有具體回答「人名」的選項 (C) 才是正解。
□ **take over** 接手（工作等）
□ **research and development division** 研究開發部
□ **takeover** [ˋtekˏovɚ] 名 接收；收購
□ **in charge** 負責

23　M🇨🇦　W🇺🇸

M: You haven't filed that report yet.
W: (A) Sorry, I've been too busy.
　　(B) Yes, it's very boring.
　　(C) There's a reporter outside.

M：妳還沒提出那份報告。
W：(A) 抱歉，我太忙了。
　　(B) 對，非常無聊。
　　(C) 外面有個記者。

正解 (A)　直述句

對於「妳還沒提出那份報告。」這個稍微帶有責備語氣的平敘句而言，以 Sorry, I've been too busy.（抱歉，我太忙了。）解釋的選項 (A) 為合理回應。選項 (B) 答非所問。選項 (C) 則試圖以 reporter 來與 report 產生混淆。

□ **file** [faɪl] 動 歸檔；提出
□ **boring** [ˋborɪŋ] 形 無聊的

24　M🇦🇺　M🇨🇦

M: Why didn't you take the 12:15 train?
M: (A) About 12 to 15 hours to get there.
　　(B) Yes, we trained there, too.
　　(C) I changed my plans.

M：你為什麼沒搭十二點十五分的火車？
M：(A) 到那裡要十二到十五個小時左右。
　　(B) 是的，我們也在那裡受訓。
　　(C) 我改變了計畫。

正解 (C)　Why 疑問句

題目問的不是「要花多久時間」，所以選項 (A) 不恰當。同時，選項 (A) 也試圖以 12 和 15 這兩個也出現在題目裡的數字來引誘上當。而選項 (B) 試圖以 train 的另一個意思來誘導答題。選項 (C) 以「計畫變更」作為「沒搭火車的理由」是合理的回應，故為正解。

□ **train** [tren] 動 訓練；受訓

25　W🇬🇧　W🇺🇸

W: Where are the new employees supposed to go for orientation?
W: (A) The main auditorium in the west wing.
　　(B) Your presentation proposals are fine.
　　(C) It's a good way to meet new co-workers.

W：新進員工應該要去哪裡參加職前說明？
W：(A) 西側樓的大會堂。
　　(B) 你的簡報提案還不錯。
　　(C) 這是認識新同事的好方法。

正解 (A)　Where 疑問句

Where 問的是「地點」，故只有具體回答出「地點」的選項 (A) 是正確答案。選項 (B)、(C) 中含有 presentation 和 co-workers 這兩個單字，容易讓人與題目裡的 orientation 和 employees 產生聯想，但是卻都答非所問，因此皆不適當。

□ **orientation** [ˏorɪɛnˋteʃən] 名（對新生或新進人員的）情況介紹
□ **auditorium** [ˏɔdɪˋtorɪəm] 名 大廳；禮堂
□ **wing** [wɪŋ] 名（建築物的）側棟；廂房

26　W🇺🇸　W🇬🇧

W: Would you like a blueberry muffin or a banana one?
W: (A) Yes, a blue bandanna.
　　(B) They are delicious.
　　(C) Hmm ... either would be fine.

W：妳要藍莓鬆餅還是香蕉鬆餅？
W：(A) 對，藍色的大手帕。
　　(B) 它們很好吃。
　　(C) 嗯……都可以。

正解 (C)　邀請、提議

一般而言，A or B 這種二選一的問題應該明確地回答其中一個，但是本題正解 (C) 的 either would be fine（都可以）也是一種常見的答法。選項 (A) 利用 blueberry 和 banana 造成與 blue bandanna 的混淆，而選項 (B) 則利用 delicious 這個容易聯想到食物的單字來誘導誤答。另請注意，如選項 (C) 當中的 Hmm ... 的發語詞在新制多益考題中經常出現，考生不妨多加留意。

第 2 回完全解析

PART 2

試題與翻譯	答案與解析

27 M 🇨🇦 W 🇬🇧

M : What attracts you to working the night shift?
W : (A) Nothing in particular.
　　(B) Yes, that track's being worked on.
　　(C) Until 11:00 at night.

M : 是什麼吸引妳去上夜班的？
W : (A) 沒什麼特別的原因。
　　(B) 對，那條鐵道正在施工。
　　(C) 到晚上十一點為止。

正解 (A)　What 疑問句

選項 (B) 利用 track's 的發音與題目裡的 attracts 混淆。選項 (C) 也不正確，因為題目問的不是「到什麼時候？」，而是「理由」。只有回答「沒什麼特別原因」的選項 (A) 才是正解。

☐ **attract** [ə`trækt] 動 吸引
☐ **night shift** 夜班
☐ **in particular** 特別地
☐ **track** [træk] 名 小徑；軌道

28 M 🇦🇺 W 🇺🇸

M : Hasn't the deadline for the project passed?
W : (A) We project 4 percent.
　　(B) No, we've still got 2 days.
　　(C) Line up here, please.

M : 案子的截止期限還沒過嗎？
W : (A) 我們預估 4%。
　　(B) 還沒，我們還有兩天的時間。
　　(C) 請在這裡排隊。

正解 (B)　否定疑問句

本題為否定疑問句，問答方式與一般 Yes-No 問句相同。只有回答 No, we've still got 2 days. 的選項 (B) 為正解。選項 (A) 中的 project 和選項 (C) 中的 line 目的都在混淆視聽，答題時要格外注意。

☐ **deadline** [`dɛd.lain] 名 截止期限
☐ **project** [`pradʒɛkt] 名 方案；企劃
　　　　　 [prə`dʒɛkt] 動 預計；推斷
☐ **line up** 排隊

29 W 🇬🇧 W 🇺🇸

W : Could you show me how to work the copier, please?
W : (A) I bought a copy of that book yesterday.
　　(B) Tea, not coffee.
　　(C) Sorry, I'm on my way out.

W : 能不能麻煩你告訴我影印機要怎麼用？
W : (A) 我昨天買了一冊那本書。
　　(B) 茶，不是咖啡。
　　(C) 抱歉，我正要出門去。

正解 (C)　How 的間接問句

Could you show me how to ...? 的意思是「能否教我如何……？」，是一種禮貌性的問句。回答 Sorry, I'm on my way out.（抱歉，我正要出門去。）來拒絕對方請求的選項 (C) 為正解。選項 (A) 以 copy、選項 (B) 以 coffee 的發音試圖製造與 copier 的混淆。

☐ **copier** [`kapɪɚ] 名 影印機
☐ **copy** [`kapɪ] 名 (書的) 一冊
☐ **on one's way out** 正要出門

30 W 🇺🇸 M 🇨🇦

W : Are you going to read through even the minor details of the contract yourself?
M : (A) No, a specialist will.
　　(B) I'll contact them later.
　　(C) It's for three years.

W : 你連合約的小細節都要自己看過嗎？
M : (A) 不會的，會由一位專家來做。
　　(B) 等一下我會聯絡他們。
　　(C) 是三年的合約。

正解 (A)　Yes-No 問句

本題為一 Yes-No 問句，以 No 起始的選項 (A) No, a specialist will.（不會的，會由一位專家來做。）即為正解。選項 (B) 利用與題目中 contract 發音類似的 contact 來混淆視聽。而題目問的不是「期間」，所以選項 (C) 也不恰當。

☐ **read through** 仔細看過
☐ **detail** [`ditel] 名 細節
☐ **contract** [`kantrækt] 名 契約

31 W 🇬🇧 M 🇦🇺

W : When's the earliest we could pick up the office supplies?
M : (A) I've picked up the list.
　　(B) I always get up early.
　　(C) Next Tuesday, I think.

W : 我們最早可以在什麼時候拿到辦公用品？
M : (A) 我已經拿到清單了。
　　(B) 我一向早起。
　　(C) 我想下星期二吧。

正解 (C)　When 疑問句

小心別掉入句中含有 pick up 的選項 (A) 這個陷阱中，也不要誤選了試圖以 early 來混淆 earliest 的選項 (B)。只有回答具體時間「下星期二」的選項 (C) 才是正解。

☐ **pick up** 拾起；獲得

PART 3

 092-093　W 🇬🇧　M-1 🇨🇦　M-2 🇦🇺

題目	題目翻譯
Questions 32 through 34 refer to the following conversation with three speakers. W : Steve, can you send these documents to Michelle in Dublin, please? M-1 : Sure. Are they important? W : Yeah. I need her to review the graphics before I go any further with this project. M-2 : Actually, you can give them to her in person, Ms. Grady. W : What do you mean, Ted? M-2 : She's in a meeting on the fifth floor at the moment. W : Oh, I didn't realize she was here in our London office. No wonder she didn't answer my calls. Then, Steve, could you ask her to drop by my office later, please? I'm on a tight deadline. M-1 : No problem. M-2 : The meeting's due to end in a few minutes. She's reserved a seat on the train for Brussels this evening and then she's going to Paris, so now's a good time to see her.	第 32 到 34 題請參照下面這段三人對話。 W ：史提夫，能不能麻煩你把這些文件發送給都柏林的蜜雪兒？ M-1：好的。這些文件很重要嗎？ W ：是啊。我需要她在我進一步進行這項案子前先看一下圖示。 M-2：其實妳可以直接拿給她，葛蕾迪小姐。 W ：什麼意思？泰德。 M-2：她現在正好在五樓開會。 W ：噢，我不曉得她人在我們倫敦事務所這兒，難怪她沒有回我電話。那麼，史提夫，能不能麻煩你請她晚點來我辦公室一趟？我的截止時間很趕。 M-1：沒問題。 M-2：會議預計再過幾分鐘會結束。她已經訂了今天晚上去布魯塞爾的火車票，接著她會去巴黎，所以現在是見她的好時機。

Vocabulary

☐ **review** [rɪˋvju] 勔 檢查；複審　☐ **graphics** [ˋɡræfɪks] 图 圖像（複數形）　☐ **in person** 親自　☐ **at the moment** 此刻
☐ **realize** [ˋrɪə.laɪz] 勔 發現　☐ **no wonder ...** 難怪……　☐ **drop by** 順道拜訪　☐ **tight** [taɪt] 晤 時間緊湊的
☐ **deadline** [ˋdɛd.laɪn] 勔 截止期限　☐ **be due to *do* ...** 預計做……

試題	試題翻譯	答案與解析
32 Where are the speakers? (A) In Dublin (B) In London (C) In Brussels (D) In Paris	說話者在哪裡？ (A) 都柏林 (B) 倫敦 (C) 布魯塞爾 (D) 巴黎	正解 **(B)** 從女子提到的 ... I didn't realize she was here in our London office. 可知，蜜雪兒在目前說話者身處的倫敦事務所，故女子與兩位男子三人都在倫敦。正解為 (B)。（即使 PART 3 一開始就是由三人對話的題型，作答時也無須驚慌。）
33 What does the woman want Michelle to do? (A) Send her an e-mail (B) Call her directly (C) Fax her some files (D) Come to see her	女子要蜜雪兒做什麼？ (A) 寄電子郵件給她 (B) 直接打電話給她 (C) 傳真一些檔案給她 (D) 來見她	正解 **(D)** 由女子拜託史提夫 (M-1) 說的 ... could you ask her to drop by my office later, please? 可知，她希望蜜雪兒能前來見她，故本題選 (D)。注意，女子說的 her 指的就是蜜雪兒。
34 What does one of the men say will happen in a few minutes? (A) A conference will end. (B) A train will leave. (C) A deadline will arrive. (D) A project will be launched.	其中一位男子說過幾分鐘會發生什麼事？ (A) 有一場會議會結束。 (B) 有一班火車會出發。 (C) 有一個截止期限會到。 (D) 有一個案子將展開。	正解 **(A)** 答案就在泰德 (M-2) 最後的發言中：The meeting's due to end in a few minutes.，所以正確答案是換句話說的選項 (A) A conference will end.。注意，meeting 與 conference 屬同義字。 ☐ **launch** [lɒntʃ] 勔 使……開始；展開

題目	題目翻譯
Questions 35 through 37 refer to the following conversation.	第 35 到 37 題請參照下面這段對話。
W : Good morning. Welcome to SunCrest Mutual. How can I help you?	W：早安。歡迎光臨日冠互惠。我能為您效勞嗎？
M : I'm going to Thailand on business soon and I'd like to know if I'll be able to use my SunCrest Debit Card there. I prefer to use that over cash or traveler's checks.	M：我即將要去泰國出差，我想知道，我在那裡能不能使用日冠簽帳卡。我比較想用這張卡，而不想用現金或旅行支票。
W : You can use your card overseas to pay for everything from plane tickets to travel insurance. Just look for the SunCrest logo on ATMs and on buildings. Any place you see that, the card is valid.	W：您可以在海外用這張卡購買各種東西，從機票到旅遊險都行。只要尋找有日冠商標的自動櫃員機和大樓，任何一個您看到有它的地方，卡片都能使用。

Vocabulary

- ☐ **debit card** 簽帳卡
- ☐ **prefer A over B** A 與 B 相比，較喜歡 A
- ☐ **overseas** [`ovɚ`siz] 副 在（或向）海外
- ☐ **insurance** [ɪn`ʃʊrəns] 名 保險
- ☐ **valid** [`vælɪd] 形 有效的

試題	試題翻譯	答案與解析
35 Who most likely is the woman? (A) A tour agent (B) An airline clerk (C) A bank representative (D) An insurance salesperson	女子最有可能是誰？ (A) 旅遊公司業務 (B) 航空公司職員 (C) 銀行業務代表 (D) 保險業務員	**正解 (C)** 女子正在為男子說明金融卡可使用的場所與辨別標誌，故四個選項之中只有選項 (C) A bank representative 最適當。 ☐ **tour agent** 旅遊業者
36 What would the man prefer to take on his trip? (A) A debit card (B) A credit card (C) Cash (D) Traveler's checks	男子出差時希望帶上什麼？ (A) 簽帳卡 (B) 信用卡 (C) 現金 (D) 旅行支票	**正解 (A)** 男子提到 I'd like to know if I'll be able to use my SunCrest Debit Card there. I prefer to use that over cash or traveler's checks.，表示他較喜歡使用簽帳卡，因此本題正解為 (A)。
37 What does the SunCrest logo on ATMs and buildings indicate? (A) The brand is popular. (B) The usage fee is low. (C) Debit cards can be used. (D) The machine is new.	自動櫃員機和大樓上有日冠的商標代表什麼？ (A) 該品牌很受歡迎。 (B) 交易手續費很低。 (C) 可使用簽帳卡。 (D) 機器是新的。	**正解 (C)** 女子最後提到 Just look for the SunCrest logo on ATMs and on buildings. Any place you see that, the card is valid.，這段話為解答關鍵。意思是，只要是有該簽帳卡標誌的 ATM 和場所，就能使用卡片，所以正確答案是選項 (C)。 ☐ **usage fee** 使用費

題目	題目翻譯
Questions 38 through 40 refer to the following conversation.	第 38 到 40 題請參照下面這段對話。

W : Excuse me, conductor. Do you know which station is next? I must have fallen asleep after we left Boston.

W：不好意思，乘務員。你知道接下來是哪一站嗎？波士頓站發車後我一定是睡著了。

M : Actually, we just left New York, so we're headed toward Philadelphia as our next major stop, before continuing on to the last stop, Washington, D.C.

M：事實上，我們剛過了紐約，所以正開往下一個主要停靠站費城，接著會繼續開往終點站華盛頓特區。

W : How long will it take us to get to D.C.? About two more hours?

W：我們要多久才會到華盛頓特區？大概再兩個小時嗎？

M : I guess, closer to three, assuming that all this snow on the rail tracks doesn't slow us down.

M：我想差不多要三小時，假設鐵軌上的這一大堆雪沒有讓我們慢下來的話。

Vocabulary

- ☐ **fall asleep** 睡著
- ☐ **actually** [ˋæktʃuəlɪ] 副 實際上
- ☐ **be headed toward ...** 開往……
- ☐ **major** [ˋmedʒɚ] 形 主要的
- ☐ **assuming that ...** 假設……
- ☐ **rail track** 軌道

試題	試題翻譯	答案與解析
38 Where most likely are the speakers? (A) On an airplane (B) On a bus (C) On a ship (D) On a train	說話者最有可能在哪裡？ (A) 飛機上 (B) 公車上 (C) 船上 (D) 火車上	**正解 (D)** 從對話裡的 station 和 rail tracks 等字即可斷定，選項 (D) 為正解。
39 What is the final destination? (A) Philadelphia (B) Boston (C) New York (D) Washington, D.C.	終點站是哪裡？ (A) 費城 (B) 波士頓 (C) 紐約 (D) 華盛頓特區	**正解 (D)** 由男子第一次發言時提到的 ... we're headed toward Philadelphia as our next major stop, before continuing on to the last stop, Washington D.C. 可知，Washington D.C. 為終點站，故正解為 (D)。注意，題目裡的 final destination 換句話說就是對話中的 last stop。 ☐ **final destination** 終點
40 When is the woman likely to reach her destination? (A) In about two hours (B) In about three hours (C) In about four hours (D) In about five hours	女子最有可能在什麼時候到達目的地？ (A) 大約兩個小時後 (B) 大約三個小時後 (C) 大約四個小時後 (D) 大約五個小時後	**正解 (B)** 女子問到華盛頓特區需要多久時間，男子回答 I guess, closer to three，所以答案是選項 (B)。注意，選項 (A) In about two hours 是女子預測的時間，答題時千萬別張冠李戴。

題目	題目翻譯
Questions 41 through 43 refer to the following conversation.	第 41 到 43 題請參照下面這段對話。
W: I hear the workshop schedule for new recruits has been put up. Have you seen it yet?	W：我聽說新進人員研討會的時程已經公布了。你看到了沒？
M: Yes, it's for the week beginning June 25. Each division will hold workshops in different rooms, but the main presentations will be held in Conference Room 21D.	M：看到了，是從 6 月 25 日開始的那週。各部門會在不同的會場辦研討會，但主要的說明會是在 21D 會議室舉行。
W: So do we need to register for them somewhere or submit our names to someone?	W：所以我們得去哪裡登記呢，還是得向誰報名？
M: Yes, we have to confirm we'll be going through our managers by this afternoon. They'll give us brochures containing all the information we need.	M：是的，今天下午之前我們必須透過經理確認我們會去參加。他們會發一本小冊子，裡面包含所有我們需要的資訊。

Vocabulary

- ☐ **workshop** [ˈwɝkˌʃɑp] 名 研討會
- ☐ **recruit** [rɪˈkrut] 名 新進人員
- ☐ **division** [dəˈvɪʒən] 名 部門
- ☐ **conference** [ˈkɑnfərəns] 名 會議
- ☐ **register for** 登記參加……
- ☐ **submit** [səbˈmɪt] 動 提交
- ☐ **confirm** [kənˈfɝm] 動 確認
- ☐ **brochure** [broˈʃʊr] 名 小冊子
- ☐ **contain** [kənˈten] 動 包含

試題	試題翻譯	答案與解析
41 Where most likely are the speakers? (A) At a conference (B) At a presentation (C) At a workplace (D) At a library	說話者最有可能在哪裡？ (A) 會議上 (B) 說明會上 (C) 工作場所 (D) 圖書館裡	**正解 (C)** 兩人正在詳細討論研討會時程，所以這應該是在一般「工作場所」中的對話，正解為選項 (C)。注意，由於話題並非會議或簡報相關的公事，故選項 (A) 與 (B) 並不適當。
42 What will happen on June 25? (A) New employees will start work. (B) A department will relocate. (C) Presentations will end. (D) Training will begin.	6 月 25 日將發生什麼事？ (A) 新進員工要開始上班。 (B) 有一個部門將搬遷。 (C) 簡報會結束。 (D) 訓練會開始。	**正解 (D)** 針對女子提到的新進員工研討會時程，男子說 ... it's for the week beginning June 25，意即新員工的研習開始日期為 6 月 25 日。正解為選項 (D)。 ☐ **department** [dɪˈpartmənt] 名 （公司的）部門 ☐ **relocate** [riˈloket] 動 重新安置；遷移至另一個地方
43 What must the speakers do today? (A) Alter the program schedule (B) Verify attendance (C) Hand in their brochures (D) Go to a conference	說話者今天必須做什麼？ (A) 變更課程的時程 (B) 確認是否參加 (C) 交出他們的小冊子 (D) 參加一場會議	**正解 (B)** 由男子最後提到的 ... we have to confirm we'll be going through our managers by this afternoon 可知，新進員工必須透過經理確認是否參加研習，故本題選 (B)。 ☐ **alter** [ˈɔltɚ] 動 變更 ☐ **verify** [ˈvɛrəˌfaɪ] 動 確認；證實 ☐ **hand in** 提出

題目	題目翻譯
Questions 44 through 46 refer to the following conversation.	第 44 到 46 題請參照下面這段對話。
M : The total will be 25 dollars and 30 cents, please. How would you like to pay?	M：總共是 25 元 30 分，麻煩您。您要怎麼付款？
W : Oh, that's more expensive than I thought. Is that the amount before, or after my store card discount?	W：噢，比我所想的要貴。那是店卡打折前還是打折後的金額？
M : After. You received 10 percent off your purchase. Here it is printed on your receipt.	M：打折後。您享有購買金額的九折。都列印在您的收據上了。
W : Oh, I see. I guess that dress was more than I thought. I'd like to pay by credit card if that's OK.	W：噢，我明白了。我想就是這件洋裝比我想的還要貴。我要刷卡付錢，假如可以的話。

Vocabulary

- **expensive** [ɪkˋspɛnsɪv] 形 昂貴的
- **amount** [əˋmaʊnt] 名 總數
- **discount** [ˋdɪskaʊnt] 名 折扣
- **purchase** [ˋpɝtʃəs] 名 購買
- **receipt** [rɪˋsit] 名 收據
- **guess** [gɛs] 動 猜測；【美】【口】想；認為

試題	試題翻譯	答案與解析
44 What is the woman doing? (A) Returning goods (B) Concluding a transaction (C) Applying for credit (D) Explaining about products	女子在做什麼？ (A) 退貨 (B) 交易結帳 (C) 申請信用 (D) 解說產品	**正解 (B)** 這是在櫃台結帳時的對話。付錢等於「結束交易」，選項 (B) 最符合題目所問的內容。 □ **conclude** [kənˋklud] 動 使……結束 □ **transaction** [trænˋzækʃən] 名 交易 □ **explain** [ɪkˋsplen] 動 解釋；說明
45 How much did the woman save? (A) 10 percent (B) 20 percent (C) 25 percent (D) 30 percent	女子省下了多少錢？ (A) 10% (B) 20% (C) 25% (D) 30%	**正解 (A)** 由男子對女子說的 You received 10 percent off your purchase. 可知，女子享有九折優惠，因此正解為 (A)。
46 What did the woman misunderstand? (A) The credit card limit (B) The item price (C) The location of the store (D) The refund policy	女子誤解了什麼事？ (A) 信用卡的額度 (B) 商品的價錢 (C) 商店的地點 (D) 退款規定	**正解 (B)** 一開始女子因結帳金額高於預期，而嚇了一跳，但是在男子給她做了說明並讓她看了收據之後，女子便說 I guess that dress was more than I thought.，也就是，她低估了洋裝的價錢，因此正解為選項 (B)。 □ **location** [loˋkeʃən] 名 位置；場所 □ **policy** [ˋpɑləsɪ] 名 政策；方針

題目	題目翻譯
Questions 47 through 49 refer to the following conversation.	第 47 到 49 題請參照下面這段對話。

W: As you know, the supplier's still refusing to increase our discount. I've been researching the market online and I think we can get the raw materials we need cheaper elsewhere.

M: That'd be great. We need to reduce costs to the level of our competitors if we're going to survive.

W: Exactly! I'd like us to buy from eastern Europe from now on. I had Ricardo in Operations look at the figures. He confirmed my research. He said we could save up to 32 percent that way.

W：如你所知，供應商還是不願意增加我們的折扣。我上網做過市調，我想我們可以從其他比較便宜的地方購買我們所需要的原料。

M：那太好了。如果我們要生存，就必須把成本降到競爭對手的水準。

W：一點都沒錯！我想從現在起，我們應該向東歐採購。我請營運部的李卡多看過數據，他證實了我的市調結果，他說這樣我們可以省下高達 32% 的費用。

Vocabulary

- **supplier** [sə'plaɪə] 名 供應商
- **refuse to** *do* ... 拒絕做……
- **research** [rɪ'sɜtʃ] 動 名 研究；調查
- **raw material** 原料
- **reduce** [rɪ'djus] 動 減少
- **competitor** [kəm'pɛtətə] 名 競爭對手
- **survive** [sə'vaɪv] 動 存活
- **from now on** 從現在起
- **up to ...** 高達……

試題	試題翻譯	答案與解析
47 What are the speakers mainly discussing? (A) Expanding their market share (B) Offering a discount (C) Lowering expenses (D) Selling new products	說話者主要是在討論什麼？ (A) 擴大市占率 (B) 提供折扣 (C) 降低支出 (D) 販售新產品	**正解 (C)** 說話者雙方明顯在討論如何降低成本。將男子提到的 to reduce costs 換句話說的選項 (C) Lowering expenses 即為正解。 ☐ **expand** [ɪk'spænd] 動 擴大 ☐ **market share** 市占率 ☐ **lower** ['loə] 動 降低；減少
48 Why does the man think that they need to change their supplier? (A) To access better materials (B) To remain competitive (C) To order online (D) To raise product prices	男子為什麼認為需要更換供應商？ (A) 為了取得更好的材料 (B) 為了保持競爭力 (C) 為了上網訂購 (D) 為了提高產品售價	**正解 (B)** 男子同意女子提出的更換供應商的意見之後，便針對該意見提出他的理由：We need to reduce costs to the level of our competitors if we're going to survive.，也就是他認為唯有如此才能與競爭對手抗衡，因此正解為 (B)。
49 What did Ricardo do? (A) Transferred to eastern Europe (B) Simplified operations (C) Saved money (D) Reviewed the data	李卡多做了什麼？ (A) 調任到東歐 (B) 簡化營運 (C) 省錢 (D) 審視資料	**正解 (D)** 答案就在女子最後提到的 I had Ricardo in Operations look at the figures. He confirmed my research.。換言之，李卡多已審視過資料，故本題選 (D) Reviewed the data。 ☐ **transfer to ...** 調職到…… ☐ **simplify** ['sɪmpləˌfaɪ] 動 簡化

題目	題目翻譯
Questions 50 through 52 refer to the following conversation.	第 50 到 52 題請參照下面這段對話。
W: Excuse me, do you have the latest Red Wolf?	W：請問一下，你們有沒有最新的「赤狼」？
M: I'm sorry ma'am, that product won't be released until Friday. Would you like to pre-order one?	M：抱歉，女士，要到星期五才開賣。您要不要預購一支？
W: Um … I'm not sure. I'd like to take a look at it first. I only want it to make calls. So, the simpler, the better.	W：嗯……我不曉得耶。我想先看過。我只是要用它來打電話。所以，愈簡單愈好。
M: Red Wolf comes in a variety of models, from the very basic to the very sophisticated. They can also be upgraded later if you want. I can get some of the previous models out for you to look at if you like.	M：「赤狼」有各種款式，從非常基本的到非常精密的都有。之後如您有需求它們也可以升級。要是您願意的話，我可以拿一些之前的型號出來給您看看。

Vocabulary

☐ **latest** [ˋletɪst] 形 最新的　　☐ **release** [rɪˋlis] 動 發行　　☐ **pre-order** [priˋɔrdɚ] 動 預購商品　　☐ **a variety of ...** 各式各樣的……
☐ **basic** [ˋbesɪk] 形 基本的　　☐ **sophisticated** [səˋfɪstɪˏketɪd] 形 複雜的；精密的　　☐ **upgrade** [ˋʌpˋgred] 動 使升級

試題	試題翻譯	答案與解析
50 What most likely is the Red Wolf? (A) A radio (B) A mobile phone (C) A Web site (D) A television set	「赤狼」最有可能是什麼？ (A) 收音機 (B) 手機 (C) 網站 (D) 電視機	**正解 (B)** 由女子提到的 I only want it to make calls. 可知，這是「打電話的工具」，所以選項 (B) A mobile phone 為最合理的答案。
51 What does the man offer to do for the woman? (A) Exchange a model (B) Upgrade a component (C) Show her some products (D) Order a product	男子提議為女子做什麼？ (A) 更換型號 (B) 升級某個零件 (C) 展示一些產品 (D) 訂購一項產品	**正解 (C)** 男子在對話最後說 I can get some of the previous models out for you to look at if you like.，提議拿一些舊型號出來讓女子鑑賞，所以正確答案是 (C)。 ☐ **component** [kəmˋponənt] 名 零件
52 Why does the woman say, "the simpler, the better"? (A) She does not need a lot of extra functions. (B) She wants to acquire the product promptly. (C) She values unique design features. (D) She strongly believes in quality over quantity.	女子為什麼說 "the simpler, the better"？ (A) 她不需要很多額外的功能。 (B) 她想要馬上得到該商品。 (C) 她重視獨特的設計特色。 (D) 她深信質重於量。	**正解 (A)** the simpler, the better 的意思是「愈簡單愈好」。女子在這句話之前向店員說 I only want it to make calls.，表示購買此產品的目的只有通話而已，因此選項 (A) 為正解。 ☐ **function** [ˋfʌŋkʃən] 名 功能 ☐ **acquire** [əˋkwaɪr] 動 獲得；取得 ☐ **promptly** [ˋprɑmptlɪ] 副 迅速地；立即地 ☐ **value** [ˋvælju] 動 重視 ☐ **feature** [ˋfitʃɚ] 名 特色

題目	題目翻譯
Questions 53 through 55 refer to the following conversation.	第 53 到 55 題請參照下面這段對話。
W: I'd like two tickets for the 1:00 showing of *Jack the Pirate*, please.	W：我要兩張一點開演的《海盜傑克》的票，麻煩你。
M: I'm sorry, but that's sold out right now. We still have tickets for the 3:00 show.	M：抱歉，那場的票現在都賣光了。我們還有三點開演的票。
W: My son and I don't really want to wait around for two hours. What else could you recommend for children under 10?	W：我和我兒子不太想等上兩個小時。你還有什麼可以推薦給十歲以下的小孩看的片子嗎？
M: *Secret Forest* might interest both of you. It's an exciting mystery based on a book. Would you like two tickets?	M：你們兩位或許會對《祕密森林》有興趣。這部電影根據原著改編，是相當刺激的推理片。您要兩張票嗎？

Vocabulary

☐ **right now** 現在	☐ **recommend** [ˌrɛkəˈmɛnd] **動** 推薦；介紹	☐ **(be) based on ...** 以 ...... 為基礎

試題	試題翻譯	答案與解析
53 Where most likely are the speakers? (A) At an amusement park (B) At a bus terminal (C) At a movie theater (D) At a bookstore	說話者最有可能在哪裡？ (A) 在遊樂園 (B) 在客運站 (C) 在電影院 (D) 在書店	**正解 (C)** 由女子一開始的發言 I'd like two tickets for the 1:00 showing of Jack the Pirate, please. 即可知，他們最有可能是 (C) At a movie theater（在電影院）。 ☐ **amusement park** 遊樂園
54 What is the woman's preferred time? (A) 1:00 (B) 3:00 (C) 7:00 (D) 10:00	女子比較想要的時間是？ (A) 一點 (B) 三點 (C) 七點 (D) 十點	**正解 (A)** 女子原本就希望看一點的電影，所以答案是 (A)。選項 (B) 的三點是可以買到票的時間，藉由女子說的 My son and I don't really want to wait around for two hours. 也可斷定，這並不是女子想要的時間。
55 What does the man suggest the woman do? (A) Wait for two hours (B) Check another area (C) Get a refund (D) Accept an alternative	男子建議女子做什麼？ (A) 等兩小時 (B) 看看別區是否有票 (C) 退費 (D) 接受別部片的建議	**正解 (D)** 男子雖然先告知了女子三點場次還有票，但是女子說她並「不想等兩個小時」，所以男子就問女子要不要看其他的兒童片，也就是建議她選另一部電影，因此正解為 (D)。 ☐ **refund** [ˈrɪfʌnd] **名** 退款 ☐ **alternative** [ɔlˈtɜnətɪv] **名** 二擇一；供選擇的備案

題目	題目翻譯

Questions 56 through 58 refer to the following conversation.

第 56 到 58 題請參照下面這段對話。

M : I'm going to the reception desk to find out the earliest time we can set up at the exhibition hall. Do you want to come along?

W : Umm ... I think I'd rather not.

M : Why is that?

W : Well, I need to stay here in the office and finish writing my notes. I have a meeting with Cirrus Planning at 2:00. They want to confirm the schedule for tomorrow and talk to me about the complimentary gifts and refreshments.

M : Oh really. That sounds pretty expensive for an investors' conference.

W : Maybe, but it's what Mr. Gupta wants, and he's the CEO. He wants everything to go as smoothly as possible.

M：我要去櫃台查一下我們可以在展覽廳布置的最早時間。妳要不要一起來？

W：嗯……，我想我還是不了。

M：為什麼？

W：嗯，我得留在辦公室這裡把筆記給寫完。我兩點要跟藤蔓企劃開會。他們要確認明天的行程，還要跟我討論贈品和茶點的事。

M：哦，是喔。這樣聽起來，投資人會議還挺花錢的。

W：也許吧，不過這是古普塔先生要的，而他是執行長。他希望一切都儘可能順利地進行。

Vocabulary

☐ **reception** [rɪˈsɛpʃən] 名 接待；櫃台　　☐ **find out** 找出；查明　　☐ **set up** 建立；設置　　☐ **exhibition** [ˌɛksəˈbɪʃən] 名 展覽；展示會
☐ **come along** 一起來　　☐ **complimentary** [ˌkɑmpləˈmɛntərɪ] 形 贈送的　　☐ **refreshments** [rɪˈfrɛʃmənts] 名 茶點（複數形）
☐ **investor** [ɪnˈvɛstə] 名 投資者

試題	試題翻譯	答案與解析

56

What are the speakers doing?

(A) Touring a site
(B) Preparing for an event
(C) Taking a break
(D) Making a presentation

說話者在做什麼？

(A) 參觀一個場所
(B) 籌備一項活動
(C) 休息
(D) 做簡報

正解 (B)

對話一開始男子說道 I'm going to the reception desk to find out the earliest time we can set up at the exhibition hall.，而女子也提及為了確認明日行程而要開會一事。根據這兩條線索得知，他們正在準備一項活動，正解為選項 (B)。

☐ **tour** [tur] 動 遊覽；巡

57

What does the woman mean when she says, "I think I'd rather not"?
(A) She is not interested in the exhibition.
(B) She hopes that she will quit her job soon.
(C) She wants to stay and work in the office.
(D) She might be able to accompany the man.

女子所說的 "I think I'd rather not" 是什麼意思？
(A) 她對展覽沒興趣。
(B) 她希望早點離職。
(C) 她想留在辦公室裡工作。
(D) 她或許能陪男子一起去。

正解 (C)

I'd 為 I would 之簡略，would rather not 意指「寧願不做某事」，是委婉表達 don't want to 的句型。本句在 not 之後省略了 come along，而她不與男子同行的理由則以 I need to stay here in the office and finish writing my notes. 做了說明，因此選項 (C) 為正解。

☐ **accompany** [əˈkʌmpənɪ] 動 陪同

58

What will the attendees receive?

(A) Presents
(B) Complimentary tickets
(C) Gift certificates
(D) Conference brochures

出席者會拿到什麼？

(A) 禮物
(B) 贈票
(C) 禮券
(D) 會議手冊

正解 (A)

女子提及 They want to ... talk to me about the complimentary gifts ....，由此可知選項 (A) 即為正解。(gifts = presents) 注意，選項 (B) Complimentary tickets 和選項 (C) Gift certificates 皆為試圖引誘誤答的陷阱，而選項 (D) 則故意選用對話中曾出現的 conference 來混淆視聽，要小心別上當了。

☐ **attendee** [əˈtɛndi] 名 與會人員
☐ **gift certificate** 禮券

第 2 回完全解析

PART 3

題目	題目翻譯
Questions 59 through 61 refer to the following conversation.	第 59 到 61 題請參照下面這段對話。
W : Something's wrong with this door. When I enter the code, nothing happens.	W：這道門有點問題。我輸入密碼時，什麼反應都沒有。
M : Haven't you heard?	M：妳沒聽說嗎？
W : Heard what?	W：聽說什麼？
M : The procedure changed last night. Now you need to swipe a security card through a reader to open the entrance.	M：程序昨天晚上改了。現在妳要拿保全卡刷過讀卡機，門才會開。
W : Do you mean my ID card?	W：你是說我的識別證嗎？
M : Not that one. You'll need to pick up a new one with a magnetic strip on the back. Talk to Susan in human resources. She'll explain everything. Then, go to IT to pick up your card.	M：不是那張。妳要去領一張背後有磁條的新卡。去找人資部的蘇珊，她會說明一切。然後，去資訊部領卡。

Vocabulary

- **procedure** [prə'sidʒə] 名 程序；步驟
- **swipe a card through ...** 刷卡
- **reader** ['ridə] 名 讀卡機
- **entrance** ['ɛntrəns] 名 入口；門口
- **magnetic strip** 磁條
- **human resources** 人事資源部

試題	試題翻譯	答案與解析
59 What happened last night? (A) A door was installed. (B) A system was changed. (C) An entrance was closed. (D) A code was updated.	昨天晚上發生了什麼事？ (A) 裝了一扇門。 (B) 有個系統被更換。 (C) 有個入口被關閉。 (D) 有一組密碼被更新。	**正解 (B)** 根據男子的發言 The procedure changed last night. 即可知，換句話說的選項 (B) A system was changed. 為正解。 □ **install** [ɪn'stɔl] 動 安裝
60 What does the man say about the woman's ID card? (A) It needs a new magnetic strip. (B) It needs to be replaced. (C) It works when slid through a reader. (D) It works at another entrance.	關於女子的識別證，男子說什麼？ (A) 需要新的磁條。 (B) 必須更換。 (C) 要刷過讀卡機才有用。 (D) 在另一個入口才有用。	**正解 (B)** 男子說道 You'll need to pick up a new one with a magnetic strip on the back.，表示舊卡有更換的必要，正解為 (B)。注意，要更換的不是新的磁條，而是背面附磁條的新卡片，因此選項 (A) 並不恰當。
61 Why does the man recommend seeing Susan? (A) She supervises human resources. (B) She manages IT. (C) She makes repairs. (D) She has more details.	男子為什麼建議去找蘇珊？ (A) 她掌管人資部。 (B) 她主管資訊部。 (C) 她負責維修。 (D) 她會說明更多細節。	**正解 (D)** 男子在最後的發言提到 Talk to Susan in human resources. She'll explain everything.，也就是說蘇珊會為女子說明一切，故 (D) She has more details. 是最適當的選項。 □ **supervise** ['supəvaɪz] 動 監督；管理 □ **make repairs** 修理

題目	題目翻譯
Questions 62 through 64 refer to the following conversation and map.	第 62 到 64 題請參照下列對話和地圖。

W: Don, would you mind going to the downtown branch office to pick up the Halvorsen portfolio for me? Sorry to ask you on such short notice. I had no idea I'd get called to an emergency meeting.

M: I think I can do that. Hopefully I won't get lost. What's the quickest way to get there?

W: After you get off the Interstate at Exit 57, just keep going straight until you hit 3rd Street, then take a left. About two blocks down you'll see a ... some kind of a dry cleaners on the right. It's got a huge sign.

M: So, it's by the cleaners?

W: Right. It's right across the street from that. 562 3rd Street is the address.

W：唐，你介不介意去一趟市區的分公司，幫我拿哈爾沃森的卷宗？抱歉這麼臨時拜託你。我也不知道我會被叫去開一個緊急的會議。

M：我想我能幫妳這個忙。希望我不會迷路。到那裡怎麼去最快？

W：你從 57 出口下高速公路之後，繼續往前直直開到第三街，然後左轉。大概過兩條街之後，你會看到右手邊有一……應該是家乾洗店。那家店有個非常大的招牌。

M：所以，分公司在乾洗店附近？

W：沒錯。就在乾洗店的正對街，地址是第三街 562 號。

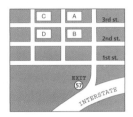

第 2 回完全解析

PART 3

Vocabulary

- ☐ **portfolio** [port`foljo] 名 文件夾；卷宗
- ☐ **get called to ...** 被叫去做……
- ☐ **emergency** [ɪ`mɝdʒənsɪ] 名 緊急狀況
- ☐ **interstate** [.ɪntɚ`stet] 名（美國的）洲際公路
- ☐ **go straight** 直向前進
- ☐ **take a left** 左轉
- ☐ **huge** [hjudʒ] 形 巨大的
- ☐ **be right across the street from ...** 在……的正對街位置

試題	試題翻譯	答案與解析
62 What is probably the woman's problem? (A) She has lost some documents. (B) She cannot find a location. (C) She has to change plans quickly. (D) She does not have a car.	女子的問題可能是什麼？ (A) 她遺失了一些文件。 (B) 她找不到一個地點。 (C) 她必須迅速地改變計畫。 (D) 她沒有車。	**正解 (C)** 對話一開始，女子就拜託男子前往市區的分公司。接著她又說 Sorry to ask you on such short notice. I had no idea I'd get called ...，由此可知女子因遇到臨時狀況而必須改變預定行程，所以正確答案是選項 (C)。
63 What is the man being asked to do? (A) Attend a meeting (B) Travel downtown (C) Clean an office (D) Sign some papers	男子被拜託做什麼？ (A) 出席會議 (B) 去市區 (C) 打掃辦公室 (D) 簽署一些文件	**正解 (B)** 答題線索就在開頭的第一句話裡。Would you mind ...ing? 是用來表達對他人客氣請求的句型，而將 going to the downtown branch office 簡潔地描述成 Travel downtown 的選項 (B) 最適當。 ☐ **papers** [`pepɚz] 名 文件（複數形）
64 Look at the graphic. Where is the downtown branch office located? (A) Building A (B) Building B (C) Building C (D) Building D	請看圖表。市區分公司在哪裡？ (A) A 大樓 (B) B 大樓 (C) C 大樓 (D) D 大樓	**正解 (D)** 做圖表題時，建議在聆聽語音之前先迅速地將圖表內容掃瞄一遍。例如本題，看到地圖就能預測題目應為問路的對話。根據女子所做的說明「你從 57 出口下高速公路後，繼續往前直直開到第三街，然後左轉。大概過兩條街後，你會看到右手邊有一……應該是家乾洗店。」可知，乾洗店應位於 C。接著再對照女子最後所言「（分公司）就在乾洗店的正對街」，因此正解為選項 (D)。

題目	題目翻譯

Questions 65 through 67 refer to the following conversation and label.

M : Hi, I just bought this shirt three days ago. I washed it only once, and didn't put it in the dryer, but still it shrunk two sizes. It's too small now. Is there any way I could exchange it for a new one?

W : I'm sorry, our refund policy only covers unused items, with the tag still on them. As to why it shrunk, let's see what the label says.

M : Oh. It must've been the water temperature. Oh well, live and learn, I guess.

W : The good news is, those shirts are now on sale. Half off. We have size large in stock, too.

M : Really? Well then, maybe I'll try again.

STYLE #55xl-navy
100% COTTON
Dry clean or machine
wash cold. Inside out
with like colors. Tumble
dry low. Non-chlorine
bleach only.

Made in U.S.A.
L
$16.99

第 65 到 67 題請參照下列對話和標籤。

M：嗨，我三天前剛買了這件襯衫。我只洗過一次，而且沒有把它放進烘乾機裡，但是它還是縮小了兩個尺寸。現在它太小了。請問有沒有什麼辦法讓我可以換一件新的？

W：很抱歉，我們的退款規定只包括未使用的新品，並且附原標籤。至於為什麼您的襯衫縮水了，讓我們看看洗標上是怎麼寫的。

M：噢。一定是因為水溫的緣故。噢，嗯，我想這就是不經一事，不長一智吧。

W：好消息是，這款襯衫目前正在打折特賣。只要半價，而且我們也有 L 碼的庫存。

M：真的嗎？嗯，那，也許我會再試一次吧。

STYLE #55xl- 海軍藍
100% 純棉
須乾洗或洗衣機冷水洗。請將裏面外翻並與同色系衣物一起洗滌。使用烘乾機時，請設定低溫。不可使用含氯漂白劑漂白。
美國製造
L
$16.99

Vocabulary

- **dryer** [ˋdraɪɚ] 名 烘乾機；吹風機
- **shrunk** [ʃrʌŋk] 動 shrink「縮小」的過去式、過去分詞
- **unused** [ʌnˋjuzd] 形 未使用的
- **as to ...** 至於⋯⋯
- **live and learn** 不經一事，不長一智
- **tumble dry** 用烘乾機（翻滾）烘乾
- **chlorine** [ˋklorin] 名 氯
- **bleach** [blitʃ] 動 將⋯⋯漂白

試題	試題翻譯	答案與解析
65 What is the conversation mainly about? (A) An incorrect purchase (B) Overpayment for an item (C) A problem with an item (D) An item being out of stock	這段對話主要和什麼有關？ (A) 買錯東西 (B) 多付了錢 (C) 某項商品發生問題 (D) 某項商品沒有庫存	正解 **(C)** 新制多益考題較以往更生活化，考生須多加熟練。由男子一開始的發言可想像此為顧客帶著所購買之襯衫至店內客訴衣服洗後縮水的情境。將此情境抽象化表示的選項 (C) 為正解。an item 指的就是襯衫。
66 Look at the graphic. How could the problem have been avoided? (A) By using cold water (B) By using hot water (C) By using bleach (D) By drying the item	請看圖表。如何能避免問題發生？ (A) 使用冷水 (B) 使用熱水 (C) 使用漂白劑 (D) 將產品烘乾	正解 **(A)** 店員聽聞襯衫縮水而查看洗標之後，男子說 It must've been the water temperature.（一定是因為水溫的緣故。）再對照標籤上寫著 machine wash cold「洗衣機冷水洗」，即可知男子並未以冷水洗滌襯衫，而使用了熱水。故本題選 (A)。注意，must've 是 must have 的簡略，應習慣其發音。
67 What does the woman suggest the man do? (A) Buy a different size (B) Wash the item again (C) Get a refund for the item (D) Purchase another item	女子建議男子做什麼？ (A) 購買不同的尺寸 (B) 將該商品再洗一次 (C) 取得該商品的退款 (D) 購買另一項商品	正解 **(D)** 女子提及 The good news is ...，告知同款襯衫正在打折，並藉此向男子推薦再次購買，因此選項 (D) 為正解。

題目	題目翻譯

Questions 68 through 70 refer to the following conversation and coupon.

W: Hi, I can use this coupon on more than one jar, right?

M: Yes, ma'am. You can only use the coupon one time, but you can use it on as many jar candles as you'd like.

W: I'd like six: four vanilla and two lavender. I could only find one lavender on the shelf. Is there another one somewhere?

M: We might have one in the stock room. If we don't, I could probably have one sent over from one of our other stores.

W: Oh, that won't be necessary. But if you have one in the back, I'll take it. Otherwise I'll take another vanilla one instead.

M: I'll go check right now.

第 68 到 70 題請參照下列對話和折價券。

W：嗨，這張折價券我可以用來買超過一罐，對吧？

M：是的，小姐。這張折價券您只能使用一次，但是您要用來購買幾罐蠟燭都可以，只要您喜歡。

W：我要買六罐：四罐香草味和兩罐薰衣草香。架上我只看到一罐薰衣草香的。請問其他地方還有嗎？

M：我們倉庫裡可能有一罐。假如沒有，我應該可以從我們別家店送一罐過來。

W：噢，那倒不需要。不過，如果你們後面有一罐，我會買。不然的話，我就再多帶一罐香草味的。

M：我現在馬上去確認。

坎蒂絲蠟燭工坊
罐裝蠟燭 $4
買一送一

憑本折價券，以定價購買一罐蠟燭時，可獲得等值或以下的商品一罐。
購買時必須出示本券。
一人限用一張。

Vocabulary

- **coupon** [ˈkupɑn] 名 折價券
- **jar** [dʒɑr] 名 廣口瓶；罐
- **more than ...** 比……多
- **as many ... as you'd like** 要多少……就有多少
- **necessary** [ˈnɛsəˌsɛrɪ] 形 必要的
- **back** [bæk] 名 後面
- **otherwise** [ˈʌðə.waɪz] 副 否則；不然
- **right now** 立刻
- **purchase** [ˈpɝtʃəs] 名 購買
- **per** [pɝ] 介 每

試題	試題翻譯	答案與解析

68

What is the woman's problem?

(A) She cannot use a coupon.
(B) She does not have enough money.
(C) She cannot find an item.
(D) She cannot get a refund.

女子的問題是什麼？

(A) 她無法使用折價券。
(B) 她帶不夠錢。
(C) 她找不到一件商品。
(D) 她無法獲得退費。

正解 (C)

女子所遇到的問題描述於第二次發言時說的 I could only find one lavender on the shelf. Is there another one somewhere? 此部分。another one 是指另一罐薰衣草香的罐裝蠟燭，將此抽象地表示成 an item 的選項 (C) 為正解。

69

Look at the graphic. How many free candles will the woman get?
(A) Two
(B) Three
(C) Four
(D) Six

請看圖表。女子將可獲得幾罐免費的蠟燭？

(A) 兩罐
(B) 三罐
(C) 四罐
(D) 六罐

正解 (B)

根據男性店員第一次的發言，此折價券可使用於不只一罐蠟燭。女性顧客說 I'd like six，她需要六罐。再對照折價券上寫道 Buy One, Get One FREE「買一送一」，所以女子只要付三罐的錢，另三罐可免費獲得。故正解為 (B)。雖然圖表內有許多資訊令人眼花撩亂，但是只要抓到「買一送一」這項關鍵，便能正確答題。注意，沒有必要將所有資訊一字一句全都接收，掌握重點提高解題效率非常重要。

70

What will the man most likely do next?

(A) Contact another store
(B) Wrap some items
(C) Take a customer's order
(D) Look for another candle

男子接下來最有可能會做什麼？

(A) 聯絡其他店
(B) 包裝商品
(C) 接受顧客訂貨
(D) 再找一罐蠟燭

正解 (D)

針對女子要的薰衣草香蠟燭，男子回答「倉庫裡可能有」，並於對話最後表示 I'll go check right now.（我現在馬上去確認。），所以正確答案是 (D)。注意，男子雖然提議幫忙從別家店調貨，但是女子說不需要 (that won't be necessary)，因此選項 (A) 並不適當。

第 2 回完全解析

PART 3

PART 4

題目	題目翻譯
Questions 71 through 73 refer to the following talk. Welcome to Leighton's Investment Division. As you'll know from reading the employee training materials we sent you, this is one of our areas of expertise, the other two being Retail and Corporate Banking. Our goals are simple: to help our clients grow their personal or business success through sound financial management. Our strategy has helped us through many decades, even in times when our competitors have struggled or failed. You'll learn more about that later. First, please switch off your phones and make sure your ID badges are visible while I take you through our secure trading floor.	第 71 到 73 題請參照下面這段談話。 歡迎來到萊登的投資部。各位從閱讀我們所寄的員工訓練資料就會知道，這是本公司的專長領域之一，另外兩項是零售和企業金融。我們的目標很簡單：透過健全的財務管理，協助客戶擴大個人或事業上的成就。我們的策略幫助我們歷經了幾十年，甚至是當競爭對手艱難掙扎或失敗時。這一點各位稍後就會更加了解。在我帶領大家進入我們的安全交易樓層時，首先請將行動電話關機，並確定身上的識別證一眼就能被看見。

Vocabulary

- **material** [mə'tɪrɪəl] 名 資料
- **expertise** [ˌɛkspə'tiz] 名 專門知識〔技術〕
- **retail** ['ritel] 名 零售
- **corporate banking** 企業銀行業務
- **sound** [saʊnd] 形 健全的
- **strategy** ['strætədʒɪ] 名 策略
- **struggle** ['strʌɡl] 動 掙扎
- **fail** [fel] 動 失敗
- **visible** ['vɪzəbl] 形 可看見的
- **secure** [sɪ'kjʊr] 形 安全的

試題	試題翻譯	答案與解析
71 According to the speaker, what can be found in the training materials? (A) Locations of all the divisions (B) Names of their competitors (C) Information about the company's expertise (D) Advice on investments	根據說話者，在研修資料裡可以找到什麼？ (A) 各部門的位置 (B) 競爭對手的公司名 (C) 公司專長領域的資訊 (D) 投資建議	**正解 (C)** 由談話開始的第二句 As you'll know from reading the employee training materials we sent you, this is one of our areas of expertise, ... 即可知，研修資料裡記載了關於公司專業領域的資訊，故本題選 (C)。
72 What is implied about Leighton? (A) It has gained a large market share. (B) It has existed for a long time. (C) It has used complex strategies. (D) It has recruited new managers.	關於萊登公司，這段談話暗示了什麼？ (A) 它獲得了很高的市占率。 (B) 它已經存在了很長的時間。 (C) 它採用了複雜的策略。 (D) 它已經招募了新的經理。	**正解 (B)** 從談話中段的 Our strategy has helped us through many decades, ... 可知，這家公司擁有幾十年的歷史，因此選項 (B) It has existed for a long time. 為正解。 ☐ **gain** [gen] 動 獲得 ☐ **exist** [ɪɡ'zɪst] 動 存在 ☐ **complex** ['kɑmplɛks] 形 複雜的 ☐ **recruit** [rɪ'krut] 動 招募
73 What will the listeners do next? (A) Take off their ID badges (B) Retrieve their mobile phones (C) Go up to the second floor (D) Tour the trading area	聽者接下來會做什麼？ (A) 把他們的識別證拿下來 (B) 取回他們的行動電話 (C) 上到二樓 (D) 參觀交易區	**正解 (D)** 談話最後提到 First, ... while I take you through our secure trading floor.，解說參觀交易樓層時的注意事項，可見他們即將參觀交易區，正確答案是選項 (D)。注意，這種預測後續行為的題目的答案常出現在結尾，所以從頭到尾都必須集中注意力。 ☐ **retrieve** [rɪ'triv] 動 取回

題目	題目翻譯

Questions 74 through 76 refer to the following advertisement.

Last month South Africa, this month Australia! Glorious Hair Care Corporation invites you to learn more about how our range of products can help protect and nourish your hair. On Tuesday, June 13, our team of expert stylists and colorists will show you how our shampoos, conditioners and lotions can leave your hair looking healthy and shiny. The team will be making particular use of our Lemon Gold One Gel, designed to let you easily control your hair during your busy day. Four lucky audience members will also be selected for a free hair styling session. The show starts at 11:00 A.M. at the Sydney Grand Hotel Ballroom, so be sure to arrive early to secure a seat. Seats will be given on a first come, first served basis. For more information visit us online at www.glorioushair.au. Next month we're holding this same event in New Zealand!

第 74 到 76 題請參照下面這段廣告。

上個月在南非，這個月在澳洲！亮麗護髮公司邀請您進一步了解，我們的各項產品如何能有助於保護及滋養您的秀髮。6 月 13 日星期二，我們的專業造型師和染髮師團隊將為您示範，我們的洗髮乳、潤髮乳和護髮霜如何能讓您的秀髮看起來健康閃亮。本團隊將特別使用我們的檸檬金一號髮膠，這項產品專為您在忙碌的一天裡輕鬆打理頭髮而設計。現場也將挑選四位幸運的觀眾朋友接受免費的髮型設計。展示將從早上十一點開始，地點在雪梨大飯店的宴會廳，請務必早點來取得位子，座位將以先到先贏的方式來安排。詳情請上我們的網站 www. glorioushair.au 查詢。下個月，同樣的活動將在紐西蘭舉行！

Vocabulary

- ☐ **nourish** [ˈnɝɪʃ] 動 滋養
- ☐ **stylist** [ˈstaɪlɪst] 名 造型師
- ☐ **colorist** [ˈkʌlərɪst] 名 染髮師
- ☐ **shiny** [ˈʃaɪnɪ] 形 閃亮的
- ☐ **make use of ...** 利用……
- ☐ **ballroom** [ˈbɔlˌrum] 名 舞廳；宴會廳
- ☐ **be sure to do** 一定要做（某事）
- ☐ **secure** [sɪˈkjʊr] 動 確保

試題	試題翻譯	答案與解析

74

What is the advertisement mainly about?
(A) A product demonstration
(B) A travel opportunity
(C) A local competition
(D) A sales campaign

這段廣告主要在講什麼？
(A) 一項產品的示範
(B) 一次旅遊的機會
(C) 一項地方性的競賽
(D) 一場銷售活動

正解 (A)

本題與全篇主旨有關。此廣告目的在於宣傳美容師與染髮師將「示範」某項產品的優點，所以正確答案是選項 (A) A product demonstration。注意，不要認為是產品「示範活動」就誤選了 (D)。

75

What feature of Lemon Gold One Gel is mentioned?
(A) Size
(B) Popularity
(C) Usefulness
(D) Price

檸檬金一號髮膠被提到的特色是什麼？
(A) 大小
(B) 人氣
(C) 實用
(D) 價格

正解 (C)

廣告中段提到 ... designed to let you easily control your hair during your busy day「專為在忙碌的一天中輕鬆打理頭髮而設計」。換句話說，該產品的特色在於實用性，正解為選項 (C) Usefulness。

76

What does the speaker imply when he says, "Seats will be given on a first come, first served basis"?
(A) There are no more seats left.
(B) People should come to the place early.
(C) The show will start earlier than planned.
(D) A light meal will be given during the show.

當說話者說 "Seats will be given on a first come, first served basis" 時，他暗示了什麼？
(A) 已經沒有座位了。
(B) 民眾應提早來會場。
(C) 活動將比預定時間提早開始。
(D) 活動當中將提供輕食。

正解 (B)

on a first come, first served basis「以先到先贏的方式」是廣告文宣中經常可見的文句。而就算不知道此片語的意思，聽到之前的 be sure to arrive early to secure a seat，也應該能判斷選項 (B) 即為正解。注意，例如 (D) 的 given 般，重複使用題目劃線部份的選項多半為陷阱，小心不要上當。

題目	題目翻譯

Questions 77 through 79 refer to the following news report.

Now for today's business news. Astar Pharmaceuticals Corporation has agreed to buy its smaller Hong Kong rival San Yin for 65 million pounds. The deal is still subject to shareholder approval but has the potential to create the United Kingdom's third biggest drug company. Astar's CEO Daniel Rice said the deal was good news for both firms, and would help cut distribution costs by as much as 36 percent — as well as provide potential entry into the mainland China market. Under Rice's direction, Astar has pursued an aggressive M&A policy over the past four years. Last summer it purchased the 900 Drug Corporation and in January this year acquired Crocus Pharmaceuticals. Shares of Astar rose by 2.75 percent at the release of this news, while San Yin was up 1.27 percent by market close.

第 77 到 79 題請參照下面這則新聞報導。

現在播報今天的商業新聞。亞斯塔製藥公司已經同意以 6,500 萬英鎊收購其規模較小的香港對手三銀公司。此交易仍須經過股東核准,但是有機會使該公司躍身為英國的第三大藥廠。亞斯塔的執行長丹尼爾‧萊斯說,這筆交易對兩家公司來說都是好消息,並將有助於削減高達 36% 的經銷成本,同時有機會藉此打入中國大陸的市場。在萊斯的運籌帷幄下,亞斯塔過去四年來採取了積極的併購策略。去年夏天,它收購了九百藥廠,今年一月則買下了番紅花製藥。在這項消息發布後,亞斯塔的股價上漲了 2.75%,三銀則在收盤時漲了 1.27%。

Vocabulary

- ☐ **deal** [dil] 名 交易
- ☐ **be subject to ...** 受……控制;須經……的
- ☐ **shareholder** [ˈʃɛr.holdə] 名 股東
- ☐ **approval** [əˈpruvl] 名 認可
- ☐ **potential** [pəˈtɛnʃəl] 名 可能性;潛力
- ☐ **distribution** [ˌdɪstrəˈbjuʃən] 名 經銷
- ☐ **entry into ...** 進入……
- ☐ **pursue** [pəˈsu] 動 進行
- ☐ **aggressive** [əˈɡrɛsɪv] 形 侵略的;侵犯的
- ☐ **M&A**（= mergers and acquisitions）併購
- ☐ **by market close** 收盤時

試題	試題翻譯	答案與解析

77

What is the report mainly about?

(A) An upcoming takeover
(B) An appointment of a new CEO
(C) An upturn in consumer spending
(D) New markets in China

這則報導主要在講什麼?

(A) 即將發生的併購
(B) 新執行長的任命
(C) 消費購買力的好轉
(D) 中國的新市場

正解 (A)

由報導的第二句 Astar Phamaceuticals Corporation has agreed to buy its smaller Hong Kong rival San Yin for 65 million pounds. 可判斷,本文應該是在談論「併購企業」的話題,故正解為 (A)。注意,以本題為例,新聞報導通常開頭就會點出主旨,所以千萬別漏聽了第一句。

☐ **takeover** [ˈtekˌovə] 名 接手;併購
☐ **upturn** [ˈʌptɜn] 名 上揚

78

What will the companies achieve as a result of the deal?
(A) Higher revenue
(B) Better products
(C) Reduced costs
(D) Improved technologies

交易的結果會使兩家公司達成什麼目標?

(A) 較高的收益
(B) 較好的產品
(C) 降低成本
(D) 技術改良

正解 (C)

題目中的 the companies 指的是亞斯塔製藥公司和三銀公司,the deal 則是指雙方合併一事。由報導中段提到的 ... the deal ... would help cut distribution costs by as much as 36 percent 可知,合併的好處是能夠削減經銷成本,所以正確答案是 (C)。

79

According to the report, what has been Mr. Rice's policy at Astar Pharmaceuticals?
(A) Increasing size
(B) Upgrading services
(C) Raising share prices
(D) Production in mainland China

根據這則報導,萊斯先生在阿斯塔製藥的方針為何?

(A) 擴大規模
(B) 提升服務品質
(C) 拉抬股價
(D) 在中國大陸生產

正解 (A)

從報導後半段中提到的 Under Rice's direction, Astar has pursued an aggressive M&A policy over the past four years. 這句話和之後的具體事例可知,萊斯先生希望透過積極的併購使公司的規模愈來愈大,故正解為選項 (A)。注意,選項 (D) 是併購之後所期待的發展,因此並不適當。

☐ **raise** [rez] 動 提高
☐ **share price** 股價

題目	題目翻譯

Questions 80 through 82 refer to the following telephone message.

Hello, this is Olivia Ross. I'm calling about the Deluxe AZ700 MP3 Player delivered from your store a week ago. The volume mechanism on the device doesn't appear to be working. I can barely hear music on it, no matter which direction I turn the dial. I've read the user manual thoroughly but I don't understand why this is happening. I know this product comes with a 12-month warranty and I'd like to bring it in to a customer service center and have someone take a look at it if at all possible. I think it needs to be replaced. This is the second message I've left, so I'd really appreciate it if someone could get back to me as soon as possible. Thanks.

第 80 到 82 題請參照下面這則電話留言。

你好,我是奧莉維亞・羅斯。我打電話來是為了上星期從你們店裡送過來的豪華型 AZ700 MP3 播放器。這個播放器上的音量調節裝置似乎壞了。我幾乎聽不到裡面的音樂,不管調節鈕往哪個方向轉都一樣。我已經把使用手冊仔細看了一遍,但是我不明白為什麼會發生這種情況。我知道這項產品有十二個月的保固,所以假如可以的話,我想把它拿去客服中心請人看一下。我認為有需要換一個。這是我第二次留言了,如果有人能儘快給我個回覆,我會十分感激。謝謝。

Vocabulary

- **mechanism** [ˋmɛkəˌnɪzəm] 名 機械裝置
- **device** [dɪˋvaɪs] 名 設備;裝置
- **appear to ...** 似乎……
- **work** [wɜk] 動(機器等)運轉
- **barely** [ˋbɛrlɪ] 副 幾乎沒有
- **direction** [dəˋrɛkʃən] 名 方向
- **I'd (really) appreciate it if ...** 如果……我會很感激
- **get back to ...** 給……回電

試題	試題翻譯	答案與解析

80

What does the speaker imply when she says, "I can barely hear music on it, no matter which direction I turn the dial"?
(A) There is something wrong with the volume dial.
(B) The directions are too complicated for her.
(C) She cannot find the dial to turn.
(D) She wants to know what music is on.

當說話者說 "I can barely hear music on it, no matter which direction I turn the dial" 時,她暗示了什麼?
(A) 音量調節鈕似乎有問題。
(B) 指示說明對她而言太複雜。
(C) 她找不到轉鈕。
(D) 她想知道正在播放什麼音樂。

正解 (A)

女子是為了所購買的 MP3 播放器而來電,由她的第三句話 The volume mechanism on the device doesn't appear to be working. 也可知,選項 (A) 即為正解。

81

What does the speaker want to do?

(A) Find a manual
(B) Extend a warranty
(C) Locate a repair shop
(D) Receive a new product

說話者想要做什麼?

(A) 尋找使用手冊
(B) 延長保固
(C) 找出維修店的位置
(D) 取得新的產品

正解 (D)

說話者在留言結尾處提到 I think it needs to be replaced.,也就是她認為有換新品的必要,因此正解為換句話說的選項 (D) Receive a new product。

- **locate** [loˋket] 動 確定……的地點

82

What does the speaker say about herself?
(A) She has had the same problem before.
(B) She has made partial repairs.
(C) She has called previously.
(D) She has received a replacement.

說話者談到了自己的什麼事?

(A) 她以前遇過同樣的問題。
(B) 她已經修好了一部分。
(C) 她之前有打過電話。
(D) 她已經拿到了替換品。

正解 (C)

女子在最後提及 This is the second message I've left,表示這訊息是第二次的留言。換言之,她之前已經因為同一件事而打過電話詢問,所以正確答案是選項 (C)。

- **partial** [ˋpɑrʃəl] 形 部分的
- **previously** [ˋprivɪəslɪ] 副 事先;以前
- **replacement** [rɪˋplesmənt] 名 替換品

題目	試題翻譯

Questions 83 through 85 refer to the following talk.

Welcome to the Warsaw City Opera House. As you already know from your sponsorship invitation, the Opera House is one of the oldest in Poland, dating back to the 18th century. However, it is now in need of serious renovation, particularly since its roof is leaking. We have received donations of 2.1 million euros from all over the region, but I'm afraid we still need more. We have therefore chosen this evening to launch a Restoration Fund with the aim of raising 2.3 million more euros. Campaign chairman Lech Havelcek will be joining us soon to explain some of the privileges that sponsorship of the theater carries, such as invitation-only shows. After that, we hope you'll join us for a Champagne Reception in the main lobby. Afterwards, there will be a short performance by classical singer Melanie Farcheau of France, accompanied by Canada's Geoffrey Regan on piano.

歡迎光臨華沙市歌劇院。如同各位從贊助邀請函中已經得知，本歌劇院是波蘭最古老的劇院之一，可追溯到 18 世紀。然而，它現在需要大幅翻修，尤其是因為屋頂會漏水。我們已收到地方各界 210 萬歐元的捐款，但恐怕還需要更多。因此，我們選了今晚來成立重建基金，目標是再募得 230 萬歐元。活動主席雷克‧哈維賽克稍後就會到場說明贊助劇院所能享有的特別優待，例如只限受邀來賓觀賞的表演。在那之後，希望各位蒞臨主廳的香檳歡迎會。然後，法國的古典歌手梅蘭妮‧法修將有簡短的表演，並由加拿大的傑佛瑞‧雷岡以鋼琴伴奏。

Vocabulary

- [ ] **sponsorship** [ˋspɑnsəˏʃɪp] 名 贊助
- [ ] **date back to ...** 追溯到……
- [ ] **in need of ...** 需要……
- [ ] **serious** [ˋsɪrɪəs] 形 重大的
- [ ] **renovation** [ˏrɛnəˋveʃən] 名 翻修
- [ ] **leak** [lik] 動 滲漏
- [ ] **donation** [doˋneʃən] 名 捐款；捐獻
- [ ] **with the aim of ...** 目標是要……
- [ ] **privilege** [ˋprɪvlɪdʒ] 名 特權；優待
- [ ] **accompany** [əˋkʌmpənɪ] 動 為……伴奏

試題	試題翻譯	答案與解析

83

What is the main purpose of the talk?

(A) To announce a schedule
(B) To perform a new opera
(C) To outline a goal
(D) To discuss problems

這段談話的主要目的是什麼？

(A) 宣布一個時程
(B) 演出一齣新歌劇
(C) 概述一個目標
(D) 討論問題

正解 (C)

這種問主旨的問題有時必須聽完全篇才能準確答題。由談話中段提到的 We have therefore chosen this evening to launch a Restoration Fund with the aim of raising 2.3 million more euros. 可推測，這段談話主要在敘述需要更進一步的募款以達目標金額，所以正確答案是選項 (C) To outline a goal。

- [ ] **outline** [ˋautˏlaɪn] 動 敘述……的概要

84

According to the speaker, how many euros have been donated so far?
(A) 2.0 million
(B) 2.1 million
(C) 2.2 million
(D) 2.3 million

根據說話者表示，到目前為止的捐款已有多少歐元？
(A) 200 萬
(B) 210 萬
(C) 220 萬
(D) 230 萬

正解 (B)

由談話中段提到的 We have received donations of 2.1 million euros from all over the region 即可知，正解為選項 (B)。注意，2.3 million 是之後希望募得的目標金額，故選項 (D) 不適當。注意，本題為數字問題，別忘了先將選項掃瞄一遍，然後將注意力放在題目裡出現的數字。

85

What is an advantage of being a sponsor?
(A) Music previews
(B) Backstage passes
(C) Free champagne
(D) Exclusive events

當贊助人有什麼好處？

(A) 音樂的預聽
(B) 進入後台的通行證
(C) 免費的香檳
(D) 獨享的活動

正解 (D)

談話後段提到贊助人享有 invitation-only shows「僅限受邀來賓參加的表演」的優待，因此 (D) Exclusive events 為正解。

- [ ] **preview** [ˋpriˏvju] 名 預演；預展
- [ ] **exclusive** [ɪkˋsklusɪv] 形 獨有的；獨享的

題目	題目翻譯
Questions 86 through 88 refer to the following talk.	第 86 到 88 題請參照下面這段談話。

Thank you for joining us in the boardroom this afternoon. I'd like to take this opportunity to introduce you all to Richard Kashumbe, senior executive in charge of marketing at Moise and Moise Marketing Company. He'll be joining us from April 1 as our new Director of Communications. Some of you may recognize Richard from the cover of *Business World Magazine*. He is a recent winner of that magazine's Marketing Person of the Year Award. He's also been praised in several other media outlets, such as the *European IT Journal* and *Fast Business Daily*. So we're excited to have Richard run our new multimedia marketing and advertising campaigns for Africa and the Middle East. After this informal "meet and greet" session — please help yourself to refreshments — Richard will be making a short presentation and answering your questions before meeting the business press later this afternoon.

感謝各位今天下午蒞臨會議室。我要藉這個機會向大家介紹在摩以斯與摩以斯行銷公司掌管行銷的資深主管理查‧卡尚貝。從 4 月 1 日起,他將來到本公司擔任我們的新傳媒總監。在座有些人或許看過理查登上《商業世界雜誌》的封面。他最近榮獲該雜誌的年度行銷人員獎。他還曾受到過另外幾家媒體機構的讚揚,像是《歐洲資訊期刊》和《快速商業日報》。所以我們非常高興理查能為我們執掌非洲與中東的新多媒體行銷與廣告活動。在這場非正式的「見面歡迎」會後——請自行取用茶點——理查將做個簡短的報告並回答各位的問題,接著稍後在下午他會與財經媒體見面。

Vocabulary

- **boardroom** [`bord͵rum] 名 會議室
- **in charge of ...** 負責⋯⋯
- **recent** [`risn̩t] 形 最近的
- **media outlet** 媒體機構
- **run** [rʌn] 動 管理;經營
- **help yourself to ...** 自行取用⋯⋯

試題	試題翻譯	答案與解析
86 Who most likely are the listeners? (A) Corporate staff (B) Business journalists (C) Media analysts (D) Market regulators	聽眾最有可能是誰? (A) 公司員工 (B) 財經記者 (C) 媒體分析師 (D) 市場主管機關	**正解 (A)** 談話前段中提及 He'll be joining us from April 1 as our new Director of Communications. 以告知聽眾理查‧卡尚貝將從四月起加入公司,接著並傳達稍後將有一場見面歡迎會的訊息。由以上線索推論,合理答案應為選項 (A)。 ☐ **regulator** [`rɛgjə͵letə] 名 管理者;主管機關
87 What is Richard Kashumbe's current occupation? (A) Marketing manager (B) Film director (C) Communication expert (D) Journalist	理查‧卡尚貝的現職是什麼? (A) 行銷經理 (B) 電影導演 (C) 傳媒專家 (D) 記者	**正解 (A)** 根據談話前段提到的 Richard Kashumbe, senior executive in charge of marketing at Moise and Moise Marketing Company 可知,理查‧卡尚貝目前是摩以斯與摩以斯行銷公司的資深行銷主管,因此正解為選項 (A) Marketing manager。
88 What will happen next? (A) Refreshments will be served. (B) A different speaker will talk. (C) A press conference will begin. (D) Questions will be taken.	接下來會發生什麼事? (A) 會上茶點。 (B) 另一位講者發言。 (C) 召開記者會。 (D) 接受提問。	**正解 (B)** 談話後段提及 Richard will be making a short presentation ...,也就是說,理查待會兒會上台報告,因此正解為選項 (B)。其他錯誤選項不是在會場中持續發生的事,就是在理查的演講結束之後才會發生的事,所以答題時要仔細聽出事件的發生順序。 ☐ **press conference** 記者會

題目	題目翻譯

Questions 89 through 91 refer to the following announcement.

Good morning shoppers and welcome to Victoria Supermarket. Those of you new to Victoria Supermarket may not know about our Special One Dollar Aisle. Everything in Aisle 3, just inside our main store entrance, costs just one dollar. <u>Yes, you heard right</u>. Not three, not two, but one dollar. And you'll be amazed at what's on offer there including leading brands! From household goods such as Sharply Floor Cleaner to tasty treats the whole family loves like Crowley's Potato Chips. Why not check it out today? This offer cannot be combined with other discounts, and items purchased in Aisle 3 do not earn Victoria Card purchase points. Cash or credit welcomed.

第 89 到 91 題請參照下面這段廣播。

各位顧客早安，歡迎光臨維多利亞超市。維多利亞超市的新顧客或許不知道我們的一元特別走道。三號走道——就在本店主要入口的內側——裡面所有商品都只要一塊錢。對，您沒聽錯，不是三塊，不是兩塊，而是一塊錢。那裡所販售的商品會讓您大吃一驚，其中還包括領導品牌在內！從犀利地板清潔劑之類的居家用品，到像克羅立洋芋片這種全家人都愛吃的零食應有盡有。何不今天就來看看？本優惠不可搭配其他折扣，在三號走道所購買的產品也無法累積維多利亞卡的購物點數。現金或信用卡都歡迎使用。

Vocabulary

- ☐ **shopper** [ˈʃɑpə] 名 購物者
- ☐ **aisle** [aɪl] 名 走道
- ☐ **be amazed at ...** 對……感到震驚
- ☐ **leading brand** 領導品牌
- ☐ **household goods** 居家用品
- ☐ **tasty** [ˈtestɪ] 形 美味的
- ☐ **treat** [trit] 名 樂事；盛饌
- ☐ **check out** 檢查
- ☐ **combine A with B** 結合 A 與 B

試題	試題翻譯	答案與解析

89

Why does the woman say, "Yes, you heard right"?
(A) To agree with an opinion
(B) To emphasize what she says
(C) To ask for permission
(D) To show her gratitude

女子為什麼說 "Yes, you heard right"？

(A) 為了同意一個意見
(B) 為了強調自己所言
(C) 為了請求許可
(D) 為了表示感謝

正解 (B)

right 在此作副詞用，是「正確地；無誤地」的意思，you heard right 則指「你沒聽錯」，表示加強語氣以肯定前面說過的事情，故正解為 (B)。

- ☐ **emphasize** [ˈɛmfə.saɪz] 動 強調
- ☐ **permission** [pəˈmɪʃən] 名 許可
- ☐ **gratitude** [ˈgrætə.tjud] 名 感激（之情）

90

What is true of the goods in Aisle 3?

(A) They are from major companies.
(B) They are unique to Victoria Supermarket.
(C) They are all edible.
(D) They are sold only in the morning.

關於三號走道產品的描述何者為真？

(A) 它們來自大公司。
(B) 它們是維多利亞超市所獨有的。
(C) 它們全部都是可以吃的東西。
(D) 它們只在早上有賣。

正解 (A)

從廣播中段提到的 And you'll be amazed at what's on offer there including leading brands! 即可知，該走道的貨品「包含名牌商品」，因此選項 (A) They are from major companies. 為正解。注意，雖然此活動為維多利亞超市的特有活動，但所販售之商品並非僅於該超市獨家販售，故不可誤答選項 (B)。

- ☐ **major** [ˈmedʒə] 形 主要的；大的
- ☐ **edible** [ˈɛdəbl] 形 可食用的

91

What are customers using Aisle 3 unable to do?
(A) Pay by credit cards
(B) Buy leading brands
(C) Receive shopping points
(D) Shop in other aisles

使用三號走道的顧客不能做什麼？

(A) 用信用卡付帳
(B) 購買領導品牌
(C) 換取購物點數
(D) 在別的走道買東西

正解 (C)

廣播末段提到 ... and items purchased in Aisle 3 do not earn Victoria Card purchase points.，意思是「於三號走道購買的商品無法累積維多利亞卡的購物點數」，所以正確答案是選項 (C) Receive shopping points。

題目	題目翻譯
Questions 92 through 94 refer to the following broadcast.	第 92 到 94 題請參照下面這段廣播。

And for today's business news. In a surprise move, the board of directors of Chow Ling Manufacturing Corporation has appointed Jason Yu Chief Executive Officer. Mr. Yu had been the company's Chief Financial Officer for the last 18 months. He will replace Michael Liggins, who is retiring. Bob Heller, the company's Business Development head, was widely expected to succeed Mr. Liggins, when he moved from rival Homestead Production in Toronto 2 years ago. Observers have reported he is now unlikely to stay with Chow Ling. Those same observers expect Mr. Yu to move quickly to reduce staff by investing in labor-saving technologies. In a statement, the new CEO said he looked forward to outdoing the record profits in the last fiscal year earned through several successful products.

接著播報今天的財經新聞。在一次出乎意料的行動中,卓靈製造公司的董事會指派了于杰森出任執行長。在過去十八個月中,于先生是該公司的財務長。他將接替即將退休的麥可·李金斯。該公司的企業發展主管鮑伯·賀勒在兩年前從多倫多的敵營「家園生產」跳槽過來時,備受期待會接任李金斯先生的位置。評論家表示,現在他不太可能會留在卓靈。同一批觀察家認為,于先生很快就會藉投資節省人力的技術,以裁減人員。在一項聲明中這位新執行長說,他期待能超越上個會計年度靠多項成功的產品所達成的創紀錄獲利。

Vocabulary

- [ ] **appoint** [ə`pɔɪnt] 動 指派
- [ ] **replace** [rɪ`ples] 動 接替;取代
- [ ] **retire** [rɪ`taɪr] 動 退休
- [ ] **succeed** [sək`sid] 動 接任
- [ ] **observer** [əb`zɝvɚ] 名 觀察家
- [ ] **be unlikely to** *do* 不太可能做(某事)
- [ ] **invest in ...** 投資……
- [ ] **labor-saving** [`lebɚ͵sevɪŋ] 形 節省人力的
- [ ] **look forward to ...ing** 期待……
- [ ] **outdo** [͵aʊt`du] 動 超越
- [ ] **fiscal year** 會計年度

試題	試題翻譯	答案與解析
92 What is the broadcast mainly about? (A) Financial results (B) Leadership changes (C) Brand development (D) Market trends	這則報導主要在講什麼? (A) 財務報告 (B) 領導人的變動 (C) 品牌發展 (D) 市場趨勢	**正解 (B)** 本題須聽完全篇來龍去脈才能正確解答。文中提及于杰森被任命為新執行長,成為麥可·李金斯的繼任者,所以這應該是與「經營團隊之換血」有關的報導,故正解為選項 (B)。
93 What is Bob Heller expected to do next? (A) Leave the company (B) Hire a rival (C) Transfer to Toronto (D) Oversee investments	鮑伯·賀勒接下來預計會做什麼? (A) 離開公司 (B) 雇用競爭者 (C) 轉調至多倫多 (D) 督管投資	**正解 (A)** 報導中段描述到 ... he is now unlikely to stay with chow Ling,he 指的是鮑伯·賀勒,亦即專家預測他會離職,所以正確答案是選項 (A)。 □ **oversee** [`ovɚ`si] 動 監督;管理
94 What has Jason Yu said he will do? (A) Increase net income (B) Raise staffing levels (C) Lower manufacturing costs (D) Launch new products	于杰森說他會做什麼? (A) 增加淨利 (B) 擴充人員編制 (C) 降低製造成本 (D) 推出新產品	**正解 (A)** 由報導最後一句提到的 ... the new CEO said he looked forward to outdoing the record profits ... 可知,新任執行長于杰森希望增加營收,因此正解為選項 (A) Increase net income。 □ **net income** 淨利 □ **launch** [lɔntʃ] 動 推出(新產品等)

第 2 回完全解析

PART 4

題目	題目翻譯

Questions 95 through 97 refer to the following telephone message and request form.

Hi Mike, it's Arleen in Sales. Thanks for setting up Room 4 for tomorrow's meeting. The number of chairs is just right. However, I have a favor to ask: Could you move the projector screen to the other side of the room? If it's by the windows, the afternoon sun makes it hard to see, even with the curtains drawn. The weather is supposed to be cloudless tomorrow. You may have to adjust the projector a little, but aside from the screen, the setup is fine. If you could call me when you get back from lunch to confirm, that would be great.

第 95 到 97 題請參照下列電話留言和申請單。

麥克你好，我是業務部的雅琳。謝謝你布置了明天開會要使用的四號會議室。椅子數量完全正確，不過，我想請你幫個忙：你能不能把投影機螢幕搬到房間的另一邊？螢幕如果靠窗的話，即使拉下窗簾，下午的陽光也會讓它很難看清楚。明天應該是晴朗無雲的天氣。你可能需要稍微調整一下投影機，但是除了螢幕以外設置都沒問題。你吃完午餐回來若能打個電話給我確認一下就太好了。

Johnson Corp.
Maintenance Request Form
Submitted by: ___Royce Brown___
Supervisor: ___Michael Halvorsen___
Location: ___Meeting Room 4___

Room Setup
- 70 chairs, 7 rows of 10
- Set up projector screen on west side of room

強森公司
維修設備申請單

申請人：羅伊斯‧布朗
主　管：麥克‧哈爾沃森
地　點：四號會議室

室內擺設
- 70 張椅子，一排 10 張、排成 7 排
- 投影機螢幕請設置於室內西側

Vocabulary

☐ **have a favor to ask** 有件事想請求幫忙　　☐ **draw a curtain** 拉上窗簾　　☐ **cloudless** [ˋklaʊdlɪs] 形 無雲的；晴朗的
☐ **adjust** [əˋdʒʌst] 動 調整　　☐ **aside from ...** 除了……之外

試題	試題翻譯	答案與解析

95

Why is the woman calling?

(A) To cancel an order
(B) To amend a request
(C) To make an appointment
(D) To schedule a meeting

女子為什麼來電？

(A) 為了取消訂單
(B) 為了修改申請
(C) 為了約定會面
(D) 為了排開會日期

正解 (B)

女子的談話與明日會議的場地布置有關。從她說的 I have a favor to ask 及之後的內容可知，女子是為了請對方協助變更擺設而打電話來，故選項 (B) 為正解。

☐ **amend** [əˋmɛnd] 動 修改；訂正

96

Look at the graphic. What does the woman want Mike to do before the meeting?
(A) Put the screen on the east side of the room
(B) Move some tables to the other room
(C) Reduce the number of chairs
(D) Change the type of projector

請看圖表。女子希望麥克在會議前做什麼？

(A) 將投影機螢幕放在室內東側
(B) 搬幾張桌子到另一個房間
(C) 減少椅子數量
(D) 更改投影機類型

正解 (A)

這種問說話者請求何事的題目，答案通常就在含有 Could you ...? 句子的段落中。女子提及 Could you move the projector screen to the other side of the room?，希望將投影機螢幕挪到會議室裡的「另一邊」。對照申請表可知原本的需求為 Set up projector screen on west side of room。也就是說，女子想請對方將已經設置於西側的螢幕移動到東側，因此選項 (A) 為正解。

97

When will Mike most likely return the call?
(A) This morning
(B) This afternoon
(C) Tomorrow morning
(D) Tomorrow afternoon

麥克最有可能於何時回電？

(A) 今天上午
(B) 今天下午
(C) 明天上午
(D) 明天下午

正解 (B)

問有關聯絡方式、時間的問題大多在整段語音的尾聲中可找到線索。本題由最後提到的 If you could call me when you get back from lunch to confirm, ... 可推知正確答案是選項 (B)，因為「吃了午餐回來之後」即指「下午」。

題目	題目翻譯

Questions 98 through 100 refer to the following excerpt from a meeting and chart.

Here are the latest data from our Sales Department, showing our four top-selling products over the last quarter. As you can see, smartphones accounted for more than half our revenue. I see an opportunity to further expand our line of smartphones, but at the same time, Marketing is putting together a campaign for our new Xenon Z27 copier, the fastest and cheapest on the market. If the campaign is well executed, I project we'll be able to double sales in that field. I'll speak with Accounting after this meeting to find out how much we can allot to the campaign, and I will report what they say at our next meeting.

第 98 到 100 題請參照下列會議摘錄和圖表。

這是來自業務部的最新資料，當中顯示出上一季本公司的四大暢銷商品。如同各位所見，智慧型手機就占了半數以上的營收。我認為這是個進一步擴展智慧型手機產品線的好機會，不過同一時間，行銷部正在為本公司的新型氙 Z27 影印機籌備一項宣傳活動，這款影印機是市面上最快速且最便宜的機型。假如活動執行順利的話，我預測我們將能夠在該領域創造雙倍業績。這場會議之後我將和會計部討論，看看我們能分配多少金額給那個活動，然後下次開會時我再跟大家報告他們是怎麼說的。

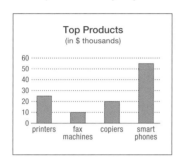

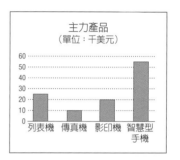

Vocabulary

- ☐ **account for ...** 占……的比例
- ☐ **revenue** [ˈrɛvəˌnju] **图** 收入；收益
- ☐ **put together** 組織；籌備
- ☐ **execute** [ˈɛksɪˌkjut] **動** 執行；實施
- ☐ **double** [ˈdʌbl] **動** 變成兩倍；增加一倍
- ☐ **allot A to B ...** 分配 A 給 B

試題	試題翻譯	答案與解析

98

Where most likely does the man work?

(A) At a printing company
(B) At an office supply retailer
(C) At a research firm
(D) At a telecommunications center

男子最有可能在哪裡工作？

(A) 印刷公司
(B) 辦公用品零售商
(C) 調查公司
(D) 電信中心

正解 (B)

此談話的情境為會議中，而男子正依圖表的數據說明自家公司商品的銷售狀況和行銷活動計畫。由圖表中的列表機、傳真機等產品類型可斷定正確答案是 (B)。

99

Look at the graphic. What figure does the man predict as a result of the campaign?
(A) $20,000
(B) $30,000
(C) $40,000
(D) $50,000

請看圖表。男子預測活動成果可達多少金額？

(A) 20,000 美元
(B) 30,000 美元
(C) 40,000 美元
(D) 50,000 美元

正解 (C)

男子的預測出現在 I project we'll be able to double sales in that field 此句中。project 有「預估；推論」的意思，double 作動詞用指「變成兩倍」，that field 在這段談話中則指行銷部正在為其籌備活動的影印機市場。再對照圖表，影印機的數據為 $20,000，因此男子的預測值應為其兩倍的 (C) $40,000。

100

What will the man do after the meeting?
(A) Help with a campaign
(B) Put together a report
(C) Make a presentation
(D) Consult with a department

會議後男子將會做什麼？

(A) 協助一個活動
(B) 整理出一份報告
(C) 做簡報
(D) 諮詢某個部門

正解 (D)

由談話最後一句中的 I'll speak with Accounting after this meeting ... 即可知，正解為 (D)。選項中的 consult with 和 a department 分別為文中 speak with 和 Accounting 的「換句話說」。注意，關於說話者接下來的行動或想法的題目，關鍵大多落在 will 這個助動詞上，不過，在口語上通常會用簡略式，例如將 I will 說成 I'll，考生須多多習慣其發音。

PART 5

101

Heart Life Corporation's new medicine will be distributed in pharmacies after _____ over a period of 18 months certifies that it is safe.

(A) test
(B) being tested
(C) tested
(D) have tested

心生命公司的新藥在經過十八個月的測試後被證實為安全無虞，即將派發給各藥局販售。

正解 (B) 動名詞

空格之前的 after 是介系詞，其後須接其受詞，四個選項當中只有名詞選項 (A) test 與動名詞選項 (B) being tested 可作受詞用，但因 test 為「普通名詞」，使用時須加「冠詞」，故本題選 (B)。注意，being tested 實為動名詞之「被動式」。

☐ **distribute** [dɪˋstrɪbjut] 動 分配
☐ **pharmacy** [ˋfɑrməsɪ] 名 藥局
☐ **certify** [ˋsɝtəˌfaɪ] 動 證明；證實

102

The entire downtown business area was filled _____ 12 hours with shoppers enjoying holiday discounts.

(A) as
(B) in
(C) on
(D) for

整個市中心的商業區塞滿了享受節日折扣的購物人潮長達十二小時。

正解 (D) 介系詞

空格後接續著表時間長度的 12 hours，所以介系詞應選擇 (D) for。

☐ **shopper** [ˋʃɑpə] 名 購物者

103

Analysts report that shopping online for groceries has _____ changed the entire supermarket experience.

(A) dramatically
(B) accusingly
(C) impenetrably
(D) combatively

分析師表示，上網購買雜貨大大地改變了整體的超市體驗。

正解 (A) 字彙

空格前有 has，空格後為 changed，亦即完成式動詞結構，因此推斷空格內應填入副詞來修飾動詞，而最合適的是選項 (A) dramatically（戲劇性地）。

☐ **analyst** [ˋænḷɪst] 名 分析家
☐ **groceries** [ˋgrosərɪz] 名 食品雜貨（複數形）
☐ **entire** [ɪnˋtaɪr] 形 整體的
☐ **accusingly** [əˋkjuzɪŋlɪ] 副 指責地
☐ **impenetrably** [ɪmˋpɛnətrəblɪ] 副 無法穿透地
☐ **combatively** [kəmˋbætɪvlɪ] 副 好鬥地

104

Chinese retailer Zin Mart predicted no _____ in profits for the year, despite a slowdown in consumer spending.

(A) deteriorate
(B) deteriorated
(C) deteriorating
(D) deterioration

中國零售業者勤瑪特預測，其年度獲利將不會惡化，儘管消費購買力趨緩。

正解 (D) 詞性

空格前為形容詞 no，因此空格內應填入「名詞」。正解為選項 (D) deterioration（惡化）。

☐ **retailer** [ˋritelə] 名 零售業；零售店
☐ **predict** [prɪˋdɪkt] 動 預測
☐ **despite** [dɪˋspaɪt] 介 儘管
☐ **slowdown** [ˋsloˌdaʊn] 名 減緩
☐ **consumer spending** 消費者購買力
☐ **deteriorate** [dɪˋtɪrɪəˌret] 動 惡化

105

In case this event is canceled, ticket holders will each _____ the full face value of their purchase.

(A) entitle
(B) receive
(C) remove
(D) object

假如這場活動取消，每位持票人皆可獲得全額面值的退票。

正解 (B) 字彙

空格內須填入以 the full face value of their purchase 作為受詞的動詞。活動中斷時，購票者「獲得」全額退費最符合文意，故本題選 (B)。注意，選項 (A) entitle（賦予資格）的用法為 entitle sb. to do sth.，所以不是正確答案。

☐ **remove** [rɪˋmuv] 動 移除
☐ **object** [əbˋdʒɛkt] 動 反對

試題與翻譯	答案與解析

106

Trascki Automobile Company has gone from strength _____ strength since entering the North American market.

(A) on
(B) in
(C) and
(D) to

自從進入北美市場以來，崔斯基汽車公司日益壯大。

正解 (D) 慣用語

go from strength to strength 是一個慣用語，意指「日益壯大」，所以正確答案就是 (D) to。

□ **automobile** ['ɔtəmə.bil] 名 汽車

107

Millions of consumers are rushing to buy the game software, leaving storeowners _____ to meet demand.

(A) conflicting
(B) contesting
(C) targeting
(D) struggling

好幾百萬的消費者一窩蜂地購買該遊戲軟體，使得店家們拚命地應付需求。

正解 (D) 字彙

突然有一大堆消費者為了買遊戲軟體而湧入店裡，而店家們為了滿足消費者，應該會「很辛苦」，因此最合理的答案為選項 (D) struggling。

□ **conflict** [kən'flɪkt] 動 衝突
□ **contest** [kən'tɛst] 動 競爭
□ **target** ['tɑrgɪt] 動 以……為目標

108

The _____ merit of Mr. Rysbecki's financial model comes from its ability to predict demand for the company's products.

(A) relative
(B) relation
(C) relate
(D) relatively

瑞斯貝基先生的財務模型相對的優點來自於其預測該公司產品需求之能力。

正解 (A) 詞性

空格後有名詞 merit（優點；長處），所以空格內應填入能修飾名詞的「形容詞」，即選項 (A) relative（相對的）。

□ **relation** [rɪ'leʃən] 名 關係
□ **relate** [rɪ'let] 動 使關聯；有關聯
□ **relatively** ['rɛlətɪvlɪ] 副 相關地

109

Mr. Kim said he would prefer _____ in the Seoul office rather than transfer to the smaller branch in Incheon.

(A) remains
(B) to remain
(C) remained
(D) had remained

金先生說他較想留在首爾辦事處，而不想調到比較小的仁川分處。

正解 (B) 不定詞

prefer A rather than B 是「比起 B 較喜歡 A」的意思。由於 rather than 後為原形動詞，故不定詞選項 (B) 為正解。

□ **transfer** [træns'fɝ] 動 調職
□ **remain** [rɪ'men] 動 留下；停留

110

CEO Gawande of IndoOne Tech was known for his honest and _____ approach to business negotiations.

(A) opening
(B) openly
(C) open
(D) opened

印度壹科技的執行長賈萬德以誠實和開放的商業談判作風而聞名。

正解 (C) 詞性

對等連接詞 and 之前有形容詞 honest（誠實的），故之後的空格內也應填入形容詞，因此正解為選項 (C) open（開放的）。注意，雖然現在分詞選項 (A) 與過去分詞選項 (D) 也可當成形容詞使用，但是與題意不符。

□ **negotiation** [nɪɡoʃɪ'eʃən] 名 談判

111

The client _____ us make several revisions to the advertising campaign literature, such as putting the logo in a more prominent position.

(A) had
(B) did
(C) permitted
(D) got

客戶要我們針對廣告活動文宣修改幾個地方，比方像把商標放在比較明顯的位置。

正解 (A) 使役動詞

這是屬於使役動詞用法的問題。＜have＋受詞（人）＋動詞原形＞是「讓某人做某件事」的意思，依照文意，選項 (A) 即為正解。注意，雖然選項 (D) got 也可用於使役，但是其句型為＜get＋受詞＋to do＞。

□ **revision** [rɪ`vɪʒən] 名 修正
□ **literature** [`lɪtərətʃə] 名 文學；印刷品
□ **prominent** [`prɑmənənt] 形 顯眼的
□ **permit** [pə`mɪt] 動 允許

112

Harris Corporation acted _____ in recruiting the very best personnel for all of its divisions.

(A) assertion
(B) asserting
(C) asserts
(D) assertively

哈里斯公司果斷地為所有部門招募最優秀的人才。

正解 (D) 詞性

修飾動詞 acted 必須使用副詞，所以選項 (D) assertively（果斷地）是正確答案。

□ **personnel** [ˌpɝsṇ`ɛl] 名 員工
□ **assertion** [ə`sɝʃən] 名 斷言
□ **assert** [ə`sɝt] 動 斷言；聲稱

113

Green World Foods emerged as the most _____ brand in a survey, with 93% of respondents feeling positive about the company.

(A) imported
(B) trusted
(C) reviewed
(D) assumed

格林世界食品在一項調查中躍居為最受信賴的品牌，有 93% 的受訪者對該公司抱以好感。

正解 (B) 字彙

本題考分詞的前位修飾。根據文意，只有「可信賴的」品牌才會「被肯定」，正解為選項 (B) trusted。

□ **emerge** [ɪ`mɝdʒ] 動 出現；浮現
□ **survey** [sə`ve] 名 調查
□ **respondent** [rɪ`spɑndənt] 名 回應者
□ **review** [rɪ`vju] 動 審查；審視
□ **assume** [ə`sjum] 動 假定

114

The emergence of satellite TV is generating a crucial _____ that even local entertainment companies can market globally.

(A) understands
(B) understandably
(C) understanding
(D) understandable

衛星電視的出現產生了一項極重要的認識，那就是，甚至連地方娛樂公司都能行銷全球。

正解 (C) 詞性

空格前出現了不定冠詞 a 和形容詞 crucial（極重要的），空格後則接續一個 that 子句。而由 a crucial 及 that 子句可斷定，空格內應填入一名詞作為 that 子句之同位語，故本題選 (C)。

□ **emergence** [ɪ`mɝdʒəns] 名 出現
□ **generate** [`dʒɛnəˌret] 動 產生
□ **globally** [`globḷɪ] 副 全世界地
□ **understandably** [ˌʌndə`stændəblɪ] 副 可理解地
□ **understandable** [ˌʌndə`stændəbḷ] 形 可理解的

115

The board of directors at Dragon Robotics Co. reacted _____ to the idea of merging with a rival corporation.

(A) positively
(B) positive
(C) positiveness
(D) positivity

龍機器人公司的董事會對於合併對手公司的想法反應正面。

正解 (A) 詞性

react to ... 是「對……做出反應」的意思。要修飾動詞 reacted 只能用副詞，故正解為選項 (A) positively（正面地）。

□ **board of directors** 董事會
□ **positiveness** [`pɑzətɪvnɪs] 名 肯定；確實
□ **positivity** [ˌpɑzə`tɪvətɪ] 名 積極性

116

Professor Shah's expertise in industrial engineering earned him an _____ reputation in his field.

(A) insurable
(B) unwarranted
(C) unintentional
(D) enviable

夏教授的工業工程專長為他在所屬領域中贏得了令人羨慕的聲譽。

正解 (D) 字彙

由句中使用的 earned（贏得）與空格後的 reputation（名聲）來判斷，選項 (B) enviable（令人羨慕的）最符合題意，故為正解。

□ **expertise** [ˌɛkspɚ'tiz] 名 專門知識
□ **insurable** [ɪn'ʃurəbl] 形 可保險的
□ **unwarranted** [ʌn'wɔrəntɪd] 形 無保證的
□ **unintentional** [ˌʌnɪn'tɛnʃən] 形 非故意的

117

Director Khan said the senior managers of the company had made a number of _____ comments regarding its reorganization.

(A) construction
(B) constructive
(C) construct
(D) constructively

甘恩主任說公司的資深經理針對公司的重組提出了一些有建設性的意見。

正解 (B) 詞性

空格之前有 a number of（一些），而空格之後出現名詞 comments，因此空格內應填入能修飾名詞的形容詞，故本題選 (B) constructive（有建設性的）。

□ **regarding** [rɪ'gɑrdɪŋ] 介 與⋯⋯有關
□ **reorganization** [ˌriɔrgənə'zeʃən] 動 重組
□ **constructively** [kən'strʌktɪvlɪ] 副 建設性地

118

The expansion of Titan Corporation's factories in Indonesia _____ as part of its goal of increasing output from its facilities in the region.

(A) will see
(B) is seeing
(C) was seen
(D) being seen

泰坦公司在印尼的擴廠被視為是該公司利用當地工廠以增加產量之目標的一部分。

正解 (C) 被動式

本句主詞為 The expansion of Titan Corporation's factories in Indonesia，故動詞使用被動式才合理。選項 (C) was seen 即為正解。

□ **expansion** [ɪk'spænʃən] 名 擴張
□ **output** ['aʊtˌpʊt] 名 產量
□ **region** ['ridʒən] 名 地區

119

Global Footwear Inc. is _____ larger than its domestic rivals, which gives it a much larger marketing budget.

(A) consecutively
(B) considerably
(C) consequently
(D) confusingly

全球鞋品公司遠大於其國內的對手，因此它的行銷預算也多得多。

正解 (B) 字彙

空格之後的 larger than 為比較級結構，因此以表「程度」的 (B) considerably（相當地）作為其修飾語最適當。

□ **domestic** [də'mɛstɪk] 形 國內的
□ **budget** ['bʌdʒɪt] 名 預算
□ **consecutively** [kən'sɛkjətɪvlɪ] 副 連續地
□ **consequently** ['kɑnsəˌkwɛntlɪ] 副 因此
□ **confusingly** [kən'fjuzɪŋlɪ] 副 令人困惑地

120

Following months of _____, Joshua Technologies publicly announced its takeover of Carpon Digital Design for £375.5 million.

(A) education
(B) speculation
(C) performance
(D) regulation

經過數個月的思索後，約書亞科技公開宣布要以 3 億 7,550 萬英鎊收購卡彭數位設計。

正解 (B) 字彙

企業在宣布併購案之前先做長時間的「思考」最為合理，因此選項 (B) speculation 為正解。

□ **following** ['faləwɪŋ] 介 在⋯⋯之後
□ **takeover** ['tekˌovə] 名 收購
□ **performance** [pə'fɔrməns] 名 業績
□ **regulation** [ˌrɛgjə'leʃən] 名 規定；調節

試題與翻譯	答案與解析

121

Lopez Telecom Co. won a contract to build a telecommunication network in Eastern Europe, _____ in a 14% rise in profits.

(A) result
(B) to result
(C) resulting
(D) will result

羅培茲電信公司拿到了在東歐建造電信網的合約，使得利潤增加了 14%。

正解 (C) 分詞構句

result in ... 是「導致……」的意思。由於逗號之前已經是一個完整的句子，因此應選表達出「結果」的選項 (C) resulting。注意，本句逗號之後的結構屬「分詞構句」。

☐ **win a contract to *do*** 獲得從事……的契約

122

The success of the Crystal Mountain Resort Hotel _____ by its low vacancy rate of only about 3% almost year-round.

(A) could determine
(B) can be determined
(C) to be determined
(D) is determining

水晶山度假飯店的成功可以取決於它的低空房率，全年幾乎都只有 3% 左右。

正解 (B) 被動式

determine 是「決定；判斷」的意思。句中沒有動詞，所以選項 (A)、(B)、(D) 都可能是答案。由於句子的主詞為（抽象）名詞 success，且空格後出現 by，因此使用被動式的動詞才合理。正解為選項 (B) can be determined。

☐ **vacancy rate** 空房率
☐ **year-round** [ˋjɪrˏraʊnd] 副 一年到頭地

123

One of the main strengths of Ms. Chou's company lies in _____ ability to uncover previously undeveloped markets.

(A) it
(B) herself
(C) hers
(D) its

周女士公司的主要強項之一在於發掘過去未開發市場的能力。

正解 (D) 代名詞

空格後有名詞 ability，故空格內應填入具形容詞功能的代名詞所有格，而表 Ms. Chou's company 之所有格的選項為 (D) its。

☐ **uncover** [ʌnˋkʌvɚ] 動 發現；揭露
☐ **previously** [ˋpriviəslɪ] 副 原先；以前

124

Attendees at the One Globe Financial Seminar will have a chance to learn _____ corporations should carefully manage their internal cash reserves at all times.

(A) they
(B) why
(C) them
(D) what

壹全球金融研討會的出席者將有機會學到為什麼企業隨時都應該謹慎地管理內部的儲備現金。

正解 (B) 關係副詞

空格前後各有一個子句，故空格內應填入連接詞。選項 (A) they 與 (C) them 並非連接詞，因此可先排除。而若填入關係代名詞選項 (D) what，則空格後應接缺乏主詞或受詞的不完整子句，此與本題結構不符，故不可選。由於空格後為完整子句，故填入關係副詞選項 (B) why 最適當。

☐ **attendee** [əˏtɛnˋdi] 名 與會人員
☐ **manage** [ˋmænɪdʒ] 動 管理
☐ **internal** [ɪnˋtɝnl] 形 內部的

125

Organic foods at Happy Face Restaurants are becoming _____ popular, as people realize the benefits of making healthy food choices.

(A) increasing
(B) increase
(C) increasingly
(D) increment

隨著民眾體認到選擇健康食品的好處，快樂臉餐廳的有機食品愈來愈受歡迎。

正解 (C) 詞性

屬「副詞」的 (C) increasingly（漸增地）是四個選項中唯一可用來修飾 popular（受歡迎的）此形容詞的選項。

☐ **realize** [ˋrɪəˏlaɪz] 動 理解；領悟
☐ **benefit** [ˋbɛnəfɪt] 名 利益；好處
☐ **increment** [ˋɪnkrəmənt] 名 增加

126

Although White Sky Airlines has lost some of its market share in recent years, it is still _____ than its rivals.

(A) establishing
(B) establishes
(C) more established
(D) most established

雖然蒼天航空近幾年來流失了一些市占率，但是它還是比對手立足更穩。

正解 (C) 比較級

空格之後出現 than，所以使用了比較級的選項 (C) more established 為正解。（考生應多練習能夠僅看選項和空格後的 than 就能立即正確回答的反應。）

☐ **established** [əsˋtæblɪʃt] 形 確立的

127

The Dancing Baby doll created a great _____ among consumers, and sold in very large numbers upon its initial release.

(A) sensation
(B) compensation
(C) determination
(D) promotion

「跳舞寶寶」玩偶在消費者之間造成了很大的轟動，一推出就賣了非常多。

正解 (A) 字彙

create a sensation 指「造成轟動」，所以本題應選 (A) sensation。其他選項皆與題意不符。

☐ **initial** [ɪˋnɪʃəl] 形 最初的
☐ **release** [rɪˋlis] 動 發行；公布
☐ **compensation** [͵kɑmpənˋseʃən] 名 補償（金）
☐ **determination** [dɪ͵tɜməˋneʃən] 名 決心
☐ **promotion** [prəˋmoʃən] 名 促銷；晉升

128

The communications department _____ the company's media coverage, both at home and abroad.

(A) monitors
(B) renovates
(C) contacts
(D) invests

通訊公關部監看與公司相關的媒體報導，不論是國內還是國外的。

正解 (A) 字彙

一個公司的通訊公關部理當「監看」媒體的相關報導。正解為選項 (A) monitors。

☐ **media coverage** 媒體報導
☐ **renovate** [ˋrɛnə͵vet] 動 翻新；修復

129

PetCare1.com is a corporation _____ has been able to tap into the multibillion dollar pet market by shipping a variety of dog and cat-related products directly to owners.

(A) who
(B) whose
(C) which
(D) what

PetCare1.com 是一家有辦法打入高達數十億美元之寵物市場的公司，靠的就是將各種貓狗相關產品直接運送給飼主。

正解 (C) 關係代名詞

本題須選出適當的關係代名詞。空格之前為先行詞 corporation，屬「物品」，因此後面應接選項 (C) which。順帶一提，先行詞為「人」時，關代用 who，而 whose 之後應接名詞，what 則因本身已含先行詞，故不會出現在名詞後。

☐ **tap into** 打入（市場等）
☐ **multibillion** [ˋmʌltɪˋbɪljən] 形 數十億的

130

Caris Coffee has _____ its commitment to donate 5% of its annual profits to charities in Eastern Kenya.

(A) confirmed
(B) contributed
(C) contacted
(D) concerned

卡里斯咖啡已經確認了它的承諾，要捐出年營收的 5% 給肯亞東部的慈善機構。

正解 (A) 字彙

企業對所做出的 commitment（承諾）進行「確認」最符合題意。正解為選項 (A) confirmed。其他選項皆與題意不符。

☐ **donate** [ˋdonet] 動 捐贈
☐ **annual** [ˋænjuəl] 形 一年一次的
☐ **contribute** [kənˋtrɪbjut] 動 貢獻
☐ **contact** [ˋkɑntækt] 動 接觸
☐ **concern** [kənˋsɜn] 動 與……有關係；掛念

PART 6

Questions 131-134 refer to the following e-mail.

To: Francesco Milletti
From: Masoud Akbar
Date: 31 August
Subject: Replacement request

Dear Mr. Milletti,

I received your e-mail yesterday. In it, you _____ the shipment of the construction
                                              131.
materials from Milan. I have pasted information from that e-mail below.

Steel beams	200
Wood beams	175
Concrete mix	500 kilograms
Glass Panes	600
Tools	34 pieces

We have checked the shipment, and most of the goods that arrived are fine.
There is one issue, however: _____ the number of glass panes noted above
                              132.
totaled what we had ordered, there were variances in quality. Some of the
panes were quite thick, for example, while others were thin. _____. We would
                                                              133.
therefore like to have 100 replacement panes _____ to us.
                                              134.
If you are able to do this before 7 September, that would be ideal, as that
would mean minimum disruption to our construction schedule. Please let me
know when we can expect the replacement units.

Regards,
Masoud Akbar

131. (A) confirmed
(B) negotiated
(C) permitted
(D) accepted

132. (A) yet
(B) despite
(C) unless
(D) although

133. (A) We really like these high-quality products.
(B) We really need all the items to be of a similar quality.
(C) These panes are normally either too thick or thin.
(D) There are no complaints whatsoever about the price.

134. (A) send (C) sending
(B) sent (D) to send

第 131 到 134 題請參考下面這封電子郵件。

收件者：法蘭西斯科‧米雷堤
寄件者：馬索德‧阿克巴
日　期：8 月 31 日
主　旨：請求換貨

米雷堤先生您好：

我昨天收到了您的電子郵件。您在信中確認了建築材料已從米蘭發送。我將那封電子郵件的內容貼在下面。

鋼樑..	200
木樑..	175
攪拌混凝土................................	500 公斤
玻璃板..	600
工具..	34 件

貨到時我們已經檢查過，大部分都很好。不過有一個問題：雖然上面記載的玻璃板總數跟我們所訂的一樣，但是品質卻不一致。例如有些板子相當厚，有些則很薄。我們必須要求整批貨的品質差不多一樣。因此，希望您能寄 100 片替換的新玻璃板過來。

假如您有辦法在 9 月 7 日前處理好這件事，那再好不過了，因為那代表我們的施工時程所受的干擾會最少。我們什麼時候可以等到替換品，請通知我一聲。

馬索德‧阿克巴上

146

131

正解 (A) 字彙

由題目的下一個句子裡提到的「收到電子郵件的資訊」及之後列出的所有內容推測，空格內應填入選項 (A) confirmed 來表達「確認」建材配送明細之意。

□ **negotiate** [nɪˋgoʃɪet] 動 談判；協商

132

正解 (D) 從屬連接詞

由於該句逗號前後兩個子句具相反的意涵，因此連接詞應表「讓步」的從屬連接詞選項 (D) although。注意，選項 (A) yet 雖然具有逆接功能，但是並非從屬連接詞，無法用於句首；選項 (B) despite 雖也可作為逆接之用，但為介系詞，無法用來連接子句。

133

正解 (B) 插入句

寄件者於前兩個句子中具體舉出其所收到的玻璃板有厚薄不一、品質不均的問題。空格之後則表達希望換貨，依此文脈推斷，最適合填入空格的即為選項 (B)，其中的 items 指的就是 panes。

(A) 我們非常喜歡這些高品質的產品。
(B) 我們必須要求整批貨的品質差不多一樣。
(C) 這些玻璃板通常不是太厚就是太薄。
(D) 關於價格完全沒有什麼好抱怨的。

□ **whatsoever** [ˌhwɑtsoˋɛvɚ] 副（置於接續 no 的名詞之後）任何事物；無論什麼

134

正解 (B) 使役動詞

＜ have ＋ O ＋過去分詞＞此句型指「使 O 被做某事」，而 would like to have ... sent to us 是「想請對方將……送過來」之意。故本題正解為 (B)。

Vocabulary

□ **shipment** [ˋʃɪpmənt] 名 裝運（物）
□ **issue** [ˋɪʃju] 名 問題
□ **variance** [ˋvɛrɪəns] 名 變化；不一致
□ **quality** [ˋkwɑlətɪ] 名 品質
□ **therefore** [ˋðɛr.for] 副 因此
□ **replacement** [rɪˋplesmənt] 名 取代；代替物
□ **ideal** [aɪˋdiəl] 形 理想的
□ **minimum** [ˋmɪnəməm] 形 最小的
□ **disruption** [dɪsˋrʌpʃən] 名 中斷；擾亂

Questions 135-138 refer to the following letter.

Ajit Rahman
22 Ackley Road
Nashville, TN
December 3

Dear Mr. Rahman,

Please find a recent summary of the _____ on your account below.
135.

Amount in account at start of period: $500,000
Withdrawal, November 13 .... $6,000
Deposit, November 15 .... $5,320
Withdrawal, November 30 .... $4,200
Ending Balance: $495,120

We'd also like to remind you that _____ for overdraft protection is highly
136.
recommended. Such protection guards you against fees which would
otherwise be incurred.

You are currently eligible for up to $5,000 in overdraft protection. Many of our
customers feel that this provides them with _____, as they know they will not be
137.
penalized if they write checks for amounts temporarily not in their accounts. _____.
138.

Sincerely,

Renee Zuiller
Account Manager
r.zuiller@d-bank.com

---

135. (A) upgrades
(B) purchases
(C) transactions
(D) investments

136. (A) applies
(B) applicable
(C) applications
(D) applying

137. (A) secure
(B) secured
(C) more security
(D) more securely

138. (A) Please e-mail me if you are interested in this program.
(B) Please let me know if this is possible at your earliest convenience.
(C) If you have any recommendations, I would like to hear them.
(D) I look forward to receiving your next report soon.

第 135 到 138 題請參考下面這封信件。

阿吉特‧拉曼
田納西州那什維爾市艾克里路 22 號
12 月 3 日

拉曼先生您好：

請參閱下列您的帳戶近期之交易明細。

開戶金額：... $500,000
提款，11 月 13 日.. $6,000
存款，11 月 15 日.. $5,320
提款，11 月 30 日.. $4,200
期末結餘：... $495,120

另外，我們強烈推薦您申請加入本行的透支保護服務。這項保障能使您免除在未申請該服務的情況下可能會被收取的費用。

您目前適用的透支保護金額達 5,000 美元。我們的許多客戶表示，本服務提供了更安心的感受，因為他們知道，如果他們開出的支票金額暫時超出帳戶結餘，並不會遭到罰款。假如您對此方案有興趣，請寄電子郵件給我。

客戶經理
芮妮‧崔勒敬上
r.zuiller@d-bank.com

135

正解 (C) 字彙

題目之句意是「請參閱下列您的帳戶近期之……明細」，並於下方列出交易明細，故 (C) transactions（交易）為正確答案。

☐ **upgrade** [ˋʌpˋgrɛd] **名** 升級
☐ **purchase** [ˋpɝtʃəs] **名** 購買
☐ **investment** [ɪnˋvɛstmənt] **名** 投資

136

正解 (D) 詞性

remind（人）that SV 此句型指「提醒某人某事」。在 that 子句中由空格至 protection 為主詞，is 為動詞。apply for 是「申請」的意思，而在此 that 子句中因須作為主詞，故應用動名詞表示之。本題正解為選項 (D) applying。注意，選項 (C) applications（申請表）為複數形，be 動詞應使用 are 而非 is，故不可選。

137

正解 (C) 比較級

provide A with B 的意思是「提供 B 給 A」。在本句中 them 指的是 Many of our customers，空格內則應填入名詞或相當語詞，故選項 (C) more security 為正解。另，由於這段是在表達「使用透支保障方案與未申請前相較，安全性較高」，因此依上下文來判斷比較級的選項非常合理。

138

正解 (A) 插入句

本題須選出何者最適合為文章做總結。這封信的目的在於提供客戶的銀行交易概要，並說明銀行所提供的 overdraft（透支）保護服務之內容及額度。最適合作為此信結論以吸引客戶對該服務產生興趣的只有選項 (A)。

(A) 假如您對此方案有興趣，請寄電子郵件給我。
(B) 這件事可行還是不可行，請儘快通知我。
(C) 假如您有任何建議，願聞其詳。
(D) 期待很快收到您的下一份報告。

☐ **recommendation** [ˌrɛkəmɛnˋdeʃən] **名** 推薦；建議

Vocabulary

☐ **withdrawal** [wɪðˋdrɔəl] **名** 提款
☐ **deposit** [dɪˋpɑzɪt] **名** 存款
☐ **remind** [rɪˋmaɪnd] **動** 提醒；使想起
☐ **be eligible for ...** 對……有資格的
☐ **penalize** [ˋpinˌlaɪz] **動** 對……處罰
☐ **temporarily** [ˋtɛmpəˌrɛrəlɪ] **副** 臨時地

Questions 139-142 refer to the following notice.

The management at Lysell Corporation _____ staff to take care of their bodies
139.
as well as their careers.

Apart from our company fitness center and health plan, we have recently
launched a Healthy Living campaign, _____ by the Human Resources
140.
Department. _____. More precisely, the campaign is designed to get our staff
141.
to exercise, eat right, and watch their weight. Already, 210 employees have
signed up for it.

Elisabeth Choi from the Human Resources Department, who leads the
campaign, recommended the staff could get in _____ in various ways, such as
142.
cycling to work instead of driving, or taking the stairs instead of the elevators.

139. (A) encouraging
(B) encouragement
(C) encouragingly
(D) encourages

140. (A) contacted
(B) converted
(C) developed
(D) declared

141. (A) However, the campaign has been running
quite smoothly.
(B) The aim of the campaign is to help our
staff improve their well-being.
(C) The communication plan would boost the
campaign's impact.
(D) Therefore, we would appreciate your
contribution to this cause.

142. (A) position
(B) place
(C) touch
(D) shape

第 139 到 142 題請參考下面這則通知。

力索公司的管理階層鼓勵全體同仁兼顧身體與事業。

除了我們公司的健身中心與醫療保險方案外,我們最近還推出了由人資部所開發出來的健康生活活動。本活動的目標在於幫助員工改善他們的健康。更確切地說,這項活動的設計是要讓員工們多運動、吃得恰當,並注意體重。已經有 210 位員工報名了。

此活動由人資部的伊莉莎白‧崔負責,她建議員工們可以用各種方式來鍛鍊身體,比方說不要開車而改騎腳踏車上班,或是不要搭電梯而改爬樓梯。

139

正解 **(D)** 詞性

空格前為名詞結構,顯然是句子的主詞。空格後則為另一名詞,而句中並未出現動詞,故判斷此名詞應為動詞之受詞。因此,空格內應填入一及物動詞。正解為選項 (D)。< encourage + 人 + to do >指「鼓勵某人做某事」。

140

正解 **(C)** 字彙

必須選出能從後面修飾空格前之 a Healthy Living campaign 的過去分詞。而由空格後面出現的 by the Human Resources Department 來判斷,由人資部「開發出」該活動最合理。正解為選項 (C)。

☐ **convert** [kən'vɝt] 動 轉換

141

正解 **(B)** 插入句

空格前一句說力索公司開發了健康生活的活動,而由空格後的 More precisely「更確切地說」可知,其後乃針對空格內容做了更具體的說明。依此文脈,填入選項 (B) 最合理。注意,句中的 well-being「健康」即指文中的 exercise, eat right, and watch their weight。

(A) 不過,本活動一直進行得相當順利。
(B) 本活動的目標在於幫助員工改善他們的健康。
(C) 該溝通計畫會提升本活動的影響力。
(D) 因此,我們很感謝您對此目標貢獻。

☐ **boost** [bust] 動 提高;增加
☐ **contribution** [ˌkɑntrə'bjuʃən] 名 貢獻

142

正解 **(D)** 字彙

本題須思考伊莉莎白‧崔在健康生活活動方面建議員工做何事。在 such as 之後描述了幾個具體例子,而依其內容可判斷,即 get in shape「使身體健康」的方法。選項 (D) 為正解。

Vocabulary

☐ **take care of ...** 照顧……
☐ **health plan** 醫療保險方案
☐ **recently** ['risṇtlɪ] 副 最近
☐ **launch** [lɔntʃ] 動 發起;推出
☐ **precisely** [prɪ'saɪslɪ] 副 精確地
☐ **various** ['vɛrɪəs] 形 不同的;各式各樣的

Questions 143-146 refer to the following e-mail.

From: David Martin, Operations Director
To: Luiz Rodriguez, Carmel Falls Manager
Subject: Georgetown Branch Opening
Date: Monday, May 5

Luiz,

As you know, the Georgetown Branch of PizzaMan Inc. is due to open this fall.

As a result, we now need to _____ staff in the local area.
143.

The Carmel Falls Branch is only 10 miles away, so we would like to offer some

of your staff the opportunity to join _____ there. We feel that their previous
144.

experience of working for PizzaMan could be extremely important in _____ the
145.

new branch a success.

Please let your employees know about this great new career option as soon as

possible. _____.
146.

Sincerely,

David Martin

143. (A) reorganize
(B) recruit
(C) outsource
(D) survey

144. (A) theirs
(B) us
(C) our
(D) their

145. (A) causing
(B) going
(C) letting
(D) making

146. (A) We will give priority to those who have been with us the longest.
(B) We look forward to serving you at our new Carmel Falls branch.
(C) This is the very first time we have treated you like this.
(D) All staff members should report to work on time each day.

試題翻譯

第 143 到 146 題請參考下面這封電子郵件。

寄件者：營運部主任大衛‧馬丁
收件者：卡莫佛斯店經理路易茲‧羅德里格茲
主　旨：喬治城分店開幕
日　期：5 月 5 日星期一

路易茲：

如你所知，「披薩人」公司的喬治城分店即將在今年秋天開幕。因此，我們現在需要在當地招募人員。

卡莫佛斯分店離那兒只有十英哩，所以我們想讓你的部分員工有機會去那裡加入我們。我們認為，他們之前在「披薩人」服務的經驗對於使新分店得以成功可能非常重要。

請儘快把這個很棒的新職涯選擇轉告你的員工。我們會將優先權給那些在公司任職最久的人。

祝　好
大衛‧馬丁

143

正解 (B)　字彙

文章從新分店開幕的話題開始敘述，而空格之後出現 staff（員工），因此空格內填入表「招募」之意的選項 (B) recruit 最合理。注意，由於後面段落討論到要調動連鎖店的人手，因此選項 (C) outsource（外包）明顯不適當。

☐ **reorganize** [ri`ɔrgə.naɪz] 動 重組
☐ **survey** [sə`ve] 動 調查

144

正解 (B)　代名詞與「格」

so 之後子句的主詞為 we，因此只有其受格選項 (B) us 和所有格選項 (C) our 可考慮。而因空格後並沒有名詞，故所有格選項 (C) 不適當，選項 (B) us 才是正解。注意，offer A B 指「提供 B 給 A」。

145

正解 (D)　字彙

空格前有介系詞 in，所以空格內必須使用動名詞，而四個選項中唯一適合與其後受詞及受詞補語搭配的是 (D) making。＜make＋受詞＋a success＞為「使……得以成功」之意。注意，假如使用 let 的話，後面接的受詞補語不能是名詞，因此選項 (C) 不可選。

146

正解 (A)　插入句

前一句提到「請儘快把這個很棒的新職涯選擇轉告你的員工」，而用來進一步說明前句內容的選項 (A) 為正解，其中之 priority（優先權）即指獲得前一句當中的 this great new career option。

(A) 我們會將優先權給那些在公司任職最久的人。
(B) 我們期待在我們的卡莫佛斯新分店為您服務。
(C) 這是我們的第一次如此地對待您。
(D) 全體員工同仁每天皆應準時出勤。

☐ **report to work** 上班出勤

Vocabulary

☐ **previous** [`priviəs] 形 以前的
☐ **extremely** [ɪk`strimlɪ] 副 非常地

PART 7

Questions 147-148 refer to the following ticket.

ADMIT ONE ADULT

Summer of Strings

An evening of classical music with the Singapore National Symphony Orchestra

Kwan Teok Hall
Doors Open: 7:30 P.M.
Performance First Half: 8:15 P.M.
Intermission: 10:00 P.M.
Performance Second Half: 10:30 P.M.

No cameras, videos or other recording devices allowed. No admittance after 10 minutes before the show starts. Please turn off all phones prior to entering. Except in the event of a performance cancellation, all ticket sales are final.

第 147 到 148 題請參照下面這張入場券。

限一位成人
夏日弦樂
新加坡國家交響樂團的古典樂之夜

官德廳
入場：晚上 7 點 30 分
上半場演出：晚上 8 點 15 分
中場休息：晚上 10 點
下半場演出：晚上 10 點 30 分

禁用相機、攝影機或其他攝錄裝置。開演前十分鐘起禁止入場。入場前行動電話請關機。除演出取消之情形外，所有入場券售出後概不退費。

Vocabulary

- **string** [strɪŋ] 名 弦樂器（用複數形）
- **performance** [pəˋfɔrməns] 名 演出；表演
- **intermission** [ˌɪntɚˋmɪʃən] 名 （戲劇等中間的）休息時間；幕間休息
- **device** [dɪˋvaɪs] 名 設備；儀器
- **turn off ...** 關閉……（的電源）
- **prior to ...** 在……之前
- **in the event of ...** 如果發生……
- **cancellation** [ˌkænsḷˋeʃən] 名 取消

試題	試題翻譯	答案與解析

147

When is the latest that ticketed guests may enter to see the performance?

(A) 7:30 P.M.
(B) 8:05 P.M.
(C) 8:15 P.M.
(D) 10:00 P.M.

持票觀眾最晚可以在什麼時間入場觀賞演出？

(A) 晚上 7 點 30 分
(B) 晚上 8 點 05 分
(C) 晚上 8 點 15 分
(D) 晚上 10 點

正解 (B)

演出上半場於 8 點 15 分開始，而依規定 No admittance after 10 minutes before the show starts.，換言之，最後的入場時間為開演前十分鐘，故正解為選項 (B) 8:05 P.M.。

☐ **ticketed** [ˋtɪkɪtɪd] 形 持有票券的

148

What is stated on the ticket?

(A) Seating may be unreserved.
(B) Refunds are not usually available.
(C) No cancellations are allowed.
(D) Performance dates are limited.

入場券上註明了什麼事？

(A) 座位可以不必先預定。
(B) 通常不可退費。
(C) 訂票無法取消。
(D) 演出限期舉行。

正解 (B)

從最後一項規定 Except in the event of a performance cancellation, all ticket sales are final. 可知，除了演出取消之外票券通常不可退費，因此正解為選項 (B) Refunds are not usually available.。

☐ **unreserved** [ˌʌnrɪˋzɝvd] 形 未預約的

Questions 149-150 refer to the following text message chain.

第 149 到 150 題請參照下面這段手機訊息。

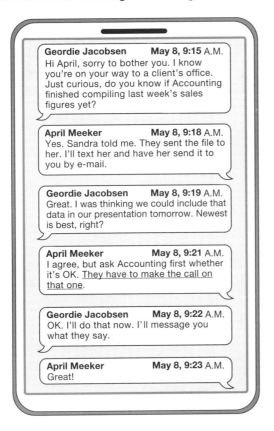

Geordie Jacobsen   May 8, 9:15 A.M.
Hi April, sorry to bother you. I know you're on your way to a client's office. Just curious, do you know if Accounting finished compiling last week's sales figures yet?

April Meeker   May 8, 9:18 A.M.
Yes. Sandra told me. They sent the file to her. I'll text her and have her send it to you by e-mail.

Geordie Jacobsen   May 8, 9:19 A.M.
Great. I was thinking we could include that data in our presentation tomorrow. Newest is best, right?

April Meeker   May 8, 9:21 A.M.
I agree, but ask Accounting first whether it's OK. They have to make the call on that one.

Geordie Jacobsen   May 8, 9:22 A.M.
OK. I'll do that now. I'll message you what they say.

April Meeker   May 8, 9:23 A.M.
Great!

喬迪・傑可森　　　　　五月 8 日上午 9:15
嗨,愛裴蘿,抱歉打擾妳。我知道妳正在去客戶辦公室的路上。我只是好奇,妳知不知道會計部把上禮拜的銷售數字彙整好了嗎?

愛裴蘿・米克　　　　　五月 8 日上午 9:18
好了。珊卓拉告訴我的。他們把檔案寄給她了。我會傳訊息給她,請她把檔案用電子郵件寄給你。

喬迪・傑可森　　　　　五月 8 日上午 9:19
太好了。我在想我們可以把那份資料加進我們明天的簡報。最新的就是最好的,對吧?

愛裴蘿・米克　　　　　五月 8 日上午 9:21
我贊成,不過還是先問一下會計部是不是 OK 吧。這得要他們決定才行。

喬迪・傑可森　　　　　五月 8 日上午 9:22
好。我現在就問。我再傳訊息告訴妳他們怎麼說。

愛裴蘿・米克　　　　　五月 8 日上午 9:23
太棒了!

Vocabulary

☐ **curious** [ˈkjʊrɪəs] 形 好奇的　☐ **compile** [kəmˈpaɪl] 動 彙整;收集(資料等)　☐ **make the call** 做主;決定

149

What is Ms. Meeker doing now?

(A) Gathering some data
(B) Preparing for a presentation
(C) Writing an e-mail to Accounting
(D) Going to a client's office

米克小姐正在做什麼?

(A) 蒐集資料
(B) 為簡報做準備
(C) 寫電子郵件給會計部
(D) 去客戶的辦公室

正解 (D)

從一開始傑可森先生說的 you're on your way to a client's office 即可知,米克小姐現在正在前往客戶辦公室的路上,選項 (D) 為正解。on one's way to ... 指「在前往……的途中」。多益改制後的新題型「(手機等)文字通訊對話」中,有可能提及直接見面談、寄 e-mail、講電話等,情境變得較為複雜。因此,看到題目想像對話雙方正在哪裡以及什麼情況之下互傳訊息相當重要。

150

At 9:21 A.M., what does Ms. Meeker most likely mean when she writes, "They have to make the call on that one"?

(A) Accounting has to give permission to use data.
(B) Accounting has to give a presentation.
(C) She has to make a phone call to Accounting.
(D) She has to forward the data to Mr. Jacobsen.

九點二十一分時,米克小姐打的 "They have to make the call on that one" 最有可能是什麼意思?

(A) 會計部必須允許使用該資料。
(B) 會計部必須做簡報。
(C) 她必須打電話給會計部。
(D) 她必須轉寄該資料給傑可森先生。

正解 (A)

They 是指 Accounting,而 that one 則指「在明天簡報上使用銷售額的最新數字」一事。make the call 是「做重要決策」的意思,將其換句話說的選項 (A) 為正解。注意,選項 (C) make a phone call 為「打電話」之意,小心不要被混淆而誤選。

☐ **give permission** 給予許可
☐ **forward A to B** 將 A 轉寄給 B

Questions 151-152 refer to the following information.

Annual Pan-Pacific Telecom Association Meeting

Macau Lotus Hotel
Pandora Room
July 7

The Association is pleased to announce that during this year's meeting, a keynote lecture will be given by Mr. Sun Liu Fan, widely regarded as the world's leading authority on global telecommunications. His research has led to the development of new insights on emerging advances in the industry. This has enabled both corporations and government regulators to maximize the benefits of this dynamic field.

Following the release of his latest book, *A World Connected*, Mr. Sun will share his most recent findings on telecommunications in emerging markets.

All those wishing to attend the lecture can get more information at www.panpacifictelecomassoc.net/lectures/.

*Fees for attending the annual meeting are not inclusive of the lecture. Those should be covered in advance through the online address noted above.

第 151 到 152 題請參照下面這則資訊。

泛太平洋電信協會年會

澳門蓮花酒店
潘朵拉廳
7 月 7 日

本協會很高興宣布，在本次年會期間主題講座將由被公認為全球電信首席權威的孫留芳先生擔綱。針對產業中的新發展，他的研究促使了新見解的形成。這使得企業與政府主管機關都能在此蓬勃領域創造出最大的利益。

在推出最新的著作《串連的世界》後，孫先生將分享他對於新興市場中電信業的最新發現。

所有希望參加講座的人可上 www.panpacifictelecomassoc.net/lectures/ 查閱詳情。

* 參加年會的費用並不包含聽講座的費用；聽講座之費用應事先經由上列網址另外支付。

Vocabulary

- **pan-Pacific** [ˈpænpəˈsɪfɪk] 形 泛太平洋的
- **telecom** [ˈtɛləkɑm] 名 電信（telecommunication 之簡稱）
- **association** [əˌsosɪˈeʃən] 名 協會
- **keynote lecture** 主題講演
- **leading** [ˈlidɪŋ] 形 第一的
- **authority** [əˈθɔrətɪ] 名 權威
- **insight** [ˈɪnˌsaɪt] 形 見解；洞察力
- **emerging** [ɪˈmɝdʒɪŋ] 形 新興的
- **regulator** [ˈrɛgjəˌletə] 名 主管機關
- **maximize** [ˈmæksəˌmaɪz] 動 使增加至最大限度
- **dynamic** [daɪˈnæmɪk] 形 有活力的；蓬勃的
- **inclusive of ...** 包含……的

試題	試題翻譯	答案與解析

151

According to the information, what is Mr. Sun renowned for?

(A) His regulatory authority over markets
(B) His financial investments into industry
(C) His many years of experience in different corporations
(D) His expertise and research in a specific field

根據上列資訊，孫先生以什麼聞名？

(A) 他管制市場的職權
(B) 他在業界做的金融投資
(C) 他多年來在不同企業的經驗
(D) 他在特定領域中的專業知識與研究

正解 (D)

第一段提及孫先生是一名在「全球電信產業」的研究專家，且對企業與政府主管機關頗有貢獻，由此可知 (D) 為正解。文中的 the industry、this dynamic field 和選項 (D) 當中的 a specific field 皆指 telecommunications（電信業）。

□ **regulatory** [ˈrɛgjələˌtorɪ] 形 管理的；控制的

152

What will attendees who want to hear the lecture have to do?

(A) Join the Association
(B) E-mail Mr. Sun
(C) Pay an extra charge
(D) Download a pass

想要聽講座的與會者必須怎麼做？

(A) 加入協會
(B) 寫電子郵件給孫先生
(C) 額外付費
(D) 下載入場券

正解 (C)

文章最後在底下註明 Those should be covered in advance through the online address noted above.，表示必須事前另外支付費用才能參加不包含在年會費裡的演講，所以正確答案是選項 (C)。

□ **extra charge** 額外費用

Questions 153-154 refer to the following instructions.

第 153 到 154 題請參照下面這份使用說明書。

The Revlar Microwave Oven User Guide

Position your oven away from sources of heat or moisture, for optimum efficiency.

Do not operate it when empty.

Use appropriate, heat-resistant cookware, including knives, forks or spoons, at all times. Keep bowls partially covered while cooking, but never seal them completely.

You may see moisture collecting on the inner walls or the door when the oven is in use. This is normal.

Cooking time varies according to quantity, as well as the fat or water content of the food. Monitor cooking progress to prevent food from drying out, burning or catching fire.

Food with skins or membranes – like whole apples, potatoes or tomatoes – must be pierced before cooking.

Clean the insides of the oven and its door after each use so that it remains perfectly dry. This will prevent corrosion.

瑞夫拉微波爐
使用指南

為達最佳效能，爐具應擺放於遠離火源或水氣來源處。

禁止於空爐時操作。

固定使用合適的耐熱餐具，包括刀叉或湯匙。烹調時應將碗部分覆蓋，但切勿完全封死。

爐具在使用時，內壁或爐門上可能會匯集水氣。此為正常現象。

烹調時間因量及食物所含之脂肪或水分而異。監控烹調進度，以免食物乾掉、燒焦或著火。

帶皮或膜的食物（例如整顆的蘋果、馬鈴薯或番茄）必須扎洞再烹調。

每次使用後都要清理爐具內部和爐門，以保持完全乾燥。這樣可避免鏽蝕。

Vocabulary

- **microwave oven** 微波爐
- **source** [sors] 名 源頭
- **moisture** [ˈmɔɪstʃɚ] 名 濕氣；水分
- **optimum** [ˈɑptəməm] 形 最理想的
- **efficiency** [ɪˈfɪʃənsɪ] 名 效率；效能
- **appropriate** [əˈproprɪɪt] 形 適當的
- **heat-resistant** [ˈhitrɪˌzɪstənt] 形 耐熱的
- **cookware** [ˈkukˌwɛr] 名 廚房用具
- **partially** [ˈpɑrʃəlɪ] 副 部分地
- **seal** [sil] 動 密封
- **vary** [ˈvɛrɪ] 動 改變
- **catch fire** 著火
- **membrane** [ˈmɛmbren] 名 膜
- **pierce** [pɪrs] 動 刺穿；打洞
- **corrosion** [kəˈroʒən] 名 腐蝕；生鏽

153

What is stated about the cookware?

(A) It should be kept away from moisture.
(B) It should not be used in an operating oven.
(C) It should be able to withstand heat.
(D) It should be sealed inside bowls.

說明書中註明廚具要怎麼樣？

(A) 應遠離濕氣。
(B) 不應於爐具運轉時使用。
(C) 應可耐熱。
(D) 應密封於碗裡。

正解 (C)

注意本題問的是有關 cookware（廚具）如何使用。選項 (A) 說的是有關 oven（爐具）的事，故不適當。而由說明書裡提到的 Use appropriate, heat-resistant cookware 可知，換句話說的選項 (C) 為正解。至於選項 (D)，文中提及「應將碗部分覆蓋，但切勿完全封死」，因此不可選。

154

What is recommended in the instructions?

(A) The oven should be operated when empty.
(B) The food should be dry before cooking.
(C) Airtight containers should be used.
(D) Holes should be poked into some food before cooking.

使用說明中建議做什麼？

(A) 爐具應於內部淨空時操作。
(B) 食物於烹調前應瀝乾。
(C) 應使用密閉的容器。
(D) 烹調前應先將某些食物戳洞。

正解 (D)

說明中提到 Food with skins or membranes ... must be pierced before cooking.，建議使用者帶皮的食物應在料理之前戳洞，換言之，選項 (D) Holes should be poked before cooking. 即為正解。

- **airtight** [ˈɛrˌtaɪt] 形 氣密的
- **poke a hole** 戳洞

Questions 155-157 refer to the following e-mail.

* E-mail *	×

From:	Kim Su-mi, Director, Han Kang Construction Corp.　KOREA
To:	Fara Suleiman, President, Malaya One Real Estate　MALAYSIA
Subject:	Consort Building
Date:	1 August

Dear Ms. Suleiman,

Following our videoconference of 29 July with our architects Franklin & Josephs, we feel it is necessary to visit your office to discuss the ongoing progress of the Consort Building project. We hope 4 August might be acceptable to you.

In your last e-mail, you also mentioned needing our assistance with some of your interior work. As you are aware, our agreement covers only the exterior of the building. However, we can recommend Maxima Space Co., headquartered in Rome. They have extensive experience with interiors, and have worked with us on buildings like yours in the past. Maxima Vice-president Ron Fascenelli has told me his corporation is quite capable of installing carpeting, furnishings, and handling painting for each of the 273 offices within the office building, in addition to other decorating needs as may be required.

I have taken the liberty of asking Mr. Fascenelli to send you a brochure package about his company by post. You can also learn more about them through their Web site www. maximaspaceitalia.com or simply e-mailing Mr. Fascenelli at ron.f@maximaspace.com.

We hope this helps you in your situation.

Yours sincerely,

Kim Su-mi

第 155 到 157 題請參照下面這封電子郵件。

寄件者：韓國漢江營建公司主任金秀美
收件者：馬來西亞第一不動產總裁
　　　　法拉・蘇雷曼
主　旨：合建
日　期：8 月 1 日

蘇雷曼女士您好：

在 7 月 29 日跟我們的建築師富蘭克林和約瑟夫開過視訊會議後，我們覺得有必要到您的辦公室拜訪一下，以便討論合建案的進度。希望您在 8 月 4 日會有空。

在您上一封電子郵件中，您還提到需要我們協助你們部分內部裝潢工程一事。如您所知，我們的合約只涵蓋大樓的外觀。不過，我們可以推薦總部位於羅馬的極大空間公司。他們在內部裝潢方面擁有豐富的經驗，過去也跟我們合作過像你們那樣的大樓。極大公司的副總裁隆恩・費森內里跟我說過，他們公司有充分的能力為辦公大樓裡的 273 間辦公室鋪設地毯、安裝家具陳設並負責油漆，而若有其他的裝潢需求，他們也能一併處理。

我已冒昧請費森內里先生將他們公司的簡介型錄冊郵寄給您。您也可以上他們的網站 www. maximaspaceitalia.com，或直接寄電子郵件到 ron.f@maximaspace.com 給費森內里先生，以了解詳情。

希望這對於您的情況有幫助。

金秀美敬上

Vocabulary

- **videoconference** [ˈvɪdɪoˌkɑnfərəns] 名 視訊會議
- **architect** [ˈɑrkəˌtɛkt] 名 建築師
- **ongoing** [ˈɑnˌgoɪŋ] 形 進行中的
- **interior** [ɪnˈtɪrɪə] 名 內部
- **agreement** [əˈgrimənt] 名 協議
- **exterior** [ɪkˈstɪrɪə] 名 外部
- **(be) headquartered in ...** 以……為總部所在地的
- **extensive** [ɪkˈstɛnsɪv] 形 廣大的
- **be capable of ...** 有……能力的
- **install** [ɪnˈstɔl] 動 安裝
- **furnishings** [ˈfɜnɪʃɪŋz] 名 家具；陳設（複數形）
- **take the liberty of ...** 冒昧做……
- **by post** 郵寄

155

What is the purpose of Ms. Kim's upcoming meeting with Ms. Suleiman?

(A) To meet construction architects
(B) To propose additional project outlines
(C) To provide updates on construction work
(D) To inspect building specifications

金小姐要去拜會蘇雷曼女士的目的是什麼？

(A) 為了會見建案的建築師
(B) 為了提報額外的建案大綱
(C) 為了提供工程進度的最新消息
(D) 為了檢查建築規格

正解 (C)

第一段裡提及 we feel it is necessary to visit your office to discuss the ongoing progress of the Consort Building project，表示她想討論「建案的最新進度」，故正解為 (C)。文中的 the Consort Building project 以 construction work（建築工程）取而代之，而 discuss the ongoing progress 則以 provide updates 來換句話說。

☐ **outline** ['aʊt.laɪn] **图** 大綱
☐ **building specification** 建築規格說明書

156

Why does Ms. Kim recommend Maxima Space Co.?

(A) They have developed many building exteriors.
(B) They dominate the market in Rome.
(C) They have done a lot of work in interior projects.
(D) They offer the lowest prices.

金小姐為什麼推薦極大空間公司？

(A) 他們研發過許多大樓的外觀。
(B) 他們在羅馬是市場的霸主。
(C) 他們做過很多內裝修繕工程。
(D) 他們的報價最低。

正解 (C)

電子郵件第二段裡寫道 They have extensive experience with interiors, and have worked with us on buildings like yours in the past.，也就是說，金小姐過去曾經與極大空間共事，並肯定該公司在內部裝潢領域擁有相當深廣的經驗，所以才會建議與他們合作。正解為選項 (C)。

☐ **dominate** ['dɑmə.net] **動** 支配；控制

157

What does Ms. Suleiman expect to receive soon?

(A) An e-mail from the vice-president
(B) Some reading material from overseas
(C) A phone call regarding construction deadlines
(D) A Web site service agreement

蘇雷曼女士預計很快會收到什麼？

(A) 副總裁寄的電子郵件
(B) 海外寄來的閱讀資料
(C) 關於工程期限的電話
(D) 網站的服務合約

正解 (B)

第三段提到 I have taken the liberty of asking Mr. Fascenelli to send you a brochure package about his company by post.，表示將會有一個來自費森內里先生的型錄包裹送達，而蘇雷曼女士人在馬來西亞，費森內里先生的公司位於羅馬，所以答案是選項 (B)。注意，是寄件者建議蘇雷曼女士可寄電子郵件與費森內里先生聯絡，而非副總裁費森內里將寄電子郵件給她，小心不要誤選 (A)。

Questions 158-160 refer to the following advertisement.

第 158 到 160 題請參照下面這則廣告。

Come Join the Team at Symington Company
We Animate the World!

Symington Company, headquartered in New Zealand, announces openings in its Riga, Latvia office.

About us: We are one of the largest companies in the Asia-Pacific region, known for our cutting-edge animation technologies. Our employees are dedicated, hard-working, and generally long-term. Our compensation packages are in most cases well above industry averages. We were chosen "Best Company to Work For" this year by the business news Web site, 21CTrade.com.
Our recent moves: We are now entering the European market. The Riga office is intended to serve as the company's base for the Eastern Europe-Russia region.

We are looking for staff in the following areas:

● **Computer Graphics & Animation**
● **Print Illustration**
● **Information Technologies**
● **Management**

All applicants must have at least 3 years of experience in their respective fields. Managerial applicants must have at least 4 additional years. Medium fluency in English required; medium or advanced fluency in Russian, German or French is preferred.

Those interested in one of the positions listed above may apply online at www.symingtonanimation.com/jobs/animation/latvia/. Callers to Personnel about this position will be directed back to this site. Faxed résumés will receive no response. Interviews will take place from October 5 to October 12 at our Riga headquarters, and those who are selected for positions will be notified by October 20. Most positions will start October 23.

一同加入賽明頓公司的團隊
我們讓世界動起來!

總部位於紐西蘭的賽明頓公司
發布拉脫維亞里加分處的職缺

關於我們:我們是亞太地區最大的公司之一,以尖端的動畫技術而聞名。我們的員工既認真又勤奮,而且普遍都任職很久。我們的薪資與福利在大部分的情況下都遠優於業界平均水準。我們今年被商業新聞網站 21CTrade.com 選為「最佳可任職公司」。

我們的近期動向:我們目前正在進軍歐洲市場。里加分處預定要作為公司在東歐及俄羅斯地區的根據地。

我們在找下列幾個領域中的人才:

● 電腦繪圖和動畫
● 平面插圖
● 資訊科技
● 管理

所有應徵者在各自的領域必須具備三年以上的經驗,管理職的應徵者則至少必須再多四年。英語須尚稱流利,俄語、德語或法語尚稱或極為流利者佳。

對上列職缺有興趣的人可上網應徵,網址是 www.symingtonanimation.com/jobs/anmination/latvia/。以電話向人資部洽詢此職缺者將會被指示回該網站。傳真履歷亦不回覆。面試將從 10 月 5 日到 10 月 12 日在里加總部進行,錄取者於 10 月 20 日之前會接獲通知。大部分的職缺將從 10 月 23 日起開始上班。

Vocabulary

- **cutting-edge** [ˈkʌtɪŋˈɛdʒ] 形 尖端的
- **dedicated** [ˈdɛdəˌketɪd] 形 專注的;獻身的
- **long-term** [ˈlɔŋˈtɜm] 形 長期的
- **compensation package** 薪資與福利
- **average** [ˈævərɪdʒ] 名 平均
- **be intended to do ...** 打算做⋯⋯
- **applicant** [ˈæpləkənt] 名 申請人;求職者
- **respective** [rɪˈspɛktɪv] 形 各別的
- **managerial** [ˌmænəˈdʒɪrɪəl] 形 管理人的;經理的
- **additional** [əˈdɪʃənl] 形 額外的;附加的
- **medium** [ˈmidɪəm] 形 中間的
- **fluency** [ˈfluənsɪ] 名 (說話或寫作的) 流暢度
- **résumé** [ˈrɛzuˌme] 名 履歷表
- **response** [rɪˈspɑns] 名 回答;回應
- **take place** 發生
- **notify** [ˈnotəˌfaɪ] 動 通知

試題	試題翻譯	答案與解析

158

What is indicated about Symington Company?

(A) It is well known in the European region.
(B) It is respected for its Web site technologies.
(C) It is famous for its award-winning products.
(D) It is noted for its generosity to its staff.

廣告中提到了賽明頓公司的什麼事？

(A) 它在歐洲地區廣為人知。
(B) 它因網站技術而備受尊敬。
(C) 它以得獎產品聞名。
(D) 它以對員工大方而著稱。

正解 (D)

廣告「關於我們」部分提及賽明頓公司所給予的薪資福利優於業界平均，且被商業新聞網站選為最佳可任職公司，所以正確答案應為選項 (D) It is noted for its generosity to its staff.。

☐ **award-winning** [əˈwɔrdˈwɪnɪŋ] **形** 獲獎的
☐ **generosity** [ˌdʒɛnəˈrɑsətɪ] **名** 慷慨；寬容

159

How much experience is required for applicants for managerial positions?

(A) Three years
(B) Four years
(C) Five years
(D) Seven years

應徵管理職的人須具備多長的經驗？

(A) 三年
(B) 四年
(C) 五年
(D) 七年

正解 (D)

這是與計算有關的問題。廣告中提到 All applicants must have at least 3 years of experience in their respective fields. Managerial applicants must have at least 4 additional years.，換言之，應徵管理職必須具備 3 + 4 = 7 年的資歷，故正解為 (D)。如果沒注意到 additional 這個字，很可能就會誤選 (B)，千萬要注意。

160

When will Symington Corporation inform successful candidates?

(A) By October 5
(B) By October 12
(C) By October 20
(D) By October 23

賽明頓公司什麼時候會通知被錄取的人？

(A) 10 月 5 日前
(B) 10 月 12 日前
(C) 10 月 20 日前
(D) 10 月 23 日前

正解 (C)

廣告文章的末尾提到 those who are selected for positions will be notified by October 20，意即錄取者 10 月 20 日前會收到通知。選項 (C) 為正解。注意，選項 (A) 是面試的第一天、選項 (B) 是面試的最後一天，而選項 (D) 則為開始上班日。

Questions 161-163 refer to the following article.

第 161 到 163 題請參照下面這篇文章。

Accounting for the New Century —in the Right Way

If your company commonly has errors in its financial reports, the accounting computer network, not the staff, is usually more to blame. — [1] —. The errors themselves are only a symptom of that underlying problem.

Consulting companies can advise you on which accounting computers to purchase. These computers are able to manage very large amounts of data, and are linked to a central network. — [2] —. Best of all, they commonly have easy-to-follow operation instructions. Consulting companies can offer advice on using these computers and teach staff to increase productivity through them.

These consulting companies also maintain industry-wide benchmarks for your accounting department. — [3] —. Their Ax Blue reports published each year provide an overview of how corporations and corporate departments in over 200 areas stay world-class. Meeting benchmarks like these ensures that your company is rising to the best practices within your industry. — [4] —.

新世紀會計──妥善之道

假如貴公司的財務報表老是出錯，責任比較大的通常是會計電腦網絡，而不是員工。— [1] —。錯誤本身只是那個潛在問題的徵兆。

顧問公司可建議您採購哪些會計電腦。這些電腦能管理非常大量的資料，並連結至中央網絡。— [2] —。最棒的是，它們的操作指令通常都很容易理解。顧問公司可提供使用電腦上的相關諮詢，並教導員工以此提高生產力。

這些顧問公司也能將您會計部的等級維持在整個業界的基準上。— [3] —。他們每年出版的艾克斯藍皮書報告為兩百多個地區的企業和公司部門提供了如何保持世界水準的概要。達到類似的標準可確保貴公司提升至業界最佳實務水平。— [4] —。

Vocabulary

- ☐ **commonly** [ˋkɑmənlɪ] 副 通常地
- ☐ **be to blame** 應該受責
- ☐ **symptom** [ˋsɪmptəm] 名 徵兆
- ☐ **underlying** [ˌʌndəˋlaɪɪŋ] 形 潛在的
- ☐ **best of all** 最棒的是
- ☐ **easy-to-follow** [ˋizɪtuˋfɑlo] 形 容易理解的
- ☐ **productivity** [ˌprodʌkˋtɪvətɪ] 名 生產力
- ☐ **industry-wide** [ˋɪndəstrɪˋwaɪd] 形 全產業的
- ☐ **benchmark** [ˋbɛntʃˌmɑrk] 名 基準；標準

161

According to the article, why do most accounting errors occur?

(A) Reports are done too quickly.
(B) Companies have insufficient data.
(C) Computer systems are inadequate.
(D) Supervisors lack management skills.

根據文章,大部分的會計錯誤為什麼會發生?

(A) 報表做得太快。
(B) 公司的資料不足。
(C) 電腦系統不適當。
(D) 主管缺乏管理技巧。

正解 (C)

第一段第一句就提到 ... the accounting computer network ... is usually more to blame.,意即會計方面出錯「通常是會計電腦網絡的問題」,因此正解為選項 (C)。

☐ **insufficient** [ˌɪnsəˈfɪʃənt] 形 不充分的
☐ **inadequate** [ɪnˈædəkwɪt] 形 不適當的

162

How are the Ax Blue reports helpful to corporations?

(A) They list the largest corporations in each field.
(B) They show how to maintain top standards in different sectors.
(C) They showcase the best managers at major businesses.
(D) They provide an overview of important markets.

艾克斯藍皮書報告對企業有什麼幫助?

(A) 它們列出各領域中最大的企業。
(B) 它們說明如何在不同部門維持最高的標準。
(C) 它們介紹各大企業的最佳經理人。
(D) 它們提供重要市場的概述。

正解 (B)

第三段提及 Their Ax Blue reports ... provide an overview of how corporations and corporate departments in over 200 areas stay world-class.,表示「他們的報告為兩百多個地區的企業和公司部門提供了如何保持世界水準的概要。」而正解就是換句話說的選項 (B)。

☐ **showcase** [ˈʃo.kes] 動 展示
☐ **major business** 大企業

163

In which of the positions marked [1], [2], [3] and [4] does the following sentence best belong?

"AxTor Consulting Group is a good example of this."

(A) [1]
(B) [2]
(C) [3]
(D) [4]

下面這個句子插入文中標示的 [1]、[2]、[3]、[4] 四處當中的何處最符合文意?

「艾克斯特顧問集團就是一個好例子。」

(A) [1]
(B) [2]
(C) [3]
(D) [4]

正解 (C)

像本題這種插入句的問題,仔細看 this、that 等指示代名詞或 his、them 等人稱代名詞所指內容非常重要。由題目裡的 AxTor 此公司名稱和 this 判斷,插入 [3] 的位置最適當,意即 AxTor Consulting Group 是「幫助企業會計部門維持在全業界標準上的顧問公司」的例子,且與之後的 Their Ax Blue reports ... 在文意上也能夠連貫。

第2回完全解析

PART 7

Questions 164-167 refer to the following notice.

BLIGO
BLIGO TRADING SERVICES
Friday, July 28

Following the senior directors' meeting last week, it has been decided that structural changes at the Bligo Hong Kong branch are necessary. The following measures are to be implemented to make operations more cost-efficient. These changes will be implemented in stages.

August 1
All help desk issues will be handled by our Bangalore, India global consumer service center. Help desk facilities in Hong Kong, including both human operators and the automated answering system, will cease.

August 20
The human resources department will utilize Web technologies for recruiting, staff management, employee benefits and other staff services to the maximum extent to decrease current costs in the department.

August 31
Personnel from the sales and marketing divisions will merge into one group, with expected staffing reductions of 42%.

While it is regrettable that some of these steps will result in job losses for the departments concerned, we are pleased to announce that several new positions have been created in our Mainland China division. Staff who are interested in applying are urged to contact Lisa Vu at lisa.vu@bligo.net for an application form.

第 164 到 167 題請參照下面這則通知。

BLIGO
布里哥貿易服務公司
7 月 28 日星期五

資深董事上週開完會之後，決定布里哥香港分公司有必要調整其組織結構。為使營運更符合成本效益，將採取以下措施。這些調整將分階段進行：

8 月 1 日
櫃台客服問題將由印度邦加羅爾的全球客服中心統一處理。香港的客服單位，包括人力接線生和自動答詢系統在內，將停止運作。

8 月 20 日
人資部將盡最大可能利用網路技術來處理徵才、人員管理、員工福利以及其他員工服務，以減少該部門目前的成本。

8 月 31 日
業務部和行銷部人員將併為一組，預計可節省 42% 的人力。

雖然令人遺憾地在採取某些步驟時將造成相關部門的職務縮編，但我們還是很高興地宣布，我們在中國大陸的分部已產生了幾個新的職位。有興趣申請的員工請速洽胡麗莎 lisa.vu@bligo.net，以索取申請表。

Vocabulary

- **structural** [ˈstrʌktʃərəl] 形 結構上的
- **measure** [ˈmɛʒə] 名 措施
- **implement** [ˈɪmpləmənt] 動 實施；執行
- **cost-efficient** [ˈkɔstɪˈfɪʃənt] 形 符合成本效益的
- **in stages** 分階段地
- **cease** [sis] 動 終止；停止
- **utilize** [ˈjutl̩aɪz] 動 活用
- **to the maximum extent** 至最大程度
- **merge** [mɝdʒ] 動 合併
- **regrettable** [rɪˈɡrɛtəbl] 形 令人遺憾的
- **urge someone to do** 催促某人做某事

試題	試題翻譯	答案與解析

164

What is the purpose of the changes being made by Bligo Trading?

(A) To improve facilities
(B) To reduce operating costs
(C) To reward performance
(D) To upgrade services

布里哥貿易做調整的目的是什麼？

(A) 為了改善設施
(B) 為了減少營運成本
(C) 為了獎勵績效
(D) 為了升級服務

正解 (B)

第一段裡提到 The following measures are to be implemented to make operations more cost-efficient.，意即「為了更符合成本效益，必須進行下列措施」，而在下文中則具體敘述了削減成本的策略，因此選項 (B) 為正解。

□ **reward** [rɪ'wɔrd] 動 報償；獎勵

165

What change is being planned for the human resources department?

(A) Fewer people will be recruited.
(B) Regular work hours will be reduced.
(C) Employee benefits will decrease.
(D) Online systems will be used.

人資部預計會有什麼變更？

(A) 將招募較少的人。
(B) 正常工時將縮短。
(C) 員工福利將減少。
(D) 將使用線上系統。

正解 (D)

關於人資部的敘述記載於 August 20 的項目裡，其中提到將應用網路技術以降低成本，因此換句話說的選項 (D) 為正解。

□ **work hours** 工作時間

166

What will happen on August 31?

(A) Sales will be emphasized over marketing.
(B) A company merger will occur.
(C) Two departments will be combined.
(D) The size of a group will be increased.

8 月 31 日會發生什麼事？

(A) 相較於行銷業績將倍受重視。
(B) 有一樁企業併購案發生。
(C) 有兩個部門會合而為一。
(D) 某集團規模將擴大。

正解 (C)

從 August 31 中的 Personnel from the sales and marketing divisions will merge into one group, ... 可知，業務部將與行銷部門整合，所以答案是選項 (C)。注意，由於不是與其他公司合併，因此選項 (B) 不適當。而人員削減和關閉香港客服處等措施都將使規模縮小才對，故選項 (D) 亦不可選。

□ **emphasize A over B** 著重 A 過於 B

167

The word "concerned" in paragraph 5, line 2, is closest in meaning to

(A) worried
(B) controlled
(C) related
(D) detailed

第五段第二行的 "concerned" 這個字的意思最接近

(A) 擔心的
(B) 控制的
(C) 相關的
(D) 詳細的

正解 (C)

concerned 在此的意思是「有關的」，而最接近此意的單字為選項 (C) related（相關的）。

□ **detailed** ['diteld] 形 詳細的

Questions 168-171 refer to the following online chat discussion.

第 168 到 171 題請參照下面這段線上聊天討論。

Rex Johnson [3:01 P.M.]
Thanks, everyone, for agreeing to this online session. It's much easier than trying to organize a meeting on such short notice. Now then, could we start with opinions?

雷克斯．強森 [下午 3:01]
謝謝大家同意這場線上討論。在這麼短的時間內，比起安排會議這樣簡單多了。那，我們現在可以開始交換意見了嗎？

Anita Doorn [3:03 P.M.]
Mai, we ran the same number of commercials as always, right?

艾妮塔．多恩 [下午 3:03]
麻衣，我們一直都是上一樣數量的廣告，對嗎？

Mai Yang [3:04 P.M.]
We did. No change from last quarter. I can't figure it out.

楊麻衣 [下午 3:04]
是的。跟上一季比沒有變化。我不知道為什麼。

Rex Johnson [3:06 P.M.]
We're marketing the same style computer with the same specs as our competitor, Sundry Corp. Still, sales are down for some reason.

雷克斯．強森 [下午 3:06]
我們目前正在推與競爭對手繁樣公司同類型、同規格的電腦，然而不知為何業績卻下滑。

Michael Boswell [3:08 P.M.]
Did we get any customer feedback from the surveys?

麥可．包斯威爾 [下午 3:08]
我們有沒有從意見調查收到任何顧客建議？

Abdullah Farooq [3:09 P.M.]
Yes, we got some. We haven't reviewed them thoroughly yet, but I saw a number of comments referencing Sundry.

阿卜杜拉．法魯克 [下午 3:09]
有，我們收到一些。我們還沒徹底地仔細看過，不過我有看到幾則評論提到繁樣。

Rex Johnson [3:10 P.M.]
Really? That's news to me. That probably means their publicity is better.

雷克斯．強森 [下午 3:10]
真的嗎？我第一次知道這件事。那可能表示他們的宣傳做得比較好。

Joe Forbes [3:11 P.M.]
We should look into that immediately. I'll do some Internet research, and I'll ask around and see what I can find out.

喬．富比斯 [下午 3:11]
我們應該馬上研究這點。我會在網路上做些調查，並且四處打聽消息看看能查出什麼。

Mai Yang [3:12 P.M.]
Good idea. Any information would help. If I know what Sundry is doing, I can get the ball rolling on production of a new commercial.

楊麻衣 [下午 3:12]
好主意。任何資訊都能幫上忙。假如我得知繁樣正在做些什麼，我就可以著手製作一支新廣告。

Vocabulary

- **the same A as B** 和 B 相同的 A
- **spec** [spɛk] 名 規格（speccifications 之簡略）
- **thoroughly** [ˈθɝolɪ] 副 徹底地；仔細地
- **reference** [ˈrɛfərəns] 動 提及
- **publicity** [pʌbˈlɪsətɪ] 名 宣傳
- **look into** 研究；調查
- **immediately** [ɪˈmidɪɪtlɪ] 副 立即；馬上
- **get the ball rolling** 開始（工作等）

168

What is the reason for the discussion?

(A) To discuss a commercial
(B) To review sales figures
(C) To analyze a customer survey
(D) To solicit input from staff

這段討論召開的理由是什麼？

(A) 為了討論一支廣告
(B) 為了檢視業績數字
(C) 為了分析顧客調查
(D) 為了徵求員工意見

正解 (D)

強森先生打出 Now then, could we start with opinions? 這段文字後，其他幾個人陸續針對廣告或業績發表意見，故選項 (D) 為正解。solicit 是「徵求；募集」的意思，input 則指「提供資訊或意見等」。強森先生在第二次發言已說了 sales are down for some reason，並和其他人討論此現象之原因，因此選項 (B) 並不適當。

169

What most likely is Ms. Yang's job in the company?

(A) She oversees advertisements.
(B) She builds computer applications.
(C) She designs Web pages.
(D) She manages sales.

楊小姐在這家公司的工作最有可能是什麼？

(A) 她負責監督廣告。
(B) 她負責製作電腦應用程式。
(C) 她負責設計網頁。
(D) 她負責管理銷售業務。

正解 (A)

楊小姐在兩次發言中針對廣告發表了意見，由此可推測她應該是在 advertisement（廣告；宣傳）部門工作，所以正確答案是 (A)。

□ **oversee** [ˈovɚˈsi] 動 監督；管理
□ **application** [ˌæpləˈkeʃən] 名（電腦、手機等的）應用程式

170

At 3:10 P.M., what does Mr. Johnson most likely mean when he writes, "That's news to me"?

(A) He was unaware.
(B) He was misinformed.
(C) He wants to tell more people.
(D) He wants to contact the media.

三點十分時，強森先生打的 "That's news to me" 最有可能是什麼意思？

(A) 他之前並不知情。
(B) 有人告知他錯誤的訊息。
(C) 他想告訴更多的人。
(D) 他想聯絡媒體。

正解 (A)

此處的 news 是「新訊息；初次聽聞之事」的意思，而 That's news to me. 則帶有類似 I'm surprised.（我很驚訝。）的語感。依上下文判斷，強森先生是在表示他之前沒聽過該件事而嚇了一跳，因此選項 (A) 為正解。

□ **unaware** [ˌʌnəˈwɛr] 形 不知道的；未察覺到的
□ **misinform** [ˌmɪsɪnˈfɔrm] 動 向⋯⋯傳達錯誤訊息

171

According to the discussion, what most likely will happen next?

(A) Customer feedback will be received.
(B) Sales will go up.
(C) A new commercial will be reviewed.
(D) A company will be researched.

根據本討論，接下來最有可能發生什麼事？

(A) 公司將收到顧客意見。
(B) 業績將提升。
(C) 一支新廣告將被檢視。
(D) 某公司將被調查。

正解 (D)

在討論的後段，喬·富比斯表示他要調查競爭對手縈樣公司的宣傳計畫，所以本題選 (D)。注意，A company 指的就是縈樣公司。

Questions 172-175 refer to the following information.

❧ Science-M Contest ❧

Sponsored by Suvar Corporation
Islamabad, Pakistan

Are you the next great scientist to come out of Pakistan?

Suvar Corporation is sponsoring a nationwide campaign to find the next generation of young geniuses from our country.

Top Prize: A full 4-year scholarship to the university of your choice anywhere within the nation. — [1] —.

Second Place: A set of 10 software educational packages from Suvar Corporation.

Third Place: Gift certificates for use at department stores in Lahore, Islamabad, Karachi and other major cities.

Here is how you can compete against the best young minds in Pakistan.

To enter the contest, you must be over 12 and under 20.* — [2] —. Entrants may submit any original creation within the following areas:

- **Robotics**
- **Software**
- **Biotech**
- **Hardware**
- **Pharmaceuticals**

All submissions must be entirely the work of the entrant, without any assistance from teachers, parents or other adults. — [3] —. If an entrant wishes to work with classmates on a submission, it must then be clearly labeled as teamwork.

The deadline for registering submissions is June 15. — [4] —. Entry inspections by a panel of judges will begin June 18, with a final winner chosen June 21.

*While anyone within this age group can compete, most top prizes in past years have usually gone to those aged between 17 and 19.

科學 M 競賽
巴基斯坦，伊斯蘭馬巴德
蘇瓦爾公司贊助

你是下一個來自巴基斯坦的偉大科學家嗎？

蘇瓦爾公司現正贊助協辦一個全國性的活動來發掘國內下一代的年輕天才。

首獎：你所選擇的國內任一大學的四年全額獎學金。— [1] —。
第二名：蘇瓦爾公司的十組教育套裝軟體。
第三名：拉合爾、伊斯蘭馬巴德、喀拉蚩和其他主要城市的百貨公司通用禮券。

巴基斯坦最優秀年輕頭腦競賽的辦法如下。

參賽者年齡必須在 12 歲以上，20 歲以下。* — [2] —。參賽者可繳交任何屬於下列領域的原創作品：

- 機器人
- 軟體
- 生技
- 硬體
- 藥品

所有報名作品必須百分之百出自參賽者之手，老師、父母或其他成年人不得提供任何協助。— [3] —。如果參賽者希望繳交與同學合作之作品，則須明確標示為團隊作品。

繳交作品的報名期限為 6 月 15 日。— [4] —。評審小組將從 6 月 18 日開始審件，並於 6 月 21 日決選出優勝者。

* 雖然任何於年齡範圍內者皆可參賽，但過去幾年大多數的首獎得主年紀通常介於 17 到 19 歲之間。

Vocabulary

- **nationwide** [ˈneʃənˌwaɪd] 形 全國性的
- **genius** [ˈdʒinjəs] 名 天才
- **scholarship** [ˈskɑləˌʃɪp] 名 獎學金
- **gift certificate** 禮券
- **young mind** 年輕頭腦
- **entrant** [ˈɛntrənt] 名 參賽者
- **robotics** [roˈbɑtɪks] 名 機器人學
- **biotech** [ˈbaɪotɛk] 名 生物科技
- **pharmaceuticals** [ˌfɑrməˈsjutɪk(l)z] 名 藥品學（複數形）
- **submission** [sʌbˈmɪʃən] 名 提交（物）
- **entirely** [ɪnˈtaɪrlɪ] 副 完全地
- **deadline** [ˈdɛdˌlaɪn] 名 截止期限
- **register** [ˈrɛdʒɪstə] 動 登記；報名
- **panel of judges** 評審團

172

What is the stated purpose of the Science-M Contest?

(A) To find marketable technical products
(B) To improve business research capabilities
(C) To help fund educational programs
(D) To discover talented people

科學 M 競賽的明訂宗旨是什麼？

(A) 尋找可銷售的技術產品
(B) 改善企業的研究能力
(C) 幫忙資助教育課程
(D) 發掘人才

正解 (D)

本文第二句提到 Suvar Corporation is sponsoring a nationwide campaign to find the next generation of young geniuses from our country.，意即「該公司是為了發掘下一代的年輕天才，所以主辦此次競賽」，因此正解為選項 (D) To discover talented people。

☐ **marketable** [`markɪtəbl] 形 具有市場性的；可銷售的
☐ **capability** [.kepəˋbɪlətɪ] 名 能力
☐ **talented** [`tæləntɪd] 形 具有才能的

173

Which is NOT listed as a gift for prize winners?

(A) Coupons for goods
(B) Educational materials
(C) Fees for tuition
(D) Travel tickets

下列何者「未」被列為優勝者的獎賞之一？

(A) 商品折價券
(B) 教育素材
(C) 學費
(D) 旅遊券

正解 (D)

由 Top Prize: A full 4-year scholarship 可先將選項 (C)（學費）排除。接著從 Second Place: A set of 10 software educational packages 則可刪掉選項 (B)。最後，根據 Third Place: Gift certificates 可知，選項 (A) 亦應被刪除。而未出現於文中的選項 (D) Travel tickets（旅行券）即為正確答案。

☐ **tuition** [tjuˋɪʃən] 名 學費

174

What rule is mentioned about the contest?

(A) Group work must be specified.
(B) Adult assistance is encouraged.
(C) Registration fees are required.
(D) Submissions require teacher approval.

關於此競賽文中提到什麼規則？

(A) 團體作品必須明示。
(B) 鼓勵大人從旁協助。
(C) 必須繳交報名費。
(D) 繳交作品須得老師批准。

正解 (A)

由作品領域分類底下的 If an entrant wishes to work with classmates on a submission, it must then be clearly labeled as teamwork. 可知，「團體作品必須明確標示」，因此正解為選項 (A)。注意，在此段之前有提到「報名作品須完全出自參賽者之手，其他成年人不得提供任何協助」，故選項 (B) 並不適當。

☐ **specify** [`spɛsə.faɪ] 動 明確記載
☐ **encourage** [ɪnˋkɝɪdʒ] 動 鼓勵
☐ **registration fee** 報名費

175

In which of the positions marked [1], [2], [3] and [4] does the following sentence best belong?

"While not necessary, a strong background in science is preferred."

(A) [1]
(B) [2]
(C) [3]
(D) [4]

下面這個句子插入文中標示的 [1]、[2]、[3]、[4] 四處當中的何處最符合文意？

「雖非必備條件，但具深厚科學背景者佳。」

(A) [1]
(B) [2]
(C) [3]
(D) [4]

正解 (B)

「具深厚科學背景者佳」是針對參賽者所設的條件，因此插入 To enter the contest, ...（參賽者須……）這個段落當中 [2] 的位置最合適，本題選 (B)。

☐ **background** [`bæk.graʊnd] 名 背景；經歷

Questions 176-180 refer to the following notice and e-mail.

第 176 到 180 題請參照下列公告和電子郵件。

June 17

Project Coordinator

Orange Tech Co.

Orange Tech is the largest telecom company in our regional markets. Recently, we were awarded a contract for the construction of satellite broadcasting systems throughout the Republic of South Africa.

To cope with this increased workload, we are searching for a reliable project coordinator to assist the operations manager in charge of this task.

Candidates must have a minimum of a BA degree, with a graduate degree preferred. They must have at least three years' experience in the field, and be able to demonstrate excellent interpersonal skills.

Knowledge of the following software applications is required:
- **TX25**
- **InfoScoop**
- **Arcana**
- **IsoFin**

Regular duties will include database management, compilation of weekly reports, installation schedule development, and resolution of any outstanding technical issues.

Please submit credentials by July 9 to Adam De Groot at the following address, adam.degroot@orangetech.za

---

6 月 17 日

專案助理
橘子科技公司

橘子科技是我們區域市場中最大的電信公司。最近我們取得了在南非共和國各地建造衛星廣播系統的合約。

為因應增加的工作量，本公司正在尋求一位可靠的專案助理來協助負責這項工作的營運經理。

應徵者至少須具備學士學位，具研究所學歷者佳。應徵者在此領域須具備三年以上經驗，並能展現絕佳的人際技巧。

須具備下列應用軟體知識：
- TX25
- InfoScoop
- Arcana
- IsoFin

日常職務包括管理資料庫、彙整週報、研擬安裝時程，以及解決任何未處理的技術問題。

7 月 19 日前請將資格證照送交亞當‧德葛魯特，電子郵件地址如下：adam.degroot@orangetech.za。

✱ E-mail ✱	✕
To:	adam.degroot@orangetech.za
From:	darren.zimbele@africatel.com
Date:	Wednesday, June 20
Subject:	Open Position

Attachments: References.doc
　　　　　　 CV.doc

Dear Mr. De Groot,

I am writing about your project coordinator position.

I graduated from Keele University, with an MSc in computer engineering two years ago. Since then, I have worked in Kampala Tech Co. as a software analyst, first in their Kimberly and Pretoria branches and now here in Johannesburg. There, I gained extensive experience working with TX25, InfoScoop, Arcana, IsoFin, and many other software packages.

Beyond my technical background, I also get on well with all sorts of people. Even while under the stress of tight work deadlines, I never get angry or frustrated.

I look forward to hearing from you soon.

Sincerely,

Darren Zimbele

收件者：adam.degroot@orangetech.za
寄件者：darren.zimbele@africatel.com
日期：6 月 20 日星期三
主旨：職缺
附件：推薦函.doc　履歷.doc

德葛魯特先生您好：

我寫信來是想應徵貴公司專案助理的職位。

我畢業於基爾大學，兩年前拿到了電腦工程理學碩士學位。之後，我就在坎培拉科技公司服務，擔任軟體分析師，早先是在金柏利和普勒托利亞的分公司，目前則是在約翰尼斯堡工作。在此公司經由操作 TX25、InfoScoop、Arcana、IsoFin 和許多其他的套裝軟體，我獲得了相當豐富的經驗。

除了我的理工背景，我跟形形色色的人也都相處融洽。即使在工作截止期限緊迫的壓力下，我也從不發怒或覺得沮喪。

期待很快收到您的回覆。

德倫‧辛貝利敬上

Vocabulary

- ☐ **regional** [ˈridʒən!] 形 地區的；局部的
- ☐ **award a contract** 授予合約
- ☐ **satellite broadcasting system** 衛星廣播系統
- ☐ **cope with ...** 對付；處理
- ☐ **workload** [ˈwɜkˌlod] 名 工作量
- ☐ **reliable** [rɪˈlaɪəb!] 形 可靠的
- ☐ **interpersonal skill** 人際技巧
- ☐ **candidate** [ˈkændədet] 名 應徵者；候選人
- ☐ **duty** [ˈdjutɪ] 名 責任；職務
- ☐ **compilation** [ˌkɑmpəˈleʃən] 名 編輯
- ☐ **resolution** [ˌrɛzəˈluʃən] 名 解決
- ☐ **outstanding** [aʊtˈstændɪŋ] 形 未解決的
- ☐ **credential** [krɪˈdɛnʃəl] 名 資格證書；憑據（通常用複數形）
- ☐ **reference** [ˈrɛfərəns] 名 推薦函
- ☐ **CV** (= curriculum vitae) 履歷
- ☐ **MSc** (= Master of Science) 理學碩士

176

What will Orange Tech require their new recruit to do?

(A) Manage a new project
(B) Get a new contract
(C) Expand into a new market
(D) Acquire a new company

橘子科技將要求其新進員工做什麼？

(A) 管理新專案
(B) 取得新合約
(C) 擴充進入新市場
(D) 收購新公司

正解 (A)

通知文第一段提及由於該公司得到建造南非共和國的衛星廣播系統之合約，因此增加了工作量而必須另聘員工，故正解為 (A)。

□ **expand into ...** 擴張至……
□ **acquire** [əˈkwaɪr] 動 獲得；收購

177

In the notice, the word "interpersonal" in paragraph 3, line 3, is closest in meaning to

(A) profitable
(B) communicative
(C) academic
(D) linguistic

公告第三段第三行的 "interpersonal" 這個字的意思最接近

(A) 可獲利的
(B) 善溝通的
(C) 學術的
(D) 語言的

正解 (B)

interpersonal 是「人與人之間」的意思，加上後面的 skill，就指「人際關係技巧」，而選項 (B) communicative（善溝通的）則最接近 interpersonal。注意，inter- 為一字首，表「互相的」之意。

□ **profitable** [ˈprɑfɪtəbl] 形 可獲利的

178

Where does Mr. Zimbele currently work?

(A) Cape Town
(B) Kimberly
(C) Pretoria
(D) Johannesburg

辛貝利先生目前在哪裡工作？

(A) 開普敦
(B) 金柏利
(C) 普勒托利亞
(D) 約翰尼斯堡

正解 (D)

由電子郵件第二段裡提到的 I have worked in ... now here in Johannesburg. 可知，他目前在約翰尼斯堡工作，所以答案是 (D)。

179

What can be inferred about Mr. Zimbele from his application?

(A) He does not have enough work experience.
(B) He does not have the required academic background.
(C) He does not have sufficient references.
(D) He does not have adequate software skills.

關於辛貝利先生可由其應徵信做出什麼推論？

(A) 他不具備足夠的工作經驗。
(B) 他不具備必要的學歷背景。
(C) 他的介紹人不夠多。
(D) 他不具備充分的軟體技能。

正解 (A)

這是兩篇文章都看過才能回答的題目。由電子郵件中提到的 I graduated from Keelee University ... two years ago. 可知，辛貝利先生只有兩年的工作經驗，而根據公告，所需求的資歷為三年。換言之，他的經歷並不充分，故正解為 (A)。

□ **sufficient** [səˈfɪʃənt] 形 足夠的

180

Why does Mr. Zimbele mention deadlines?

(A) To emphasize his attention to details
(B) To highlight his computer skills
(C) To show his leadership background
(D) To demonstrate his patience

辛貝利先生為什麼提到截止期限？

(A) 以強調他注重細節
(B) 以突顯他的電腦技能
(C) 以展現他的領導力背景
(D) 以顯示他有耐心

正解 (D)

電子郵件最後提到 Even while under the stress of tight work deadlines, I never get angry or frustrated. ，可見辛貝利先生想強調「他可在任何困難之下都會堅持到底」，所以本題應選 (D)。

□ **highlight** [ˈhaɪˌlaɪt] 動 使……變得顯眼
□ **demonstrate** [ˈdɛmənˌstret] 動 演示

Questions 181-185 refer to the following advertisement and e-mail.

Branson Lawn & Garden Co.
We make the exterior of every home a lovely one.

| Lawn care | Garden care |
| Bush, tree and hedge trimming | Special services as required |

Deposits accepted but not required.
Handling both commercial and residential projects. Our clients include:
- XSoft Computer Corporation
- Briar City Park
- Leviston Apartment Complex
- And homes all over the city

Voted Number 1 Landscaping Service by City Life Magazine

Drop by our office
at 302 Beckridge Way
or contact us at:
info@bransononline.com.
You'll be glad you did!

Our Management Team:
Linda Wu ———— President
linda.wu@bransononline.com
Armando Benitez —— Personnel manager
armando.b@bransononline.com
Mary Listz ———— Client Project manager
mary.l@bransononline.com
Frank Cole ———— Equipment manager
frank.cole@bransononline.com

*On the job seven days a week, through all four seasons. All work done from November 1 through April 1 requires additional fees.

E-mail

From:	michelle017@northtel.com
To:	linda.wu@bransononline.com
Date:	Monday, May 25
Subject:	Your Company

Dear Ms. Wu,

Thank you for taking the time to talk with me on the phone earlier today. After doing so, I think I might be interested in hiring your company for some landscaping projects around my home. Ordinarily, I enjoy taking care of my yard and garden on weekends, but I'm so busy at the office nowadays it's hard for me to devote as much time to it as I used to.

I think that if you carried out the work we discussed for me every fourteen days, I could keep the greenery around my home looking good. So I'd like to start with that sort of schedule. However, weekly visits might be required during spring, when everything grows very fast. If your company also does snow removal, I might also have monthly work for you in winter, or more frequently according to the snowfall.

I understand you will be sending out one of your managers tomorrow who is responsible for customer cost estimates. During that meeting I would like to discuss the service contract, including all labor, equipment and other factors. I would prefer a complete total of that in your estimate, rather than being surprised later by unanticipated prices.

Best regards,

Michelle Walker

第 181 到 185 題請參照下列廣告和電子郵件。

布蘭森草坪花園公司
我們專為每個家庭打造美輪美奐的外觀。
　　草坪維護　　　　　　花園維護
樹叢、樹木與籬笆修剪　　特別指定服務

接受訂金但非必要。
商業與住宅案件皆受理。我們的客戶包括：
● XSoft 電腦公司
● 荊棘市立公園
● 雷維斯頓公寓社區
● 以及市內各地的住家

我們的經營團隊：
吳琳達──總裁
linda.wu@bransononline.com
阿曼多・班尼特茲──人事經理
armando.b@bransononline.com
瑪莉・李茲──客戶專案經理
mary.l@bransononline.com
法蘭克・柯爾──器具設備經理
frank.cole@bransononline.com

《城市生活雜誌》票選第一的造景公司
您可親洽我們的辦事處，地址是貝克瑞吉路 302 號，或傳電子郵件至 info@bransononline.com。保證滿意！

* 我們一年四季、一週七天都營業。11 月 1 日至 4 月 1 日的各項作業須加收費用。

寄件者：michelle017@northtel.com
收件者：linda.wu@bransononline.com
日期：5 月 25 日星期一
主旨：貴公司

吳小姐你好：

謝謝您今天稍早抽空和我通電話。在我們講完後，我想我可能會有意願請貴公司來我家周邊做一些造景工程。平常我很喜歡在週末打理院子和花園，但最近我辦公室的事情很忙，所以很難跟之前一樣在上面花那麼多時間。

我想假如你們每十四天幫我處理一次我們所討論的事，我就可以讓我家周圍的綠景維持美觀。所以我希望以這樣的時程開始。不過，春天的時候什麼都長得非常快，屆時你們可能每週都必須來一趟。假如你們公司也做除雪，我可能也會把冬天每月一次的工作交給你們，或是更頻繁一點，視降雪量而定。

我知道你們明天會派一位負責幫顧客估價的經理過來。見面時，我想討論一下服務合約，包括所有的人工、器具設備和其他事項。我希望你們在估價時能一次把總金額算出來，而不要在事後突然冒出一些我並沒有預期的費用。

蜜雪兒・沃克上

Vocabulary

- **lawn** [lɔn] 名 草坪
- **hedge** [hɛdʒ] 名 樹籬
- **trimming** [ˈtrɪmɪŋ] 名 修剪；整理
- **landscaping** [ˈlænd.skepɪŋ] 名 景觀美化
- **ordinarily** [ˈɔrdn.ɛrɪlɪ] 副 通常地
- **carry out** 執行
- **greenery** [ˈgrinərɪ] 名 綠色植物
- **snow removal** 除雪
- **frequently** [ˈfrikwəntlɪ] 副 頻繁地
- **snowfall** [ˈsno.fɔl] 名 降雪（量）
- **send out** 派出
- **responsible for ...** 負責……
- **estimate** [ˈɛstə.met] 名 估價
- **factor** [ˈfæktə] 名 因素；要素
- **unanticipated** [ˌʌnænˈtɪsə.petɪd] 形 未預料到的

181

What is implied about Branson Lawn & Garden Co.?

(A) It accepts online payments.
(B) It offers big discounts.
(C) It has a good reputation.
(D) It does interiors as well as exteriors.

廣告中暗示布蘭森草坪花園公司如何？

(A) 它接受線上付款。
(B) 它給的折扣很高。
(C) 它的信譽良好。
(D) 它既做外觀，也做室內。

正解 (C)

由廣告右下角圖框裡寫的 Voted number 1 Landscaping Service by City Life Magazine. 這個句子就知道布蘭森草坪花園公司備受好評，故正解為選項 (C)。

182

What is stated about Branson Lawn & Garden Co.?

(A) It serves only corporate clients.
(B) It requires a deposit before beginning work.
(C) It limits projects during some seasons.
(D) It charges more during certain periods.

廣告中提到布蘭森草坪花園公司如何？

(A) 它只服務企業客戶。
(B) 它在動工前要收訂金。
(C) 它在某些季節有限定工程。
(D) 它在某些時期收費較高。

正解 (D)

由廣告最下方的 All work done from November 1 through April 1 requires additional fees. 可知，該公司在某些時期會加收費用，因此正解為選項 (D)。廣告約中段部分提到 Handing both commercial and residential projects., 表示不論企業或個人，該公司都提供服務，所以選項 (A) 不適當。另，文中也提及訂金並非必要，故選項 (B) 亦不可選。

☐ **corporate client** 企業客戶
☐ **charge** [tʃɑrdʒ] 動 收費

183

How often does Ms. Walker want initial service?

(A) Every week
(B) Every other week
(C) Every month
(D) Every other month

沃克女士希望初期服務多久一次？

(A) 每週
(B) 每隔一週
(C) 每個月
(D) 每隔一個月

正解 (B)

沃克女士在電子郵件第二段裡寫道她希望對方 every fourteen days（每十四天）過來一次，換句話說即每隔一週一次，故選項 (B) 的 Every other week 為正解。注意，選項 (A) 是春季、選項 (C) 是冬季可能會需求的頻率。

184

Who will Ms. Walker meet tomorrow?

(A) Linda Wu
(B) Armando Benitez
(C) Mary Listz
(D) Frank Cole

沃克女士明天會跟誰見面？

(A) 吳琳達
(B) 阿曼多·班尼特茲
(C) 瑪莉·李茲
(D) 法蘭克·柯爾

正解 (C)

電子郵件第三段裡的 one of your managers ... who is responsible for customer cost estimates 指「負責顧客估價的經理」，而由廣告中的經營團隊一覽表可知，擔任顧客專案經理的是 Mary Listz，所以正確答案是選項 (C)。

185

What is one request made by Ms. Walker?

(A) Getting a comprehensive quote
(B) Receiving fast performance
(C) Confirming top equipment
(D) Understanding project details

沃克女士提出的要求之一是什麼？

(A) 得到涵蓋一切的報價
(B) 獲得快速施工
(C) 確認設備是頂級的
(D) 了解工程的細節

正解 (A)

沃克女士提到 I would prefer a complete total of that in your estimate, rather than being surprised later by unanticipated prices., 意即她希望對方能一次報總價，而不想在事後看到有出乎意料的費用，換言之，選項 (A) Getting a comprehensive quote 即為正解。

☐ **comprehensive** [ˌkɑmprɪˈhɛnsɪv] 形 總括性的
☐ **quote** [kwot] 名 報價

Questions 186-190 refer to the following letter, voucher, and Web page.

October 27

Richard Yeoh
Laxfield Office Supplies Corporation
7861 Clayton Plaza
Denver, CO 98775

Dear Mr. Yeoh,

I was sorry to hear that your stay at our hotel in Portland, Oregon, was less than satisfactory. You should not have had your seminars exposed to the noise from work crews renovating our lobby and main entrance. I understand that at many points your presenters struggled to be heard because of that.

Unfortunately, when taking your reservation for the Premier Gold Room, our receptionist made a mistake by overlooking the fact that it was adjacent to the areas under renovation. As a Sunshine Hotels Card member, you are entitled to nothing less than top-class service.

To make up for your inconvenience in some small way, I hope that you will accept the voucher enclosed.

With very best regards,

Josef Loos

Josef Loos
Vice President
Sunshine Hotels, Inc.

10 月 27 日

楊理查
拉克斯菲德辦公用品公司
克雷頓廣場 7861 號
科羅拉多州丹佛市 98775

楊先生您好：

很抱歉聽說您對在我們波蘭的奧瑞岡飯店的那段期間並不滿意。您的研討會不該受到工程人員整修大廳與大門的噪音所影響。我了解正因為如此，您的講者有很多時候必須喊得聲嘶力竭才能讓聽眾聽見。

令人遺憾的是，在接受您預訂首金廳時，我們的接待人員犯了一個錯誤，該員忽略了它的隔壁場所正在整修這件事。因為您是陽光飯店卡的卡友，理當受到最頂級的服務。

為了多少能補償對您造成的不便，希望您能收下隨附的優惠券。

陽光飯店副總裁
約瑟夫·魯斯敬上

Sunshine Hotels Inc.

Taking care of you 365 days a year!

Guest Voucher

This voucher entitles the bearer to a 50% discount on our hotels anywhere in the United States or Canada, including our Royal Suite or Deluxe Suite rooms.

Voucher No. A982JQRV08

Expires December 27
Non-transferable, single-use only

Sunshine Hotels Card members receive an additional 10% off. Valid only for online reservations at www.sunshinehotels/vouchers/. Please enter voucher number noted above.

陽光飯店公司
全年無休照顧您！

貴賓券

持有本券者於美國或加拿大各地的本飯店皆可享對折優惠，包括皇家套房或豪華套房。

券號 A982JQRV08

到期日 12 月 27 日
禁止轉讓，僅限使用一次

陽光飯店卡的卡友可再打九折。限網路訂房有效：www.sunshinehotels/vouchers/。請輸入上列券號。

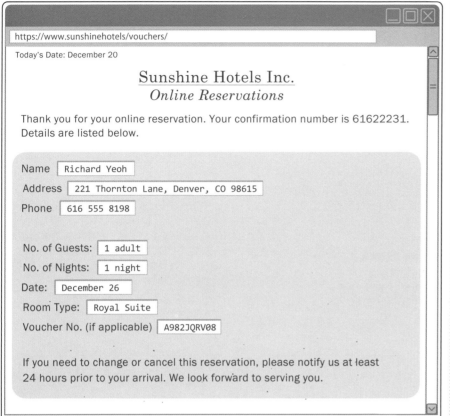

陽光飯店公司
線上訂房

感謝您的線上訂房。您的確認編號是 61622231。詳細預約內容如下。

姓名 楊理查
地址 科羅拉多州丹佛市 98615 桑頓巷 221 號
電話 616 555 8198

房客人數：成人 1 名
住宿天數：1 晚
日期：12 月 26 日
房型：皇家套房
優惠券號碼（如適用）A982JQRV08

若您須變更或取消訂單，請至少於抵達 24 小時之前告知。我們非常期待為您提供服務。

第 2 回完全解析

PART 7

Vocabulary

- **voucher** [ˋvautʃə] 名 優惠券；兌換憑證
- **satisfactory** [ˌsætɪsˋfæktərɪ] 形 令人滿意的；符合要求的
- **(be) exposed to ...** 暴露於……
- **presenter** [prɪˋzɛntə] 名 發表者
- **receptionist** [rɪˋsɛpʃənɪst] 名 接待員
- **overlook** [ˌovəˋluk] 動 看漏；忽略
- **adjacent to ...** 與……毗鄰的
- **be entitled to ...** 有……的權力或資格
- **nothing less than ...** 不能比（最好的）少
- **top-class** [ˋtɑpˋklæs] 形 最高級的
- **make up for ...** 補償……
- **enclosed** [ɪnˋklozd] 形 隨信附上的
- **bearer** [ˋbɛrə] 名 持有人
- **non-transferable** [ˌnɑntrænsˋfɝəbl] 形 不可轉讓的
- **valid** [ˋvælɪd] 形 有效的
- **if applicable** 如果適用

試題	試題翻譯	答案與解析

186

What is the purpose of the letter?

(A) To confirm a reservation
(B) To explain facilities
(C) To reply to an inquiry
(D) To make an apology

這封信的目的是什麼？

(A) 確認訂房
(B) 說明設施
(C) 回覆查詢
(D) 致歉

正解 (D)

信件一開頭就對客人住宿期間的不滿道歉，之後在第三段裡說 To make up for your inconvenience in some small way, I hope that you will accept the voucher enclosed.，表示隨信贈送折價券以聊表歉意，故正解為 (D)。

☐ **make an apology** 道歉

187

What problem occurred at the seminars?

(A) Baggage was not delivered.
(B) Speakers could not be heard.
(C) Locations were changed.
(D) Presentations were rescheduled.

研討會上發生了什麼問題？

(A) 行李沒送到。
(B) 講者說的話聽不到。
(C) 地點被更換。
(D) 簡報的時程被變更。

正解 (B)

由信件第一段最後一句話 I understand that at many points your presenters struggled to be heard because of that. 可知，研討會中的發表者受到噪音干擾而必須聲嘶力竭地講話，所以正確答案是 (B)。注意，speakers 為文中 presenters 的另一種說法。

188

In the letter, the word "way" in paragraph 3, line 1, is closest in meaning to

(A) manner
(B) condition
(C) payment
(D) portion

信件第三段第一行的 "way" 這個字的意思最接近

(A) 方式
(B) 狀態
(C) 付款
(D) 部分

正解 (A)

in some small way 此慣用語是指「以微薄的物品或簡單的方式」，通常用來聊表心意。而 way 此單字雖然有各種意思，但依上下文判斷，此處最接近 manner（方式），因此本題選 (A)。另，in some ways 為「就某種涵義而言」之意，小心不要混淆了。

189

What is the maximum discount available to Mr. Yeoh?

(A) 10%
(B) 50%
(C) 60%
(D) 70%

楊先生可享有的最大折扣是多少？

(A) 九折
(B) 五折
(C) 四折
(D) 三折

正解 (C)

該折價券開宗明義地表示持券者可享 50% 的折扣，且於最後一段註明了卡友可再享 10% 之優惠。而由信件第二段結尾處的 As a Sunshine Hotels Card member, you are entitled to ... 即可知，楊先生具有卡友身分，因此他所能夠享有的折扣最多為 50% + 10% = 60%，也就是「四折」。(C) 為正解。

190

What is indicated about Mr. Yeoh?

(A) He had seminars at a hotel near his office.
(B) He reserved the wrong room for the seminars.
(C) He will stay at a Sunshine Hotel on December 20.
(D) He was given a voucher valid for two months.

關於楊先生，文中暗示了什麼？

(A) 他在公司附近的飯店裡開了研討會。
(B) 他訂錯了房間給研討會使用。
(C) 他將在 12 月 20 日留宿於陽光飯店。
(D) 他獲得了一張效期兩個月的優惠券。

正解 (D)

信件註記的日期為 October 27，優惠券到期日為 December 27，亦即有效期間為兩個月，因此選項 (D) 為正解。由信件抬頭可知楊先生的公司位於美國科羅拉多州 (CO)，但是從信件開頭的內容可知研討會是在波蘭奧瑞岡的飯店舉行，故選項並不適當。而雖然楊先生表達了因噪音而感到不滿，但並非是因為他訂錯了房間，故選項 (B) 不可選。最後，對照網頁即可知楊先生的預定住宿日期為 12 月 26 日，故選項 (C) 亦不正確。

Questions 191-195 refer to the following advertisement, form, and e-mail.

Thorren Industries

This Week's Top Properties!
Philadelphia, Pennsylvania

■ *Downtown Office Space in Historic Building—18 Winston St.*

Entire 3rd floor (just under 8,000 sq. feet) in gorgeous historic brownstone, in the heart of downtown. Beautifully restored turn-of-the-century interior, but with all modern amenities including air conditioning and computer facilities.

$13.00/sq. feet/year

Listing No. 32330

■ *Modern and Convenient—Portmandieu Mall, 4325 Poplar Way*

Two adjacent showroom properties (about 3,000 sq. feet each) in quiet suburban location, in first-floor-only building. Up-to-date facilities. Just 30 minutes from downtown via expressway, Exit 351.

$13.00/sq. feet/year

Listing No. 32338

■ *Spacious Renovated Warehouse—2000 Industrial Drive*

Huge warehouse building, totally renovated. Easy access to the center of town, just 20 minutes by bus. Total 41,000 sq. feet. Landlord willing to subdivide, will rent space according to tenant needs.

$15.00/sq. feet/year

Listing No. 41323

For inquiries regarding the above properties, please visit our Web site at www.thorrenind.com/inquiries.

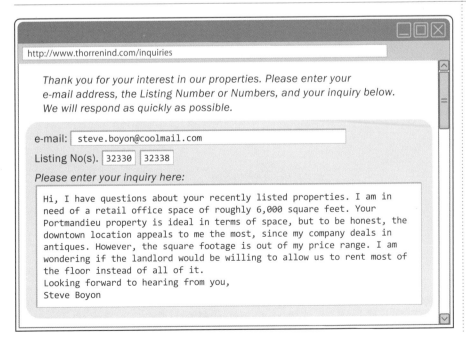

http://www.thorrenind.com/inquiries

Thank you for your interest in our properties. Please enter your e-mail address, the Listing Number or Numbers, and your inquiry below. We will respond as quickly as possible.

e-mail: steve.boyon@coolmail.com

Listing No(s). 32330 32338

Please enter your inquiry here:

Hi, I have questions about your recently listed properties. I am in need of a retail office space of roughly 6,000 square feet. Your Portmandieu property is ideal in terms of space, but to be honest, the downtown location appeals to me the most, since my company deals in antiques. However, the square footage is out of my price range. I am wondering if the landlord would be willing to allow us to rent most of the floor instead of all of it.
Looking forward to hearing from you,
Steve Boyon

—多倫產業—
本週的超級物件！
賓州費城

■ 歷史古蹟建築裡的市中心辦公空間—溫斯頓街 18 號
整個三樓（將近 8,000 平方英呎）皆為華麗古風的赤褐色砂石建築，位居城市心臟位置。完美整修完畢的十九世紀末二十世紀初之室內裝潢，但是備有全現代化設施，包括空調和電腦配備。
13 美元 / 平方英呎 / 年
目錄編號 32330

■ 現代化且便利—波普勒街 4325 號波特曼多商城
兩間相鄰的展示廳物件（各約 3,000 平方英呎），地處閑靜郊區，位於全一樓建築物內。配有最新設備。由高速公路 351 出口僅須 30 分鐘可抵達市中心。
13 美元 / 平方英呎 / 年
目錄編號 32338

■ 寬廣的整修完倉庫—工業路 2000 號
經全面整修完畢的超大空間倉儲建築，進出市中心十分便利，搭乘公車僅須 20 分鐘。總面積 41,000 平方英呎。房東願意以分割方式依房客需求出租空間。
15 美元 / 平方英呎 / 年
目錄編號 41323

詢問上列物件相關問題，請上我們的網站 www.thorrenind.com/inquiries。

http://www.thorrenind.com/inquiries

感謝您對我們的物件有興趣。請在底下輸入您的電子郵件地址、目錄編號，以及您的問題。我們將儘速回覆。

電子郵件：steve.boyon@coolmail.com
目錄編號 32330 32338
請在此輸入您的問題：

您好，我對你們最近登錄的物件有些疑問。我需要一個大約 6,000 平方英呎的零售業用辦公室空間。就空間大小而言，你們的波特曼多物件很理想，但是老實說，地點位於市中心最吸引我，因為我們是收售古董的公司。不過，每平方呎單價超過我的預算範圍。我在想房東是否願意允許我們承租該樓層的大部分面積，而非整層樓。
期待您的回覆。
史提夫・波揚

* E-mail *	✕
To:	steve.boyon@coolmail.com
From:	anetta.fasiq@thorrenreal.com
Date:	May 12
Subject:	Listing No. 32330

Dear Mr. Boyon,

Thank you for your interest in this property. We have contacted the landlord, Mr. John Fedder. Unfortunately, he has informed us that the property cannot be subdivided. However, he commented that he has spent a lot of time and money having the building restored, and seemed delighted by the nature of your business. He has graciously offered to negotiate a better price per square foot. If this is of interest to you, please contact me via e-mail, or by phone at (612) 555-8181. I will contact him immediately and arrange for you to meet as soon as possible.

Regards,

Anetta Fasiq

收件者：steve.boyon@coolmail.com
寄件者：anetta.fasiq@thorrenreal.com
日期：5 月 12 日
主旨：目錄編號 32330

波揚先生您好：

感謝您關注此物件。我們已經聯絡房東約翰‧費德先生。很遺憾地，他告知我們那塊地不能分割出售。不過，他提到他花費了大量的時間和金錢整修那棟樓，並且似乎對您事業的性質感到相當高興。他很殷切地提出要與您協商出一個較理想的每平方呎單價。如果您對此有興趣，請寫電子郵件或打手機 (612) 555-8181 與我聯絡。我將立刻與他聯繫，並儘速為兩位安排見面。

阿妮塔‧法西克敬上

Vocabulary

- ☐ **property** [ˈprɑpətɪ] 名 不動產物件
- ☐ **amenity** [əˈminətɪ] 名 生活便利設施
- ☐ **(be) willing to** *do* **sth.** 願意做某事
- ☐ **tenant** [ˈtɛnənt] 名 房客；承租人
- ☐ **appeal to ...** 吸引
- ☐ **in the heart of ...** 在……的中心
- ☐ **suburban** [səˈbɝbən] 形 郊區的
- ☐ **subdivide** [sʌbdɪˈvaɪd] 動 把（土地等）分割出售
- ☐ **in need of ...** 需要……
- ☐ **deal in ...** 經營
- ☐ **restore** [rɪˈstor] 動 整修
- ☐ **landlord** [ˈlændˌlɔrd] 名 地主；房東
- ☐ **according to ...** 根據……
- ☐ **roughly** [ˈrʌflɪ] 副 大約
- ☐ **in terms of ...** 就……方面而言
- ☐ **graciously** [ˈgreʃəslɪ] 副 親切地；殷勤地
- ☐ **be of interest** 感興趣的

試題	試題翻譯	答案與解析

191

What most likely does Thorren Industries specialize in?

(A) Retail merchandising
(B) Real estate
(C) Building renovation
(D) Construction

多倫產業最有可能專營什麼？

(A) 零售業
(B) 不動產業
(C) 建物翻修業
(D) 建築業

正解 (B)

多倫產業為廣告（第一篇文章）裡出現的公司，其中介紹了三個不動產物件，因此本題應選 (B)。

☐ **specialize in ...** 專門做……

192

What is the purpose of Mr. Boyon's inquiry?

(A) To negotiate a lower price
(B) To complete a lease
(C) To ask about rental terms
(D) To give feedback on a property listing

波揚先生詢問的目的是什麼？

(A) 為了交涉一個較低的價格
(B) 為了完成一個租約
(C) 為了詢問出租條件
(D) 為了對物件目錄發表意見

正解 (C)

波揚先生在表單（第二篇文章）當中提及兩個物件，並針對市中心的物件和收件者商量部分承租之可能性，因此正解為選項 (C)。注意，雖然有提到「超過預算」，但並不是在交涉價格，故選項 (A) 不適當。

☐ **term** [tɜm] 名 條件；條款（常用複數形）
☐ **feedback** [ˈfidˌbæk] 名 反饋的信息

193

What does Mr. Boyon indicate about the property on Poplar Way?

(A) The space is ideal.
(B) It is too expensive for him.
(C) It is not conveniently located.
(D) It does not have adequate facilities.

關於波普勒街上的物件，波揚先生表示什麼？

(A) 空間很理想。
(B) 價格太昂貴。
(C) 座落位置不便利。
(D) 沒有適當的設備。

正解 (A)

波普勒街上的物件即廣告裡的第二個物件。由波揚先生在詢問表單裡寫的 Your Portmandieu property is ideal in terms of space ... 可知，選項 (A) 即為正解。

194

What is implied about Mr. Fedder?

(A) He is fond of antiques.
(B) He specializes in renovation.
(C) He can rent out parts of his property.
(D) He has contacted Mr. Boyon.

關於費德先生，文中暗示了什麼？

(A) 他很喜歡古董。
(B) 他專門做翻修。
(C) 他可以出租部分的不動產物件。
(D) 他已經與波揚先生聯繫。

正解 (A)

根據電子郵件，費德先生是第一項物件的房東，並且欣喜於波揚先生的「事業性質」，而波揚先生於詢問表單中提及 my company deals in antiques「我的公司經營古董收售」。由此可推測費德先生是一位古董愛好者，因此正解為 (A)。

☐ **be fond of ...** 喜歡……

195

In the e-mail, what does Ms. Fasiq say she can do for Mr. Boyon?

(A) Help reduce the rental price
(B) Accelerate the rental process
(C) Recommend a different property
(D) Renovate some facilities

在電子郵件中，法西克小姐說他可以幫助波揚先生做什麼？

(A) 協助降低租金
(B) 加速租賃手續
(C) 推薦其他物件
(D) 翻修一些設備

正解 (A)

電子郵件中段的 He has graciously offered to negotiate a better price ... 提及房東答應協商價格，最後還說 If this is of interest to you, please contact me ...。由這兩個線索可知，選項 (A) 即為正解。

☐ **accelerate** [ækˈsɛləˌret] 動 加速；促使提早發生

Questions 196-200 refer to the following draft slide and e-mails.

X-Cola Consumers: Survey Responses
by Age Group (DRAFT 1)

Age Group	Number of Responses
20-29	705
30-39	142
40-49	117
50+	51

Hansen Food & Beverage Corporation
X-Cola Market Research Team
Julia Arbenz, Team Leader

Note to Eric: Here's the first draft of the slide for the presentation on Wednesday, for your review. Please e-mail me as soon as possible with any feedback. Thanks! — Julia

X 可樂消費者：調查回答
依年齡分組（草稿 1）

年齡層	回答數
20-29	705
30-39	142
40-49	117
50+	51

漢森食品飲料公司
X 可樂市場調查小組
組長茉莉亞・雅本茲

給艾瑞克的提醒：這是星期三簡報要用的投影片初稿，請你看一下。如果有任何建議，請儘速用電子郵件寄給我。謝謝！—茉莉亞

* E-mail *

To: Julia Arbenz <j.arbenz@x-cola.com>
From: Eric Bradshaw <eric.b@x-cola.com>
Date: January 14, 11:56 A.M.
Subject: Consumer data, first draft

Hi Julia,

Thanks for your hard work. At a glance, the data doesn't look that different from last year's. First, it might be good to make the table into a chart. Also, this year, could we add data for consumers between the ages of 13 and 19? In other words, teenagers, but we can label this group "young adults."

The reason I ask is, our senior staff have already proposed diverting more money to ad campaigns for people 30 and over, but personally I'm a little hesitant to concur with that idea.

If you have any survey data on young adults, would you send it to me, as well as your thoughts? I'd appreciate both.

Thanks,

Eric Bradshaw
Marketing Director, Hansen Food & Beverage

收件者：茉莉亞・雅本茲
　　　　<j.arbenz@x-cola.com>
寄件者：艾瑞克・布雷蕭
　　　　<eric.b@x-cola.com>
日　期：1 月 14 日上午 11:56
主　旨：消費者資料初稿

嗨，茉莉亞：

謝謝妳的努力。乍看之下，這份資料看起來跟去年的沒什麼不同。首先，將表格改成圖表也許會很不錯。而且，今年，我們可不可以把年齡介於 13 歲到 19 歲的消費者的數據加進去？換句話說，也就是青少年，不過我們可以將此族群歸類為「輕成人」。

我之所以會問是因為，我們的資深員工已經提出建議要轉移更多經費給三十歲以上者的廣告活動，但是我個人對同意這個提議是有點遲疑的。

如果妳有任何關於輕成人的調查資料，能不能連同妳的想法一併寄給我？我希望妳兩者都能附上。

謝謝

漢森食品飲料公司行銷部主任
艾瑞克・布雷蕭

* E-mail *	
To:	Eric Bradshaw <eric.b@x-cola.com>
From:	Julia Arbenz <j.arbenz@x-cola.com>
Date:	January 14, 1:02 P.M.
Subject:	Re: Consumer data, first draft

Hi Eric,

I just checked the data you requested. Surprisingly, the number of responses was even lower than the 50+ age group in the survey results I sent in the first draft.

However, that might be because teenagers simply don't bother to return as many surveys as people in older age brackets. So, in actuality, the number of teenage consumers might be greater.

In any event, from a research perspective, I am inclined to side with your opinion. If you would like me to convey that to the senior staff, please let me know. I'll be sending you an updated slide momentarily.

Best wishes,

Julia

收件者：艾瑞克・布雷蕭
      <eric.b@x-cola.com>
寄件者：茱莉亞・雅本茲
      <j.arbenz@x-cola.com>
日　期：1 月 14 日下午 1:02
主　旨：回覆：消費者資料初稿

嗨，艾瑞克：

我剛查了一下你所要求的資料。令人驚訝地，跟我上次寄的初稿調查結果相較，其回答數甚至比五十歲以上的年齡層還要低。

不過，這可能是因為年輕人懶得回問卷，並沒有像年長者族群答得那麼多。所以，實際上，青少年消費者的人數可能更多。

無論如何，從調查觀點而言，我傾向支持你的意見。如果你要我跟資深員工傳達這一點，請讓我知道。我會立刻寄給你一份更新的投影片。

茱莉亞上

Vocabulary

- [ ] **draft** [dræft] 名 草稿
- [ ] **at a glance** 乍看之下
- [ ] **in other words** 換句話說
- [ ] **label A B** 將 A 分類為 B
- [ ] **divert money to ...** 將錢挪至……用
- [ ] **personally** [`pɜsn̩lɪ] 副 就個人而言
- [ ] **be hesitant to** *do* sth. 猶豫做某事
- [ ] **concur with ...** 同意……
- [ ] **bracket** [`brækɪt] 名 類別；階層
- [ ] **in actuality** 實際上
- [ ] **perspective** [pə`spɛktɪv] 名 看法；觀點
- [ ] **be inclined to do** 覺得……；有……的傾向
- [ ] **side with ...** 同意；支持
- [ ] **convey A to B** 將 A 傳達給 B
- [ ] **momentarily** [`momən.tɛrəlɪ] 副 立刻

196

What most likely is Julia's job position?

(A) Team assistant
(B) Senior manager
(C) IT specialist
(D) Marketing analyst

茱莉亞的職位最有可能是什麼？

(A) 小組助理
(B) 資深經理
(C) 資訊科技專家
(D) 行銷分析專員

正解 (D)

茱莉亞為調查結果投影片之製作者；根據表格底下的資訊，茱莉亞是 X 可樂市調小組的組長。由第一封電子郵件可推測，行銷部主任艾瑞克是她的上司，而再從兩人信中所討論的內容判斷，茱莉亞的職位最有可能是 (D) 行銷分析專員。

197

What is indicated about the number of teenage consumer responses?

(A) It is significantly small.
(B) It has increased proportionally.
(C) It is the same as last year.
(D) It is as was expected.

關於青少年消費者回答數，文中指出什麼？

(A) 數量明顯很少。
(B) 數量成比例地增加了。
(C) 數量和去年一樣。
(D) 數量正如期待。

正解 (A)

第二封電子郵件開頭提到 I just checked the data you requested.，這是指第一封電子郵件中艾瑞克所要求的青少年調查數據，而茱莉亞表示 ... the number ... was even lower than the 50+ age group in the survey results ...。再對照第一篇文章裡的消費者調查結果，五十歲以上者占最少比例，僅有 51 人，而青少年族群的回答數比這還要少，故本題應選 (A)。

□ **significantly** [sɪgˋnɪfəkəntlɪ] 副 顯著地
□ **proportionally** [prəˋporʃənəlɪ] 副 成比例地

198

What does Julia imply about ad campaign money?

(A) It should be spent on ads for younger people.
(B) It has already been raised by her team.
(C) It is sufficient for more ads to be made.
(D) More funding is needed for further research.

關於廣告活動的經費，茱莉亞暗示什麼？

(A) 經費應該要花在主打年輕人的廣告上。
(B) 經費她的團隊已經籌措到了。
(C) 經費足夠再多做幾個廣告。
(D) 需要更多資金做更進一步的調查。

正解 (A)

茱莉亞於第二封電子郵件第三段裡寫道 I am inclined to side with your opinion（我傾向同意你的意見）。而艾瑞克的意見在第一封電子郵件裡有提到：「資深員工已提出建議要轉移更多經費給三十歲以上者的廣告活動，但是我個人對同意這個提議是有點遲疑的。」換言之，兩人打算利用青少年的數據，反對該提案，因此選項 (A) 為正解。另注意，side with ... 和 concur with ... 這兩個表「同意」的用法也是本題破解關鍵。

199

In the second e-mail, the word "brackets" in paragraph 2, line 2, is closest in meaning to

(A) lengths
(B) ranges
(C) differences
(D) targets

第二封電子郵件第二段第二行的 "brackets" 這個字的意思最接近

(A) 長度
(B) 範圍
(C) 差異
(D) 目標

正解 (B)

bracket 是名詞，指「區分為同類的一組（人）」，而即使不知道這層涵義，由此單字為接在 people in older age 的名詞來思考也可推知答案。對照調查結果，包含 20-29、30-39 等，依年齡「分層」列出，所以意思與 bracket 最接近的應為選項 (B) ranges（範圍）。另，調查表和第二封電子郵件第一段當中的 age group 的 group 也是同義詞。

200

What does Julia say she will do next?

(A) Reexamine the data
(B) Contact senior staff
(C) Call Eric
(D) Provide a new slide

茱莉亞說她接下來會做什麼？

(A) 重新檢查資料
(B) 聯繫資深員工
(C) 打電話給艾瑞克
(D) 提供新的投影片

正解 (D)

本題答案就在茱莉亞於第二封電子郵件的最後一句話：I'll be sending you an updated slide momentarily.，選項 (D) 即為正解。其中以 provide 取代 send、a new slide 取代 an updated slide 來換句話說。

Notes

新多益全真測驗：速戰速決 400 題

作　　者 / 入江泉
審　　訂 / 宮野智靖
執行編輯 / 游玉旻

出　　版 / 波斯納出版有限公司
地　　址 / 100 台北市館前路 26 號 6 樓
電　　話 / (02) 2314-2525
傳　　真 / (02) 2312-3535
客服專線 / (02) 2314-3535
客服信箱 / btservice@betamedia.com.tw
郵撥帳號 / 19493777
郵撥戶名 / 波斯納出版有限公司

總 經 銷 / 時報文化出版企業股份有限公司
地　　址 / 桃園市龜山區萬壽路二段 351 號
電　　話 / (02) 2306-6842

出版日期 / 2023 年 5 月二版一刷
定　　價 / 600 元
I S B N / 978-626-96783-8-9

ⓑ 貝塔網址：https://www.betamedia.com.tw

喚醒你的英文語感！

Get a Feel for English !